Praise for *The Game* series:

'Flawless'   The Book Lovers blog

'Perfect for summer'   Must Read Books or Die blog

'I devoured this book in the span of hours. DEVOURED. As
in: could not put it down'   Lovin' Los Libros blog

'An emotional rollercoaster'   The Three Bookateers blog

'A series you don't want to miss'   Paperbook Princess blog

'Romantic, fun . . . perfect summer reads'   Bookcrush blog

By day, *New York Times* and *USA Today* bestselling New Adult author Emma Hart dons a cape and calls herself Super Mum to her two children. By night, she drops the cape, pours a glass of juice and writes books.

She likes to write about magic, kisses and whatever else she can fit into the story. Sarcastic, witty characters are a must. As are hot guys. Emma likes to be busy – unless busy involves doing the dishes, but that seems to be when all the ideas come to life.

You can find Emma online at:
emmahart93.blogspot.com
@EmmaHartAuthor
/YAAuthorEmmaHart

In The Game *series*:

The Love Game
Playing for Keeps
The Right Moves
Worth the Risk

EMMA HART

THE LOVE GAME

&

PLAYING FOR KEEPS

HODDER

The Love Game first published in ebook in 2013 and *Playing for Keeps* first published in ebook in 2014 by Hodder and Stoughton
An Hachette UK company

This omnibus edition first published in paperback in 2014

1

ISBN 978 1 444 79720 6

Printed and bound by CPI Group (UK) Ltd, Croydon, CR0 4YY

Hodder & Stoughton policy is to use papers that are natural,
renewable and recyclable products and made from wood grown
in sustainable forests. The logging and manufacturing processes
are expected to conform to the environmental regulations
of the country of origin.

Hodder & Stoughton Ltd
338 Euston Road
London NW1 3BH

www.hodder.co.uk

Contents

THE LOVE GAME

Chapter One

I hated him on sight.

I'm not a hateful person. In fact, I'm actually really friendly, but something about Braden Carter rubs me the wrong way, and has ever since I first saw him five weeks ago.

Maybe it's the arrogant, smug smile on his face when girls eye him admiringly, or maybe it's the undressing with his eyes thing he does to said girls. Maybe it's the bragging, the I-don't-give-a-crap attitude or the knowledge he can get any girl on campus. Or, rather, any girl in the state.

Maybe it's because I'm attracted to him when I most definitely do not want to be, combined with the fact he reminds me of everything I left at home in Brooklyn.

I shake those thoughts off and carry on looking around the room of the frat house as if he doesn't exist. It's hard to do – especially when he has three girls on his arm and other unmentionable body parts. Did I mention the guy is sinfully hot?

He has this messy, sun-kissed blond hair with natural highlights that most girls would – and do – pay a fortune for. His eyes are so blue they're almost electric, and his skin is naturally tanned from the California sunshine. I'm sure I don't need to mention his perfectly lean, muscular body because, after all, this *is* California and surfing since you can walk is a requirement to life.

'Stop ogling him.' Kayleigh steps up next to me and nudges my shoulder.

'That's about as likely as me doing a striptease for the whole house,' I reply.

'Honey, I can name several guys that would *not* walk away from that.'

Kyle winks at me across the bar in the kitchen and I sigh. 'They can keep dreaming. Never gonna happen, Kay.'

'Shame.' She grins at me. 'I can't say I'd walk away either.'

I shake my head, but I'm smiling. Since the day Kay walked into our dorm room five weeks ago, she's been open about her sexuality. She's bisexual and doesn't care who knows. I respected her from the second we met. Her openness is refreshing to me.

'You're incorrigible,' I mock scold.

'Hey, if the shoe fits!' She winks and snaps her fingers towards Kyle. 'Drinks, mofo!'

'Wait your turn, ya pain,' he replies, pouring two vodka shots and handing them to someone at the end of the bar.

'I bet he'd jump to it if it was you askin',' she whispers not so quietly.

'Now you're talkin', Kay!' Kyle turns and hits me with his thousand-watt smile. 'Would you like a drink, gorgeous girl?'

'I'm fine, thank you.' I smile politely. 'I'm sure Kay will take one, though.'

'Bull. Shit.' Kay leans forward and slaps a hand on the bar surface. 'Four vodka shots, Kyle. Tonight I'm showing Miss Maddie how it's done.'

'Right on!' He turns and lines up four shot glasses.

'Kay,' I hiss. 'You know I don't drink!'

'Didn't,' she corrects. 'Didn't drink. You do now.'

'Kay.'

'Maddie,' she mimics my tone of voice and accepts the glasses Kyle slides to us. 'One, two, bam. That's how we're doin' this, baby girl. No thinkin', no messin'. Down them both.'

'This is such a bad idea,' I mutter, picking up both glasses and peering at the strong smelling liquid. 'If I vomit, you're cleaning it up.'

'Always.' She winks. 'Ready? One, two, bam!'

Tip. Swallow. Tip. Swallow.

My throat burns as the alcohol slides down it, and I pat my chest as if that'll stop the red hot feeling. Kyle smirks at me.

'Thought you didn't drink?' he asks.

'I don't,' I reply, putting the glasses down.

'She's gonna be a hard one to crack.' Kay wipes her chin. 'Sure you haven't ever drank before, Mads?'

I shrug one shoulder, the lie falling easily from my lips. 'Obviously I've drunk alcohol, just not enough to get me drunk.'

'This changes tonight!' Kay bangs the counter again. 'Kyle, six more shots.'

'Of?'

'Of whatever the fuck you wanna put in the glasses.'

'Make it twelve,' Lila says, sliding in next to me. 'Three for me, three for Megan when she gets here.'

'Twelve? How many glasses do you girls think I have?' Kyle jokes and opens another cupboard. There's a shelf of shot glasses neatly lined up.

'I'd hate to be whoever cleans those tomorrow,' I say.

'Braden.' Kyle laughs. 'I just get to serve them to your beautiful faces. Unlucky for him, but definitely lucky for me.' He leans forward and places three glasses in front of me with a smile that would melt any other girl's heart. I raise an eyebrow and wait patiently as he hands everyone else their shots.

'Did I miss anything?' Megan shuffles between me and Lila, her blonde hair bobbing as she bounces excitedly. 'Ooh, so many shots? What's the occasion?'

'Maddie's getting drunk!' Kay announces, lifting up the first glass.

'No way!' Megan tilts her face towards me. 'For real?'

'Apparently,' I reply dryly.

'Aw shucks, Mads. It's fun!' She wiggles her body and Kyle's eyes move to her chest. Megan's very well-endowed in the boob department and likes to let the world know.

'No more talkin'!' Lila huffs, picking up a glass. 'One, two, three, bam?'

'Yah, duh!' Kay laughs and picks up the second glass.

I take a deep breath and pick up two glasses. What the hell is wrong with me tonight? I don't drink, at least, not like this. I can't be out of control.

'Bam!' Kay shouts.

One. Two. Three. Fire.

Whee.

I blink a few times and swallow. 'Holy sh-crap.'

'It's working,' Lila giggles. 'Maddie doesn't swear, ever!'

'I didn't swear,' I protest. 'Crap is not a swear word.'

'Fine, you almost swore.' She rolls her dark, kohl-lined eyes. 'I will have one naughty word out of those pretty pink lips before the night is up!'

I resist the urge to roll my eyes.

'I'd like a few things out of those pretty pink lips,' Kyle comments, winking at me.

'Fuckin' pig!' Kay punches his arm over the bar.

'Jesus, Kay. Your fist made of fucking iron?' He rubs his arm.

'For you, Kyle honey, my fist can be whatever you want it to be.' She winks and stands up straight, grabbing my hand. 'Come on, baby girl, we're goin' to shake our booties!'

I shoot Lila a 'help me!' look and tug on Megan's shirt.

'Woah, okay, I'm comin'!' She turns and drags Lila along too.

The front room is crowded. Music pumps from speakers and bodies grind in the middle of the floor. A couple is making out on the sofa and – oh my god. Nope, that's definitely gone past making out.

I look away and allow the girls to drag me into the writhing mass of people. The alcohol is spreading through my body, and I relax a little, knowing I'm done for the night on the alcohol side. No point pushing my luck.

Megan grabs one of my hands and urges me to dance, to let go. Crazy. That's what this is. Drinking and now dancing. These girls are ruining me.

'Lighten up, baby girl!' Kay shouts. 'Mr Carter himself is watchin' your sexy little body!'

Fantastic. Just what I want – to be the next on his to-do list. The next on a very, very long list.

'He can keep looking,' I reply, seeing him watching from the corner of the room. 'Looking is as close as he's gonna get.' I turn my back to him, and Lila shakes her dark hair out, moving towards me.

'Someone needs to take his ass down a peg or two,' she says. 'Lord knows he hit every branch on the way down the beautiful tree, but he's sure perched at the top of the ego one.'

'Right,' Megan agrees. 'But he's always been like that. That's just Braden.'

Megan and Braden both come from the same town and from what she's said, their parents are quite close so they grew up together. Besides us, she's about the only girl at the party that isn't falling at his feet.

'You know what?' Kay says. We glance over at him and another blonde is wrapped around him.

'What?' I say and turn away from him with a look of disgust on my face.

'That boy needs to know what it's like to do what he does. What it's like to be humped and dumped.'

All eyes turn to me. I shake my head, stepping back. 'Oh, no. No, no, no way!' I turn and leave the room, pushing my way through the kitchen to the yard, all three girls on my heels.

'Mads, it'll be fun!' Lila takes my hands and bounces. 'Come on!'

'Um.' Megan looks at the house then at me. 'I guess it wouldn't hurt.'

'No.' I shake my head again.

'You only have to hump him once,' Kay reasons. 'Besides, he's not exactly bad to look at, is he? I could imagine smacking that ass.'

'Then you do it!'

'Oh, no.' Megan sighs. 'She can't. Kay might be bi but everyone knows she prefers girls, so he won't go there. Lila has a boyfriend who happens to be his friend, and I grew up with him. He's like my brother or something. You're the only one that can do it.'

'I don't understand what we'll get out of this.' I look at each of them.

'Satisfaction of knowing the guy finally wanted what he

couldn't have,' Kay shrugs. 'Come on, Mads. It'll take two weeks, three, tops.'

'A month maybe,' Megan adds. 'After that, he'll get bored and give in or he'll be in love with you. He's always watching you, Mads. Even in class when you think he isn't. And he refuses to talk about you to me, so I know he's attracted to you. Usually he gives me a play-by-play over his weekend conquests.'

'Plus Megs knows how his mind works,' Lila says. 'So we have that advantage.'

'You're not going to take no for an answer, are you?' I sigh and rake my fingers through my hair.

'Nope.' Kay shakes her head.

'Oh, hell. I have a feeling I'm gonna regret this.'

'Maddie Stevens. Your mission, should you choose to accept it.' She grins and puts her hand out. Lila and Megan put theirs on top of hers. 'Is to play the player at his own game. Do you accept?'

I inhale deeply, every bit of my mind screaming at me to say no and run. Play the player. The guy I hate because he embodies everything I wanted to leave behind when I left Brooklyn.

Instead of running, I place my hand on the pile in front of me. 'Accepted.'

Chapter Two

Braden

I have no fucking idea who this chick is who's hanging onto my arm. I'm pretty sure I've never seen her in my life, but she's kinda hot with nice tits so I guess she can stay for a bit. She's not hot enough to bang though, so she won't be around for that long.

Blondie presses her lips against my ear, and I hide my cringe by looking around the frat house. My eyes find Maddie Stevens – Princess of University of California, Berkeley.

She's sitting at the bar with that bi girl. Shit, what's her name? Oh, never mind. Megan and Lila are sitting with her, and I watch as they knock back shot after shot of whatever it is Kyle is throwing down their throats tonight. She shakes out her auburn hair and the bi one drags her up.

My eyes sweep her body, and I'm vaguely aware Blondie is now sitting on my lap. Two hard globes press against my chest, and I know instantly she's got fake tits. They were way too good to be true.

Megan takes Maddie's hand, and she smiles, almost shyly. She starts to move to the beat of the music and *fuck*, there's nothing shy about that. She puts her free hand in her hair, looks at the floor and her hips move perfectly in time. She glances up through her eyelashes and smiles again, more confidence in it this time.

'She's so fucking hot,' Aston says, appearing next to me. Ryan steps up behind him.

'Maddie?' I ask, my eyes still on her moving body.

'Who's Maddie?' Blondie purrs. Fuck, she still here?

Maddie looks up, her bright green eyes taking in Blondie on me. Her lip twitches in disgust, and she turns away.

'No one you should worry about, babe.' I peel her off me. 'Be a doll and get me a beer.'

She flutters eyelashes caked in mascara. 'Of course.' She hops off of me and I pat her ass, turning my attention back to the guys.

'Who was that?' Ryan asks.

'Good question, dude.' I shrug. 'Some chick.'

I catch sight of Maddie pushing her way through the crowd, Megan, Lila, and bisexual girl following her.

'Hey, reckon the girls would be pissed if I chased after her?' Aston asks, following her with his eyes.

'Megan would beat the shit out of you.' Ryan nudges him and leans against the arm of the sofa. 'Lila and Kay, too, actually.'

Kay. That's the bisexual girl.

'Maddie would likely kick my ass, too,' I add, looking at them. 'You'd need to get that girl down the aisle before she dropped her pants for you.'

'Marriage? Fuck that.' Aston shakes his head. 'I'm too hot for that shit, dude.'

He isn't far off, at least not in the eyes of the girls here. He's never short of a quick one or two on a weekend.

'Marriage?' Ryan repeats. 'Nah, you just gotta make the chick fall in love with you. Make her fall in love and bam, there it is. Piece of ass, and a hot one, too.'

I tilt my head slightly, studying them both. 'She's like a fuckin' china doll, though. If you did it too hard, she'd break.'

'I'd break it,' Aston says. 'Just without the love shit.'

'I reckon you could do it.' Ryan takes a swig of beer and glances at me.

'A week?' Aston taps his chin.

'Nah,' I say.

'A month,' Ryan says with finality. 'She ain't gonna be easy to break, but she'll give it up in a month. You could do it, Braden.'

'Dude, you realize that's your girlfriend's friend? You're askin' me to get her to fall in love with me, fuck her, then dump her.'

Not that I wouldn't mind a chance to fuck Maddie Stevens. In fact, I'd pay for that damn chance.

Ryan shrugs. 'Like Lila will ever find out. This shit stays between us three. Braden Carter seducing a girl ain't exactly gonna be out of place, is it?'

'Do it.' Aston grins. 'Make her fall in love with you. If anyone can, you can.'

'Dunno.' I lean back and look at the dance floor. She's back – all four of them are.

She's doing that hip thing again, swaying them from side to side. She shakes her hair out and laughs. Lila exaggerates a wink over to Ryan, and he smirks. Lila turns back and says something, making Maddie look over her shoulder. Her green eyes meet mine. I smile slowly, the smile that gets me anything. I wink. One side of her glossy pink mouth curls up, and she looks away again, her hair flicking with the movement of her head.

'Well?' Ryan nudges my head. 'You gonna do it?'

'Challenge accepted, boys,' I say, resting my arms behind my head. 'One month from now, Maddie Stevens will be in love with me and in my bed. You can count on that shit.'

Chapter Three

Maddie

I roll over, wincing at the light coming in through the curtains. How much did I drink last night? Too much, clearly.

'Good morning, sunshine!' Kay shouts and kicks the dorm room door shut.

'Nope, not over here.' I bury back under my covers.

'I have coffee and muffins!' She pulls the covers down and I groan, opening my eyes.

'Why? Why?'

'Why what?'

'Why do I feel like I just got run over by a herd of wilde-beest?'

'One, I have no idea what a wilderbeast is, and two, it's called a hangover.' Kay holds out a Starbucks take-out cup and my favorite blueberry muffin.

I sit up and take them from her. 'Thank you. Why are you not feeling this way?'

'I'm one of the lucky ones.' She snickers and chucks herself on her bed. 'I don't get hangovers. You, however, do, it seems. Megs is the same. She'd usually be in bed all day.'

'Sounds good to me.' I take a sip of the coffee.

'But not today,' she sings. 'Today we're getting down to business.'

'Down to business?'

She raises her eyebrows at me. 'Do you remember our deal last night? Your mission, Ms. Bond?'

Ah. Play The Player. 'I thought we were joking.'

'When have I ever joked about anything as serious as sex?'

'Fine, fine.' I give in and sigh. 'What do you mean, down to business?'

'We need to draw up a plan of attack!' She crosses her legs, Indian-style, and bounces twice on the bed.

'A plan of attack,' I repeat dumbly.

'Uh, duh! You think we can go into this blind? Oh no, honey.' She shakes her head. 'Braden Carter has got more charm than the Irish leprechauns—'

'Which don't exist.'

'And that means he's dangerous. You're trying to make him fall in love with you, yet if he lays it on thick you could end up falling in love with him.'

'There would be no hump and dump, which would defeat the object of Play The Player.' I sigh.

'Precisely!' She claps once. 'So we need to figure out a fool-proof plan that ensures while he's losing his heart, you aren't losing yours. Because that would just be disastrous.'

''Kay, I don't know.' I sigh again. 'Braden Carter doesn't fall in love. If he has a rulebook, that's it, right above the rule that says rules are for losers. I have a month to do this, right? I just don't know how it's possible.'

'Nothing is impossible if you believe in it enough.'

'But I don't know if I believe in it.'

'You will,' she says confidently. 'You will.'

'I hope you're right,' I reply. 'Because this is looking like a fail before it's even started.'

'Knock knock on your cock,' Lila opens the door and Megan follows her in, a large roll of paper and marker pens tucked under her arm.

'What is that?' I ask, taking it in.

'Operation Play The Player,' Megan answers, sitting on the floor between our beds. She unrolls the paper, uses two books to hold it flat and writes 'OPTP – Operation Play The Player' at the top of the sheet.

I shake my head in disbelief. Am I actually doing this? I was under the impression that college meant growing up, but

I was wrong. I feel like I'm thirteen again and trying to trick my lifetime crush into admitting he's crushing on me too.

'Stop shakin' your head.' Lila jumps up on my bed next to me. 'It's gonna be okay. You can do this.'

'You guys do realize that in terms of love and relationships, a month is short, right? And in terms of Braden Carter, a month is a lifetime?' I question. 'Who says he won't get bored after a week and go and find one of his floozies to warm his bed?'

'You have to stop him from doing that,' Megan says softly. 'You have to make him never want to leave your side. I give you a week to reel him in, get him interested, and then this is in the bag.'

'A week?'

'If you can get him to be by your side in a week, he'll fall in love in three,' she clarifies, uncapping a blue pen. 'Stage one. Attachment.' She jots it down on the paper, giving me until next Sunday.

'Hold up, this isn't even starting until tomorrow!'

'Wrong.' Kay shakes her head.

Lila nods in agreement with Kay. 'The guys are having a football game in the yard of the frat house later. We're all heading down there.'

I huff. 'Fine. It starts tonight.'

Megan flashes me a grin, green pen in hand. 'Stage two, next week, is Public Appreciation and Attachment.'

'Which translates to what, in my terms?' I frown.

'Hand holding, public kissing, exclusivity.'

I snort. 'You guys have a hell of a lot of faith in me, you know.'

'Stage three, week three,' Kay continues. 'Almost Sex and Public Knowledge Relationship.'

'Everyone will know?'

'Well, yeah.' Lila raises an eyebrow at me. 'Humping and dumping will be so much more satisfying if everyone we know, and then some, knows.'

'It seems a little . . . harsh.'

'You have to be cruel to be kind, baby girl,' Kay says.

'They're right,' Megan agrees without looking up from the paper. 'I don't much like the idea of hurtin' him, but he needs to sort his head out. If he's this bad five weeks into college, I dread what he's gonna be like in two years. He needs to get a clear message and soon.'

'Why not just talk to him?' I try. 'Why go to extreme measures?'

'Because Braden Carter only understands things in extremities.'

'Okay, so say this works.' I tap my finger against the bed. 'And he does fall in love with me. I'll hump and dump him and then what? You know he won't leave it. He'll fight to get me back. What do I do then?'

Everyone stops, and Megan sits back, putting the end of the pen in her mouth. Kay tilts her head to the side, and Lila chews her thumbnail.

'I didn't think about that,' Megan says quietly. 'If Bray has one thing going for him—'

'Besides the obvious?' Lila snickers.

'Besides the obvious.' Megan smirks. 'It's that he goes after what he wants. Girls, I hate to say it, but Maddie has a point. If he falls in love with her and she walks away, he'll go bat shit crazy trying to get her back. He won't let her go easily. If at all.'

My eyes widen.

'But what if Maddie falls in love with *him*?' Lila asks. 'What if she can't hump him and dump him?'

'Please.' I shake my head. 'Braden embodies everything I hate. He's arrogant, egotistical, and a pig. I'm not likely to fall in love with *that*.'

'But he's also funny, really caring, and beneath his man slut exterior, he's the kind of guy you'd take home to meet your mom.' Megan sighs. 'I know him, Mads. If he wants something he'll do whatever it takes.'

'So we remind her every day of why she hates him.' Kay shrugs.

'It might not be enough.'

'It will be,' I reply firmly. 'It will be.'

'Okay, back to the original issue. If he falls in love.' Lila rocks back and forwards, swinging her legs.

'Then we deal with that when it gets here.' Kay shrugs. 'I don't know what else we can do.'

Ugh. 'Okay, what's the last stage?' I ask.

'Stage Four, Hump and Dump.' Megan writes it and underlines it with a flourish. 'I don't think I need to elaborate on that one.'

'No,' I agree. 'You don't need to.'

I look over her shoulder at the colorful piece of paper on the floor. It's split into four, color coordinated, and every stage is explained. I sigh, wondering what the hell I've let them talk me into this time.

Chapter Four

Braden

I rub my face with the bottom of my shirt. The high fall temperatures aren't football-playing weather for most of the guys in this house, even I struggle sometimes and I've played it since I could throw the damn ball.

'Break,' Tony Adams calls. 'Please?'

I shake my head. 'You're a fuckin' wimp, Adams.'

'Sorry, I'm from Maine and not used to these desert temperatures.'

'We don't live in the desert, idiot.' Kyle slaps the back of his head and we head back to where all the girlfriends – and Maddie – are sitting.

'Fuckin' may as well be,' Adams grumbles. I shake my head, grab a bottle of water and head over to Megan and the girls with Ryan.

'"Ladies."' I smile at Maddie, and she smirks.

'Turn down the charm, Casanova.' Megan laughs and tugs me to sit. 'No one here is interested.'

'Except me.' I wink at Maddie.

'Yes, Braden, we all know about your vested interest in yourself,' Lila says and rolls her eyes.

'Ryan, control your girl,' I joke.

'Watch it, Carter,' Lila retorts. 'Or I'll control your ass to Timbuktu.'

I grin and catch Maddie's eye. She's laughing silently, looking hot as hell in a short sun dress that shows off long lean legs.

'So, Maddie.' I lean back.

'So, Braden,' she replies, looking up at me through her thick curly eyelashes.

'Move your ass,' Kyle says, sitting in next to me. 'Hey, guys, Maddie.' He nods towards her.

'Kyle.' She smiles widely at him and my hackles rise a little. I knew the guy was rude, but fuckin' hell.

'How are you, gorgeous girl?'

'Good, you?'

'Better for seeing you, that's for sure.' He winks and she smiles.

I narrow my eyes slightly, and Megan nudges me.

'Jealous, Bray?'

I snort. 'Of Kyle? Yeah, right.'

'Okay,' she whispers disbelievingly. 'But you're turning into a walking green-eyed monster.'

'Whatever, Meggy.'

'Seriously, Bray, if you wanna talk to her, just talk. She won't bite.'

'I might like it if she does.'

'You're such a pig!' She shakes her head. 'I can see you're interested in her, so just ask her out.'

'I don't do dates, Meggy, you know that. If I decided to take her somewhere, I have no idea where.'

'You'd take her out?' She grins.

'I'm not saying yes or no,' I reply. 'But I might consider it.'

'Starbucks. She likes their blueberry muffins.' She smiles, satisfied and amused. 'Just let her get to know you. Not walking horn-dog Braden, the real Braden.'

'Maybe.' I look back at Maddie, and she's looking at me and Megan with her eyes slightly narrowed. She shakes her head, and I glance at Megan questioningly. She looks away, and I shake my head. Girls. I'll never fucking understand them.

A date. Why didn't I consider that shit when I agreed to Aston and Ryan's plan last night? Why did I think dates wouldn't come into it? Of course they fucking would, and they are.

Aston calls for us to start playing again, and I get up, handing Maddie my water bottle with a wink. She half-smiles as she takes it, and I can feel her eyes on me as I go back to play.

Kyle pulls his top over his head, and I know this has turned into a pissing contest.

It's no secret to any of us that Kyle has his sights set on Maddie, and if I wanna complete the challenge the guys set, I gotta take it up a notch.

I glance over my shoulder, and her green eyes are on Kyle. Fuck no. I grip the bottom of my shirt and yank it over my head, stretching after and chucking it to Megan. She wrinkles her nose, and I laugh, noticing Maddie's eyes are back on me.

Good.

Kyle narrows his eyes at me, and I smile a shit-eating smile, knowing he looks like a ten-year-old boy compared to me topless.

We all get into position, and the game starts again. Kyle and I seem to come head to head more than often, and I know he's trying to make me look like a prick. Fortunately, everyone already knows I am one and when it comes to football, he can kiss my fuckin' ass.

He catches the ball, and I tackle him. He falls face first on the grass and curses.

'What the fuck, Braden?'

'Slipped. Sorry.' I grin.

'Slipped my ass!' He gets up and comes towards me.

'Woah, woah!' Ryan jumps in between as my muscles tense. 'Turn the testosterone down a notch, guys. It's just a game of football.'

'Yeah, Kyle, turn it down,' I goad him.

'If you're tryin' to convince her you're the better one out of the two of us, then good luck. She isn't as stupid as your usual clientele.'

I start forward, and Ryan puts a hand on my chest. 'Dude, no. Go and chill.'

I take a deep breath and nod once. 'Fine.'

I kick the ball away and turn back to the girls.

'Can't you even play a game of football without turning it into a pissing contest, Bray?' Megan laughs.

I shoot her a look, grab my shirt, and take my water from Maddie.

'Everything okay?' she asks softly.

I sip the water and look down at her. 'Yeah, everything's okay, Angel.'

'Good.' She smiles up at me, and Kay sighs.

'I'll move over,' she says in a mock annoyed tone.

'Oh, Kay,' I say and sit in the spot she just vacated. 'How did you know?'

'You look like you could rest your back against the wall.' She winks and Megan laughs.

'Or against Maddie.' Lila giggles.

I look at Maddie, and her cheeks flame a little. 'I'd rest a whole lot of things against Maddie, none suitable for public viewing, though.'

Her mouth opens and closes once. Megan, Lila and Kay all roar with laughter, and I nudge Maddie.

'I'm sorry. Did that embarrass you?'

'Nope.' She squeaks the word out. 'Not at all.'

I laugh and put an arm around her shoulder. 'I think it did, and I'm sorry. That wasn't my intention.'

'It's okay,' she replies, a little tense in my hold.

'No, it's not,' I insist.

'Game's over!' Megan calls, and they all stand. I get up and offer Maddie my hand. She places hers in my larger one, and I pull her up, grinning down at her.

'Thank you.' She smiles and takes her hand from mine, making to follow the girls.

'Hey, Maddie?' I ask.

She stops and turns back to me, tucking a piece of hair behind her ear. 'Yeah?'

'We have English Lit together tomorrow, right?'

'Yeah.'

'Do you have a class before?'

'Nope, it's a free. I usually head to the library to study.'

'Make an exception tomorrow?' I ask, leaning against the wall, facing her.

'What for?' She smiles a little.

'We could grab a coffee before class. I hear you like the

muffins in Starbucks.' I tug a lock of her hair and amusement shines in her eyes.

'Braden Carter, are you asking me on a date?' She raises an eyebrow.

'Um.' I look around, and Megan has her back to me. She nods once, sharply. 'Yes. I am, yeah.'

'Say it,' she demands.

'Say what?'

'I wanna hear you say you're asking me on a date, 'cause this has to be a historical moment.'

'Hey!' I protest. 'Fine. Maddie, would you like to go on a date to grab coffee tomorrow before English?'

She smiles widely. 'I'd love to.'

'Meet you outside Starbucks about half an hour before class, then?'

'It's a date,' she agrees and turns around, heading towards the girls.

I let out a breath and shake my head. Fuckin' hell.

Chapter Five

Maddie

I detour to the dorm room after my morning class. I shut the door behind me loudly and lean against it, shaking my head.

I'm about to go on a date with Braden Carter, resident playboy, all because of a stupid dare. But is it the dare that's stupid, or me for agreeing to it?

I think I'm voting for both.

I run my brush through my hair and touch up my make-up, glancing at the sheet on the wall. Stage One, Attachment. Today's goal is to leave him wanting a little more, to make him come back tomorrow. I sigh and leave the room, running down the stairs and out into the California sunshine. My floaty skirt swishes as I walk towards the campus Starbucks, butterflies going crazy in my stomach. Why do I have butterflies? I hate this guy. It's not even a real date.

That thought doesn't stop the extra loud beat of my heart when I see him. He's leaning against the wall outside, headphones in, and his head is bobbing to whatever he's listening to. His hands are in the pockets of his slim fit, dark blue jeans. As if he can feel me watching, he looks up and electric blue eyes collide with mine.

He smiles as I approach him, and the butterflies turn to stampeding elephants. I feel sick.

'Hey there, Angel,' Braden says and reaches to open the door for me.

'Hey,' I reply, walking through the door. 'Thank you.'

'You're welcome.' He puts a hand on my back and guides me towards the counter. 'What are you having?'

'A grande double chocolate chip frappucino, please.' I smile at his confused face. 'What?'

'Chocolate chips in coffee? Why?'

'Why not?' I shrug. 'It's yummy.'

'Okay, I'll try that.'

'What do you normally have?'

'Uh, normal coffee. You know, like a normal person drinks?' He laughs.

'Are you saying I'm not normal?' I raise an eyebrow as we reach the counter.

'Not at all.' He smiles. 'Hi, can I have, er, what was it again?' He looks at me sheepishly.

I sigh, roll my eyes and shake my head. 'Can we have two grande double chocolate chip fraps please?'

'And two blueberry muffins,' Braden adds, looking down at me. I blush slightly, and he slides his hand round so it's holding my waist. The barista steals glances at him as she prepares our drinks. It's all I can do not to roll my eyes again. We take our drinks, and Braden pays.

'Is it always like this for you?' I ask as we sit down.

'Like what?'

'Girls staring at you.'

'Who was staring?'

'The barista. Did you not notice?'

He shrugs one shoulder carelessly. 'I don't pay much attention to it. If they're good enough to catch my eye then I'll pay them attention.'

'Oh, I feel so privileged,' I say sarcastically.

'Hey.' He raises his eyebrows. 'I'm on a date with you, so you're not just good enough, Maddie. In fact, you're probably too good.'

I sip my drink and pick a piece of muffin off, popping it into my mouth. 'So why are you here then? If I'm too good.'

'Because I'll never know unless I try, right?' he asks. 'Like this coffee. I never knew how good it was until I tried it. I'll never know if I'm good enough for you unless I try.'

Wow. Braden wants in my pants. *Bad.*

'You win that one.' I smile.

'And Kyle has his eye on you. I don't do well with competition.'

'Ah, so that's what yesterday was about.' They were fighting over me?

Neanderthals.

'There's a slim chance of you bein' right there, beautiful.'

'I'd say there's a really good chance.' I sigh. 'You really were fighting over me? Me? Wow.' I shake my head.

'Don't sound so shocked, Maddie. We're not the only guys in that house that have an interest in you,' he admits.

'You just thought you'd get in there first?' I comment wryly.

'Yes. I mean, no. I mean. Fuck.' He groans. 'This is so not the way I wanted this to go.'

I raise my eyebrows and glance at the clock.

'Yes. I thought I'd get in there first, but only because I'd get stupidly jealous if I saw you with one of those guys.'

'Right,' I say. 'We need to get to class. It starts in five minutes.'

Braden sighs, and we both stand. I wrap my hands round the take-out cup and back out of the door. We walk back towards the main campus in silence, and I almost wish we didn't have class together. This no talking thing is tense, even if I do hate the guy.

'Maddie,' he says, pulling me aside before we walk into the room. 'That wasn't supposed to go like that. I'm sorry.'

I look towards the open class door. 'It's no big deal, Braden. I mean, you don't date, right? Now you know for sure you don't.'

He reaches forward and tucks my hair behind my ear. 'It is a big deal, to me it is. Let me try again. Please?'

I narrow my eyes and look at him. 'Are you asking me for a second date?'

'Yeah,' he says in a soft voice. 'I am askin' you for a second date.'

'I'll think about it, and then I'll call you.'

'You don't have my number.' He gives me a small smile.

I walk towards the classroom and look back at him when I reach the door. He's still standing by the side, watching me with that same smile playing on his lips.

'Then I guess you'll just have to wait, won't you?' I smirk

and Megan rounds the corner. Her eyes shoot between both of us.

'How long?' Braden asks.

'However long I feel like making you wait.' My smirk changes to a grin. 'Come on, you'll be late for class.'

I walk through the door with Megan, and we slide into our seats.

'Second date?' she whispers in my ear.

'Yep,' I reply. 'He just doesn't know that yet.'

Chapter Six

Braden

I watch her all through class. Make me wait? I don't do fucking waiting, but here I am.

Waiting.

I shake my head at my thoughts and try to focus on the lesson but it's impossible. The girl I'm supposed to be making fall in love with me is calling the shots. I guess that's what happens when you fuck up the first date, right?

Fucking hell. This is a mess already, and it's only day two. And where the hell am I supposed to take her for a second date?

Class ends, and I follow Maddie and Megan out. I tug on Megan's hair as I pass her and brush my fingers down Maddie's arm. She glances up at me and smiles. I wink at her and walk in the opposite direction, back towards the frat house.

Ryan's sitting on the sofa with his feet up when I get there. 'How'd it go?'

'I fucked up, naturally.' I chuck myself next to him. 'I have no fuckin' clue about this dating shit, man. I can't believe you're making me do this.'

'I'm not making you do anything,' he replies. 'You agreed to this.'

'Yeah, well, providing she agrees, I have to find a place to take her for a second date.'

Ryan laughs.

'What's so funny?'

'Braden Carter is asking me for dating advice!' He chuckles. 'Never thought I'd see the day.'

'Never thought I'd see the day I went on a damn date,' I grumble.

'Try this Friday.'

'Friday? That's four days away and a party night.'

'What better way to show her you're serious than skipping out on your own party?' Ryan raises his eyebrows.

'And where do I take the princess for our date?'

'To the beach? Have a walk under the stars,' Ryan suggests in a girly voice and sighs.

'Great,' I mutter. 'And until then?'

'Pop up when she least expects it. Spend time with her.' He shrugs. 'That shit worked with Lila.'

'Right. She said she spends free time between classes in the library. That?'

'Find out from Megan when her free time is, if she won't get suspicious.'

'Dude, she told me where to take Maddie for our first "date". I'm pretty sure Megan has her own freakin' agenda.'

He looks at me knowingly. 'Then make sure you keep to ours and not fall into hers.'

'I don't fall in love, Ry.' I snort at the idea. 'And especially not with princesses like Maddie.'

'Yet you're willing to pretend to get her in bed.'

'Desperate times call for desperate measures, my friend. I always get what I want, and I want Maddie in my bed.'

'In that case, I hope you know what you're doing. We all know what Megan is like when she gets an idea in her head.'

'Megan's ideas can stay in her head. I never paid attention to them as a kid, and I won't start now. Besides, it's not like this thing with Maddie is even real. It's all a game, man.'

'A love game?' Ryan chuckles.

'Something like that. Except the one who falls in love, loses.'

'And Braden never loses, right?' Ryan smiles wryly.

'Right.'

Chapter Seven

Maddie

I knock on Lila and Megan's door before pushing it open. Both of them are stretched out on their beds doing schoolwork, and I drop myself on the floor between them, letting the door shut itself.

'Where's Kay?' Lila asks, glancing at me.

'She's, um, entertaining.'

'Oh.' Her mouth drops open slightly.

'Yes. Oh.'

'Who this time?' Megan rolls over.

'Darla somebody.' I shrug. 'I have no idea, and I'd rather not know to be honest. It's not like I'll see her again.'

She nods. 'Mhmm. Heard from Bray?'

'Why would I have? He doesn't have my cell number.'

'Why not?' Lila smiles.

'Because I'm holding out on him.'

'Because he fucked up the first date, asked her for a second, and she hasn't answered him yet,' Megan clarifies.

'You didn't?' Lila exclaims. 'Oh, nice one, Mads. That's definitely gonna keep him coming back.'

'It's not about that.' I pick at some lint on my jeans. 'I see the way he walks all over girls, and it makes me sick. I won't be like that, running and falling at his feet just because the infamous Braden calls my name. If I'm gonna play this guy at his own game and make him fall in love with me, he's gonna respect me while he does it.'

Megan smiles. 'And that, honey, is why you are the perfect girl for the job.'

Lila nods her agreement. 'It's true, and it's why it's gonna work. You know what you're doing.'

Because I know how to handle pig-headed, arrogant male assholes.

'Whatever. I just want to get it done with. The idea of pretending to fall in love with him makes me feel sick.'

Megan's phone chimes, and she grabs it from the side. She smirks at whatever is on screen and types back quickly.

'Anything interesting?' Lila asks her.

'Nope,' she replies, rolling over onto her back. 'So, where are we on OPTP?'

'Holding out on the second date. Making him sweat.' I lean against the bed, and she grabs a notebook.

'And when are you going to give him an answer?'

'Umm.' I haven't thought about that. At all. 'Wednesday, I guess.'

They both nod. 'Wednesday is good. That gives him time to plan something for this weekend.'

'But aren't we supposed to be "exclusive" next week?' I look between them, confused.

'You will be.' Megan snaps the notebook shut. 'You have two classes together, right? So you'll see each other then and one of your free periods matches.'

'So?'

Lila groans. 'Have you ever dated before?'

'Once,' I admit.

'Once?' She sits up. 'Just once?'

'Yes.'

'Why?'

Because all the guys in Brooklyn were tools. 'Just . . . because.'

'Wait a minute.' Megan sits up and looks at me. 'Maddie, honey. Are you a virgin? 'Cause if you are we won't make you do this.'

There it is. My out. For some reason, though, I'm not taking it.

'No,' I reply with a smirk. 'I'm not a virgin.'

'Phew.' She flops backwards. 'I'd never make you lose your virginity like that.'

'What are we doing then?' Lila asks. 'Are Mads and Braden gonna spend not-a-date time together?'

'Yes,' Megan replies. 'Starting tomorrow. I'll switch seats with him in English. He sits with Aston and I'm sure it won't take much to convince Aston I'm interested.' She wrinkles her nose.

'You're not?' I ask her. 'He is kinda hot.'

'I admit his short hair is kinda sexy, but he's also a bit of a bitch for a straight guy. He spends so long getting ready.'

Lila grunts. 'Have you met my boyfriend? Ryan is just as bad.'

They carry on talking about Aston and Ryan, and I zone out, picking at my nails. First dates, now time outside of that and seating arrangements? This is getting crazy.

I mean, I guessed it would happen eventually, but it's just too soon. How am I supposed to spend so much time with a guy I hate?

I twirl a lock of hair around my finger, humming quietly to myself as I enter the library. A quick glance at the clock reads 10.55 a.m. I'm five minutes early to meet Megan – not that it means anything since she's always late anyway.

I sit at my usual table at the back and dump my bag on the table, knocking an earphone out in the process. With a sigh, I put it back in and pull out my English work I've been procrastinating. If there's one thing I hate, it's Shakespeare. I just don't understand him – there's too much tragedy in his work. I'm definitely more of a Disney's happily ever after girl.

I guess if you've suffered enough tragedy in your life, happily ever after becomes something to reach out for.

I open the workbook to the right page and spin my pen in my fingers. The letters blur in front of my eyes and I rub at them to clear them.

I can't concentrate, and I know why. It's this challenge. It's getting to me already. *He's* getting to me already.

Damn Braden Carter, damn my girls, and damn whoever

created the minefield that is the game of love. I'd sure love to shoot Cupid in the ass with his own arrow.

'That book must be really interesting,' a smooth, silky voice says over my shoulder. 'You've been staring at it for five minutes.'

'Braden,' I acknowledge, not needing to look to see if it's him. The hairs standing on the back of my neck are indication enough.

'Want some company, Angel?' He slips into the seat next to me.

I look at him. 'Apparently you're staying, anyway.'

His blue eyes twinkle with amusement. 'Is that a yes?'

'That's an "I'm meeting Megan but whatever."'

'Actually, you're not.' He nudges my foot with his. I frown. 'She said she had to run somewhere so asked me to come and let you know. Since I have a free period I thought I'd join you. If you don't mind.'

Sneaky little witch! 'I guess not, then. I'll warn you though, I don't talk much when I'm studying.'

'Neither do I.' He smiles at me, and I inwardly sigh. I appear to be sighing an awful lot lately.

I set my iPod on shuffle and put the other earphone in. I turn my attention back to Shakespeare's *Much Ado About Nothing* and attempt to sift through the old language. It doesn't go well.

I've been fighting against thrices and m'ladys and hasts for way too long when I feel Braden's arm rest across the back of my chair. He grasps a bit of my hair, teasing it between his fingers. I ignore him. Or, I try to.

He's sitting next to me, so casually. He's chewing his pen and flicking through pages of what looks like a chem book. He's also oblivious to the fact I'm looking at him.

I'm looking at him? Sheesh. I turn my attention back to the book, with him still playing with my hair, and carry on dissecting the scene for Mr Jessop.

An earphone falls out of my ear.

'Ready?' Braden asks.

'For what?' I frown.

'To go to class?' He smirks. 'You really do get lost in studying, don't you?'

'Sometimes,' I answer, shoving everything into my bag. I stand, and he takes my bag from me. 'I can carry my bag, you know.'

'I know.' He starts walking, and I follow him, shaking my head. He holds the library door open for me, and I pass through it, holding my hand out.

'Bag. Please.'

'Why won't you let me carry it?'

I raise an eyebrow. 'Braden, I don't think I've ever seen you carry someone else's bag for them.'

He shrugs and puts a hand on my back, leading me towards our English room. 'You're not anyone else.'

I purse my lips, and my eyes widen when I see Megan sitting in his normal seat next to Aston. I glare at her, and she smiles sweetly.

'Apparently I'm sitting with you.' Braden smiles.

'Apparently.' I sit down and he hands me my stuff. 'Thank you. It was unnecessary, but thank you.'

'Any time.' He turns to me, blue eyes bright under his messy mop of blond hair. 'Have you decided if I get that second date yet?'

I turn my eyes to the front as Mr Jessop walks in. 'I'm still thinking.'

Braden leans in to me, his mouth millimeters from my ear. 'You'll give in, Maddie.'

'Will I now?'

'Yep,' he breathes. 'I'll have that second date, and a third, and then more.'

'You're really confident for someone who messed up on the first date.'

'And that's why you'll give me more dates. They're chances to redeem myself.'

He's right. He'll get more dates, of course he will.

Just not for the reason he thinks.

Chapter Eight

Braden

I'm pretty sure dating isn't supposed to be this fucking hard. A simple yes or no answer would do. All this waiting is driving me up a damn wall. So why am I waiting outside her dorm block for her?

Because it's Wednesday, two days after our first 'date' and two days before our second 'date'. In which I will miss my own damn party for her.

The door opens, and Kay steps in front of me.

'Any reason you're stalkin' my dorm, Carter?' She puts a hand on her hip and looks me over.

'Maddie around?'

'You could call and ask that, you know. Lurking outside girls' dorms isn't a good look for you.'

I clench my teeth. 'Just answer the fucking question, Kay.'

'Yes.' She rolls her eyes. 'She has class in half an hour.'

'Any chance you could call her down, like now?'

She sighs and pulls her cell out. She holds a button and puts it to her ear. 'You have a stalker down here.'

She hangs up and storms past me.

'Thanks, Kay!' I call after her and she flips me off. Bitch.

I run my fingers through my hair, and Maddie appears at the door. Two girls run past her into the building, giggling, and she shakes her head.

'Isn't stalking a little below you, Braden?' She smirks at me, her pink, glossy lips turning up at one side. Her green eyes are wide and lined with a soft brown liner, her auburn hair pulled to one side revealing her very lightly tanned neck.

'You tell me, Maddie,' I reply. She leans against the wall, and

I mimic her movement. 'Will you come on another date, or do I have to stalk you some more?'

She plays with a piece of her hair, sliding her fingers up and down it. It makes me wonder what else she could slide her fingers up and down.

Not the fucking time, Braden. Make her fall in love, don't take her on the damn sidewalk.

'Maybe,' she replies, bringing me back to the conversation. Except now my brain is focused on the way her lips move when she talks.

'Maybe you'll go, or maybe I have to stalk you some more? I gotta say, Angel, I'm down for either.' I rake my eyes down her body, the tight tank top and cut-off shorts, and back up. 'Stalking could definitely have its perks.'

She gasps and slaps my arm. Ouch. That stings. 'You're a pig.'

'So I keep being told.' I sigh. 'At least I'm an honest one.'

'True.' She laughs. 'I guess it depends what you have in mind for this second date.'

'I guess you'll just have to wait and see.'

'Because you have no idea?'

Shit. She's too smart. 'I just have a few things to finalize.'

'Presumptuous,' she challenges.

'I prefer to think of it as hopeful,' I counter, laughing. 'What do you say, Maddie? Please?'

She bites the corner of her thumb, and I shove my hands in my pockets.

'Okay,' she agrees. 'One more date.'

'Really?'

'Really, Braden.' She closes her eyes for a second and turns to the door. She punches the code in and opens it, looking at me over her shoulder through her lashes. 'Mess this up, and there won't be another. I don't do games.'

She steps through and the door swings shuts. I turn and walk down the sidewalk.

Maddie does do games. The only difference is, she doesn't even realize she's playing it.

*

I have no idea what to do for this 'date'. Honestly, trying to get an idea out of my no-dating brain is like getting water from a stone. It's fucking impossible. I'm considering the walk on the beach shit Ryan suggested, but I can't just leave it at that. Can I?

Fuck this. When life gets hard, ask Google. Google knows everything.

I pull my laptop from under the bed and start it up, my leg shaking. The hassle I'm going through just for sex should be illegal in every damn state. Do people do this in real life?

This is crazy. I'm going crazy.

I double-click the browser, and it opens onto Google. *Where to take a girl for your second date*, I type. I hit enter and my cell rings. I trap it between my ear and shoulder as I trawl through the search results.

'Yep?'

'Have you spoken to her yet?' Meggy asks.

'Yep. I waited outside her dorm block earlier.'

'I'm sorry? You did what?' She laughs. 'You actually waited outside for her?'

'I wanted my answer. You know I'm impatient.' I click a link that looks promising.

'Okay. And what did she say?'

'She said yes. What, were you expecting her to say no?'

'I was fifty-fifty.' I know she's smirking, and I'd love to wipe it off her cheeky little face.

'She was always gonna say yes, Meggy. You know that.'

'Whatever. What are you doing now? Do you have anything planned for your big date?'

'I'm working on it,' I answer vaguely.

'That's a no.' She sighs. 'Do you have any idea what you're doing?'

'If you'd be quiet for two minutes, I'd have ten.'

'Are you doing what I think you're doing?'

'It depends what you think I'm doing.'

'Braden William Carter, are you on Google?'

Shit. 'Uh . . .'

She sighs heavily down the phone. 'Go on. Hit me with what it says.'

'Okay.' I scroll down. 'Dinner out, dinner in, a movie, the opera – the fucking opera? No chance. Okay, umm, a picnic, rollerskating, coffee – tried and failed – bowling. Bowling? That could work.'

'You could grab food at the alley,' Meggy suggests. 'You'd have fun.'

'But would Maddie like that?'

'Are you actually asking me if she'd like it? Is Mr Insatiable going soft?'

'Fuck off.' I laugh. 'I don't get this dating thing and you know it. Help me out here.'

'Are you dating her to get in her pants, Bray?' She asks the question so fast I double-take.

Yes. 'No. Why would you ask that?'

'Maybe I'm having a hard time believing you actually like her and want more than sex.'

That's because you're right. 'I like her, Meggy. She's beautiful and smart and funny—'

'And you sound like a robot.'

'I'm trying here.'

'You've always been trying, Bray. So what are you gonna do?'

I sigh. 'Bowling, walk on the beach, then if she wants we can head back here for the party.'

'Sounds good. Bye now.' She hangs up, the call clicking off in my ear. I sometimes wonder if I'd kill her if she wasn't like my little sister.

I dial up the bowling alley and ask for a lane for two on Friday night. The girl at the other end of the phone giggles when I give her my name, and I exhale slowly. Sometimes – and I'd never tell anyone this – the fawning girls gets a little old. I book the alley and hang up pronto.

I chuck my cell down, shut the laptop, and lean my head back against the wall. Date two? Sorted.

Chapter Nine

Maddie

I stare at my phone in disbelief. I left Brooklyn six weeks ago and now, only now, has my brother, Pearce, remembered me. This text message is the first time we've spoken since I came to Berkeley. Well, the first time he's spoken. I sent a text message when I got here to let him know I was safe, and then that was it. Until today.

I look again at my phone. I don't know why I expected any different from him. He would only get in contact if and when he wanted something. And like usual, it's money. I don't want to know what he wants it for, but judging by the fact he's asked for eight hundred dollars, I'd say it's rent. All because his arrogant, selfish ass can't hold down a job long enough to support our suicidal father.

I rub my forehead and try to block out the memories, telling Pearce I'll call up the bank and wire the money to Dad's account. Not that it makes a difference. Pearce will use it on what he wants anyway, thinking of Dad second.

A wave of guilt crashes into me for leaving Dad, but I remind myself it's what he wanted, what she would have wanted for me. Pearce has always been too self-absorbed to make something of his life. I got the brains, and that's why she saved the money for me to access when I turned eighteen.

My college fund, she called it one day. Said she'd been saving since she knew I was coming, that she wanted me to have a good life. She'd been saving for Pearce too, but he bought a car and god knows what else. She'd be ashamed if she could see him now. She'd be so mad.

I squeeze my eyes shut, banishing those thoughts from my

mind. Three years and the wound is still too fresh, too raw. The pain still trickles out the way blood trickles from a paper cut, but it's bearable. It's just a part of my life. Another part that I should have left behind when I left Brooklyn. But, like all good tragedies do, it's followed me.

I decide to skip out on going to the library for my free period, instead choosing to work from the safe bubble of my dorm. Plus, going to the library means bumping into Braden.

The Californian equivalent of my brother.

My thoughts fall to our 'date' tomorrow night. He must want in my pants really badly if he's still waiting. Usually he'll hang for half an hour – if you show your interest, good. If not, he's onto the next. Yep, you can't deny he doesn't mess around when it comes to his sex life. In fact, a part of me almost respects him for going after what he wants.

A part the size of my baby toe. The rest of me still thinks he's a pig.

I wonder what Mom would think if she knew I was doing this challenge. As an independent, strong woman, she'd probably be a little proud that I'm gonna put him in his place. As a mother, she'd warn me to be careful and not lose my own heart in the process. I snort at the idea. Lose my heart to Braden Carter?

Never going to happen.

'Casual,' Kay shouts from the bathroom.

'No, casual dressy,' Lila argues, shaking her head.

'Lila, they're bowling.' Megan huffs. 'She needs to be casual yet comfy. I'd say a casual dress or a nice top and those tight jeans you have.'

'The ones that give my ass its own ass?' I raise a brow.

'Yes. We need to show him what's on offer.' She moves towards my drawers.

'Make me sound like a promotional display at Target, why don't you?' I roll my eyes. 'Besides, I thought we were making him fall in love with me, not turn him into a walking erection.'

'The way to Braden's heart is through his dick.' She takes

the jeans, shuts the drawer with her hip, and passes them to me. Kay roars with laughter and comes back into the room.

'Braden has a heart?' She laughs. 'Funny, Megs, funny.'

'Hey.' Megan turns and points her finger at her. 'He does. It's just wrapped up in latex and usually between some girl's legs.'

'Nice,' I mutter, taking the jeans. Lila pats my arm sympathetically.

'It won't be that bad, Maddie,' she reassures me. 'Besides, if you tell him you wanna head back to the party afterward, we'll be there and you can escape for a few minutes.'

'But it's gonna be like, two hours.' I watch Megan rifle through my closet. 'Two hours alone with Braden. This is gonna be torture. You guys don't even understand it.'

'You can't hate him that much, Mads.' Megan turns. 'Can you?'

I sigh, looking at the carpet. 'You have no idea. I wasn't joking when I said he was everything I hated.'

'Then don't do it.' Kay spears me with her gaze. 'Give up. Quit.' She shrugs a shoulder.

'What?' I frown.

'If it's that bad, then back out. We won't hold it against you, but it'll be you wondering whether or not it would have worked.'

'Don't do your reverse psychology trash on me, Kay.' I sniff, standing and moving to my closet. I pull out a long, white top with a floral design and grab my white gladiator sandals. 'You all know I won't give up. I'll just have to suffer for your amusement.'

I turn and storm into the bathroom to get changed. Quit. I might be annoyed I have to do this, but I'm not going to give up. I said I would do it, and I will.

I change quickly, brushing my hair and securing it into a ponytail with a band. A quick brush of mascara on my lashes, a hint of bronzer along my cheekbones followed by a slick of gloss on my lips, and I decide it's as good as it's gonna get.

Kay whistles when I walk back into our room.

'Sexy lady!' She winks and I crack a smile at her.

'Good enough?' I spin and bow.

'Perfect,' Megan declares. 'Braden won't be able to resist you.'

I move to the mirror and slightly tease my bangs. That's what I'm worried about.

A horn beeps outside and Lila squeals, running to the window. 'He's here!'

'Great,' I mutter, grabbing my purse. 'Have fun without me, and try not to think of me too much, yeah?'

'You'll be fine, baby girl.' Kay grins at me. 'Shake your ass, flick your hair, and bat those eyelashes a few times. Do that, and this is in the bag!'

'Right.' I sigh, waving over my shoulder as I shut the door behind me. I skip down the stairs, not wanting to prolong this 'date'.

I can see him through the window of the main door. His hands are in the pockets of another pair of washed-out dark jeans, a black top covering his muscular torso. I open the door, and he smiles at me, his blue eyes brightening under his blond hair.

I get why girls fall over him. That smile is disarming.

'Maddie.' He says my name softly. 'You look beautiful.'

He's laying it on thick tonight, apparently. 'Thank you. You don't look so bad yourself.'

'You mean you can deal being seen in public with me?' He raises his eyebrows, and I smile, stepping into the evening sunshine.

'Maybe. Although, be warned, if we see anyone we know I *will* hide.' I follow him to his car – a black Jetta. Of course. I bet he doesn't foot the bill, though.

He opens the door for me, and I climb in, sinking into the leather seats. Stylish.

'Nice car,' I compliment as he gets in next to me.

'Thanks.' He grins. 'Graduation present. I worked hard for this baby.' He pats the dashboard and starts the engine, pulling away from my block smoothly.

'I'm sure you did,' I mutter, looking out of the window.

'What?' He glances at me quickly.

'Nothing.' I wish I'd backed out earlier. In three days I've had two chances to throw my hands up and say 'stuff it', and I haven't. Why? Because I'm probably borderline clinically insane. Failing that, I'm just damn stupid.

Hearing from Pearce yesterday has just reshaped Braden in my mind. When I look at him, I see all the things my brother did to my old best friend. I take a deep breath and let it out slowly. I won't think of that today. I won't think of how I saw him destroy her and our friendship in the process.

'You look like you're thinking too hard, Angel.' Braden shifts in his seat, and I realize we've pulled up to the bowling alley. I turn to him.

'Just thinking about my family, that's all,' I reply, unclipping the seatbelt. I hear his door open and close, then mine opens. He's playing the gentleman game. 'Thank you,' I say and accept the hand he gives me.

'I'm sorry,' he says, locking the car and putting a hand on my back. 'I forget you're from Brooklyn. It must be hard being away from your family.'

What's left of it. 'Sometimes. Sometimes I'm glad of the freedom I have now.'

'I bet.' He smiles down at me. 'Do you speak to them much?'

'Is this twenty questions?' I'm amused.

'Would you be annoyed if I said yes?'

'Not at all.' I let out a small laugh. 'Last I heard, a girl was lucky if Braden Carter asked her name.'

He smirks down at me and pulls me towards the counter. 'Then you should consider yourself *very* lucky.' He looks up at the girl behind the counter who beams at him, twirling her hair round her finger and sticking out her chest.

He's clearly on a date. Do these girls have no morals?

Not that I'm bothered. It's just sickening.

'I have a lane booked for six thirty. Under Carter?' he says, ignoring her obvious attempts at getting his attention. Woah, he's good.

'Of course, we have you booked in here. In fact, I think I

took the call.' Boobs beams even wider and crosses his name off the list with a flourish. Ugh. Go look in a mirror and practice being a Barbie doll. She's practically a life-size one anyway.

'I'm sure you did.' Braden smiles politely, albeit tightly at her. It doesn't look forced. Whoa, hold on there. Could Mr Playboy hate all that attention? Surely not. Another glance at him. Yep. He's definitely not impressed. I file that bit of information away for the dissection of the date tomorrow with the girls. *Interesting.*

'Maddie?' He taps my side. 'What size shoes do you need?'

'Oh, um, a seven, please.' I smile sweetly at Boobs. She gives me an icy look and grabs a pair of shoes. I look at the size when she slides them to me. 'They're a nine,' I tell her. 'I said *seven.*'

She snatches them back and passes me another pair. Sevens.

'Thank you.' I give her another sweet smile and follow Braden to the seats opposite to change our shoes.

'Feisty,' he whispers when we sit down.

'She gave me the wrong size.' I put my socks on from my purse. 'Plus I'm pretty sure she's jealous.'

'Oh, this again?' He winks at me. I roll my eyes and hand him my sandals as we stand.

'Try not to get sucked in by her chest when you hand them back.'

'Why, Maddie.' He steps closer to me, hooking a finger under my chin and tilting it upwards. 'Are *you* jealous?'

I bat my eyelashes twice. 'Would you be annoyed if I said yes?'

He laughs loudly and runs his thumb across my jaw. 'No, Angel, I wouldn't be annoyed. In fact, I'm pretty sure I'd like it if you were jealous. That, and I can see you and jealousy being crazy sexy. We'd probably have to leave if you were.'

He hands the shoes to Boobs and comes back to me, sliding his arm round my waist.

'That would be unfortunate,' I whisper, biting my lip to stop myself laughing.

'Not from where I'm standing,' he says into my ear in a husky voice.

Play. The. Game.

'Then I might just be jealous.'

'You are?' He raises his eyebrows.

'Yes, but there's a bowling ball over there with my name on it and a guy standing next to me whose ass I have to kick. So yes, leaving would be unfortunate.' I spin from his hold and walk backwards, grinning. His lips curl up in an amused smile, his eyes sparkling.

'Then let's make a deal. If you kick my ass, I get to touch yours.'

Here we go. Round one, ding ding.

'Braden, you don't lose then,' I say innocently, my hand on the blue ball I always use.

'I know.' He stops in front of me, and I bite my top lip. He looks down at my mouth. 'I don't like to lose.'

I release my lip and my heart pounds. Is that a challenge, or a promise? 'Neither do I,' I whisper. 'So prepare to get your ass kicked.'

I haul the ball from the stand and turn to our lane. I feel him tug my hair as he comes up behind me.

'I'm going to enjoy touching your ass, Maddie.'

'I'm going to enjoy kicking *your* ass, Braden.'

'Feisty,' he repeats, grinning again.

I smirk at him and step up to take the first bowl. In a roundabout way, this is actually kinda fun.

Chapter Ten

Braden

Maddie reaches up and tugs her hair from its holder. Her fiery red curls fan out around her shoulders, settling with one last bounce down her back. The end of her hair is inches from her ass – the ass I got to touch earlier, per winning conditions.

She won, but I did get to touch that pert little butt, so I'd call that a win-win situation.

'So,' I begin as we walk across the sand. 'You never answered my question earlier.'

'What question?' She looks at me with those big green eyes of hers.

'Do you speak to your family much?'

'My dad and I talk about once a week, usually on Sunday. It's become kind of a habit. My brother? Not so much.' She shrugs a shoulder.

'Aren't you close?'

She snorts, shaking her head. 'About as close as two opposite poles.'

'What about your mom? Do you ever speak?'

She stops by the edge of the water, drawing a line in the sand with her toe. Her eyes mist over a little, and I move next to her. She looks up, and there's pure, raw pain in her eyes. Pain I can't even begin to understand.

'My mom died three years ago,' she whispers softly, dropping her eyes again. 'She was a victim of a drive-by shooting.'

Shit. 'I'm sorry,' I say lamely. What the fuck do you say to that?

'Don't be.' Maddie looks at me. 'Did you shoot her? No. It's not your fault. Don't apologize for what someone else did.'

I reach up and tuck her hair behind her ear. What is it about her hair?

'I'm sorry you had to go through that.'

Her eyes are startlingly clear as she takes in my words. She doesn't flinch, doesn't cry, and doesn't break. Is her heart made of stone?

'So am I,' she finally replies. 'But it's done. There's no point in dwelling on what could have, should have, or would have been, because that doesn't make it any better for anyone. In fact, it probably makes it worse. She's gone. I can't change that, I can only live with it. And I do,' she continues, quieter. 'I live with it every day, and I'm always gonna miss her, but just because she's gone doesn't mean I can't be the person I'm meant to be.'

Shit, that's insightful. What do you say to that? How is this little girl able to render me speechless? I have an answer for everything.

Granted, it's usually a swear word or sex-related, but it's still an answer.

I slide my hand from her shoulder down her arm. I slip my fingers between hers and squeeze gently. 'You're really strong, you know that?'

'No. I'm just me.'

'Doesn't change it. You are strong.'

'What about you?' she says suddenly, the mist clearing from her eyes. That's all I'll get out of her today. But if she opens up, she trusts me, right? That is what it means? And trust leads to love. Where is Megan when I need her?

Shit. I'm a prize dick for thinking about that shit when she's just bared her soul to me.

'Not much to tell.' We start walking again, our clasped hands swinging slightly between us. 'Grew up in Palm Springs with Megan, lived the good, easy life, then spread my wings and came to college.'

'With Megan.'

'Yeah. We made a pact we'd go to college together. I'm only two months older than her, and we saw each other every day as we grew up. She's like my sister.'

Maddie nods, and I can tell she understands. It's a relief because it'll make the whole 'dating' thing easier, but not even the guys get why I'm so protective over her. Touch her and you die kinda protective.

'I think it's nice you're so close,' she says. 'I miss having that closeness with someone. Maybe I'll find it again one day.'

'I'm sure you will. Who knows? We might be that close one day.' God, I really am laying it on thick today.

She turns up to me, a smirk on her lips and her eyebrows quirked. 'Presumptuous.'

'I prefer hopeful.' I grin. She laughs and shakes her head. 'Seriously.'

'Okay, Braden.' She's still shaking her head. 'It'll be a miracle if this . . .' She motions between us. '. . . lasts beyond tonight.'

'Is that what you think?' I challenge her, stopping in front of her and holding her other hand.

'Why wouldn't it be? I've had your attention for oh, six days. That's a miracle in itself.'

I shake my head. She's fucking smart, and now I have to play it just as smart. It's all a game. Love or be loved. I don't do the first one, so it's gonna have to be the second. Megan's made me watch enough chick flicks in my life. I can fake this mushy shit.

'Angel,' I say softly, running my thumb across her cheek, across the tiny freckles I've never noticed until now. 'What if I ask you to give me a chance?'

'A chance? At what?'

'A chance to be more than your friend.'

Her eyes flick across my face, checking my sincerity. Luckily I'm good at holding a mask in place.

'And?' she asks.

'And what?'

'And what if you mess up? What then?' Maddie looks down.

'Then I give you full permission to set Kay on my ass,' I say quietly, tilting her face up. 'I promise. I'm not perfect, Maddie, I'm nothing like perfect, and I'm the first to admit it. But, if you'll let me, I'll try and be perfect for you. So you can have that closeness you want.'

I'm a prick.

'Fine,' she says after a moment. 'One chance, Braden. That's all.'

I smile slowly at her and rest my forehead against hers. My breath fans across her mouth, and she closes her eyes. Kiss her, and I've sealed the deal.

I lower my lips to hers, and my fucking phone rings. I sigh and step away from her, putting it to my ear.

'What?' I snap.

'Oho, did I interrupt something?' Ryan snickers.

'You have the worst timing ever.' I glance at Maddie, and she blushes a little, looking away.

'Do I now?'

'Yep. What do you want, asshole?'

'Are you coming back here? Lila wants to know how your date went. She's having fuckin' kittens here, man.'

I cover the bottom of my phone with my hand and look at Maddie. 'Wanna head back to the house? The girls are there already.'

'Sure.' She smiles up at me.

'We're on our way,' I say into the phone. 'See you in a few.' I hang up and shove it back into my pocket. 'Asshole.'

Maddie chews the inside of her lip to control her laughter.

'Hey.' I nudge her and take her hand in mine again. 'Don't laugh.'

'Sorry.' Her eyes glimmer with amusement.

'No you're not.'

'You're right. I'm not.' She shrugs and grins, tugging me along. 'Come on. I bet Kay already has my shots lined up, and she'll drink them if I don't!'

I look upwards and shake my head, following her back to my car.

I have a girlfriend. A fake girlfriend, but still a girlfriend.

Who the fuck would have thought?

Chapter Eleven

Maddie

We enter the house, and music pounds against us. Braden reaches for my hand, linking his fingers through mine. I let him, squeezing his hand lightly, and he pulls me through the packed house. We surface in the kitchen where Kay, Megan, and Lila are sitting by the bar.

'I'm gonna go find Ryan.' He leans down and whispers in my ear. 'Wait for me by the bar?'

I nod and step forward, releasing his hand. I smile at him over my shoulder, and he winks. Jesus. It's been twenty minutes and already, I'm tired of pretending I give a shit about any of it. Although, I am questioning why I opened up to him earlier. Maybe it's because I don't care and I know it's vital to him falling for me. Pity, right? Poor little Maddie. I scoff at myself.

Megan slides her arm through mine the second I reach her. 'Well?'

'Game on,' I whisper, smirking at Lila and Kay.

'Whoooooooop!' Kay yells and waves to Kyle. 'Eight shots, two each, one two bam!'

'You got it!' Kyle winks at me. I smile politely at him. As far as the University of California, Berkeley is concerned, I'm in a relationship with Braden Carter. Not that Kyle will understand that.

'Good night?' he asks as he slides the glasses to us.

'I'd say it was,' Lila giggles, holding up a shot. We all grab a glass and throw it back, followed by the second one.

'And why's that?' He leans forward, moving his face towards mine.

'Because she has a boyfriend.' Megan smirks and turns.

'You're kidding,' Kyle deadpans.

'Um, or not.' I shrug a shoulder.

'You're with Braden?'

'She is,' Braden says, coming up behind me. 'Problem, Kyle?'

Kyle looks up, and rage is written all over his face. 'Yeah, actually. Yeah, there is.'

'Then please, share why you're so much better than I am.'

Kyle glances at me, and I step to the side.

'Animals,' I mutter. Lila nods her agreement.

'No, Maddie.' Braden looks at me. 'I wanna know what he thinks *he* can give you that *I* can't.'

'Bray . . .' Megan warns.

'What I can give her that you can't? Maybe a secure relationship full of trust, where she won't be worried if you're gonna run off and fuck one of your whores.' Kyle looks at him in disgust. 'And the rest. There just isn't enough time in a day to describe how much of a prick you are to girls.'

'Hey!' Megan protests, slapping her hands on the counter. 'Out of order, Kyle.'

'He asked.'

'Yeah, and now *I'm* telling you that's enough!'

'No, Meggy, let him carry on.' Braden's face is like stone.

'Aren't you gonna step in?' Kay whispers.

'What's the point?' I shrug. 'They'll still have this pissing contest. Besides, it'll get what we want.'

'What's that?'

'Attention on our relationship.'

She slaps my shoulder. 'Smart girl.'

'Braden, we all know you're not gonna hang around for her. You just wanna fuck her and move on. You aren't worth shit on someone's shoe. Why not let her have someone who'll treat her right and not like one of your sluts?' Kyle says loudly.

Braden launches himself over the bar, kicking a bottle of vodka over and sending it smashing to the ground. He grabs Kyle's shirt and pins him to the wall.

'You wanna fuckin' repeat that, Kyle?' Braden hisses through clenched teeth.

'Oh, sake.' Megan sighs, shaking her head.

'I would, but I think you heard me the first time,' Kyle replies. 'Besides, not exactly showing your girl how much of a decent boyfriend you are, are you?'

'Yeah, Kyle, that's right. *My* girl. Maddie is *mine*, and don't you forget that.' Braden lets him go and glares at him. 'Try anything with her and a bottle won't be the only thing getting fuckin' broken.'

'Okay.' Ryan slips in. 'Show's over, boys. Kiss and make up or get the fuck away from each other.'

'Oh, better late than never,' Lila mutters. 'He'd be late to his own damn funeral.'

I snort and cover my mouth with my hand. Not the time. I drop it and look back towards Braden.

Megan says something to him, and he turns to look at me, a hint of regret in his blue eyes. I hold my stance, keeping his eye contact. Megan says something else, and he nods, moving forward. He takes my hand silently and leads me from the room.

'Party on, guys. Nothing to see!' Ryan yells as we head upstairs.

Braden leads me up two flights of stairs and unlocks a door. His room.

It's spotless. For some reason, I'm surprised, and I glance at him quickly. The dark covers on the bed stand out against the standard white walls, and a desk piled up with books sits in the corner. The only way you can tell it's a teenage boy's room is by the large screen TV attached to the wall above an Xbox. Naturally.

'Maddie?' He shuts the door and raises a hand to my face. 'I'm sorry, Angel. I didn't mean for that to happen.'

'You seem to do a lot of things you don't mean, Braden,' I reply.

'I know. Always around you.' He smiles wryly. I shrug one shoulder. 'I don't want you to think any differently of me because of that.'

Play the game, Maddie.

'Because of what?'

He quirks a brow and smiles. 'The fact I nearly punched him in the face.'

'Why would I think any differently? Isn't that what you're supposed to do?' My eyes flicker to our clasped hands and back up to him.

'I think so.'

I laugh. 'Wow, you really don't date.'

'Didn't, I didn't. I don't know if you noticed, but half the people downstairs just saw me go all protective over you.'

'Ah, yes. The caveman performance. Me, Braden. Maddie, mine. That?'

He chuckles. 'Yes, that.'

'Well I doubt anyone's gonna try and take me now,' I say. 'I think it's kinda obvious who thinks I belong to them.'

'Who thinks?' He steps closer.

'Yes, thinks.' I narrow my eyes slowly. 'I don't belong to anyone but myself. My body and my life are mine to control, and being someone's girlfriend isn't gonna change that.'

'Usually, at this point, I'd admit how turned on I am but I think I'll just go for this: Maddie, you're mine. Like it or not, you are.' He cups my cheek.

'Your girlfriend. That's it. I still don't belong to you.'

'Why are you turning this into an argument?' he growls.

'I'm not!' I protest. 'I just don't do that caveman thing, okay?'

'You are!'

'Now who's arguing?'

'Maddie.'

'Braden.'

'Do you ever shut up?'

'No. I don't.'

'Fantastic. I had to pick the girl who always talks.'

'Then I'll go and talk to someone who'll listen that isn't stuck in the Stone Ages!' I snatch my hand from his and spin towards the door.

'No you won't!' He growls again and pins me to the door.

'Stopping me already?' He's infuriating. Why am I doing this stupid challenge again?

'No, I'm just wondering if you're better at kissing than you are at talking.' His eyes fix on my lips, and my tongue flicks out, wetting them.

'Maybe I am, but if *you* keep talking you'll never find out, will you?'

He drops his head and softly presses his lips against mine. One of his hands slide around my waist, pulling me against him, and the other slides through my hair. I gasp as he gently sucks my bottom lip, and he takes his chance, slipping his tongue into my mouth. My hands grip his arms, slide across his shoulders, and link behind his neck.

He's soft yet probing as he kisses me, and I can't help the sprint my heart has entered. I simultaneously hate him and want him, and those feelings collide inside me, mixing into something indiscernible.

Heat spreads through my body, and Braden pulls me even closer to him. I'm flush against him, feeling every curve and definition of muscle on his torso. I unlink my hands and slip them upwards into his hair, wrapping my fingers around it.

'Maddie,' he whispers against my mouth, pulling back slightly. 'We have to stop, or I won't be able to.'

Stop? Stop what? The kissing? Oh. Really?

'Okay,' I reply.

'Angel, it's only because I know you're not like most girls. We'll go further when you're ready, okay?'

I nod, and he kisses me again, a lingering touch on my swollen lips.

He slides his hand down so they're both on my back and dips his head into my neck. He buries his face in my hair, and I turn my head into him, letting him hold me.

In this second, I'm not thinking about the challenge. I'm not thinking about Brooklyn, or why I hate Braden. All I'm thinking is that kiss was the best damn kiss I've ever had.

And that could be a problem.

Chapter Twelve

Braden

I wake up and shake my head at myself. Yesterday runs through my mind on fast-forward, and I remember – I have a girlfriend. Fuck. That's weird.

And then there was Kyle. The guy has a real stick up his ass about me being with Maddie – and not that I blame him, if I was him, I probably would too. I know what half the people at the party last night were thinking. They were wondering why Maddie is so different from the others and what's so special about her. The girls were cursing her for taking what they wanted, and the guys were slinking back into their dark corners, their chances at seducing her shot to hell.

Well, fuck them all.

'Well?' Ryan opens my door.

'Don't bother knocking,' I say sarcastically, putting my phone down. 'I love it when assholes barge in on me.'

'Uh, yeah.' He raises an eyebrow and shuts the door, sitting on my desk chair. 'What was that shit about?'

'I was about to kiss her. Seal the deal on this challenge then you fuckin' called me.'

'Shit, man. Sorry. If I'd have known—'

'You'd be damn psychic.' I laugh and sit up in bed. 'Doesn't matter.'

'You sealed it then?'

'Last night after my caveman performance.'

'Caveman performance?' He snickers.

'Her words, man, her words.' I smirk and grab my phone, waving it in his direction. 'Do you mind? I have to text my girlfriend.'

Ryan lets out a loud laugh and slaps his leg. 'Fuck me, that's a good one. Did you just say girlfriend?'

'You deaf? Course I did.'

'Wait, you're serious?' He stops laughing.

'Dude, we're official. You should have known it wouldn't have taken me long to make it exclusive.' I waggle my little finger at him. 'See this? She's wrapped right round it.'

Chapter Thirteen

Maddie

'See this?' I waggle my little finger around the room. 'He's wrapped right round it.'

'I don't doubt it,' Megan smirks. 'I saw him go mental on Kyle, remember?'

Kay leans back on her bed, crossing her arms behind her head and sighing happily. 'This shit is entertaining. And so fuckin' satisfying.'

'Satisfying?' Lila looks at her.

'Yeah. Braden Carter, Mr Playboy himself is wrapped around little old Maddie's baby finger. He's like a fly in a spider's web.'

'Except I'm not gonna eat him for dinner,' I remind her. 'I'm no cannibal.'

'Well.' She rolls over slightly and waggles her eyebrows. 'You could always—'

'Stop,' Megan orders. She holds her hand up. 'No further, Kayleigh. That is quite enough.'

'Filthy mind.' Lila giggles. I grin, and Megan pulls out the OPTP plan.

'So, we're a day ahead of schedule.' She runs a finger down it. 'Good going, Mads. What's happening today? Are you seeing each other?'

'Uh, I'm not sure.' I smile sheepishly. 'But I finally gave him my number.' Kay woots. 'So he'll probably call or something.'

My phone chimes, and I reach for it.

'Speak of the devil,' Lila smirks.

Morning, Angel. Free today?

I look up from the message, shake my phone and grin. 'Bingo.'

Slow, mischievous smiles break out on the three faces in front of me, and I know it's about to go down. Megan licks her lips.

'Don't text back yet.' She uncaps her pen. 'After last night, Stage Two should be pretty easy. He went all protective on your pretty ass, and everyone at the frat party would have seen it, heard it, or heard of it.'

'No one will believe it, though,' Lila points out.

'Then whenever you're in public, you make sure you're touching, laughing, or kissing.' Kay sighs. 'Not hard, guys. Jesus.'

Megan chucks the pen cap at her. 'Attitude, Kayleigh.'

'Shut up.' Kay chucks it back.

'Kids.' I laugh. 'What's the plan? I know one is coming.'

'It is.' Megan scribbles something, putting an exaggerated dot at the end. 'You'll double date with Ryan and Lila one night this week.'

'What?' Lila and I say simultaneously.

'You'll double date with Ryan and Lila,' she repeats.

'What?'

'You. Will. Double. Date. With. Ryan. And. Lila,' Kay says slowly, pronouncing each word perfectly.

'I heard it the first time,' I say through clenched teeth. 'No offence, Lila, but if there's anything worse than dating Braden Carter, it's double dating with Ryan.'

'You're actually kinda lucky it's Ryan,' Lila muses. 'He's a pain in the ass, but Aston is way worse.'

'This is true,' Kay agrees. 'But Aston is one hot mofo.'

'I thought you preferred girls?'

'I do. Doesn't mean I don't like a bit of—'

'Okay!' I interrupt to Kay's laughter. 'When is this date happening? I need to mentally prepare myself.'

'And text Bray back,' Megan replies.

'Oh, yeah.' I unlock my phone and look at the screen. 'Um, what do I say?'

They all sigh. 'What did he say?'

'Asked me what I was doing.'

'Then tell him you're free.'

'Okay.'

Morning :) nothing planned. You?

I press send and shrug. 'Seems easy enough.'

I was hoping to see you. Maybe we could redo the coffee thing? he replies.

I'm sure we can. Meet you there in a half hour?

See you then.

'I'm meeting him at Starbucks in a half hour,' I announce.

'I'm coming!' Megan caps the pen and grins.

'Doesn't that defy the date thing?' Lila raises an eyebrow.

'No.'

'How doesn't it?'

Megan sighs and rolls her eyes. 'Me and Bray are like family, right? Everyone always thinks there's something between us – and there absolutely is not, like, ew – so by seeing the three of us together, everyone will know they're serious. They'll see that there's nothing between me and Bray, that there *is* between him and Mads, and that she accepts the closeness of our non-related brother-sister relationship, therefore solidifying the belief that Braden and Maddie are dating. Seriously dating.'

'But there's nothing between us.' Confusing. Remind me why I'm doing this again?

Because I hate everything he represents to females. And he's a good kisser.

And that's totally contradictory.

'You know that. I know that. Lila and Kay know that, but, Mads, Braden *doesn't*.' She straightens out her outfit.

'Neither does the rest of campus,' Kay finishes. 'So, to the rest of the world, there is something between you.'

'Great.' I sigh. 'You couldn't challenge me to something easy or fun, could you?' Because I absolutely did not have fun last night. Dammit.

'Never.' Lila taps a message out on her phone. 'Everyone's going to the beach tonight. Another chance to spread the word that Braden Carter has been reeled in.'

Kay grins. 'Spread the word? I'm on it.' She grabs her cell, and I shake my head.

'Shall we leave them to it, Megs?' I stand up and grab my stuff. 'They look like they have it under control.'

Megan's light blue eyes sparkle. 'Let's go.'

Chapter Fourteen

Braden

I hear Megan's laugh before I see her and Maddie round the corner. Company. Brilliant. I know what she's doing here. Meggy will give me the creepy silent 411 with her eyes-thing she does.

Ignoring my best friend of a lifetime, I focus on Maddie. If I was going to fake date someone, then fuck me, I chose a gem with her. Her figure is obvious even in a denim skirt and simple shirt – she's not skinny and she's not overly curvy. She has a perfect mixture of toned muscle and curve that has me itching to run my hands across every inch of her bare skin. That kiss last night didn't help matters. I felt that damn body against me.

Shaking off my x-rated thoughts, I grin at her when she stops in front of me. She smiles at me, and I bend down slowly, cupping her head and capturing her soft lips with mine. One of her hands rests on my waist to steady her, and the other grips the arm holding her. She responds to the kiss almost eagerly, and I'm in no hurry to pull away.

This girl can do crazy shit with her mouth on mine. I'm not gonna lie and say I don't want that mouth elsewhere on me, 'cause I do, but until that happens I could stand here and kiss her all damn day.

Megan coughs discreetly, and I reluctantly release Maddie.

'Good morning, Angel,' I say softly.

'Good morning.' She bites her top lip and looks up at me with those pretty little eyes.

'Good morning, Bray. I'd ask you how you are today, but you seem pretty damn good,' Megan says sarcastically.

'Good morning, Meggy.' I wrap my arm around Maddie. 'I'm fine and dandy this morning. How are you?'

'Oh, you heard me then?' She rolls her eyes. Maddie smirks next to me.

I tug on her hair. 'I'd have to be seriously hearing-impaired to *not* hear you.'

'That, or busy playing a serious game of tonsil tennis.' She opens the door to Starbucks and winks at me.

'No tonsils involved,' Maddie replies casually. 'I haven't had my coffee yet. If he'd tried that, I would have bitten him.'

Maddie Stevens, biting me? Yes. Fucking. Please.

'Sounds promising,' I mutter. Megan elbows me.

'Pig.'

'You should know I'm a pig.' We approach the counter. 'I don't know why you're surprised.'

'What can I get for you?' the barista says. I think it's the same one as the other day – and she's hot. Dark where Maddie is fiery and maybe a little more meat on her bones. Still, I'd give her one. Or two.

'I got this.' I wink at Maddie. 'Two grande double chocolate chip fraps.'

'Impressive.' She looks up at me and smiles.

'I got it right?'

'Yes, but you forgot the muffins.'

I laugh and pull her a little closer to me. 'And two blueberry muffins.'

'And I'll have a caramel frap with extra cream,' Meggy puts in. 'He's paying.'

I shrug as if to say 'what can I do?' but I don't care. It's fucking coffee.

The barista bustles around making them and sets them on the counter, sticking her chest in my direction. Her name tag tells me she's Amanda. Like I care – her name is irrelevant.

I pick up a coffee and hand it to Maddie, training my eyes to ignore the way Amanda's boobs are popping out of her blouse. Shit, this exclusive shit is hard work. Maddie takes the coffee and curls right into my side, shooting Amanda a look. Oh yeah, the girl has it bad for me.

'He has a girlfriend, obviously.' Meggy picks up her cup. 'Don't be so cheap.'

I smirk, and Maddie sputters on the mouthful of coffee she's just taken. I rub her back soothingly. 'You okay, Maddie?'

'Fine,' she squeaks. 'Just fine.'

Meggy smiles at Amanda and turns to the plush sofas in the far corner of the room. I lead Maddie over and slide in next to her, making sure my leg touches hers. She settles her coffee on the table and picks at her muffin the same way she did on Tuesday, popping small pieces between those lips of hers.

I'd love to be that muffin right now.

I watch, mesmerized by the way she licks her lips after every bite, her tongue flicking out daintily to wipe away the crumbs. I'd love to be those crumbs too.

'Braden?'

I turn to look at Meggy. 'What?'

'I said, are you going to the beach party tonight?' A slow, knowing smile breaks out on her face. She caught me watching Maddie. Busted.

'Depends,' I answer, sliding my hand onto Maddie's thigh. Her skin is silky smooth, like marble. My dick stirs, and I instantly imagine those thighs wrapped around my waist . . . My legs . . . My neck . . .

'On what?'

'If my girl is going.' My eyes meet hers, and I draw gentle circles on her bare skin. Fuck. I'm actually torturing myself.

'Lila said earlier that she and Ryan are going. I don't mind,' she says. 'It could be fun.'

'Then yes, I'm going,' I tell Meggy. Her lips purse into an amused smile, and I graze my teeth along my bottom lip. 'What?'

'Nothing.' She relaxes back into her seat. 'Nothing at all.'

Fucking liar.

The door opens, and I glance over. I glance again – and one

of the girls is Blondie from last weekend. The one I blew off. This could be a little awkward.

She looks over at me and wiggles her fingers. 'Hi, Braden!'

I see Maddie's eyes flick towards her, back to me, back to her. I know she's making the connection, and I know what she's thinking. Shit.

I take my hand from her thigh and link my fingers through hers, bringing her hand to my mouth and pressing a soft kiss to her knuckles. She looks at me and her eyes are guarded, hardened, and definitely not showing the playful look she had in them earlier.

'Do you always ignore the girls you sleep with?' she asks quietly, looking at a spot on the wall behind me. Meggy gets up, mumbling something about needing the ladies room. Whatever.

'Maddie, I didn't sleep with her.' I tug her hand. 'She tried, but I wasn't interested. Not after I saw you that night.'

At least that isn't a lie.

Her green eyes collide with mine. 'I don't know whether to believe you or not. She looks like she knows you pretty well.'

'If she does it's because she spent the better part of twenty minutes rubbing her surgically enhanced body up against me while I watched you.'

She scoffs and shakes her head. 'Wow. Is that a compliment or an insult?'

I don't think I'm supposed to answer that. Am I? Girls are fucking complicated.

'Believe me when I say I've only got eyes for you. I'm not interested in anyone else.' When we're alone. I turn her face towards mine gently and lean in. 'Just you, Angel, okay? Not Blondie over there.'

I brush her lips with mine. This might be a game, but I could get used to kissing her.

She smiles against my mouth. 'Blondie? Don't you even know her name?'

I pull away so our foreheads are touching. 'No, like I said,

I was too busy watching you to care if her name was Laura or fuckin' Popsicle.'

Maddie giggles and I grin.

'Okay,' she says softly. 'I believe you.'

'Good,' I mutter and kiss her again, for longer this time.

That was a fucking close call.

Chapter Fifteen

Maddie

'The whole "do you always ignore the girls you sleep with?" line was magic, Maddie. Pure freakin' magic.' Megan laughs across the room. I pause, my mascara wand suspended in mid-air and smile at her through the mirror. I'm glad she's thinking about the plan, because I'm not.

I'm too preoccupied with how I feel when he's touching me. When he did the hand on thigh move earlier I wanted to castrate him. Really, I wanted to rip off his gentlemanly parts and rub them against a cheese grater. Repeatedly. When he started rubbing my leg, I wanted to punch him, yet when he took his hand away I wanted to grab it and demand he left it there.

That thought makes me feel slightly ill. I wanted Braden Carter to touch me, and when he did I enjoyed it. I damn well enjoyed that innocently sexy move he did with the pad of his thumb against the inside of my leg. This plan is getting dangerous.

It's a week in and already I can feel a little crack against my attraction to him. Yeah, the same attraction I locked away in a steel box complete with heavy duty padlock and a coded password.

What gets me is how I could be disgusted with him one minute and kissing him the next. And I didn't care. I still don't care. Ugh, how can I like kissing someone I hate so much? I need to remember this is a game, and to win I have to play. I have to play by the rules. *His* rules. The only way to win is by playing by the rules of the player.

Sex governs the game. It's the aim, the grand prize. Anything other than sexual attraction and feelings of sexual want don't have a place here, not on my watch.

One week down and three to go. He's feeling more than just sex with me, that much is clear. My act is believable, and I know he's falling for it. And me.

I just have to remember to hate him.

My hair blows in the wind, and I scrape it round my neck, holding it to one side. The breeze is a welcome addition to the too-hot fall weather, so I don't mind. I just wish I'd thought to bring a hairband with me.

Lila hums loudly as we step onto the sound, following the sounds of laughter and cheering to the far end of the beach. The whole freshman year is here, it seems, and music is pumping from somewhere. A bonfire is being set up, and I hear Megan's groan.

'Why do they need a bonfire? It's still eighty degrees out.'

'Because they're cool.' Kay laughs. 'Dicks.'

I grunt my agreement and look through the crowd, my eyes searching for Braden. Do I get five minutes to actually enjoy this party before I'm forced into playing the doting new girl-friend?

Apparently so.

We find a spot, and Lila immediately begins to examine the sand for pebbles and driftwood. God help any piece of drift-wood that scratched or grazed her leg. Apparently deeming it safe to sit, she settles down and leans back against a tree. Megan shakes her head, and both she and Kay drop themselves to the sand. I follow suit, but more conservatively than they did it.

I run my fingers through my hair, loosening small tangles from the soft curls at the ends. Sand shifts behind me. Two hands grip my waist, and I jump, letting out a shriek.

'What the –' I turn to look straight into bright blue, amused eyes. 'Braden. You scared me.'

'I'm sorry, Angel. I thought I'd surprise you,' he replies, shifting and moving closer to me.

'I think you achieved that,' I mutter, hating the way his skin feels against mine. Or am I hating the fact I like how it feels? I don't even know.

He rests his chin on my shoulder, pressing his cheek against mine. 'I thought you were starting the party without me, girls.'

'Like we'd ever do that,' Kay says in a fake pleasant tone. 'We all know you're the life and soul of the party, Carter.'

'Put your claws away, kitty.' Lila shoves a plastic cup in her face. 'Then shut up and drink.'

'Yes, zookeeper.' Kay rolls her eyes, and Lila smirks before turning to Braden.

'Where's Ryan?'

'He's grabbing beer from the car with Aston. They'll be here in a minute,' Braden replies, moving his head so his breath fans across my cheek.

'Lila, can I have a drink?' I ask her. I need something to stay sane tonight.

'My work is done.' Kay throws her hands up, her cup resting in the sand. 'I have successfully corrupted Maddie.'

'Not completely,' Megan half-smiles. 'She still doesn't swear or sleep with everything in sight.'

'She isn't going to, either,' Braden mutters. 'The sleeping with everything part, that is.'

'Because you're a fine one to talk.' Lila raises an eyebrow.

'Hey.' He points a finger at her. 'I was single then. I'm a changed man.'

I want to roll my eyes. Several times. Of course he is – and if he isn't, he soon will be, courtesy of yours truly. Because I can do this.

Lila rolls her eyes for me, and Ryan and Aston approach us. Ryan beelines for Lila while Aston casually sits near Megan. Oh ho, does someone have a little crush? No, that would be stupid. The only thing he has a crush on is what's inside her panties.

'You're quiet,' Braden says softly to me.

I smile and turn my face into him. 'I'm just listening.'

'Oh, you can listen?' He tickles my side slightly, and I wriggle.

'Don't tickle me.' I squirm.

'Why? Are you ticklish?'

'I'm not. Nope. Not. At. All.'

'I bet you are.'

'I'm not!'

He moves his fingers against my waist, and I squeal, moving and wriggling in his hold to get away.

'Braden, stop!' I sputter out through controlled laughter.

'Not until you say you're ticklish,' he teases and tickles me some more.

I shriek and fall backwards, kicking up a little bit of sand. He comes down with me, half lying on me, his arm still around my waist.

'Say it,' he whispers, looking into my eyes.

'No,' I whisper back. 'I won't give in.'

'Neither will I.' He drops his head, and his lips capture mine, soft and warm. My eyes flutter shut, and my hand rests against his neck. My fingers press into his skin, holding him to me.

Braden flicks his tongue out and runs it along my bottom lip, sucking it gently into his mouth. His teeth graze it slightly, nibbling as he releases it. I ignore the gasp wanting to escape from my mouth and the heat spreading down through my body. It pools in the pit of my stomach like molten lava, a swirling, boiling mass of want and need.

And then I remember that I hate him.

'Hey,' I groan. 'No distracting me with kisses.'

He pulls his head up and grins at me. It's a kind of sexy grin, and one I'd melt at if it was anyone other than Braden. Yes – Braden. Playboy, player, user of women for his own pleasure.

Yep. That did it.

I slide to the side of him and sit up, shaking sand out of my hair.

'Watch where you're flingin' that shit.' Kay bats at my hair. 'That could take my eye out. It's a lethal fuckin' weapon, Mads!'

'Oh, shut up, you.' I flick her with the ends of my curls and notice the others have disappeared. 'Where did everyone go?'

'They went to get food from the barbecue while you and Casanova were sucking face.'

I shake my head. She can be crude sometimes, but it's just her. I wouldn't want it any other way.

'Hey, Kay.' Braden leans round me. 'Isn't that your friend over there? Darla or whatever she's called?' Oh, great.

Kay huffs. 'If you wanna be alone, just say.' She stands, gives me a playful salute, and saunters off to where the blonde bombshell that is Darla is standing.

I turn my face and look out past the fire and the partying to the water as it rolls up the sand. It's always the same at the parties. Whether it's a frat party, a dorm party, or a beach party. I always feel like the only one not enjoying it.

After six months of following my old best friend round them while she chased after my brother, only to get her heart broken, can you blame me? No. I don't blame me either.

'You're somewhere else,' Braden observes. Remembering I hate him would be so much easier if he wasn't already so tuned into me.

'Just thinking,' I reply, keeping my eyes trained on the clear blue sea. 'You don't have to stay here, you know. You can go find the guys.'

'No.' He leans against the tree and pats the space next to him. Sigh.

I crawl backwards and sit next to him, curling into his side as he wraps an arm around me. I rest my head on his shoulder, and he lifts my legs so they're resting over his. He brings his knees up, and I'm wrapped around him like a blanket. His cheek leans against the top of my head.

I can feel the eyes of people from the party on us. It's making my hairs stand on end, making me want to get up and run away from this whole fake production.

But then – then there's a little part of me enjoying it.

Chapter Sixteen

Braden

I learned three things last night.

One, Maddie Stevens fits in my arms perfectly. Two, I want to fuck her, badly. Like, really fuckin' badly. And three, her hair smells like apples.

It's been nine days since Ryan and Aston challenged me to make Maddie fall in love with me, giving the limit of a month to do it. I won't need a damn month at this rate. She's falling – and she's falling hard and fast. I give it ten days, and I'll prove to them I can do it and then I'll walk away from her.

Because, let's face it, if I was a falling in love kinda guy, I'd fall in love with someone like her. Under that curvy body, fiery hair, and behind those pretty green eyes is a girl unlike anyone I know. I'm also pretty damn sure I won't meet anyone like her either.

And that's the problem. When she smiles at me, really smiles, I can see her turning me into a falling in love kinda guy. That makes her dangerous, too fuckin' dangerous, and I gotta get her in bed and walk away before it's too late.

She's tapping a message out on her cell with her brow furrowed as she walks around the corner towards me. Her hair is swept to one side, hiding her face from the rest of the world. I step out from where I was waiting in the stairwell and grab her hand, twirling her into me.

She looks up at me with wide eyes and leans against my chest. 'Dammit, Braden! You have to stop doing that to me.'

'Doing what?' I grin down at her.

'Scaring me,' she huffs, pocketing her phone.

'Everything okay?' I push her hair back from her face.

'Yeah, just my brother.' She frowns again and shakes her head. 'Doesn't matter. He's just being his usual stupid self.'

'Sure?' I smooth the frown lines out with my thumb.

'Yep,' she says brightly. A little too brightly. She smiles but there's no light in it, not like there was last night. And I'll be damned if I wanna find out what's going on instead of wanting to fuck her in every possible way right now.

It's because she's Megan's friend. That explains the whole caring thing that's starting to go on here. Of course.

I kiss her forehead and link our fingers. We leave the stairwell and head towards the campus cafeteria. It's not the best food in the world, but I know she has a class in half hour. I swear she takes every damn class possible.

We follow the line through and find a small table in the corner. I've already noticed she hates being the center of attention.

She's picking at her food and barely eating any of it. I want to talk to her, but I haven't got a clue what to say. I must be the most insensitive guy ever, but feelings have never mattered much to me. To me, the only feelings that mean anything and are real are in the bedroom.

Until I look into Maddie's sad eyes. Then her feelings are very, very real.

Instead of talking, I settle for sliding my hand across the table and taking hers in mine. I've seen guys do it in those stupid movies Meggy's made me watch. Maddie looks up and gives me a sad, worried smile and I figure it's comforted her some.

What the fuck do I know?

'Hey, Braden.' A girl with long, blonde hair approaches me. The perfect distraction.

If I wasn't in this fucking fake relationship.

'Hi?' I reply. I'm pretty sure I should know her name, but I'm drawing a blank.

'So I was wondering if you were free tonight. We could,

y'know, pick up where we left off last time?' She twirls some hair round her finger and juts out a hip.

Fuck. Why does this shit keep happening?

'No, sorry.' I say, feeling Maddie's eyes on me. 'I'm not available anymore.'

'What do you mean, not available?' Blonde girl looks between us. Are all the girls I sleep with blonde? Shit.

'As in, I have a girlfriend.'

'Who happens to be sitting right across from him,' Maddie mumbles. There aren't enough 'shits' for how I feel right in this moment. Why is it always chicks that can mess up my carefully laid plan?

'Oh, yes. I didn't notice you there.' Blonde girl turns to Maddie. 'I mean, you're not his *usual* type, honey.'

'Maybe that's why I'm his girlfriend, and you're a discarded weekend fuck whose name he can't even remember, *honey*.'

Did *Maddie* just cuss? Holy fuck. She did. Did she get abducted by aliens overnight?

I look between the two girls. Blonde girl is staring daggers at the side of Maddie's head, while she carries on casually picking at her food as if she hadn't just said something completely out of character.

'Maybe you should go.' I nod towards the blonde girl. She gives Maddie one last evil glare and turns back to me, a sweet smile on her face.

'When you're done with her, call me, okay?' She turns and walks away, exaggerating the sway of her hips.

'You have a really bad taste in girls,' Maddie says when blonde girl has disappeared.

Apparently so. 'Are you included in that?'

She looks up at her, her previously sad eyes now as cold as ice. This look would freeze hell, I'm sure of it.

'Don't fuck with me, Braden. Not today. I'm not gonna sit here and deal with a bunch of fake-boobed whores coming up to me and telling me how I'm not your "usual type".' She snatches her hand from mine and gets up, storming past me.

I lean my head back, sigh, and get up to follow her. Why, oh *why*, is this *so* fucking *hard*?

I follow her out the doors to an area shaded by trees. She's standing there, sunlight glinting off the top of her head where she's not fully under the cover of trees. Her arms are folded over a heaving chest, and she leans against a tree trunk, resting her head back against the rough bark of the trunk.

'Now, Angel,' I say, approaching her. 'Why don't you tell me what that was all about?'

'I'm not in the mood to discuss your previous bed-mates, Braden,' she replies, her eyes closed.

'I'm not talking about that.' I move closer to her. 'Why don't you tell me where those cuss words came from, because I'm pretty sure I haven't heard you cuss. Ever.'

'A bad day. A slip up. Ignore it.'

'Why would I ignore it?'

'Because I said to.'

'If you're having a bad day, talk to me. It's what I'm here for, right?' I pause. 'I said I wanted to be there for you, so let me.'

She laughs bitterly and shakes her head. Her eyes open and that hardened, guarded look is glossing over the bright green I'm getting so accustomed to.

'My life before Berkeley and yours were very, very different. You can't even imagine it, so there's no point in talking. You wouldn't understand.'

'Then help me to.' I put a hand against the trunk, standing in front of her. Her eyes meet mine. 'Help me understand. Help me help you.'

She bites her top lip. 'Not today,' she whispers. 'I just can't talk right now.'

I slide my hand behind her neck and tug her to me, pressing her body against me. She flattens her hands against my stomach and pushes back.

'No,' I say into her ear. 'If you won't talk to me, Maddie, let me hold you. I can do that, at least.'

She freezes, stuck in a state of indecision, before relaxing into me and wrapping her arms around my waist.

'I'm sorry,' she murmurs. 'For being a raging bitch.'

'Don't be,' I reply, stroking the back of her head. I saw that in a movie too. 'I'm sorry.'

And I am. I just don't know what the hell I'm sorry for.

Chapter Seventeen

Maddie

My brother, currently three thousand miles away, still has the ability to mess my day – and my mood – up. And apparently, the ability to nearly mess up nine days of hard work with Braden.

But, really, who the hell walks up to someone in a college cafeteria and asks to finish what they started? It's vile, and reminds me exactly why I'm doing this. It also reinstates the hate for Braden I lost when he held me the way he did after my outburst.

I sigh, and my thoughts return to Pearce. Anger bubbles inside me, and I have the crazy urge to chuck my phone clear out of my dorm window. It would be so, *so* satisfying to see it smash into a million pieces on the sidewalk. Or, of course, I could just get a new number. That's probably the better idea, but nowhere near as invigorating.

I'm not surprised he's contacted me so soon after last time. I figured he wanted the money for rent, but I was wrong. Oh, so wrong.

There's one big difference between Pearce and Braden that I have to acknowledge. That difference would be in the form of illegal drugs.

Pearce turned to it when Mom was killed. It was his 'escape'. There's nothing wrong with wanting an escape, but when that escape gives you a bigger down after, you have a problem. My darling brother solved that by getting more of the escape.

And this time he's run up a bill so bad that the eight hundred dollars already transferred from my bank doesn't even cover half of it.

Naturally, he told whoever he gets it from he'd get the money, assuming I'd hand it over like I always do, but this time I said no. I told him I wasn't going to bail him out anymore, and he went crazy.

His text message yesterday morning was informing me he was making arrangements to be here, and I should expect to see him next week sometime.

I click my tongue. Two different lives merging. Everyone here knows I have an older brother back in Brooklyn but they don't know the details. Besides Kay, Megan and Lila, only Braden knows about Mom being killed. No one never asked, and I've never felt like offering up that information.

But Pearce, here? The idea scares me, because I know what he's like. After all, didn't I watch him dominate, control and drive my best friend to attempted suicide, all because of his drug addiction and inferiority complex?

'Argh!' I rub my eyes with the heels of my hands, digging them in as if it can pull away the memories of last year. I should be so lucky.

The bright colors of our Operation Play the Player poster catch my eye. Day ten, and I'm even more determined than ever to see this through. For what feels like the hundredth time in two days, I build a wall around my heart.

Despite everything bad, Megan was right. Braden is caring, sweet, and thoughtful. He does have a heart, somewhere, at least.

But, so did Pearce before he ripped out Abbi's heart.

I walk across the lawn towards Braden's frat house. We haven't really spoken since my outburst in the cafeteria yesterday, so I know I need to 'patch things up' for the sake of the plan. All I really want to do is run away and hide somewhere Pearce can't find me.

Lila lets me in at the door. 'He's out the back, come on.'

I smile gratefully at her, but I still sigh.

'Hey.' She wraps an arm around my shoulders. 'It'll be okay. Even if he does show, we'll all be there. Promise. You won't be alone.'

'I know.' I drop my eyes to the ground as she opens the door.

'Time out!' Braden calls. I look up again, and I'm met by a sweaty, shirtless Braden jogging towards me. His face breaks out into a smile, and he hops onto the small porch. 'Hey, Angel.'

'Hey,' I say quietly. 'Braden—'

'If you're gonna apologize about yesterday, then stop right there.' He steps towards me and brushes some hair away from my eye. 'We're all entitled to a freak-out once in a while, right?'

'Right.' I smile at him. 'So, we're good?'

He laughs. 'Maddie, we never weren't good. I just figured you needed time to cool down.'

I nod in agreement, and he reaches out to tuck me into his side. We rest back on the porch, our backs to the rest of the field. My hand rests on his stomach, and with my decision to finish this fresh in my mind, I take the game up another level.

I trace the grooves in his torso with the tip of my finger, my thumb brushing the solid packs of muscle as I go. His grip on my waist tightens as I approach the subtly defined 'v' by the waistband of his shorts. I feel him shiver, and his free hand clamps down onto mine an inch before I reach his shorts.

'Maddie,' he whispers in a deeper voice than I've ever heard him use. 'If I were you, I'd stop there.'

Bingo.

'Why?' I smile, amused, and look up at him. 'I was only wondering if that muscle went as far down as it looks like it does.'

He turns to me, his electric blue eyes clouding over with desire. 'It goes further.'

I bite my top lip, pulling the corner of it into my mouth and glance down at our clasped hands. He clears his throat, and I snap my eyes to his.

'Sorry,' I whisper. 'Just curious.'

Braden moves his head down, putting his lips next to my ear. 'Angel, you can be curious all you like, but unless you want my frat brothers to see what you look like in your birthday suit, it's wise if you stop right there.'

Warmth erupts in my belly. Holy . . . I swallow. This is totally turning around on me. I can't even do justice to the turned-on tone of his voice. It's a husky, masculine sound that vibrates right through my body. I can feel it wrapping around every inch of my skin.

'Okay,' I breathe out. 'I'll stop.'

I slide my hand out from under his and up his body, reaching his shoulder and trailing it down his arm. Goose-pimples erupt in my hand's wake, and he makes a growling sound deep in his throat. I control my smile, linking my fingers through his bigger ones.

I said I'd stop. I didn't say when.

He exhales loudly, his breath fluttering my hair. 'Maddie.'

'I've stopped.' I bite my lip. 'Sorry.'

He shakes his head, smiling and leans his forehead against mine. I look up into his eyes, my eyelashes tickling my skin. He rubs the tip of his nose against mine and gently tips his head so his lips brush mine. I move up to my tip toes, squeezing his hand. I wrap my free arm around his neck gently, returning the kiss.

So I like kissing the guy I hate. Shoot me.

'Hey, Carter! Put my girl down!' Kay yells, a door slamming behind her. I smile against Braden's lips and drop back down from my tip toes.

'Hey, Kay,' I greet her, turning round.

She looks between me and Braden. 'You two are like a walking porn movie.'

'Hey, can't I kiss my girl now?' Braden looks at her. 'It's not my fault if I want to show her off.'

I blush a little. A forced blush. A very forced blush. No, I'm lying. It wasn't forced at all. *Crap*.

'You can.' She sniffs. 'Just not when I'm around.'

Megan slaps the back of her arm. 'Don't be so fucking grumpy. It's nice to see them happy!'

I smile at her.

'Thank you, Meggy.' Braden grins at her. Kay huffs, flips him off, and turns to join Lila and Ryan. 'Man, she really hates me, huh?'

'It's because you don't have a vagina.' Megan giggles. 'At least, I hope you don't.'

'I can assure you,' Braden replies, looking right at me. 'There is no vagina in my pants.'

I bite my lip again to stop myself from grinning like crazy.

So I skipped a stage. This one is way more fun.

Chapter Eighteen

Braden

I'm fucked. Genuinely fucked.

Maddie's hand trailing down my stomach equaled an instant, rock hard, raging hard-on. My dick standing to attention so fast it could well have been doing an army drill.

I curse the fact she's not like my usual girls. Usually, a suggestive smile and a wink is all that's needed. But no, I have to wine and fucking dine Maddie. I might as well serenade her under the fucking stars – and you know what? If I could sing, I damn well would.

Because I have to want what I can't have, all the time. And Maddie? Maddie is at the top of that list. Hell, she's at the top of every fucking list I own.

She is so damn untouchable, like a rare stone in a museum surrounded by laser lights. I feel like a ninja, dodging one more laser light daily and getting one step closer to worming my way into her heart.

But then, do I want her in love with me? The problem with this challenge is that it's not just a quick roll in the hay. I have to get to know her, I have to pretend to care about her – but when does pretending start becoming real?

I know her mom was killed. I know she's not close to her brother, that she loves her dad, and I also know that when she's in a bad mood her dirty mouth can rival mine on a good day. And that's sexy, on her.

Prim, proper Maddie going bad is the biggest fuckin' turn on I've ever had.

Shit.

I get up, slamming my bedroom door behind me. I can't

stay in my room thinking about her. I practically run into Aston and Ryan at the bottom of the stairs and grab their arms, shoving them through the front door and round the side of the house.

'Dude? What the fuck?' Aston rubs his arms.

'You two.' I look between them. 'Are driving me fucking crazy.'

'What?'

'This challenge. Do you know how hard it is to have that hot piece of ass rubbing up against me, knowing I can't drag her off to fuck her?' I resist the urge to slam my fist into the wall.

Ryan smirks. 'You agreed, bro. I was only kidding, but then you agreed. You can't back out now. She's wrapped around your little finger.'

'Yeah, and that's the problem.' I look at him pointedly. 'I don't want her wrapped around my little finger. I want her wrapped round my fucking dick.'

'So just drag her off to bed,' Aston suggests. 'You two were gettin' pretty cozy last night, if you get what I mean.'

'It hasn't even been two weeks, man.' I shake my head. 'I can't even consider that until next week. She's attracted to me, and she's falling, but she's not fallen. She won't do it until she's full on in love with me. It doesn't help that girls I can't even remember keep coming up and asking me for another go.'

Both guys burst out laughing.

'Dude, you're joking, right?' Aston leans against the wall.

'I fuckin' wish.' I rub my forehead. 'It's like, they see me with my fake girlfriend and all of a sudden I'm the sexiest thing on this damn campus.'

'I bet that isn't going down well,' Ryan muses. 'With Maddie, that is. I bet you're loving it.'

'Actually, I fuckin' hate it.'

'You're joking? You actually hate it?'

'It's about as enjoyable as a hole in the head. That's how much I hate it. It doesn't help with the trust thing at all – especially since I can't remember them.'

Aston chuckles. 'Send 'em my way next time. There's always space in my bed.'

'I'm sure there is,' I reply dryly. 'What do I do about Maddie, though? She's driving me mad. She's like a walking sex advert to my brain.'

'Fuck her,' Ryan says simply. 'You fuck her, get her out of your system. Just sooner than you already planned.'

Meggy's blonde hair bounces as she sits on my bed. 'So, you and Maddie.'

'What about us?' I glance at her.

'You look pretty into her.'

Do I? 'That's 'cause I am, Meggy.'

'Really, Bray? Because I know how well you can act. You can't hide anything from me.'

And that's the fucking problem. 'I'm not acting. I like her.'

'Or do you like the sex you could get out of it?'

Seriously? 'Meggy.'

'Bray.'

I look at her, and she raises her eyebrows. 'I like her, I do. I mean, what's not to like?'

She leans back against the wall and crosses her arms across her chest. Her eyes bore into me, and I squirm slightly under her intense scrutiny. Shit. Why can she do this to me? *How* does she do it?

'I love you, Bray. You're like my brother, but if you're fucking her about, I will castrate you and hang your balls as a wind chime in the frat house front-room window.' Ouch. I wince.

'I'm not fucking her around.' Much.

'Braden William Carter,' she snaps. 'I mean it. I can read you like a book, and what you say and what you mean are two different things. But y'know what? What you mean and what you think are two different things, too.'

'Please, Meggy,' I say sarcastically. 'Enlighten me on what I say, what I mean, and what I think.'

'What you say is that you want to be with her. What you mean is you want to sleep with her, and what you think is letting yourself feel for her what you do, in your heart, means you're a pussy.'

'What do you mean, letting myself feel something for her? I just admitted I like her.'

'Yes, Braden,' she says wryly. 'But that's not what you mean. I'm not stupid. You're on some kick here with Maddie, and while it's not my business, I care about both of you. Unless you pull your brain from your dick, you're gonna end up hurt. Both of you will. Sex isn't everything.'

'I'm not in it for the sex.' I hate lying to her, but it has to be done.

'I call bullshit on that and every other lame-ass excuse you have stored in your brain, whichever part of your body it's currently residing in.' She jumps off the bed, crosses the room, and jabs a finger in my chest. 'You need to stop thinking you're the next Hugh Hefner and start thinking about how you actually feel. Your friends don't control you, Bray.'

'You just say that 'cause you think they're assholes.' I smirk.

'That's because they *are* assholes. Don't let them make you think that you should spend the next four years of your life at this college fucking everything with a pulse, because while you're busy getting it on, your future could be right in your line of sight. And y'know what else? Unless you open your eyes, you'll miss your future. She'll come and go so fast you'll blink, and you'll miss it.' She exhales and moves to the door. 'Decide if Maddie is something with a pulse, or something more than that. She's been through too much to deal with your man-whore bullshit. Sit back and ask *yourself* what she is, not Tweedledick one and Tweedledick two.' She yanks the door open and slams it behind her.

'Fuck off,' I mutter, grabbing a pillow from the bed and chucking it at the closed door. 'Fucking future. Bullshit.'

I'm almost nineteen. Who the fuck finds their future at this age?

Chapter Nineteen

Maddie

I've checked my cell obsessively since Monday. It's Wednesday, and I haven't heard a thing from Pearce. If he was telling the truth, a week from now I'll be looking into his pitiful eyes.

And that scares me.

I don't want him here, and there's only so much longer I can pretend and not tell the girls exactly what's happening. I don't want to keep it from them, but there isn't much I can do. If he isn't coming, then there's no need to tell them the gritty details of my life in Brooklyn. If he does come . . . Then it might be too late.

I hate not knowing. I hate the uncertainty that encompasses my brother in a thick cloud. Nothing with him is ever definite, except drugs. But then again, when is anything with anyone ever definite? It's not. Not ever.

I swallow my sigh, tapping my pen against the table. I glance at the clock for the thousandth time in ten minutes. The second hand is moving at a snail's pace, zero point zero miles per hour, it seems.

For the first time in my life, I actually want to see Braden. When he's around I have something to focus on, the challenge, the game. The need to win the game he doesn't even know is being played takes over.

But, does that compare me to my brother? Playing someone for your own satisfaction?

No. No, it's different. Meggy said the plan is for Braden, to make him a better person. I don't get satisfaction from it. Just frustration.

But it's still two lives merging into one. I'm sitting here, in class, the bad girl from Brooklyn, yet when I walk out of the door and see him, I'll be the California college good girl.

Finally the bell rings, and I grab all my stuff, all but running from the classroom. The air in it seems stifling, heavy with the silence from my brother. Every thought I've had in the last ten minutes swarms around in my mind, over and over and over.

I feel dizzy. I can't breathe, too much is creeping up on me. My brother and the events of the last year are creeping up on me from three thousand miles away. I put a hand over my eyes, determined to battle the hallways and get outside to the fresh air, to where I can breathe.

Two arms grab me, and in my panicked state, I scream. I'm pressed against a hard body and I recognize the woody smell. Braden. My hand not holding my books grips his shirt. I need something to ground me. It's an almost desperate move, but I don't care.

'Sssh,' he whispers. 'I've got you. You're okay.'

I close my eyes and breathe deeply as he wraps his arms around me tightly. I bury my face into his chest. Grounding. Centering. I remember the breathing from the yoga classes I did in senior year of high school and chant the instructions in my mind, breathing in deeply, breathing out deeply.

The noise around us dies down, and I realize that I have no idea how long I've been standing in Braden's arms.

'Okay, Angel?' he asks softly.

'Yeah,' I whisper. 'I think so.'

He runs a hand through my hair, his fingers tugging lightly at knots in my curls. 'I didn't mean to scare you a minute ago. You looked like you were about to faint.'

'So you thought you'd come riding in like a knight in shining armor?' That thought is amusing.

'Something like that.' He chuckles. 'What's up?'

'Oh, nothing,' I dismiss it and pull back, smiling up at him.

'Don't lie to me, Maddie. I can see in your pretty green eyes that something is bothering you.' He runs his thumb down the side of my face. I fight to keep my eyes open. 'Talk to me.'

'It's just my brother.' I look down.

'I remember you saying you don't get along.'

'That's an understatement.' I snort. 'He mentioned something about coming here . . . And I . . . I don't want him to. I don't want him to come here.'

'So tell him.'

'It's not like that. You don't just *tell* Pearce things.'

'Then what do you do?'

'It doesn't matter.' My eyes flick up to him and back down again. 'It doesn't matter.'

Braden cups my chin, forcing my face upwards, but I keep my eyes trained downwards.

'Maddie, look at me.' I shake my head. 'Maddie. Please.'

The tenderness in his voice cuts me and I break, looking back up at him. 'What?'

'It does matter, okay?' he says softly. 'It always matters.'

'No, it doesn't.'

'Why won't you talk to me?'

Because when you're like this, soft and caring, it's hard to remember that I hate you and this is a game. 'I just can't talk about it, Braden.'

He sighs. 'Why won't you let me in? Let me help you.'

Because you're the first person outside of the girls to actually care about me and show it since the day she died – and caring isn't good for anyone. Not when everything you think you know is a game.

'Why?' I look at the roller-skates in front of me. 'Why? Why? Why?'

'I bet Megan thinks she's fucking hilarious,' Lila grumbles, looking at the skates with the same disdain I am.

'Why did we even let her organize this?' I mutter.

'I have no idea, but I'm never doing it again.'

'I am so with you there.'

Not only are they roller-skates, they're pink. Flippin' pink. I do not do pink.

'Come on, you two!' Ryan skates up to us as if he's been doing it his whole life, which he probably has.

'Uhh.' Lila's still frozen in place, staring at the skates.

'Really, babe.' Ryan skates up to her. 'It's not that hard.'

'Damn, Ryan,' she huffs. 'How many times do you think I've ever skated in Washington? Really?'

'I kinda figured everyone had at some point.' He looks at me. 'Don't tell me – you've never skated either, right, Maddie?'

'That would be correct,' I answer, finally looking up from the skates. 'It's not really an "in" thing in Brooklyn, funnily enough.'

'Damn city girls.' He shakes his head.

'Ah, they aren't that bad.' Braden skates backwards down the sidewalk towards us.

'Fucking show-off,' Lila mutters.

'I heard that, Lila.'

'You were supposed to, Braden.'

He stops in front of me. I look up at him. 'What?'

'You've actually never skated before?'

'No.' I fold my arms across my chest. 'No. Never.'

'Come on.' He takes my hands. 'Put them on and try it. I promise it's fun. Just try it, once.'

I look at the skates and back to him. He has a pleading, hopeful look on his face. 'Will you stop with the puppy dog eyes?'

'Cross my heart.' He crosses his heart.

I sigh and sit down. 'Fine.' I grab the skates and after taking my shoes off, I slip my feet in, only to fumble with the confusing buckles afterward.

Braden sighs and shakes his head. 'Come here.' He bends down at the waist and tightens them all for me, snapping them into place.

He grabs my hands, hoisting me up, and I squeak as I roll forwards and straight into him. I put my hands on his chest to steady myself, ignoring the heavy pounding of my heart.

'You're fine.' He smirks, amused.

'Yep,' I reply. 'I'm fine.'

'Let's go.' He grins and takes my hand, moving back from me.

I look forward and find Ryan pulling Lila along. Her feet are shoulder-width apart, and her legs are shaking. She looks a bit like a newborn foal trying to walk for the first time, and I giggle silently, knowing I probably look the same.

She glances over her shoulder at me and mouths '*help me*'. I shrug helplessly as Braden moves a little faster and I jolt forwards.

'Okay, slow, slow, slow!' I protest, waving my free arm in the air.

'Oh my god, Maddie,' he groans. 'Really?'

'Yes! I've never done this before, ever.' I grunt. 'Like, *ever*, Braden.'

'Fuck this,' Ryan snaps. 'Crash course!' He skates around Lila and grips her waist before pushing her along the sidewalk. She screams out loud, and her hands go to where Ryan's are on her waist to steady herself.

'Ryan, you asshole!' I hear her shout before they disappear from view. I laugh and bend over at the side. Braden lets go of my hand and—

'No, no, no, Braden! Don't you dare!' I try to turn, and I feel his hands on my waist, his breath on my ear.

'Crash course, Angel.'

'No –' My protest turns to a scream as we shoot off down the concrete the way Lila and Ryan did. 'Oh my god, oh my god.' I want to shut my eyes but no, that's not a good idea.

My heart is hammering against my chest, and I find myself gripping Braden's hands, my fingers slipping between his.

'It's not that bad.' He laughs into my ear.

'That depends on which side you're on,' I reply, my back going stiff. 'Braden, I want to stop.'

'No.' He slides one of his arms around me and pulls me to him so my back is flush against his chest, both of our arms wrapping my stomach. 'See? I've got you. It's fine, beautiful.'

'This is crazy. Never again is Megan organizing a date.'

'Yeah, she got a good one with this.' He laughs again, and I shake my head.

'No, no, she didn't. This is terrible.'

'Really? I would have thought that being up against me would be a good thing.'

'Maybe it would be if I could actually focus on the fact I'm pressed against your body.'

'Well, then.' He spins so he's in front of me, skating backwards.

'Braden, you can't see where we're going!'

'That's your job.'

'Oh my god.' I try looking over his shoulder, but I can't. He's too tall, dammit. 'You're too tall!'

'Then you just have to trust me.' His lips take mine in a searing kiss, and I gasp inwardly, grabbing hold of him tightly. His hands find my waist and pull my hips against him, our speed slowing slightly. He goes to deepen the kiss, his tongue tracing between my lips, and I nip his bottom lip before I open to him. My fingers tangle in his hair as our tongues meet, starting an intricate dance of want.

For a second, I forget the game. I forget the fake relationship. I forget the fact I'm on rollerskates and Braden isn't—

'Oomph!' Braden grunts, hitting the grass. I laugh, rolling off him.

'I told you we didn't know where we were going!' I say through my laughter, blades of grass tickling my ears.

'Hey.' He rolls towards me, propping himself up on his elbow. His hair flops down towards my face, casting little shadows over my face. 'I totally knew where we were going until you distracted me.'

'*I* distracted *you*? Oh no, mister. You kissed me, not the other way around.'

'And I didn't hear any complaints about that.'

'Maybe that's because there weren't any.'

'Oh, yeah?'

'Yeah.'

'Then let's try again.'

I arch into him as he presses himself against me, his tongue slipping straight between my lips. I grip his hair again, holding his mouth against mine. He runs a hand down my side, igniting a blazing trail of goose-pimples beneath my clothing. My leg bends, leaning against his hip, and his hand finds my thigh, holding it underneath. His fingers stroke and probe the bare skin gently, and I press myself closer to him, on fire everywhere he's touched me.

He pushes his hips into me and I can feel him against my other thigh, hard and ready. I whimper deep in my throat, want for the guy I hate overtaking any other feelings in my body. It builds up, climbing higher and higher, and I know if we weren't in public there's no way I wouldn't end what he started.

I'm half considering it, and we're in the middle of a park.

His teeth graze my bottom lip as he pulls away. My eyes open to a mass of cloudy, electric blue need in his. He breathes out heavily, his eyes fixated on mine.

'Maddie, I—'

'There you are! Oh, shit!' Lila calls. 'I didn't see anything. I promise. Carry on. I'm leaving now.'

I giggle and rest my forehead against Braden's shoulder, the moment between us broken.

'There's nothing to see, Lila,' Braden calls to her. 'Just a kiss.'

'Oh. Get up then!'

We both laugh, and Braden stands up, offering me his hands to help me up. I wrap my fingers around his, and he tugs me up, surprising me with another kiss before pulling me along after him through the park.

I swallow and let him guide me. The game is quickly reaching levels I'm not ready for.

Chapter Twenty

Braden

There are too many levels in this game, and I'm not ready for the one it's climbing to. That level has a big fat fuckin' neon sign declaring the game over, and reality starting. Reality, with Maddie?

Reality, with anyone?

When I was six, I assumed I'd grow up and marry Meggy, like all little kids do. You marry your favorite person, and at six that's your best friend, right? Yeah. What a laugh.

Now, Meggy is my little sister. She's the one person I'd go to hell for. I'd take a bullet for her, I'd kill for her, and I will protect her until she doesn't need it anymore – and I'll probably do it even then.

Saturday marks two weeks since this game started, and with every day that passes I get to know Maddie a little more. She's guarded. There are a lot of secrets behind those pretty green eyes, despite how revealing they are for her emotions. I want to know what those secrets are, because despite it all, I'm starting to fucking care about her.

I'm starting to care about the sadness that appears and the wall she puts up whenever her brother is mentioned. Ever since we spoke about him two days ago, she's been more and more fidgety. She keeps checking her phone, the clock, her phone, the clock. It's a repeated cycle that is driving me fucking insane because I have no idea what's going on.

'Update?' Ryan sticks his head in my door.

'Getting there.' I don't look up from the TV where I'm playing – but not focusing on – the Xbox.

'How close is getting there? Two weeks left.'

'Just over.'

'What?'

'Just over two weeks.' I take off a zombie's head. 'Don't sweat it, man. I'm fine.'

'I could tell that from the show you two put on in the park.'

'Fuck off,' I reply, a protective streak suddenly sparking in my body. 'It's gotta be done, you know that.'

'Alright. Whatever, Braden.'

My door clicks shut, and I shake my head. Megan's words come back to me. *Decide if Maddie is something with a pulse or something more than that.*

I shoot several zombies in a row. Eh. What the fuck does she know anyway?

I die. I drop the controller on the floor and huff, lying back on my bed. Stupid game. Stupid challenge.

I hear a light knock at my door. 'Come in.' I raise my head from the pillow, and Maddie pushes the door open, her arms full of books. I jump up and take them from her, letting her shut the door.

'Afternoon.' She smiles and takes her books back.

'Good afternoon, Angel.' I smile back at her, bending for a quick kiss. 'I didn't realize you were bringing the library with you. If I knew, I would have met you there instead.'

'Oh, ha ha ha. Funny.' She drops the books on my desk. 'I still have to do that English paper.'

'Which one?'

'On the themes of love in *Much Ado*.'

'You haven't done it yet?' I raise an amused eyebrow.

'No.' She shakes her head. 'I've been somewhat distracted lately. You would know all about that, Braden.'

I grin and walk to her, wrapping my arms around her waist from behind. I push my face into her hair, still grinning. 'My fault?'

'I'd say it's a high possibility,' she murmurs in response. 'So now I have to write it.'

'Really?' I move my hand across her stomach, her hip, and leave it to rest at the top of her thigh. 'You're here, in my room, and you want to do schoolwork?'

'Braden!' She slaps my hand. 'Yes. It is possible, you know, to be in a room with a girl and not have sex with them.'

'But it's not possible with you.' I breathe into her ear and brush my lips along her lobe, placing soft kisses down her neck. She shivers.

'Braden,' she warns.

'Fine.' I sigh. 'I'll just sit here and watch you, then.'

'Are you actually going to do that?' She spins in my arms and looks up at me.

I drop my head and capture her lips, cupping her ass and holding her to me. I suck on her bottom lip, putting my hand in her hair. She grips my waist, and I dip her back slightly, deepening the kiss. Her hands slide to my back, her fingers spreading.

My dick hardens, and I walk backwards, pulling her towards my bed. She falls back without any resistance. One of her hands finds the hem of my shirt and slips under it, her palm hot against my bare skin. The urge to rip her clothes off is too much, way too much.

I pull my lips from her mouth and ghost them along her jaw, stroking her thigh at the same time. She tilts her head back, and I kiss down her neck, my tongue flicking out at the tender spot where her neck meets her shoulder. She moans, and I carry on exploring the top of her body with my mouth, kissing along the tops of her boobs.

My tongue traces inside the cup of her bra, her skin hot and soft.

'Braden,' she whispers in a breathless voice.

'Maddie,' I mumble against her skin, my breathing hard. Her chest is rising and falling in a steady rhythm, her heart pounding.

I slide my hand inside her skirt, my fingers slipping to find her underwear. She wears a thong. *Fuck.*

Her breath hitches and with my thumb gliding across the smooth material of her underwear, I pull my lips from her skin and meet her eyes.

'Angel?' I say softly.

Her eyes are full of heat, and she grips my hair tighter,

moving her hips into me. Her movements answer my question, and I drop my mouth to her jaw, pressing little kisses to her.

I move my hand under the fabric and my finger slips inside her, gliding through the wetness easily. Her muscles tighten at the invasion, and her fingers dig into my back. My thumb creeps up, finding her clit, and I rub it in slow, gentle circles. Another finger inside her and her hips buck.

She moans again and I cover her mouth with mine, swallowing it. Her tongue runs along my top lip and I follow it with mine. I sweep the inside of her mouth, stroking her tongue in a similar way to how my fingers are stroking her below.

Her breath catches. Her muscles tighten.

I rub harder, move faster, kiss deeper. She cries out my name before she relaxes, her muscles limp and her breathing fast. I end the kiss and remove my hand, pulling away with regret.

Her eyes open slowly, the sparkle in them a contrast to the flushed red hue of her cheeks. Her hair is fanned out across my white sheets, her lips slightly parted.

And she looks fucking beautiful.

'What . . . Was that?' she breathes out.

'That, Angel, was an orgasm,' I reply, grinning at her.

'I know that.' If she could, she'd slap me now. 'But where did it come from?'

'Can I tell you a secret?' I run my nose along her cheek, and she nods. 'I've wanted to do that since I saw you.'

Another truth.

She laughs silently and turns her face, kissing me softly. 'Oh. Are you happy now?'

'Very,' I murmur against her lips. 'Are you?'

'Mm,' she murmurs back. 'I think so.'

'Good.' I kiss her once more and brush some hair from her forehead. 'Now you can do your English work.'

She laughs – out loud this time – and smiles. 'Give me a minute.'

Maddie closes her eyes, and I roll to the side of her, pulling her body into me while she recovers from her orgasm.

I know three more things.

Maddie Stevens is fucking beautiful after an orgasm.

I know I'd like to put that look on her face many, many more times.

And last, her apple-smelling hair drives me fucking insane. For real.

Chapter Twenty-One

Maddie

I get it. I understand why every girl goes crazy about Braden Carter, because that guy can do crazy stuff with just his fingers.

But I still hate him. And I hate even more than I can't just say it.

'Umm.' I hide my face.

'You've done it already?!' Lila shrieks, jumping up.

'Oh my god, no!' I wave my hands. 'No, no, no!'

'But you've done something, haven't you?' Kay asks, her eyes wide with humor. 'I can tell.'

'Y-yes.' I mumble.

Megan licks her lips, smiles, and uncaps her pen. 'So, do tell.'

'I'm not telling you that!' My cheeks burn.

'Oh!' Kay laughs. 'Priceless! She's embarrassed over a game! Oh my god. It gets better, guys.'

'Go away,' I mutter. 'I just . . . I'm not giving sordid details.'

'Come on,' Megan grins. 'Just say it. We've all done it all.'

'You guys,' Lila scolds and turns to me. 'Maddie, did you have sex with Braden?'

'No.'

'Did you, you know, blow his whistle?'

I snort. 'Blow his whistle?'

'Did you suck his lollipop?' Kay lies on her stomach, shaking with silent laughter.

'Ew! No!' I laugh.

'Okay, then.' Lila shrugs. 'Well, did he bite your burger?'

I fall backwards on my bed, my stomach tensing as I laugh harder than I've laughed in ages. I'm pretty sure tears are stinging my eyes.

'Bite . . . My . . . Burger?' I take a deep breath. 'What, on earth, is that?'

Kay tries and fails to get the words out, waving her hand dismissively before burying her face in her pillow.

'It's, licking, um, y'know.' Megan shakes her head and laughs. 'I can't. I can't do it.'

'Oh! Oh, oh no. No burger biting.'

Megan nods and gives me a thumbs up.

'Okay, so was there bean flicking?' Lila continues, her shoulders bouncing.

'I'm not even . . .' I shake my head. 'Going to ask.'

'It's just, uh. How do I put this?' Lila leans her head back.

Kay looks up. 'Did he play with the bait while he went fishing?'

Megan collapses on the floor laughing hysterically, her whole body shaking. 'I . . . Oh.'

I look at Lila, and she shakes her head, dropping it so she can't see me.

'Um, yes?' I guess, trying to keep my giggles in.

'Woohoo!' Kay shouts and my cheeks flame.

'I can't believe I just told you that. I actually can't believe it,' I mumble.

'Oh, what do I write for that?' Megan wipes under her eyes.

'Write? Wait, what?!' I sit up. 'You can't write that on the plan!'

'I have to,' she replies. 'It's so we can keep track.'

'So wrong, Megs.' Lila shakes her head.

'Put fishing.' Kay snorts. 'No one is gonna know what that means.'

'Oh my god.' I cover my face with my hands. I hear Megan uncap the pen lid and the scratchy sound of the pen moving against the paper. 'Oh, my god.'

'There.' She sits back. 'Fishing, in week two. Definitely ahead of schedule, my little player.'

'That's a good thing, right?'

Lila nods enthusiastically. 'Oh, yeah. This was just a rough idea. If you can get it done before the month is up, even better.'

'Sounds like it'll be done before the week is up,' Kay says slyly.

'What, two days?' I shake my head. 'He's not in love with me yet. Wasn't that the point?'

'True,' she acquiesces.

'He's getting there, though,' Megan offers. 'I can see it in his eyes.'

'You think he's falling in love with me after like, twelve days?' I snort. 'Yeah, okay, Megs. This isn't some trashy romance novel where you get that crappy insta-love. There's no supernatural pull from the fates demanding we be together as soul mates for all of eternity while fighting off the bad guys. Love takes time. It takes work. It's not just something you throw yourself into because if you do it right, you'll only ever have to fall in love once. I only intend to fall in love once, and when I do, I won't be falling in two weeks' time, and Braden probably won't either. People like Braden don't fall in love like that. But the point is, you can't control love. You can't make it happen.' I get up and look out the window.

'But isn't that what you're doing now?' Lila asks softly, her gentle brown eyes focusing on me. 'Trying to control love, to make it happen?'

'No. I'm just trying to beat it to the finishing line. It's just a game. Love is like Clue – you might take a few wrong turns, but you'll get there in the end. For Braden, I'll be a wrong turn, and he'll barely be a blip on my radar.'

'So because we're not in a book, it means you can't be in love instantly?' Megan raises her eyebrows.

'Yes. This isn't a dream world, it's reality, and reality is a bag of balls.'

She snorts. 'But what if you were in love before you knew it? It's been scientifically shown that we're automatically attracted to people who "match" with our pheromones.'

'Gross,' Kay mutters.

'So why can't you just fall in love as easily as that?' Megan continues, unaffected. 'What if love is instant, but our human brains aren't yet advanced enough to know? What if each of us have a soul mate? What then?'

'Then the world would be a better place,' I reply quietly. 'Because no one would get hurt. That's an ideal, Megs. The real world isn't ideal. There are rules you have to play by – unwritten rules, granted – but they're still there. Break them and you're back a level. Follow them and life is perfect. With this plan, I'm just skipping a few rules. I'm going to beat the game.'

'I'd like to believe we have someone out there for us that's perfect for us,' Lila says quietly. 'I'd like to think the natural way of life governs even that.'

'I wouldn't,' Kay grumbles. 'Fuck having someone in control of my life and love.'

'That's because you don't believe in love, Kay.' Megan looks at her pointedly.

Kay returns her look. 'Neither do you.'

Megan gives her a small smile, a soft smile that somehow manages to brighten her whole face. 'Oh, I believe in love, Kay. I believe that each of us have someone out there that will love us no matter what. I like to believe that. Otherwise, what would be the point? Love is beautiful, it's free from judgment and it never condemns. It enlightens, it embraces, and it makes even the hardest day worth living through. Who wouldn't want to believe in that?'

'You've been reading too many romance novels, Megs.'

'So what? We all have to get our hope from somewhere, and if getting lost between the pages of a deep book gives me hope, then I'll keep on getting lost, all the while hoping that one day I'll have a real love I can get lost in. Because it will happen, to each of us. One day we'll get so lost in love that we won't be able to find our way back out.'

My eyes flick up, and I can see the top of the frat house across the street. Third floor, second window from the right. Braden.

'How do you know, though?' I look back to Megan.

She gives me the same small smile she gave Kay. 'Oh, I don't know. But I hope, and at the end of the day, without love, hope is all we really have, isn't it?'

Chapter Twenty-Two

Braden

I rub her hair between my fingers, watching her intently. She fidgets under my intense scrutiny, and all I can think of is the way she fidgeted underneath me as she came.

She sighs and wriggles, shifting away from me. A slow smirk breaks out on my lips, and I twirl the same lock of hair around my finger. She runs a hand through her hair. I drop her hair, immediately picking it back up when she drops her hand back to the table. This is fun.

'Mr Carter, are you concentrating?' Mr Jessop asks me.

'Yes, Sir.'

'On my lesson, or Miss Stevens here?'

'That would be the last option, Sir.' I turn my head and grin. 'But at least I'm concentrating, right?'

'Yes.' He hides his smile. 'As lovely as Miss Stevens is, do you think you could concentrate on my lesson for the last ten minutes of class instead?'

Maddie looks at me and smiles. I wink at her.

'I'll try, Sir, but I'm not promising anything.'

Mr Jessop shakes his head and turns back to the board.

I drop Maddie's hair, letting my forearm rest across the back of her chair. She glances at me, and I raise my eyebrows innocently.

'What?' I mouth.

She shakes her head, her lips curving upwards, and bites her pen. Her plump lips seal around the pen cap, and she spins it in her mouth, her lips puckered. Fucking tease.

I move my hand to her shoulder and begin to trace light circles on her bare skin, eliciting a shiver from her. Bingo.

I face forward, pretending to concentrate on the lesson but in actuality, I'm focusing on the way Maddie's lips are around that pen. I'm jealous of that pen. Really fuckin' jealous.

I shift in my seat slightly. This girl is turning me into a walking hard-on, and it's all because my dick isn't used to waiting for what it wants. I'm not used to waiting for what I want. Is class over yet? No? *Fuck.*

Maddie looks at me out of the corner of her eye, the green in it brighter from her amusement at the situation. Her eyes bore into mine as I turn my head slightly. My finger trails up to her neck, her hairline, and back down. She shivers again, stronger this time.

'Stop it,' she hisses at me quietly.

'Why?' I whisper back. 'I thought you liked that.'

'Braden, we're in class!'

'And?' I grin cockily at her. 'Maybe I'm having a fantasy about taking you on my desk, and this class isn't helping that thought.'

Her mouth opens, and her pen falls out. Blood rises in her cheeks, flushing them.

'Oh my god,' she mutters.

'What?' I chuckle silently.

'I can't believe you just said that.'

'Why? It's true. I am imagining having sex with you on my desk.'

The bell rings, and she gathers all her stuff up, shaking her head with her still-flushed cheeks. I shove my stuff into my backpack and join her round the front of the desk. I slip my arm round her waist and cup her hip as we leave the classroom.

'I don't get it,' she says as we make our way outside.

'Get what, Angel?'

'How you managed to think of that in the middle of studying Moby . . . Y'know what? Never mind.'

I laugh out loud. 'Yep, I was pretty sure I heard the word "dick" at some point at the beginning of class, and you just confirmed it.'

'But how did you get from a whale to . . . Yeah.'

'Maddie, if someone says "pussy cat" I instantly think of sex. Same with Moby Dick, whale or otherwise.'

'Say if you go into a restaurant, what if someone ordered something to do with sausages? Would that make you think of sex?'

'Yeah, probably.'

She giggles and sits at the base of a tree. The sun is glinting off her hair, making the copper hues even shinier. I sink to the ground next to her and dig my hand into my backpack.

'What are – oh!' She exclaims, seeing the blueberry muffin I produce. 'When did you get that?'

'I ran by before class. Thought I'd surprise you.' I grin at her genuinely delighted face. I'm actually happy she's happy – that I've managed to make her happy. Yep, I'm starting to care about this girl and how she feels. Shit.

'Oh!' She touches my cheek. 'Thank you. That was thoughtful.'

I put my hand on top of hers and gently turn my face into it, pressing a kiss to the pulse on her wrist. She takes the muffin from me and begins to eat it in her normal way. I've discovered it's not just a muffin thing. She actually picks most of her food apart as she eats it.

'Why do you do that?'

'Do what?' She puts some more muffin in her mouth.

'Pick it apart. You do it with all your food.'

'Oh.' Her voice is so quiet I barely hear it. 'I didn't eat much after Mom died, and what I did eat, I picked at. I guess it's become a kind of habit. I never realized.'

My foot is so far in my mouth it's probably about to come out my ass.

'I'm sorry, Angel, I didn't realize.' I put my arm around her, and she lays her head on my shoulder.

'Why would you?' she asks softly. 'Actually, you're the first person that's noticed it. Well, the first person that's ever mentioned it, anyway.'

Have I really watched her that much in the last two weeks that I'm picking up on her habits? Yeah, I have.

Fuck.

The game, Braden. The game.

'Come stay with me tonight?'

She leans her head back, sad eyes meeting mine. 'Why?'

I kiss her. 'Because I want you to.'

'I'll be at the house anyway. For the party.'

'Fuck the party.' I shake my head. 'Don't go. We'll grab a movie and some junk food. We'll spend the night upstairs in my room, then tomorrow we'll go out and get breakfast.'

She blinks a couple of times. 'Really?'

'Really.' I smile. 'You sound surprised.'

'I am, a little.' She smiles back shyly. 'Okay.'

'You'll stay?'

She nods once and moves her face into my neck. 'I'll stay.'

'Good.' I rest my cheek on top of hers, and I'm happier than I should be.

'She's staying, here?' Ryan's eyes bug out of his head.

'You deaf? That's what I said, isn't it?'

'You're skipping the party for a fucking sleepover?' Aston raises his eyebrows and sits back, laughing. 'Fuckin' hell. You want in her pants, bad.'

'So what if I do? That's the whole reason for this, isn't it?'

'That it is,' Ryan agrees, taking the Xbox controller off Aston.

'Then don't sound so fuckin' surprised.'

'This gonna be over tomorrow then, Braden?'

'Chances are, no,' I answer. 'I'm not forcing her into anything.'

'Since when did you give a fuck?' Aston half-glares at me.

'Since Maddie isn't like the girls I usually fuck around with, all right?' I drop my controller on the floor.

'Don't tell me you're starting to fall for her.'

'Fuck off, Aston.' I shake my head. 'You know as well as I do, I have to be careful with Maddie. Mess her around too much and Meggy will kick my ass.'

'You can handle Megan.' Aston smirks. 'Never thought I'd see the day Braden Carter was controlled by a girl.'

I lean around Ryan and punch him in the arm. 'Fuck *off*, Aston! Don't be a prick.'

'I was just sayin', man.'

'Well, don't,' Ryan interrupts. 'I'm already in a relationship, and it's perfectly normal to have your girl stay over, *without* sex, Aston. It's hard for your playboy mind to comprehend, but it can be done. If that's how Braden wants to play it, then that's how he's gonna play it.'

'He's getting so caught up in being the perfect boyfriend he's forgetting about the sex.'

I snort. 'You've seen her, right? If you think I forget about sex around Maddie, then you're more stupid than you look.'

'Oh, so you're not falling then?' He smirks, amused.

'Not a fucking chance, man.' I smirk back. 'The only thing on my mind around her is when I'm gonna do her, where I'm gonna do her, and how many times I'm gonna do her.'

I hope.

Chapter Twenty-Three

Maddie

'Forget your pajamas.'

'Why would I forget my pajamas?'

'Because then you either have to sleep in your underwear, nude, or in one of his shirts,' Megan explains.

'And there's nothing sexier than a girl in a guy's shirt,' Lila adds. 'I wear Ryan's all the time. It's guaranteed sex.'

'I'm not at the sex stage yet, Lila.'

'So? It's almost week three, right?' She looks up at the poster on the wall, tracing her finger along the steps. 'So that means sexual seduction can commence.'

I dump my bag on my bed and sit down on Kay's opposite it. 'You pack my bag then.'

'Yes!' Megan scrambles up from my pillow and attacks my dresser, pulling drawers open. 'Oooh! This!' She turns, holding up a black silky underwear set I bought months ago, yet never wore. She tugs off the labels and Lila empties my bag. The underwear goes in, along with my make-up, hairbrush, and clothes for tomorrow.

Lila zips it up. 'Done.'

'Really? Underwear, clothes, and minimum toiletries? That's it?!' I shriek.

'Yes!' Megan turns to me with her hands on her hips. 'Seduction not comfort, Maddie! You need to tease him, so that when it comes to you giving your hot ass up to him he's not gonna resist.'

'He wouldn't resist anyway,' I say dryly, the memory of us in his room flashing behind my eyes. Nope, he wouldn't resist.

'Yes, but like you said, he's not in love. Yet.' Megan smiles slyly.

'Whatever,' I huff and grab the bag. 'Can we go now?'

'Yep!' Lila grabs her purse, and the three of us file out of my room. 'Hey, is Kay going tonight?'

'She is . . .' I trail off. 'Wait, I don't even know where she is.'

'If we don't know, it probably means we don't want to,' Megan summarizes.

'And that's the truest thing I've heard all day.' Lila snickers. 'Do you think she's with Darla?'

I shake my head. 'Since when did Kay go back for seconds?'

Lila shrugs, and we leave the main campus, crossing the road to the frat house. A few people are milling around outside, and Lila pushes straight through the girls huddled on the porch to inside. Megan grabs my hand and pulls me through. I ignore the dirty looks several of them give me.

I'm not surprised that most of the people downstairs are girls. I'm also not surprised that one is trying her best to rub up against Braden. I *am* surprised at how he's pushing her away.

Woah.

He glances up and catches my eye. I lean against the banister of the staircase and raise an eyebrow. His face breaks into a grin, and he pushes around the girl throwing herself at him, much to her disappointment, and stalks towards me. He's eating the room up as he moves, and I find myself swallowing at the look in his eye.

He stops in front of me, sliding his hand around my neck and into my hair. His lips meet mine, slowly, softly, and I'm momentarily taken aback by the tenderness there. I put a hand on his waist and move closer to him, rubbing his back slightly with my fingers.

'Hey, Angel,' he whispers against my mouth.

'Hey, Braden,' I whisper back. 'Miss me that much, huh?'

His blue eyes twinkle down at me. 'Maybe I did.'

I smile at him.

'Hey, Braden, are you down here tonight?' A low voice purrs behind us. Seriously? Still?

'Nope.' He turns, still holding me tightly. 'I'm spending the night with my girl.'

'Maybe some other time, then?'

'Or not.' I smile sweetly at the dark-haired girl and curl into Braden's side. He chuckles quietly.

'Come on, tiger, let's get you upstairs,' he says into my ear.

'Is that an invitation?' I flirt.

He smiles against me. 'Maybe later.'

I laugh quietly, and he leads me up the stairs. His room is still as clean as ever, and I'm actually surprised. I thought all guys had messy rooms.

I put my bag on the floor at the end of his bed and lie down on it, rolling to my side. 'What?'

'Make yourself comfy.' He smirks.

'Oh, I am.' I grin at him sassily.

He shakes his head and comes over to me, bending over me. 'Those jeans don't look too comfy. Maybe you should remove those. For maximum comfort, of course.'

'And how long have you been waiting to use that line?' I ask playfully.

'Actually, I just thought it up then.'

'Oh, he's handsome *and* quick-witted. What a catch.'

'Handsome, huh?' He quirks his eyebrow and leans down closer to me. 'Tell me more.'

'Is your ego hungry from the female conveyor belt no longer running through the bedroom?'

'No. Far from it.' He touches the tip of his nose to mine. 'My ego is delighted that you're still hanging around, actually.'

I close my eyes and smile, ignoring the spark of pleasure that shoots down my spine at his words. I tilt my head and brush my lips across his softly, and he strokes my cheek with his thumb.

It's hard to believe that Mr Hump 'Em and Dump 'Em can be so tender.

'I'm gonna put the movie on,' he says. 'Or it'll never get watched.'

'Fine,' I pout, remembering the game. I feel like I have

multiple personalities. A double life – the Brooklyn Maddie and the California Maddie. Yet, the California Maddie has two, maybe three different Maddies rolled into it. The friend Maddie, the game Maddie and then . . . maybe a Braden Maddie.

I wish I knew what Maddie I really was.

'What movie is it?'

Braden wrinkles his nose. 'Uh, good question.'

I laugh, and he pulls a box out from under his bed. 'Chances are, most of these belong to Megan, so there could be anything in here.'

I shift on the bed, turning sideways, and I hang my head over the side of the bed. Braden bats my hair away.

'Hey!' I protest.

'It tickles.' He grins, opening the box. He's right. It's full, and at least three-quarters of visible movies belong to Megan.

'Wow.' I look in the box. 'What are we watching?'

He shrugs. 'I don't know.'

'You told me to come here to watch a movie.' I half-smile at him. 'Did you even have anything in mind then?'

'Uh, no?' he says sheepishly. 'It was a spur of the moment thing, Angel.'

I sigh and start digging through the box. 'Guys. If you want something done, do it yourself,' I mutter.

'Does that account for orgasms too?'

'What?' I stop, blink and look at him.

'The do it yourself thing.' He grins, and I laugh, hiding my face.

'No, they are an exception to that rule.'

'Oh, good.' He kisses the side of my mouth. 'Because I'd hate to never give you another one.'

My cheeks heat up and yet again I wonder about his ability to make me blush.

'I like it when you blush.' He presses his cheek against mine.

'Why?' I smile. 'Oh wait, let me guess. It reminds you of an orgasm?'

'Mind reader.' He brushes his lips along my cheek, his breath hot on my ear. 'It reminds me of when *I* made you come. That's exactly why I like it.'

His hand moves to cup my other cheek, and I tilt my face into his. He moves his face, and his mouth finds mine, taking it in a kiss that damn near takes my breath away. My arm stretches, my hand rests on the side of his neck, and my lips caress his.

I nip his bottom lip and he moves to stand, helping me roll over on the bed. His arms scoop me up and reposition me in the center of the bed, his body on top of me, pressing into me. Hard.

He probes my mouth with his tongue, and I meet his kiss with the same fervor. My free hand snakes to his back and under his shirt as he sweeps his tongue through my mouth, eliciting a silent moan from me. His back muscles flex under my fingers as he shifts slightly, and my fingers dig into his skin.

One of his hands is in my hair, tangled in the curls, and the other is exploring my body. It slides down the curve of my waist to my hip, down my thigh and back up again. His thumb brushes the underside of my breast, and even fully clothed, I feel it as if it was skin on skin.

His mouth travels across my jaw and down my neck, peppering hot kisses across my skin – and suddenly, suddenly it's not enough.

I want it all. Not because of the challenge, or because it's what the girls want.

I want him because *I* want him.

And I don't know what to do about that.

'I could kiss you all day,' Braden whispers.

I smile, unable to form any words, and hold him close to me.

I'm spinning in my own mind. Want is okay. Want is a natural thing, right? Like Megan said – pheromones or something. It's human nature to be attracted to someone, especially someone like Braden. It's okay that my body and my mind aren't on the same page. Yep. Perfectly okay, because want isn't love.

'Shall we watch that movie?' Braden asks.

'Yeah,' I reply. 'Whichever one.'

He nods and kisses my temple, getting off the bed, and me. Despite the temperature still being above sixty, I'm suddenly cold.

Braden puts a disk in the DVD player and pulls off his top, giving me a chance to admire his chest. Not that I haven't before, but it definitely feels much more appropriate to do so as his 'girlfriend'. He's all smooth, sleek muscle. He's not overly built, but he's lean and defined in a way that would make most girls cry. It probably has made most girls cry.

And I'm back in the game, with just that thought. Operation Play the Player. Everything about him screams player, and every scream just reminds me of why I can't want him. Why I shouldn't want him. Every scream reminds me of Pearce and Abbi.

I drop my eyes as he hands me my bag. 'You can get changed here, or in the bathroom across the hall.'

'Umm, I think I forgot my pajamas.' I glance up at him and smile.

'Oh.' He turns, opens a drawer and pulls out a shirt. 'Here.' He grins, and I take it from him, sweeping past him.

In the bathroom, I strip and put on the black underwear Megan insisted I wear. I pull Braden's shirt over my head, feeling the tickle of the hem at the top of my thighs. A quick run of my brush through my hair and I step back into the hall – straight into Kyle.

Well, this is awkward. I haven't really spoken to him since last week when Braden ended up pinning him to the wall.

'Uh, hey, Kyle.' I say quietly.

'Maddie,' he responds, his eyes pinned to my legs.

I clear my throat, and he looks up. 'How are you?'

'Fine. You?'

'Yeah, I'm good.' I glance behind him towards Braden's shut door.

'So you really are then? With him?'

'Kyle.'

'Sorry.' He holds his hands up. 'Just . . . Be careful, yeah,

Mads? I don't want to see him hurt you. You're too good for that.'

I touch his arm. 'I won't, Kyle, don't worry.'

Braden's door opens, and he looks at us for a second before he registers it's Kyle I'm talking to. 'Not chatting my girl up again, are you, Kyle?'

'Wouldn't dream of it, Braden,' he replies, his eyes on mine. 'She's all yours.'

I look down and step around him towards Braden.

'Good thing, too. I'd hate to slam you against the wall again.'

I scoff, shaking my head and push past him into his room. What is it with males and their need to be absolute neanderthals?

I chuck my bag down, and he shuts the door. 'What was that about?'

'You're asking *me* that?' I raise my eyebrows and look at him. 'What was *that* about, Braden? Can I not even talk to Kyle now?'

'Of course you can, but excuse me for being a bit pissed when you're talking to him wearing my shirt.'

'Isn't that the point? Wearing *your* shirt. It's obvious who I "belong" to, as you so eloquently put it last week, so there's no need to go all caveman on anyone who speaks to me.'

'How did I go caveman? 'Cause I don't get it.'

'"I'd hate to slam you against the wall again,"' I imitate his voice. 'You'd love to pin him against a wall again for talking to me.'

'So what if I would? You're my girl.' He walks towards me and I tilt my head back to look at him.

'I'm not your property, Braden, and I won't be treated like I am!'

'You're mine, Maddie.' His hand cups my chin, and I knock it away.

'Don't treat me like I'm your possession, Braden, because that possessive streak doesn't go down well with me.' I turn, and he grasps my waist, pulling me back against him. His arms wrap around my waist, holding me tight to him.

'I'm not possessive over you, Maddie,' he says into my ear. 'I'm protective, and there's a difference. I'd never try to control you or tell you what you can and can't do, but I know every guy in this frat house wants to be me right now – especially Kyle. And you know why? It's because you're so fucking beautiful.' My breath catches in my throat. 'They all want you, but *I* have you, and there's not a chance I'm gonna risk one of them taking you from me, all right? So yes, Angel, yes, you are fucking mine!'

Chapter Twenty-Four

Braden

'You think I'm beautiful?' she whispers softly. Of course, that would be what she hears.

'Yeah.' I turn her face up to mine. 'I do. You *are* beautiful, Maddie. Inside and out.'

And I'm being completely fucking honest. She's not hot, or fit, or bangable. She's beautiful, she's sexy and she's sweet.

She closes her eyes and, when she opens them, they're glistening with tears. Oh fuck.

'Did I say something wrong?'

She shakes her head and spins in my arms, sliding her arms around my waist. Her cheek presses against my chest and I feel her take a deep breath. I hold her to me tightly.

'No,' she whispers. 'No, you didn't.'

'Then why are you crying?'

Her shoulders shake, and she looks up at me, a smile on her face even though her eyes are filled with tears. 'Because it makes me happy.'

'Good,' I whisper and kiss the corners of her eyes, kissing the tears away. 'I like making you happy, Maddie.' And I do. For some reason, I do.

I pull her over to my bed and climb in, pulling the covers back and patting the space next to me. She slides in, my shirt raising up. I catch a glimpse of black silk panties. Holy . . .

Doing my best to ignore the inappropriate thoughts running through my mind, I wrap my arms around her and pull her close to me, spooning her. She hugs my arm, and I breathe in the sharp apple scent of her hair, the ends tickling my nose.

She's molded to my body like she was made to fit there, and

it's fucking unnerving. I'm not sure anyone else could fit against me the way she is right now.

I trace my finger along her arm and after a while her breathing evens out. I shift up to see her face. She's asleep – her eyes are closed, and her thick eyelashes are fanned out across her cheeks. Her lips are puckered in a slight pout, and I'd love to kiss them right now. I won't wake her though.

I lie back down next to her and pull her tighter to me, letting my eyes close shut.

I'm woken by an elbow in my cheek.

'The fuck?' I mumble and sit up, remembering Maddie next to me. 'Maddie?'

I open my eyes, and she's shaking her head, still asleep. The TV casts a harsh glare over her, and I can see her lips moving, mumbling in her sleep. What's she saying?

'Maddie? Angel?' I push hair away from her face and she jolts awake, breathing frantically. Tears I didn't notice are streaming down her face. 'Maddie?'

'Just a dream,' she whispers to herself. 'Just a dream.'

'Angel, are you okay?'

Her eyes focus on me for the first time. She nods. 'Just hold me. Please, Bray.'

'You know I will.' I tuck her into me, facing me this time – and I realize she called me Bray.

'Thank you,' she whispers, slipping her legs between mine and holding me tightly. Tears are still falling from her eyes. I can feel them as they drip from her eyes onto my shoulder and onto my pillow. I have no idea what to do. I have no idea why she's crying. I'm lost.

I make soothing noises in her ear and smooth her hair until she's quiet again.

There's more layers to this girl than I'll ever understand – but I'm starting to want to understand.

Maddie picks a piece of her muffin off and eats it.

'How do you stay so skinny?' I ask, amused.

'What do you mean?' She tilts her head to the side.

'I'm pretty sure I've seen you eat one of those muffins every single day for two weeks.'

'Only two weeks? I'm pretty sure I've eaten one of these muffins every day for at least eight months.' She casually shrugs a shoulder.

'And you look like that?' My eyes roam her body shamelessly.

'Fast metabolism.'

'Not that it would be an issue if you didn't have one. I'm sure I could think up a way to burn off those extra calories.' I wink at her, and she smirks.

'I'm sure you could think of several ways,' she replies. 'Unfortunately, so can I, none of which probably agree with yours. They're all exercise.'

'I never said mine weren't exercise.'

'Sex does not count as exercise.' She looks at me pointedly. 'In *any* position.'

'It burns calories,' I argue. 'That counts as exercise.'

She sighs and shakes her head, but I can tell she's trying not to laugh. What? I make a damn good point.

'It's not a recognized form of exercise, Braden.'

'You called me Bray last night. I liked it.' I scrape her hair from her face with my fingers.

'Did I? When?'

'You, um . . . You had a nightmare, and I woke you. Then.'

'Oh.' She puts the muffin down. 'Sorry.'

'Hey.' I make her look at me. 'Don't be sorry. Do you have them often?'

Her eyes move from my face, looking out at the crystal clear water in front of us. 'Sometimes. Less than I used to.'

'Why do you get them? I mean, what do you dream about?'

The silence is telling. I know what she's going to say before she even says it.

'The day my Mom died.'

'Maddie, we don't have to talk about this—'

'Talking helps, sometimes. I've just never had anyone to really talk to.'

I take her hand, slipping my fingers through hers. I rub the back of her hand with my thumb. 'If you want to talk about it, then we'll talk.' I want her to talk to me about it.

She takes a deep breath, and in the silence, I wonder if she's going to speak. But she does.

'I have the nightmares because I watched her die.'

Fuck.

Chapter Twenty-Five

Maddie

I remember it. I remember it like it was yesterday. Every detail is etched into my mind, and when I let myself remember – like now – it plays out like an old movie strip. The memories are cracked, a little fuzzy in some places, and sometimes the sound goes, but I still remember. I still know. I know it all.

'We'd been out for a girls night. It wasn't anything unusual. Once or twice a month, Mom insisted we had some girl time, and we headed for dinner and a movie, maybe some shopping. It was our time where we caught up on life. We talked boys, music, clothes. Everything.'

'It sounds like you were close.'

'We were.' A small smile graces my lips. 'She was my best friend.'

'Tell me about her.'

'Everyone says I look like her, but I don't think so. Mom was beautiful. Sure, we had the same hair and the same green eyes, but she had this inner goodness that radiated out of her. She was always happy and smiling, always ready to lend a hand. She worked at a local youth center with young people who were addicted to drugs or homeless. Sometimes, when I'd go with her to volunteer on a weekend, I'd hear them talking about how amazing she was. She always brightened their day. Everyone loved her.

'But that night . . .'

We had been to the movies since it had been my choice for that particular girl's night.

'Let's get some cotton candy,' Mom suggested, spying a vendor across the street.

'That's silly, Mom. It's eleven o'clock! Dad will be up waiting for us.'

'Oh, come on, Maddie Moo. Don't be a spoilsport.' She parked the car across from the vendor. 'It'll only take two minutes. Promise.'

I sighed. 'Okay, but you're crazy.'

She opened the door, glancing at me over her shoulder, her light, flowery smell seeming to strengthen in her excitement. She grinned, her eyes wide and mischievous, just like a child's. I couldn't help but grin back at her – she had the kind of smile that was infectious. I watched as she left the car and rifled through her purse for some change as she approached the vendor.

Bangs echoed from maybe a block away. Fireworks!

I rolled my window down and stuck my head out – then I heard the scream. Someone was screaming over and over. The bangs were getting louder and tires screeched—

'Maddie get down!' Mom yelled.

I began to shake and sat back in the car, wrenching the seat belt off me. I slid down my seat as the bangs ricocheted off the city buildings around me. I looked for Mom and then . . .

Bang.

She began to fall.

I screamed.

A car sped past, the bangs finally registering in my brain as gunshots.

I crawled over the seats, reaching for the driver's side door. 'Mom! Mom! No, Mom!' I yanked the door open and fell from the car, scrambling to my feet. Gunpowder and smoke filled my nose, the thick smell wrapping around me.

A crowd had gathered, and I pushed my way through, shoving bodies and people away, screaming her name, needing to see her because she had to be okay, she had to be. Mom couldn't leave me because she was always meant to be there, always.

Alwaysalwaysalways.

★

Braden reaches up and removes my hands from my ears, bringing me back to the here and now.

I can still hear the ringing from the shots in my ears. I can still hear the screams that drowned out the city nightlife. I can still feel the adrenaline as it pumped through my body, the fear as recognition dawned. It's still so real.

'That's where it gets fuzzy. I remember hearing sirens, and I remember being held back. I remember breaking free and shaking Mom to get her to wake up. She didn't. She couldn't. She'd taken a direct hit to her thigh. In the time it took for me to get out of the car and to her, she'd bled out. Alone, on a cold sidewalk in Brooklyn. She'd gone, and I never did anything to save her. I never should have let her leave the car for her stupid cotton candy.'

Fingers swipe under my eyes at the silent tears falling there. Braden moves and crouches in front of me, cupping my face. I look into his eyes, blue eyes, full of sorrow and sympathy.

'You're so strong, Angel,' he says softly. 'Not many people would have got through that and still be here today, going on the way you do. You're amazing, you know that, right? I bet if she could see you now, she'd be so, so proud of you.'

I nod silently. He kisses my forehead and kneels down, pulling me into his arms. The gentle sea breeze teases my hair as I curl into him, needing the comfort and safety he can provide me.

I've never told anyone the whole story. Even when Dad forced me to speak with a counselor, I never spoke about it. She was mine. The last memory of her was mine.

But not anymore. I've shared it, in the place she was born and raised.

I brought her home.

The guys all huddle in the middle of the yard, all shirtless and glancing over at us flirtatiously. Kay shakes her head and flips them off.

'Fuckin' animals,' she mutters. 'Parading round half-naked like they're King of the fuckin' frat.'

I laugh into my hand silently.

'Don't you start laughin' at me, Mads. You and Carter are like the King and Queen of this place, and Lila and Ryan are like the Prince and Princess. Or should that be Princess and Princess?'

'Hey!' Lila chucks a chip at her. 'He's a pretty boy, but he's my pretty boy, Baker.'

'Got it, Princess.' Kay winks, and Lila grins at her.

There's something relaxing about having a secure, close friendship with people that can make you laugh. The chat at the beach with Braden is still weighing heavily on my mind, but being here, with these girls, makes it all seem better.

Braden looks over his shoulder at me and grins devilishly. I can't help but smile back, and my stomach flip-flops. Ugh.

'Love is in the air, doo doo doo doo doo doo!' Kay sings, waving her bottle of soda around.

'Get lost.' I chuck a piece of candy at her, and she catches it, shoving it in her mouth.

'Thanks, baby girl.' She winks.

'I like seeing him happy,' Megan says, watching the boys line up to start playing. 'I haven't seen him like this in a long time. It's almost gonna be a shame to end it in two weeks, maybe even a few days.' She glances at me.

'You know the rules of the game, Megan,' I reply, picking some grass. 'Four weeks. That's all we allowed.'

She stares at me out of the corner of her eye, a knowing gleam that's only meant for me. 'If Braden lets you go.'

Translation: if you can end it.

Sometimes, it's really annoying how observant she can be.

'He will,' I say with more confidence than I feel, my eyes watching him as he runs and jokes with his frat brothers. 'He won't hang around, Megs.'

'Okay,' she acquiesces. Reluctantly. Ugh – I'm so fed up of hearing about this.

I turn my attention back to the yard and watch as they throw the ball to and fro. Braden catches it and makes a run for the end zone – which is marked by two t-shirts. Sweat drips from his toned upper body, and his back muscles ripple as he runs.

It's enough to make me want to chain my legs together, because he is *hot*. Especially when he's sweaty and shirtless.

He dives, scoring a touchdown. The guys on his team congratulate him, and he winks, motioning me over to him. I tilt my head to the side questioningly. He jogs over to me, looking too much like perfection for my liking, and bends down to grab my hands. He pulls me up from the ground, wraps an arm around my waist, and tilts me back.

He kisses me hard, his lips a searing flame on mine. I grab his hair and hold on, one of my feet leaving the ground. He slips his tongue between my lips quickly, and I meet his every movement.

Slowly, he pulls back. I smile, and he looks at me with heated eyes.

'Now I feel like I've celebrated.' He chuckles, righting me.

'You just wanted to show off.' I trail my finger down his chest. His fingertips dig into my back slightly.

'When I have a beautiful girl like you to show off, who can blame me?' He smirks and puts his mouth by my ear. 'And stop your finger where it is, or we'll go and continue our celebration inside.'

I swallow. Right now, that sounds kinda good.

I ping the waistband of his shorts. 'You have a game to play,' I remind him. And me. 'Go and play it.'

He smirks again and kisses me once more. For luck, I guess. Not that he needs any. I drop back to the floor as he runs back and take my candy back from Kay.

'Wowee, I don't think I've ever seen a real foot-poppin' kiss!' Megan grins.

'A foot what?' Kay raises her eyebrows.

'A foot-poppin' kiss,' Megan repeats. 'From *The Princess Diaries*? With Anne Hathaway?'

'Do I look like I've watched the fucking *Princess Diaries*, Meg?'

'I never know with you.'

'I'll make sure to put it on my Christmas list. I'm sure it's *fascinating*.'

Megan leans over and punches her in the arm. 'No need for sarcasm, Kayleigh.'

'With you, Megan, there's always a need for sarcasm.'

'Shut up.'

I shake my head, smiling, and chuck a piece of candy at them both. Lila giggles and copies me. Megan shrieks, Kay yells. Before I know it, we're in the middle of a junk food fight, and I'm lying on my back on the grass, holding my stomach as I laugh.

I sigh and wipe tears from my eyes. I can't remember the last time I laughed so hard.

Chapter Twenty-Six

Braden

I hate Sundays. There's something so fucking dull about them.

So maybe that's why I'm at the beach. Contrary to popular belief, I'm not the biggest fan of sun, sea, and sand. Nor am I the next champion surfer.

But Maddie wanted to come, and the rules of the game state that what Maddie wants, Maddie gets. So, here I am. Getting sand up my shorts and, if I'm not careful, a crab pincer around my balls.

'You didn't have to come with me. I'm capable of sunbathing by myself,' Maddie says, lying on her back on the sand.

I roll onto my side and prop myself up on my arm. 'And why would I not come? I like spending time with you.' I drag my finger across her flat stomach, and she squirms.

'Because.' She shrugs a shoulder.

'Because?'

'Yep. Because.'

I flip over and straddle her. She squeals and pulls her sunglasses off, flinging them to the side. She looks up at me, and I grin wolfishly.

'What?'

'Why are you sitting on me?'

'I felt like it.'

'You felt like it.'

'Yep.'

'Why?'

'Because.'

'Because?' She raises an eyebrow.

'Yep. Because.' I grab her hands and thread my fingers

through hers. Her lips quirk up at one side, and her eyes show the amusement she feels. I stare at her, just watching her, and taking her in.

The light tan on her skin sets off her auburn hair, making her green eyes stand out even more. Her curled lips are plump and shiny, begging me to kiss them.

I do.

I drop my head and brush my lips across hers. Her fingers tighten around mine, and her lips pucker, softly massaging my bottom lip. I pull back, opening my eyes and watching as hers open slowly.

'What was that for?' she asks softly.

'Because I can.'

'Fair enough.' She smiles. 'But you can get off me now. You're in my sun.'

I laugh and roll off her, flopping next to her again. She places her sunglasses back over her eyes. My eyes rake down her body, every curve available for my viewing pleasure. And boy, it's a fucking pleasure all right.

'Stop undressing me with your eyes.'

'Hate to tell you, Angel.' I run my hand down her side. 'But there isn't much to undress. Not that I'm complaining.' My fingers gently probe the soft, bared skin under her bikini top.

'Braden,' she warns.

'What?' I move my hand across her ribs.

'Braden!'

'What?'

'There are other people around!' she hisses.

'And?' I kiss her cheek, close to her ear. 'I'm allowed to touch my girlfriend.'

'Mmm.' I'll take that as an agreement.

I find her lips again and run my tongue along her bottom lip. She squeaks and opens her mouth in surprise. I take the chance, sweeping my tongue into her mouth. Her hand claps down onto my neck as she kisses me back, her tongue swirling in a way that makes all the blood in my body rush straight down to my dick.

I shift a little, putting my fingers in her hair and running them through to the ends.

'I think you need a cold shower,' she mutters against my lips, running her nails down my arms. All my hairs stand on end at that innocent, yet damn sexy move.

'There's a sea over there. Care to join me?'

'I'm unsure if it's a smart or stupid move, but I will anyway.'

I move and get up, holding my hands out for her. She takes her glasses off, slips her hands into mine and jumps up, grinning at me. I raise an eyebrow and she runs off down the beach, giggling to herself.

I shake my head and take off after her. I'm close enough to hear her loud, high-pitched squeal when she runs into the water. She turns straight away and runs towards me. I laugh and grab her round the waist, lifting her up, and run into the water.

'Braden, no! It's cold!'

'That's the point!'

She kicks and clings to my neck. I wade through the water until we're waist-deep and drop her, letting her slide down my body. Big mistake.

I clear my throat and she glances up at me through her eyelashes. She smiles and shoves me. I lose my balance and fall backwards into the water. I bounce back up, sputtering, and focus my gaze on her. She's so in for it now.

'I'm sorry! No, no!' She holds her hands out.

'No, that's it now.' I shake my head and move towards her.

'No!' She squeals when I tackle her.

We fall into the water, her legs kicking in a feeble attempt to get away. She pushes herself up on my shoulders and as I surface, I cup her ass and hold her against me.

'You—'

My lips on hers silence her. Her hands find my hair and she holds on tightly, gripping it between her fingers. One of my hands comes to rest on her waist, and her feet lock around my waist, holding her in place and tight against me.

My dick rubs against her, making her whimper and press into me tighter. My fingers dig into her ass and back as she rises up slightly, pushing my head back. She kisses me harder, taking control.

She stops and whispers, 'People are watching us, aren't they?'

I glance over to the beach and two little boys, about six, are staring at us with their mouths wide open. 'Yes.'

She blushes and slowly turns her head to them.

'Ewwwww!' They shriek and run across the beach.

I laugh, and Maddie buries her face in my shoulder. She unhooks her legs and slides down, her hands smoothing the wet skin of my chest. I rest my cheek on her head, still laughing, and she pokes me.

'It's not funny. They probably think they just watched a live porn show.' She moves her head and glares at me.

'Angel, they were little kids. To them, you're a girl and that means you have cooties.'

Her narrowed eyes gleam in amusement. 'Do I? Have cooties?'

'I'm not sure,' I shrug a shoulder. 'I haven't decided yet.'

'Well, if I do . . .' She smiles innocently. 'You should consider yourself infected.'

She blows a raspberry on my chest and slips from my arms, giggling as she tries to run back towards the beach. I can't help it – a huge laugh erupts from me, and I rub my face, shaking my head. She turns her body, looking at me and covering her mouth with her hand. She ducks, her wet hair coming to rest over her shoulders and shining copper in the sun.

There's a lightness in the way she teases me, the way she can make me laugh so easily. It's a lightness that isn't usually there in her, and I kinda like it.

Chapter Twenty-Seven

Maddie

I smile absently to myself as I make my way out of class. I hug my books to my chest, and my hair falls to the side, hiding one side of my face. Ever since I spent the afternoon at the beach with Braden yesterday, I've felt better than I have in a long time. I'd like to believe it was the mix of sun, sea, and sand, but I'd be lying.

I'm pretty sure *he* is the main cause of my happiness.

'Hey, Maddie.' Kyle falls into step beside me.

'Hey. How are you?' I glance up at him, thinking – not for the first time – it's a shame I don't see him as anything other than a friend. Though he's not as built as Braden, his chestnut-brown, wavy hair and equally brown eyes are captivating, all the same. He's taller than me, shorter than Braden, but he has a good heart and I know he'll be a great boyfriend to someone one day.

But why am I comparing him to Braden?

'Good. Look, I'm sorry if you guys ended up fighting on Friday. I never realized Braden was so . . . so . . .'

'Protective?' I offer dryly, echoing Braden's word.

'Um, sure.'

'Don't worry about it.' I bump his shoulder. 'He just . . . I don't know.' I shrug.

'I have no doubt you put him straight, anyway.' He grins at me.

One side of my mouth curls up. 'Of course I did. I conveniently reminded him I was wearing his shirt, not yours.'

'Yeah.' Kyle coughs and looks away. Is he blushing? Wait, what? 'Well, gotta go. See you soon, Mads.'

'Uh, okay?' I frown as he walks off, waving over his shoulder.

'Okay, Angel?' Braden slides an arm around my waist.

'Yes. Just Kyle being weird.' I shake it off and smile up at him.

'Kyle's always weird.' He drops a quick kiss to my lips, and we leave the building, turning towards the road that will take us to Starbucks. Oh, yum.

'No, he blushed.' I tilt my head, and I realize. 'Oh! *Oh.*'

'What?'

'He thinks we had sex on Saturday.' I giggle. 'Oh. He must have felt really awkward.'

'Why would he?' Braden says in a tight voice.

'Don't start that.' I slap his chest. 'Because I mentioned I was wearing your shirt, that's why. He must have assumed.'

'Good.' He laughs and tugs me a little closer. 'He might back off now.'

'He was never coming onto me.' I roll my eyes. 'He may have given you that impression, but we're just friends.'

'Sure you are, beautiful. Maybe it's a good thing he knows that now,' he says sarcastically.

'Why, Bray, are you jealous?' I raise an eyebrow, and he pulls Starbucks' door open, glancing at me.

'Of Kyle? No. Why would I be?'

'You sound jealous to me.'

'I'm not.'

'Then why do you sound it?'

'I don't!'

'Yes, you do.'

'I'm not arguing about this, Maddie.'

'I'm not arguing,' I respond. 'I'm asking, and you're not answering. There's a difference.'

He reels off our usual order to the barista and tucks some hair behind my ear. 'You are arguing.' He smirks. 'And you don't even realize it.'

I narrow my eyes at him and realize he's right. Damn him!

'Fine. You're not jealous. Whatever.'

'Oh, shut up.' He tugs me towards him and kisses my temple. 'You're cute when you're angry.'

'I'm not angry!'

'Of course not.' He grins and grabs our order.

I huff and walk over to a table with a sofa and two chairs. I sit in one of the chairs and stare at him.

'Making a point, Angel?'

'Not at all.' I smile sweetly and take my coffee and muffin. 'I just wanted to sit here.'

'Fine,' he says, sitting in the chair opposite me. He watches me as I sip my coffee and pick at my muffin the same way I always do. It's unnerving. He's eating and drinking, yet he's not even taking his eyes away from me for a second. I don't even know if he's blinking.

I don't know if I like it or not. But hey, at least I'm playing the game right, right?

Right.

It's almost funny how sometimes, just sometimes, it feels so real that I forget about the game.

'You're thinking again.'

'I'm thinking about how hard you're staring at me.'

'Maybe I like staring at you.'

'Maybe I don't like you staring at me.'

'I think you're in an argumentative mood today, Maddie.'

'I think you –' I stop and tilt my head to the side, finally meeting his searing gaze. 'Huh. You could be right there. How about that?' I grin.

He fights to control his smile, his already bright eyes brightening even more. 'It's been known to happen.'

'You being right?'

'Yep. In fact, it happens all the time.'

'Mr Always Right?' I raise a skeptical eyebrow.

'I'm male. Of course I'm always right.'

I laugh. 'Okay, sweetie,' I say with a smile. 'Here's the thing – you're male, and even though you like to think you're always right, you're not. I'm female and it's naturally wired into my brain to be right. I'm sorry to burst your bubble.'

Braden looks at me slowly, stirring his coffee absently. 'You say that, but every time I look at you I know you're beautiful, and I'm absolutely right on that one. So in this case, I'm Mr Always Right, because you'll always be beautiful.'

I pull the corner of my top lip into my mouth, trapping it between my teeth. I can feel a faint blush rising up my cheeks, and I glance down, uncomfortable.

Just when I'm reminded of the game, he goes and says something like that, reminding me that to him, this is real.

'Hey.' He gets up and moves towards me, crouching down in front of me. 'I didn't mean to embarrass you.'

'You didn't,' I say softly and look up, holding his gaze. 'I just . . . I don't know.'

He cups my chin and runs his thumb across my cheek. 'You're not used to being told you're beautiful, are you?'

'What makes you say that?'

'The first time I told you, you cried. And now you're hiding.'

'The only people who ever said it were my parents. And since Mom died, Dad doesn't have much of a mind for anything.'

He rests his forehead against mine, and I close my eyes, fighting the tears that seem to spring up every time my parents are strung together in one thought. I can think of them separately, but when one is dead and the other wants to be, it's hard to group them together.

Because, really, Dad is all I have left in my family.

'Believe it,' Braden whispers softly. 'Believe it, Angel, because you are beautiful. I'm not blind, and I'm not stupid – okay, maybe I'm kinda stupid sometimes –' I smile. 'But I know you're beautiful. I see it every day.'

I lick my lips. 'I'll never believe it, Bray, but I'll let you win this one.'

'Oh, you'll let me, will you?' he murmurs, amused.

'Yep.' I take his free hand in one of mine, lacing my fingers through his. 'I'll let you.'

'So kind of you.' He chuckles and rubs his nose against mine, his lips coming to rest softly on mine.

I tighten my grip on his hand and kiss him back, wondering what I'm doing.

*

'So, we're all heading to Vegas this weekend,' Megan says casually, picking some lint off her jeans.

'Why?' I look up from the laptop.

'Braden's birthday.'

'I'msorrywhat?' I slam the laptop shut. 'You're kidding.'

'No.' She smiles. 'Did I forget to tell you? Oops.'

I chuck a pillow at her head. 'Yes, you freakin' did! Nothing like short notice, Megan. Sheesh!'

'Well, you don't have to worry. We've booked the rooms. You're sharing with Braden, Lila is with Ryan, I'm with Kay, and Aston is sharing with a couple of the guys from their house.'

'Are we the only girls going?'

'Braden's orders.' She smiles slyly.

'Who would have thought?' I play with a strand of my hair.

'Who would have thought what? That he's said no girls besides us, or that you had an electric shock type jolt of panic go through your body at the thought you didn't know it was his birthday?' Her eyes gleam with a knowing no one should have. *No one.*

'The girls,' I reply, averting my gaze from her. I only panicked that I didn't know because of the challenge, right? Right. Right. Yep.

'Mmhmm.' She hums it out and lies back on the bed. 'I totally believe you.'

'Megan, I do not have feelings for Braden Carter.' Not discernible ones, anyway.

'I never said otherwise, Maddie.'

My phone buzzes under my pillow and I grab it, opening the incoming text without glancing at the screen.

I'll see you in two days.

I think my heart just stopped beating. What?

My hands begin to shake, and I close it down, tapping on my Messages and opening it. Yep.

Pearce: *I'll see you in two days.*

I drop my phone and stare at it as if it's burning a hole in the comforter on my bed. I push my hair away from my face and tilt my head back, trying to still my shaking hands.

'Maddie?' Megan asks, sitting up. 'What's wrong?'

I shake my head, unable to form any words. It doesn't matter, I want to say. Maybe I can arrange to meet him somewhere away from campus where no one else will have to see him.

Where no one else will have to find out the truth about what happened to my Mom, my Dad and my brother. Because, ultimately, they will. Drug addicts like my brother aren't exactly commonplace around here.

Megan places her hand on top of mine. 'Maddie, you have to calm down, honey.'

I blink and focus on her, and I realize I can't breathe. I'm breathing too hard. Too fast.

Fuck.

I close my eyes and focus on the techniques I learned in yoga last year. Yes, yoga. Relaxation. In, out. In, out.

When I feel like I can answer the inevitable questions, I open my eyes. Megan's eyes are full of concern, full of worry.

'You wanna tell me what that was about?' she says softly, handing me a glass of water she must have gotten sometime while I was calming down.

I accept the glass and sip it, looking down. 'I guess I don't have a choice.'

'You always have a choice.'

'No, I don't. He's made sure of that.' I look out the window.

'Who has?'

'My brother.'

'What's he doing, Mads?'

'He's coming here. He wants money, and I won't give it to him. Not anymore.'

'So tell him that when he gets here, and he'll leave.'

I look at her, almost sadly, because compared to me, she's led a sheltered life.

'You don't tell my brother anything, Megs. He'll do whatever it takes to get the money he needs to feed his habit.'

'His habit? Oh, you mean, drugs?'

I nod.

'Then he can get his own damn money!' She squeezes my hand.

'I wish it was that easy. When I meet him, I'll have to hand it over. I know I will.'

'You're going to meet him alone?'

I nod again.

'Hell fucking no!' She explodes, standing up. 'Do you hear me, Maddie? Hell. Fucking. No. I don't wanna know what you mean when you say "he'll do whatever it takes to get the money he needs" so I ain't gonna find out! When you meet your brother, you ain't gonna be alone.'

'Thanks, Meg, but—'

'No goddamn buts!' She shakes her head vehemently. 'No buts! I love you, Maddie, and I can see you're absolutely petrified of him. I don't know why that is either, but I'm not letting you walk in there alone. If you don't wanna give him your money, then you damn well don't, and if he lays one finger on you, Braden will break his legs.'

I sigh, focusing on a spot on the wall behind her. 'It's not that simple—'

'No, it is. The bottom line is I'm not letting you see your brother alone, and if that means you're not left alone for the next fucking month, then you won't be alone, do you get that? You're one of my best friends, and I care about you, and that means you don't have to do anything alone. Friendship means never having to be alone, it means there's a constant wall of solidarity even when everything else is crumbling around you. If he's the crumble in your life, then I'll be the damn wall!'

Tears spring to my eyes unannounced, and I smile gratefully at her. 'Thank you, Megan. Thank you.'

She wraps her arms around me, and I cry silently into her shoulder for five minutes.

Friendship. Never having to be alone.

For the first time since my Mom died, I don't feel alone.

Chapter Twenty-Eight

Braden

'No, Mom. She's not a "weekend buddy", as you put it,' I groan into the phone.

'Well Megan told Gloria you were dating, and when Gloria told me this morning over breakfast, I told her that was silly, that my boy isn't a dating kind of boy. She was adamant though, Braden, that you were dating this Maddie girl.'

'That's because I am.'

My mom has never been speechless before now. She has an answer for everything, and I guess that's where I get it from.

'You *are*?' she shrieks, delighted. 'Oh, Braden! Thomas, Thomas! Gloria was right! Braden has a girlfriend!'

I cringe at how high she's squealing to my father. I hear his baritone voice declaring, 'That's lovely, darling, I'm so happy for him, but could you possibly turn down the strangled cat a notch or two?'

I snort into my fist.

'Oh, what's she like, Braden? I must meet her. Oh, I'm so happy for you,' Mom babbles.

'Honestly, Mom, I'm dating her, not marrying her.'

'I know, I know, but she's your first girlfriend!'

'No she isn't.'

'Yes, darling, she is. You usually just sleep with them, and I know sleeping is all you do. Now, I've never been one to get involved in your business because, well, boys will be boys and all that. In fact, your Uncle Calvin was exactly the same when we went to college. Anyway, I'd just love to meet her.'

'I've been dating her for like, two weeks. Can you let me, y'know, be with her first?'

'Oh, you mean you haven't *done it* yet? Oh, good for her.'

'Mom, not like that!' Kill me. Just fucking shoot me now. 'Be in a relationship with her. Let us get to know each other before I introduce her to my family, okay?'

'Oh, well I suppose.' She's pissed. Oh well. Damn Megan!

'I have to go, Mom,' I lie. 'I have to get to class.'

'Of course you do. Now, be good, and make sure you use protection. I'm happy for you, Braden, but not that happy, do you understand?'

'Yes, Mom.' I grit my teeth. 'Goodbye, Mom.'

'Goodbye, Braden.'

I put the phone down and sigh. Good god, I love my mom, but she's a fuckin' nightmare sometimes. Not to mention embarrassing. Really embarrassing.

I shake my head and glance out the window. Being directly opposite the main campus, I can see people coming and going. A fire-red head next to a blonde one catch my eye as they leave the gates, and I grin. I jump up onto my bed and push the window open, putting my fingers into my mouth and whistling loudly.

Maddie jumps, and Megan gives a perfunctory look over her shoulder, notices me, and gives me the finger. I laugh, return the gesture, and Maddie looks up at me smiling. She waves and I wink at her, blowing her a kiss. She laughs and shakes her head. She turns away, and they head towards Starbucks.

Damn Starbucks. The one near campus probably remains open on Maddie and Megan's money alone.

I grab the remote from the side and flick the TV on, reaching out with my leg to press the Xbox's start-up button with my toe. I don't have a class for two hours . . . I might as well put it to good use and get some practice in killing zombies.

Chapter Twenty-Nine

Maddie

If Pearce was telling me the truth, I should see him at some point today.

I don't think it'll be quite the brother-sister reunion he was hoping for.

Since Megan explained the situation to the girls – and I think she also told Braden, even if she won't admit it – I'm constantly surrounded. If there isn't Megan at my side, Kay is, or Braden, or Lila. Even Ryan walked me to class. That was creepy.

My body is warring with itself. My gut tells me that Pearce will be here while my head tells me it's not possible. After all, if he has the money to travel across the country, he has it to pay off his debts. Right? Not in his eyes. As much as I want to ignore it, I know he'll show.

I fidget all the way through my classes. I barely listen to anything any of the professors say, and even Braden doesn't joke his way through English like usual. He spends the hour running his fingers through my hair. Strangely, it relaxes me. A little. Sort of.

When dinner approaches and I still haven't seen Pearce, a part of me relaxes and lets my guard down. Of course, the reason I haven't seen him could be because I haven't left campus all day. I haven't even been close to leaving campus because I know if I'm here, I'm safe. Not even Pearce will go that far.

At least, I'm hoping he won't.

I didn't even go to Starbucks. I sent Braden instead. He was only too happy to go for me, providing I stayed sitting between Aston and Ryan on the green. I could have killed him. Aston spent the whole time examining my chest.

So for all I know Pearce is standing just outside the campus limits waiting for me.

I don't want to find out.

But I have to leave campus eventually. Tonight, in fact. To see Braden.

The game. Reality. It's all starting to mix. Feelings are clashing with feelings, and I'm starting to wonder what's real – if anything is real anymore.

I can separate my feelings about Braden and Pearce, and that scares me. They should be lumped in the same box with the same feelings and the same thoughts and the same fears. They shouldn't be separate. They shouldn't be discernible from one another.

'Eat,' Lila orders, shoving my plate back in front of me.

'I'm not hungry,' I lie through the twisting of my stomach. Nerves.

'I don't give a shit if you're hungry or not. You haven't eaten anything except half a blueberry muffin today. That's the first time you haven't finished one since we started college, so you're damn well eating it.' She gives me a hard look, and I narrow my eyes, grabbing two fries. I shove them in my mouth and exaggerate my chewing the way an insolent six year old would.

'There. I've eaten something.'

Lila glares at me. 'Not good enough.'

Kay puts a hand on her shoulder. 'Let me handle this, Princess.' She turns to me. 'Eat the fuck up.'

I stare at her, meeting her hard look. My lips twitch slightly, but I hold in my smile. Kay raises an eyebrow, and I copy her.

'I thought I was in a college cafeteria, not a damn kindergarten playground,' Megan quips, sitting down.

I smile and pick my fork back up, stabbing some more fries. 'Fine. You win. I'll eat.'

'All of it,' Lila demands.

'Some of it. I won't be able to eat it all.'

'She's right.' Megan looks at them both. 'She's barely eaten, so if she eats all of it she'll make herself sick.'

'I ain't cleanin' up no damn vomit!' Kay folds her arms across her chest. 'No fuckin' way.'

'You swear like a sailor.' Lila looks at her pointedly. 'Have I ever told you that? Your potty mouth could give Braden, Aston and Ryan a run for their money – and they swear more than anyone I've ever met.'

'Why thank you.' Kay grins. 'I'm choosing to ignore the last half of that speech, because on a bad day, I'd appreciate being called more manly than actual men, but those three aren't much of a comparison to a girl.'

Megan snorts. 'She has a point.'

'Braden isn't as bad as Ryan and Aston,' I mutter. 'Aston has more hair products than all of us put together, and Ryan spends as long on his hair daily as I do in a week.'

Lila pouts for a second then nods begrudgingly. 'I suppose you have a point.'

'At least I know what to be this New Year.' Kay winks. 'First Mate Kay at your service.'

'I dread to think how many people you'll be of service to on New Years Eve,' Megan says dryly.

Kay shoots her a look, and I laugh, looking down.

'What are you laughin' at, Stevens?'

I look up at Kay. 'The fact you look *so* offended, yet you know it's absolutely true. Maybe we should get someone to reel you in, girl, 'cause you're a female Braden.'

Her eyes widen, and she looks at me in utter shock for thirty seconds. Lila gasps, and Megan shakes with silent laughter.

'Well, damn.' Kay shakes her head. 'You could be right there.' She pauses, touching a finger to her lips for a second. 'But at least I have variation. Males, female, gay, straight, y'know. Braden just goes for blondes.'

'Which is why I'm almost surprised this is working.' Lila smiles. 'Because Maddie is definitely not a blonde.'

'There's nothing wrong with being blonde,' Megan huffs.

'Of course there isn't.' I pat her naturally blonde hair. 'But your hair is a nice blonde, not bottle blonde like the usual rats that rub against him.'

'Jealous, Maddie?' Kay's eyes flare with excitement.

'About as jealous as I will be this weekend when you make out with a female stripper in Vegas.'

Kay blinks. 'I didn't even think of that. Maybe I'll take Aston with me. See if the little boy can handle it.'

Megan's eyes flicker to Kay and back again, but I'm the only one who catches the slight hardening of them. *Oh.*

'Let's go,' Lila says and stands, giving a resigned sigh at my half-full plate.

'Where are we going?' Kay groans.

'Frat house,' Megan replies, picking up her water bottle and dumping her plate.

'I spend half my fuckin' life in that house full of testosterone-filled dicks.'

'Don't be such a misery bum.' Lila pokes her. 'Maybe if you liked those dicks a little more it wouldn't be so much hassle for you.'

'I'll have you know I like dick just fine, thank you very much.'

'Too much information.' I mime throwing up.

Kay tugs my hair, and we step into the evening sunshine. One thing I definitely prefer about California is the weather. You just don't get this kind of sun in Brooklyn.

I hum silently to myself, pretending not to notice that I'm actually off-campus. I mentally kick myself – I moved here to get away from my brother. I'm not in Brooklyn anymore, he doesn't have his asshole friends to back him up, and I'm not staring into the glassy eyes of a suicidal best friend.

I'm in California. I have *my* friends to back *me* up. I'm not alone.

I'm stronger than I was six months ago.

I won't give in.

'Maddie?'

I freeze.

Pearce.

I turn, slowly raising my eyes upwards. His brown hair is messy, his face pale and thinner than when I last saw him.

There's no light in his eyes, no happiness in the smile plastered on his face.

'What, no happy greeting for your brother?'

'What are you actually doing here, Pearce?' My voice comes out stronger than I feel, and I'm thankful. I won't give in.

'What do you think I'm here for? I need your help, Maddie.' He steps towards me. 'I'm in trouble, sis. I just need your help.'

'You always need my help. Problem is, you won't help yourself, will you?'

'You know why I do it. I miss her—'

'Don't you dare use her as an excuse!' Anger rises inside me, overcoming the fear, and I take a step forward, away from the girls. 'Don't you dare use Mom as an excuse for your habit. You were into it before she died, so don't you stand there and feed me that bullshit!'

'It's not bullshit, Maddie. Really.'

'I miss her too, every damn day I miss her, Pearce, but it doesn't mean I have to turn to the closest narcotic to escape from it. Life is what you make it, and this is what she'd want me to make of mine. It's why she left me – left us – a college fund. She's probably turning in her grave at what her beloved son is doing now.'

'Mads, is that –?' Kay puts a protective hand on my arm.

'It's no one.' I shake her arm off. 'Go home, Pearce. I won't help you anymore. I won't keep bailing you out.'

'I need you to, Maddie,' he begs. 'It'll be the last time, I promise.'

'It's always the last time, though, isn't it, huh? Every. Single. Time. You say it's the last fucking time, and it never is, is it? It might be the last time you do whatever you're on now, but what's next? Ice? Heroin? Come on, Pearce! What next?!' I can't even register that people are staring. I don't even care I'm somehow right outside the frat house.

'That's shit, Maddie, and you know it! I just need your help!'

'And I've said no!' I walk up to him, jabbing him in the chest with a shaky hand. 'I'm your sister, not your fucking keeper! You're twenty-two, sort your shit out! You can't keep running to me because your sorry ass can't keep a job down to support Dad. I've been here two months and I've had to pay Dad's rent because *you* are too busy getting jacked up!'

He grabs my arms. 'And it's me that has to watch him move closer to killing himself every day while you're sunning it up here in California!'

'Getting an *education*!' I shove him away from me. 'So that one day I can support Dad and get him the help he needs to move on!'

'So why won't you do it for me?!'

'Because you're a waste of air, Pearce.' I say it quietly but coldly. 'I used to look up to you so much. You used to take me everywhere and we'd do anything. I knew we'd drift apart when you got to high school, but you changed into the people you used to despise. Mom used to work with drug addicts, for fuck sake! You knew what drugs would do to you, but you still did it. You still played around, and now, look at you.' I look him up and down. 'You're not the brother I know. In fact, I'm pretty sure you're not even my brother at all.'

'What?' He grabs my wrist, squeezing it tightly.

'You're not my brother. Not anymore.' I fight to get him to loosen his grip. 'How much have you put us through since Mom died, huh? First you played Abbi, made her fall in love with you while you controlled her and abused her because of the drugs, then you drove her to attempt suicide. I lost my best damn friend because you're fucked up! Dad told me to come here, far away from Brooklyn, where I could have a fresh start, and you just have to mess that up, don't you? You have to drag your sorry ass down here because you can't help but run up a goddamn bill for your drugs. You keep thinking "oh, good little Maddie, she'll bail me out." Not this time, Pearce. You and your habit can fuck off back to Brooklyn and stay there!'

He glares at me, the expression in his green-blue eyes as hard as rock. I stare back up at him, and the tension between us is palpable. For the first time, I admit my feelings about my brother to myself.

I hate him. It's a real hate, one that tinges everything and infects every happy memory I have of him. It's wrapping around the memories as I glare at him and wiping them out. As if they were never there.

With the loss of the memories, I lose a part of myself, but the rest of me strengthens.

I won't give in.

'I have no idea who you are, but it would be a smart idea to remove your hand from my girl,' Braden says in an icy tone.

I don't know where he is. I can't see him. I'm shaking, adrenaline and fear pumping through my body.

'I'm her brother.' Pearce laughs bitterly.

'All the more reason to get your fucking hands off her.' I feel Braden's hands on my arms. One of them moves to my wrist, and I fight my wince as he grips Pearce's wrist, squeezing until he releases me. I let my wrist hang limply down by my side, not wanting to give my brother the satisfaction of knowing he's hurt me.

'This is none of your business,' Pearce bites out.

'It's my business if you're hurtin' my girl, brother or not.' Braden pulls me into him. 'You'd better leave, because I can guarantee I'm not the only one here protective over Maddie. There's a house full of boys in there that would happily come and kick your ass for hurtin' her.'

'It's between—'

'Nothing.' I say. 'There is *nothing* to talk about, Pearce. I've made it clear where I stand, and I won't help you. You've wasted your time coming here.'

I stare him down until he steps back, hate and anger spitting from his eyes.

'Fine,' he snaps. 'Fine. I guess I'll have to find another way.'

'It's about time,' I reply coldly.

'Mom would be devastated you weren't helping me,' he throws at me as he steps back.

'Fuck, that's enough!' Braden yells.

'Get the fuck out of here before I put you out of here,' Ryan threatens, holding Lila behind him and stepping up next to

Braden. 'I mean it. No one talks to one of our girls that way. You have thirty seconds to get out of my fuckin' sight.'

'I'm goin',' Pearce says, throwing me one last look before he turns and walks down the sidewalk.

Whispers start up around us. I can imagine it. Good little Maddie – that's her brother? Bullshit. It's all bullshit.

'Inside,' Braden says softly to me, leading me towards the house. 'And you all can fuck off.'

He pulls me through the door and up the stairs to his room. He shuts the door, and my legs buckle. I barely grab his desk before he snatches me back into his chest. I can't breathe. My heart is pounding, my chest is tight, and I'm shaking more than I knew possible.

I just stood up to my brother.

'Sssh,' Braden soothes. 'He can't get near you anymore, Angel. I promise you. I won't let him.'

Tears sting my eyes, and I let them roll out, trickling down my cheeks. I fist his shirt in my hands and hold on tightly, the fear leaving me slowly.

'Come here.' He lifts me and carries me across the room, lying me down on the bed. He lies next to me, pulling my sobbing body into him. He tucks my face into his neck and holds me as close to him as I can get, so close we're practically one person. The covers go over me, and he tucks them under my chin.

Braden rocks us slightly, and I slowly begin to calm. In here, in this room, I'm safe.

With Braden, I am safe.

I don't know how long we lie here in silence, with him just holding me as if he's never going to let go. I don't think I want him to let go. I think I want him to keep holding me, to keep on keeping me safe.

I take a deep breath, and he kisses my forehead. I open my mouth to speak – to explain I guess – but he interrupts me.

'No, Maddie. Don't worry. It's getting late, you get some sleep.'

We must have been lying here for a long time.

'I can't sleep in my jeans,' I mumble in a thick voice.

'Shit,' he mutters, kissing my forehead again and getting up. He goes to his dresser and passes me a shirt. 'Here, wear this.'

I smile gratefully at him and quickly change, aware of his hot eyes on me. When I'm done, he strips to his boxers and climbs back into his bed. He puts his arm out.

'Come here.'

I move over and curl into him, resting my head on his shoulder. My leg hooks over his, and my arm rests over his waist. His arm holds me to him while the other strokes my hair in a rhythmic beat.

I relax, and it doesn't take long for my thoughts to take over in my vulnerable state.

All the fighting I've done for the last two odd weeks has been futile. It's been a defense mechanism to protect myself, keep me safe so I didn't get hurt while I played the game.

But that's the problem. I've been so busy playing the game, I didn't notice when the game played me.

Somehow, the rules of the game have changed somewhere along the way without my knowledge.

Because I'm falling in love with Braden Carter.

Chapter Thirty

Braden

When she's lying in my arms, like she is now, she's vulnerable.

Only, I didn't realize just how vulnerable she was until last night. I also didn't realize how strong she was, how much fire is in her.

I look down at her. Her hair is fanned across my pillow, and her lips are parted slightly, her breath crawling over my bare chest. She looks peaceful when she's sleeping, like there aren't a thousand demons running around in her head and her heart. Like she isn't protecting herself from anything and everything.

My hand moves from its resting place on my stomach, and I smooth hair away from her face. She sniffs and moves closer to me, causing me to pull her even closer. My lips press against her forehead, and she slides an arm across my stomach, her fingers brushing the bare skin above the covers.

I'm not sure when I started to care for her so much. It could have been the day at the beach when she told me about her Mom, or it could have been when she went crazy at that girl in the cafeteria – when she went badass. It could have happened during one of our crazy make out sessions, or maybe it was while I was pretending to focus in English while I played with her hair.

Or maybe it was there all along.

Maybe I always cared about her, and I just buried it under sex.

I don't know. All I know is, now, I do care, and the game is becoming something more. It's becoming more real than anything I've ever known. It's becoming something I can hold on to. Something Maddie can hold on to.

I'm something she can hold on to.

'Good morning,' she says in a sleepy voice, yawning and rubbing at her eyes.

'Good morning, Angel,' I whisper softly. 'How are you?'

She pauses for a second, her green eyes clouding over. 'I'm not sure. I feel good, but I feel bad too.'

I kiss her forehead again, smoothing out her furrowed brow.

'I did the right thing yesterday, didn't I?' Her voice is full of doubt as her eyes travel up to mine. 'Telling him no? Not helping him.'

'I think so,' I answer honestly.

'He is my brother, though.'

'Hey.' I tilt her face up. 'You had a reason for saying no. He's obviously put you through something so bad that you don't feel like you can help him anymore. That's okay, Mads. He can't keep taking without giving you something back.'

She nods. 'You're right. Everything he's put me through . . .' She closes her eyes and shakes her head. 'I won't do it anymore. I won't be a doormat.'

I stroke her hair because I don't know what to say.

'I was five when I met Abbi. She was my first friend in kindergarten. We went through school together, right up until high school,' she says suddenly, breaking the silence between us.

'You don't have to—'

'No, no, I do.'

'Okay, Angel.'

Her eyes glaze over, and a small smile plays on her lips. 'We did everything together. We were literally attached at the hip. If Abbi started a ballet class, I did too. If I quit and tried gymnastics, Abbi did too. That's how it was. Everyone said we must have been separated at birth because we were so alike, so attached to each other. I thought we always would be.

'When Mom died three years ago, Abbi was my rock. As my world fell apart and Dad got depressed, she was there to help me cope. She'd be there after school every day, cleaning and helping me cook. After Mom, I was the only one that could cook a decent meal – and since Mom had taught us both to cook, it made sense that she would help.

'But it changed when we started senior year. I knew that one day it would change. Maybe we wouldn't go to the same college or one of us would get a serious boyfriend. Well, one of us got a boyfriend. It wasn't me, and I didn't expect Abbi's boyfriend to be my brother.

'Pearce lost it when Mom died. He'd already been at high school for a few years when she was killed, so he'd been going to parties and stuff. He'd been trying out drugs, playing here and there, since he was about fifteen or sixteen, probably, so it was an easy vice for him to turn to. He sank deeper and deeper, going more and more into the habit, trying stronger and stronger drugs. Dad was too broken himself to stop him, and Pearce ate up his college fund from Mom doing drugs.

'So, yeah, I was surprised when Abbi and Pearce started dating. I mean, we were both honor roll students, so it was an absolutely cliché good-girl-falls-for-bad-boy scenario.' Maddie pauses, collecting her thoughts, and I carry on tracing my finger along her arm.

'He seemed to treat her kind of well at first, I suppose. He'd be a jerk when he needed a fix, but he'd buy her flowers and stuff to apologize after. I tried warning her off, after all, I'd seen him spiral downwards, but she was determined she could save him.' She rolls her eyes.

'Save him. It was the stupidest thing I'd ever heard. In my mind, the only person that could save Pearce was Pearce. I'd tried talking to him after Mom died to no avail. I tried over and over until I couldn't do it anymore. Mom always said you couldn't help someone unless they wanted helping. That was her mantra since she worked with addicts.

'But Abbi wouldn't listen. At all. So, I went with her to his parties. She'd never admit it, but she was grateful. She wasn't a fan of his friends – neither was I, mind you, but I'd never let her go into that by herself. I'd been going to them for about

two months, somehow keeping up honor roll while Abbi
dropped it, when it all kicked off one night.

'Pearce didn't have enough cash on him to pay for his fix.
The prices had gone up because his dealer's supply was getting
low, and he didn't know. Pearce was at the stage where he
needed a fix, badly, and when it all got crazy, Abbi tried to
calm him down. He swung and caught her in the face. She
went flying across the room. Her nose was gushing blood, and
I ran straight to her side. Pearce didn't care. He just wanted
his next fix. That was all that mattered to him.

'I ended up coughing up the extra cash, and it was the worst
thing I ever did. He took it that since I helped him once, I'd
do it again. He didn't seem concerned he'd hit Abbi – I still
don't know if it was deliberate or accidental, but I do know it
wasn't the last time.'

'Did you stop going to the parties?' My muscles are taut at
the thought of her being in a place like that.

She nods. 'I went to see Abbi the next day and told her I
wouldn't go anymore and that she should break it off with
Pearce. She refused. She told her parents she'd slipped on some
ice and hit the pavement and that's why her nose was bleeding.
It was November, so no one batted an eyelash at it. I felt terrible.
I was letting her go to those parties by herself. It wasn't long
before she was there as much as Pearce, although she never
actually touched the drugs. She'd just have a few drinks.

'Over the next six months, she seemed to have an extra
bruise every time I saw her. Whenever I asked her, she'd say
she fell down the stairs, got pushed into a wall, or slipped in
gym. Pearce pleaded innocence when I confronted him. He
said he didn't know what she did when he was getting his fix.
Slowly Abbi became someone I didn't know. Where she was
once outgoing, carefree, and extroverted, she folded into herself.
She became weak and dependent on my brother. And fright-
ened. She was so scared of him. I would hear them arguing all
the time, but I reminded myself she chose that. She chose to
be with Pearce.

'I tried talking to her one last time, a last-ditch attempt to bring her back, but she wouldn't have it. Whatever it was Pearce had done to her, he'd broken my best friend.'

I hold her tighter to me when I feel her start to shake, and I know what she has to say next won't be good.

Chapter Thirty-One

Maddie

'I remember finding her. Her parents were out of town on business, and her Mom hadn't heard from her so she asked me to check on her. I went.' My hands shake, and my voice is flat, my body numb to the emotions as the night I discovered her plays in my mind.

'Abbi? Abbi, are you in there?' I had knocked on the door frantically. 'I'll break in if I have to! C'mon, Abs, your mom is worried about you.'

Nothing. She didn't reply. I banged harder. 'You have five seconds to reply or I'm coming in!'

I counted in my head using the Mississippi numbers. One Mississippi. Two Mississippi. Three Mississippi . . . We might not have talked in a month, but she was still my best friend.

'Okay, I'm coming in!' I warned one last time and stepped back, kicking the lock on the door a few times. The wood splintered, and I held it open. I stopped dead at the sight before me.

Abbi was lying in the bath fully clothed, the tub half full with her arm hanging over the side. Blood dripped from numerous lines and scratches all up her arm, and a small brown bottle caught my eye. My shaky hand reached out to grab the bottle. Paracetamol. The easiest way. Mom had taught us that – sixteen tablets would be enough if you went long enough without being discovered. Who knows how long Abbi had been locked in her bathroom?

'Oh, Abbi,' I sobbed out and dropped the bottle. It landed on the floor with a deafening clatter in the silence. I backed into the door frame, trying to stop my legs from buckling. I took my phone from my pocket, and my trembling thumb typed out nine one one.

Did she have a pulse? I didn't know. Was she breathing? I didn't know. I was scared to touch her. I was scared to move her. *Please don't be dead,* I thought. *Please don't die on me too.* First I'd lost Mom, I couldn't lose Abbi too. I couldn't lose both. *Pleasepleasepleasepleaseno.*

I hung up after giving the information and stayed staring at her still body. Her chest rose slightly, and a sliver of relief ran through me. She was alive. Maybe.

But why? Why? Why would she do it?

'I knew why, of course,' I whisper. 'Pearce had driven her to it. He'd broken her so much that every piece of her was shattered. He'd destroyed her. The only thing she had left to do was exist.'

'Oh, Angel.' Braden holds me tight.

'She's alive. She's in an "institution" for mentally ill teens outside of Brooklyn. She's alive, but she's not really living. Sometimes I wonder if she'd be better off not here, then I feel terrible.' Tears are warm as they coast down my cheeks. 'I still don't know everything Pearce did to her, and I'll never find out. I don't want to know. The idea of it scares me.'

'You feel guilty, don't you?'

'Yes. If I'd just stayed with her, maybe I could have protected her more. I don't know, Bray. Maybe if I'd stayed by her side and not let her be alone, she'd still be, well, normal, I guess.'

'It's not your fault. You didn't do it.'

'I know that. I do, but I hate that I had to find her. It's a good thing I did, though. The paramedics said if I'd left it another few hours before going round, she would have died. She'd taken that many tablets and cut herself all over. She didn't stop at her arms. Her thighs and stomach were covered beneath her clothes. She was wearing black so I didn't see them, but the water in the bath kept the cuts open. She knew exactly what she was doing. It wasn't a cry for attention, it was a real attempt.'

I swipe at my cheeks, and Braden kisses the corners of my eyes. 'That's why you hate your brother?'

152   *Emma Hart*

I nod. 'Because he made me lose everything. I'd already lost Mom, and I lost Abbi. Maybe not in the same way, but she's still not the person I knew. She never will be again.'

'I'm so sorry you had to go through all that. I really am.' He kisses my forehead. 'You know your brother will never come near you again, right? If he does, I'll kick his fuckin' ass, Maddie. I promise you that.'

I nod and press myself to him. 'I know.'

'He won't hurt you anymore,' Braden whispers, his arms wrapping my body completely in a blanket of safety.

And I believe him.

'Let me in, you great big buffoon!' Lila shouts, hammering her fist against the door. 'We have a road trip to start!'

'It's. Eight. A-fucking-m!' Kay snaps and pulls the door open. I sit up, rubbing my eyes.

'And it's going to take us eight hours to drive there, so get your lazy ass out of bed and finish packing!' Lila tugs her bag through the door followed by a grumpy Megan. Megan does not do early mornings.

She chucks a brown envelope at me. 'Yours.'

'What is it?' I yawn and pick it up.

'Open it and find out.'

I rip it open and tip it upside down. A plastic cream-colored card falls out, and I stare at it. 'Is that?'

'Fake ID?' Lila beams. 'Yep.'

'And why do I have a fake ID?'

'Because we're going to Vegas,' Megan says dryly, raising an eyebrow. 'And you can't go to Vegas and *not* have a fake ID.'

'Um, okay.' I shrug and put it on the nightstand, climbing out of bed.

Kay walks out of the bathroom, changed into her clothes for the day, and still grumbling about the 'Fuckin'' ungodly hour of the morning that should never be seen on a weekend.'

I laugh and pull my sweats from my drawer. Hey – it *is* eight a.m., and an eight-hour journey.

I head into the bathroom, change, and apply a bit of make-up, and get back out again.

'Are you packed?' Lila asks, tapping away on her cell.

'No. I wasn't expecting to leave at fucking eight a.m.,' Kay replies.

'Oh, goodness.' Megan looks at her. 'Someone's happy this morning. You're just a little ray of sunshine today, aren't you, Kay?'

'Please don't go there,' I beg as I put the last of my things into my mini suitcase. 'Just, don't even go there. She'll have you going all day.'

'It's—'

'Eight a.m. Get. Over. It.' Megan throws my pillow at Kay's head and I shake my head.

'Okay, the guys are ready and driving over now,' Lila announces.

'Wait, who's going with who? Where are we even staying?' I grab my fake ID and slip it into my purse.

'Um.' She holds up a finger and taps some more on her cell. 'Okay, Maddie travels with Braden, Megan and Kay with me and Ryan, and Aston with the rest of the guys. We're staying at Treasure Island, and Maddie and Braden are sharing, me and Ryan are, Megan and Kay and Aston with the guys.'

I look at Megan. 'She has a schedule on her phone, doesn't she?'

She nods serenely. 'It's been there for a week.'

'Fuck ya schedule, Lila,' Kay says, standing and hoisting her bag onto the bed. 'I'm packed, you're packed, and we're all packed. Let's move.'

Lila glares at her, stands, and grabs her bag. I sigh deeply, knowing this weekend is either going to be a great success or a great big flop.

Right now, I'm thinking flop.

I lock the dorm room door behind us and by the time we get to the bottom of the stairs, the guys are all parked up outside. Braden steps out from his Jetta and shoots a disarming smile my way. I smile back at him and let the main door shut behind me.

He walks towards me, taking the bag from me wordlessly and replacing it with his hand. He tugs me to the car and pops the trunk, putting my bag carefully next to his.

'Braden, you ready?' Aston leans out the window of his four-by-four.

Braden gives him a thumbs up. 'You go on. We'll be right behind you.'

I wave at the girls and watch as the three other cars pull away from the dorm room and campus. Braden drops the lid of the trunk, and I look up at him.

'What was that for?'

He turns quickly, cupping my head, and his lips find mine. I tilt backwards, leaning against the car. His knee slips in between mine, and I grab his shirt when he unclasps our hands and puts his on my waist.

His lips are hot and sweet as they massage mine, and I taste chocolate chips and coffee. I nibble his bottom lip.

'Did you buy me coffee?' I murmur.

'It's in the car.' He pulls back, eyes twinkling.

'So, that's what that was all about.'

He rights me and drops another kiss onto my lips. 'No. That was because I wanted to kiss you, because sitting next to you in a car for eight hours without kissing you is going to be a damn nightmare.'

'We can take a pit stop, you know. I want McDonalds for lunch.'

'Angel,' he says in a low voice. 'These might be sweatpants, but they happen to fit you really well, especially around that ass.' He slides his hand down across my hip and cups my ass, his fingers flexing as he pulls my hips against his. 'So if we stop, it won't be for fucking McDonalds.'

I swallow, my heart thudding in my chest. Apparently, with the realization I'm falling in love with him comes the realization that he can turn me to a puddle of red hot, bubbling, needy, desperately-wanting-him mush.

'Point taken,' I say in a somewhat strangled voice. 'Let's go, before we never leave.'

'Don't tempt me,' he whispers and kisses the spot below my ear.

I slide from his grip and open my car door, getting inside. He wasn't lying – sitting in the cup holder is a coffee from Starbucks, and a muffin is sitting on the dashboard. He put that there before he got out. I smile and take it.

'Thank you,' I say as he starts the car up.

'Anytime.' He smiles over at me, and I smile shyly. I break a piece of the muffin off and lean over before he pulls away, putting it by his lips.

He opens his mouth, and I drop it between his lips. He closes his mouth, and as I pull my hand away, his lips brush the ends of my fingers. The simple contact sends a shiver through me, and I look down as if that'll hide my reaction. He coughs, clearing his throat and pulls away from the dorm block.

Good move.

Chapter Thirty-Two

Braden

Saying that being in a car with Maddie for eight hours would be a damn nightmare was the biggest fuckin' lie I've ever said.

It's hell. Every motel we pass by I want to park in, rent a room and take her in there and not leave until tomorrow. Every. Fucking. Motel.

But I don't want to fuck her. Oh no, not Maddie. I want to *make love* to her. I want to kiss every inch of that soft, golden skin, run my hands over every curve, and move inside her until she screams. Because I already know she does, and now I've admitted to myself that I feel something for her – and I mean really feel something for her – I want it to be more than a quick fuck somewhere in a parking lot. I want it to be special. More than anything I've ever experienced.

She drops her bag at the bottom of the king bed in our room in Treasure Island and looks around. Mom offered to book me a suite, but somehow I knew this would be enough for Maddie. Judging by the look on her face, I was right.

'Is it okay?' I perch on the green chair in the corner.

She nods. 'It's beautiful.' She smiles, one of her light smiles that makes me smile back.

I knew it would be. The understated browns and greens of our room are calming and exactly what she needs after the week she's had because of her brother. Me?

I just need Maddie.

'Wanna go grab some food?'

'Uh, sure. Can I change first?' She gestures to her sweatpants.

'Sure, go ahead, Angel.'

She pulls some clothes from her bag and heads towards the

en-suite bathroom, stopping on the way to kiss the corner of my mouth. She walks away, her ass wiggling, and I smile as I watch her go. I stare at the place her ass was for a good five minutes after she's shut the door.

I shake my head and secretly wonder if she's a witch and has cast a spell on me. No, she's too pretty for that. I shake my head again.

Thank fuck for this fake ID Megan managed to get, because I need a damn beer with this dinner.

The bathroom door opens, and Maddie steps out. I glance her way. The skin-tight, black jeans she's wearing leave little to the imagination, and the hot pink top that flares from her boobs down makes me wonder exactly what's hidden underneath it. Her hair is piled high on top of her head with a few loose curls framing her face. She crosses the room, not noticing I'm practically drooling, and opens the mini suitcase. After some rummaging, she pulls out some black pumps with hot pink heels and slides her feet into them. She straightens, smooths her top in the full length mirror, and turns to me.

'Is this okay?'

I blink. Swallow. *Shit.* She looks fucking beautiful. 'You look fucking beautiful.'

She smiles. 'Thank you. Megan said to dress up, so . . .' She holds her hands out. 'I dressed up.'

'I like you dressed up,' I mutter, walking over to her. I run my hands down her arms and take her hands, my eyes sweeping her from head to toe. 'Yeah. I definitely like you dressed up. I like it a lot.'

She glances down then up at me through her lashes. 'It's not too much?'

I shake my head and step closer to her, closing the distance between us. 'No, it's perfect.' I kiss her softly. 'Now I feel like I should be wearing a shirt.'

'Maybe you should be.' She smiles.

I grin at her and kiss her once more before turning away. I find a white shirt from my bag and a pair of dark jeans. I strip – no going into the bathroom like Maddie did – and change, feeling her eyes on me the whole time. I face her as I do up the buttons of my shirt, and her eyes are fixed on my chest. A small, smug smile graces my lips.

'Is my collar straight?' I ask, tilting my head back and exposing my neck.

'Mm? What?' She snaps back to it. 'Oh, not quite.'

Her heels are soundless against the carpeted floor as she steps up to me and reaches up to adjust my collar. When she's done, she smooths her hands down my chest and kisses my neck, brushing her lips along the hollow of my collarbone afterward.

'Hey,' I whisper huskily. 'None of that, or we won't be going for dinner.'

She smirks and steps back, letting her fingers trail down my body. 'Stopping.'

I step forward. 'You don't have to stop, Maddie, I'm just saying . . .'

'Well, I'm hungry.' She bats her eyelashes. 'Where are we eating?'

'I was thinking Phil's Italian Steakhouse.'

She purses her lips for a moment. 'Expensive.'

'And my treat.'

'You can't exactly take me for dinner on your birthday weekend, Bray.'

'Hey.' I step closer to her again, resting my hand on her hip and holding her chin. 'You're my girl, so my birthday or not, if I wanna treat you, I'm gonna treat you, okay? And tonight I wanna treat you. You can pay for dinner tomorrow on my actual birthday.'

She sighs. 'Well, okay, but you should know we're only going for pizza tomorrow night.'

Her eyes glimmer, and I grin at her. She smiles back. 'Pizza is fine.'

'Good.' She leans up and kisses me. 'Now feed me.'

'Yes, ma'am.' I take her hand and pull her from the room, slipping the key card into my pocket.

She leans into my side on the way down in the elevator. 'Are the others meeting us there?'

'No.' I kiss the top of her head. 'Dinner tonight is just for us.'

'Oh yeah?'

'Yeah.' I squeeze her hand, and we step out. 'See, I realized we haven't been for dinner yet, and according to Google that makes me a bad boyfriend.' I wink, and she laughs.

'You googled it? Really?'

I half-smile at her. 'Only so it could be perfect for you.'

She stops laughing and leans up, touching her lips to my cheek. 'It's perfect anyway.'

I stroke my thumb across the back of her hand. 'Come on, let's get some food.'

The low light of Phil's Italian Steak House is perfect for dinner. Despite the place being packed – making me thankful I'd thought to book a table before we left college – there's something intimate about it.

Maybe it's because I've never really taken the time to be with Maddie before now. Maybe because it's finally more than just sex. I don't fuckin' know.

But being in this casino now with everyone makes me wish we were back in the restaurant.

Maddie runs her finger around the top of her wine glass.

'Okay, Angel?' I put a hand on her back.

She looks up and smiles. 'I'm fine. You?'

'Fine.' I kiss her quickly.

Megan powers through our crowd and takes Maddie's free hand. 'I'm stealing her. Go be a boy and play poker or something!'

'What are we gonna do?' Maddie asks and shrugs at me.

'There's a hot bartender over there, and I want his number!' Megan laughs, and I shake my head. Aston's head snaps round and watches her as she leaves. My eyes flick between them – okay, between them and Maddie.

Aston better not have designs on Megan because I'll break his fuckin' neck if he does.

The girls disappear into a throng of people, and I join the guys. 'Poker?'

'Poker,' Ryan agrees, finishing his beer and putting the glass on the bar. We all move into the poker room to a mercifully free table. After sitting, Ryan signals to the dealer that he's got it. He deals in a way that only growing up in a casino can teach you. His smooth way with the cards means there's no chance anyone other than the person the hand belongs to will have seen it. That's what you get when your Dad owns a casino in Atlantic City, I guess. You also get to deal at your own table if you know the casino owner, apparently.

'Game on,' Aston grins.

Ten minutes in, Aston is panicking as his pile of chips dwindle slowly.

'You have the shittest poker face I've ever seen,' Ryan announces. 'And I've seen a lot, Aston.'

'Slot machines are just back in there if you want 'em.' I wink.

'Fuck off,' Aston says. 'Slot machines are for girls.'

'And poker is for men who don't wobble their bottom lips when they have a shit hand.' Ed laughs.

The rest of the guys join in the piss-taking and after a few minutes, I break it up.

'All right, guys, come on,' I wave my hand. 'Give the poor baby a break. It's not his fault the only card game he can play properly is fuckin' Old Maid.'

The table roars with laughter, and someone clips me round the back of the head.

'The fuck?' I turn and Megan is standing there with her eyebrows raised. 'I thought you were getting some waiter's number.'

'I got it.' She waves a little piece of paper before tucking it into her purse. 'But we got bored and want to do something else. Lila suggested hitting a club, either in or out of the hotel.'

I look at the guys, and they don't object.

Ryan shrugs. 'Sounds good to me.'

'You only say that 'cause you're whipped, Ry.' Jake punches his arm.

Ryan shows his hand. 'You'd say the same thing if you shared a bed with her. She's a fuckin' animal.'

Megan tosses a chip at his head. 'Pigs! Do you think Lila discusses your sex life with us?'

'I know she does,' Ryan laughs. 'You all discuss your sex life. It's like a bunch of grannies being together at bingo.'

'You're all just a whole lot hotter.' Aston winks at Megan, and she rolls her eyes.

'Can we go? These shoes do have a wearable time limit, you know.' She cocks her leg to show the bright blue pumps with daggers for heels. 'And I think Aston's had enough of you guys ripping on him now.'

We laugh and throw the cards down, deciding to call it even.

'Hey, Megan,' Aston slinks up beside her. 'If those shoes get too much later, and you need a hand getting to your room, you know where I am.'

I clench my fists, watching as she turns to him and touches his chest, batting her eyelashes.

'Aston, honey, if I'm gonna get someone to take me to bed, it'll be someone more qualified than you. Say, someone who can play more than just Old Maid. You think on that and come back when you've at least learned to play Go Fish, get that?' She beams and spins on her heels, stalking out of the poker room, leaving him staring after her dumbfounded.

'And that, my friend,' I slap his shoulder, 'is what happens when you try your dirty tricks on a girl with more class than a month of your bed-warming whores.'

'Because you'd know all about that,' he replies dryly, following us out to the main hall.

I spy Maddie, twirling a piece of hair around her finger and laughing with Lila. 'Actually, I would.'

I walk up behind her and circle her waist with my arms. 'Ready to go?'

'Mhmm.' She turns her head into me, and we all head to the floor that holds the Kahunaville party bar.

Chapter Thirty-Three

Maddie

The Kahunaville party bar is tiki. Maybe Hawaiian. Personally, I always thought they were the same – and maybe they are.

Or maybe that's the wine already clouding my vision, so perhaps the margarita Megan just handed me isn't a smart idea. I'll drink it anyway because these girls have successfully corrupted me from the good girl I was a few weeks ago, to the semi-bad girl I am now.

I say semi-bad because I haven't had sex yet. Glancing up at Braden next to me, I think I might have to remedy that tonight. Then we'll have a pretty little Brooklyn Maddie and California Maddie with a dash of Braden Maddie all rolled into one.

What a delightful little package *that'll* be.

I accept Lila's hand when she holds it out to me to dance. My thoughts are getting morbid, and I won't let my past ruin this weekend for Braden. He deserves a good birthday.

Servers dance between tables, swaying their hips and the flair bartenders throw cocktails shakers around. If I was ten years younger, I'd absolutely want to be a flair bartender when I grew up. But I am grown up – sort of. And it's not really that great, is it?

Oh, sheesh. Apparently alcohol depresses me.

And makes me talk shit.

Shoot me.

I move with Lila to the beat of the music, and it doesn't take long for Megan to join us, shaking her hips in a way that has every guy besides Braden and Ryan fixating their eyes on her. I giggle.

'Where's Kay?' Lila asks.

'Not sure.' Megan shrugs. 'I think she hooked up with someone doing a table in the casino. She said she'd text.'

'Check your phone,' I say. 'Before we all get too drunk.'

Megan nods and reaches into her purse for it. 'Yep, she hooked up with that guy.'

'A guy?' Lila and I say in unison. 'A *guy*?'

'Yep.' Megan throws her head back and laughs. 'Well, hey, she was right. She does like a bit of—'

'Bamboo stick?' Lila interrupts. I laugh again.

'Where do you come up with this?' I look at her.

'Well she can't exactly say dick out loud here, can't she?' Megan smirks. 'You just did.'

'Shit.' Lila covers her mouth. 'So I did. Oh well, I am twenty-one.'

'For a weekend,' I whisper, and we all laugh.

'Are you compromising my girl?' Braden asks, stepping up smoothly behind me.

'I always compromise her,' Megan replies, unaffected. 'You're just never around to see it.' She grins, and I look away, knowing she's referring to Play the Player.

Yeah, sorry, I kinda failed on the whole '*don't fall for him*' thing. My bad.

Braden brushes his lips across my ear. 'Leave the compromising to me.'

He's had whiskey, I can smell it – but he's not drunk. Have we danced that long? Apparently.

His hand creeps around to my stomach, his fingers splaying outwards. His body presses against me. 'Let's get you a drink.'

I nod and silently allow him to lead me back to the bar. He takes me to a corner and, after ordering me whatever the hell a daiquiri is, sits me on a stool. He nudges my legs open and stands between them, one hand on the bar and another on my waist.

'Did you know that when you dance, your hips do this thing where they move?'

'I think that's the general idea.'

Emma Hart

'No, but they move in this way that makes me wish we weren't in public,' he breathes, his fingers digging into my skin. 'Because, see, they give me all kinds of crazy fuckin' ideas about how those hips would move beneath me.'

My heart pounds in my chest, and I swallow, trying in vain to steady my breathing. 'Is that right?'

'It is.' He kisses my jaw, and I grip his shirt. I turn my face so my mouth ends up near his ear.

'Who said we have to stay in public?' I breathe out, feeling the want building up inside me. I let go of his shirt and let my hand fall down, my fingers brushing across his jeans and the evidence of just how turned-on my dancing has made him.

I'm not a virgin, not exactly well experienced, but something about Braden makes me lose all inhibitions. He makes me feel sexy.

His hips jerk, and he slides me across the stool so my body slams into his, the throbbing space between my legs hitting him. I take a sharp breath in, my back going straight.

'Then let's go.'

He tugs me up and waves for the bartender to give one of the girls my drink. With my hand firmly clasped in his, he pulls me through Kahunaville and towards the elevator outside the bar.

The doors ping open, and he pulls me in. He hits the button for our floor, and I find my back pressed against the cold, mirrored wall.

His electric blue eyes are heated, cloudy, misty. Needing, wanting. It's like our eyes are two opposite poles, held together by a damn strong attraction neither of us can fight.

'Maddie, are you drunk?' he asks.

'No. I'm not sober, but I'm not drunk.'

He strokes my side. 'Because we're not doing this if you are. I'm not gonna take advantage of you.'

I grip his chin. 'I'm not drunk, Braden. I know exactly what I'm doing. What we're doing.'

'Good.' He steps back as the doors open and I follow him

through towards our room. He swipes the card through the door and holds it open for me, allowing me to pass through.

Braden shuts the door behind him, turning to face me slowly. The look in his eye has my heart pounding furiously against my chest like it's trying to escape.

His slow, calculated steps swallow up the room as he comes closer to me. All breath leaves my body as he tickles his way across my cheek, fluttering my hair. He raises his hand and runs it along the side of my head, pushing my curls back and tilting my face up to him. He grips my waist gently, his fingers flexing, and steps closer to me.

My chest heaves as I struggle to breathe, struggle to *remember* to breathe through the need enveloping me. My legs are beginning to shake with it and after the performance in the bar and being so close in the elevator, I know if it doesn't happen soon, I'll go crazy. He kisses the corner of my eye, trailing his lips down towards my jaw.

He pulls his head back, and the cloudy blue eyes I've come to know so well collide with mine. My chest heaves, and I lick my lips. He drops his gaze, and I feel his resolve leave in the way he pulls me towards him.

His lips find mine. Hot, soft, and slow. He kisses me so thoroughly yet so gently I want to cry. My hands wind around his neck, and I hold him to me, gripping the collar of his shirt. Our feet move in sync as we move backwards towards the bed, our lips locked the whole time. He stops me before I drop backwards and pulls away, looking into my eyes.

His hands slide under my shirt and gently roll it up my body, over my head and along my arms. My swollen lips part as he removes his.

I'm lowered back to the bed, and the second my back hits the mattress I hook my legs round his, kicking off my shoes. He kisses me again, his lips even hotter than last time. I respond greedily, flicking my tongue across his lips. He groans, and I feel his tongue meet mine.

His hands skim my waist, my stomach, my breasts. Every kiss, every touch, every breath – it all finds its way to the pit of my stomach. That red hot pool of lava is back and bubbling fiercely, demanding it gets the eruption it so desperately needs. The eruption I so desperately need.

I slide my hands across his back as his lips brush kisses along my jaw and down my neck. I shiver, the expectation already too much. He smiles against my skin, allowing his tongue to draw lazy circles down my chest. My back arches, and I press into him, his erection hitting my center.

'Beautiful. So, so beautiful.'

He unclasps my bra, and it falls to the sides. He takes one breast in his hand, the other in his mouth. I gasp. Loudly. His tongue swirls around one then the other and I tighten my leg muscles, my fingers digging into his muscular back.

'Braden.'

He ignores me, his mouth leaving me once again, only to ghost down my stomach. I'm panting – I can't focus on anything but the feel of him. The need for him. Want for him. Only him.

Kisses dot along just above the waistband of my jeans. The button is released, and he stops kissing me again. I glance down at him.

Holy. Crap.

He grips the zipper between his teeth, his eyes fixed on mine. I'm lost. I'm lost in the heat of his gaze, the electric blue fire burning there.

Slowly, he pulls my zipper down. With his teeth. His nose brushes the satin material waiting there for him, and my whole body twitches. He unwraps my legs from his, gently peeling the material down me. One leg first, his hands smoothing over the newly bare skin. My other leg rests on his shoulder, and he focuses on that, taking my jeans off completely.

Taking my foot in his hand, he kisses up my instep to my ankle, to my calf. Kisses rain up my leg, getting higher and higher and closer and closer until –

The other leg. The same pattern, the same places, the same kisses. His mouth is millimeters away from me, from the lava pool waiting for him. His fingers hook in the waistband of my thong, making them follow the same path as my jeans.

Hot breath across my hips. A hotter mouth descending slowly. An even hotter tongue making contact.

I gasp and moan simultaneously. One of Braden's hands presses on my stomach to stop the buck of my hips while the other reaches round to cup me behind, holding me to him. His tongue swirls and strokes and slips and slides. His mouth sucks, lips brush and teeth graze. Sensation builds, and I'm whimpering out moans, my hands gripping the cover beneath me, fisting it. My head thrashes side to side until –

I scream.

He kisses up my stomach slowly and in my half-dazed state, I hear the sound of another zipper being pulled. Material hitting carpet. Foil ripping.

Braden kisses me softly, and I can taste myself on him. His hand slips between my open legs, and I feel him move, his tip settling against me. My legs wrap around his waist, offering myself to him. My hands are on his back as he moves in, slowly.

I'm stretching to take him, and he swallows the moan that leaves me. The sensitive skin can't take it – I can't take it. He moves out slowly, finding a steady rhythm that has me going crazy.

'Braden, please,' I whisper against his neck, sucking lightly on his skin.

He slides a hand behind my back, and the other cups the back of my head. I graze my teeth along his shoulder, and he drops his head into my neck, kissing me repeatedly.

I clench my muscles once, and he loses pace, picking back up faster. Yes. This is what I want – what I need. I move with him, my hips undulating against his and I arch my back.

Breathing heavy. Forceful kisses. Desperate touches.

He kisses me hard as the sensation takes over, and I cry out his name, my whole body tensing as the waves roll over me. He falters, stops, and I feel all the air leave his lungs. He relaxes on top of me, his kiss slowly becoming softer.

We lie there, together, and when he discards the condom in the wastepaper basket and pulls me against him under the sheets, I know it's game over – but not in the way I thought.

It's supposed to be over. *We're* supposed to be over.

But when his every touch tells me I'm beautiful, every look tells me I'm sexy, and every smile tells me I'm all he wants, what's really over is my part in the game.

What's just beginning, is the very thing I set out to avoid.

And because of that crazy little thing called love, I don't even care.

'Hash House A Go Go,' Braden suggests, glancing at the screen on his cell. 'Their food looks really good.'

'Okay.' I lean over the bed and kiss his cheek. 'Your choice.'

'We can go somewhere else.'

'No. It's your birthday, we'll go to this a go go place.'

'You're going to insist on paying, aren't you?'

I grab my purse and stop by the door. 'Of course I am.'

He groans and pockets his cell, standing up. He grabs a light jacket from the chair and stops behind me, reaching for the door handle. He touches his lips to my bare shoulder, and I turn my face to him, smiling.

'You know what I'd really like for breakfast, Angel?' he murmurs against my skin.

'No idea, but I'm sure you're about to tell me.' I smirk.

'I'd really like breakfast in bed. With you.'

'With me being the breakfast?'

He chuckles and moves my hair away from my face with his nose. 'You learn fast.'

He opens the door, and Megan freezes, her hand in a knocking position.

'Maybe another time,' I mutter and step away from Braden. He lets out a tortured breath.

'Good morning, Meggy. Can I help you?' he deadpans.

She blinks, offended. 'Well, I was coming to offer to buy you breakfast, but if you're gonna be like that, I'll make you buy your own, you grumpy shit.'

Braden laughs and wraps an arm around her shoulders. 'Maddie is already buying mine.'

Megan kisses his cheek. 'Happy birthday, stud. And no, she's not.' She looks at me. 'I'll buy breakfast.'

'Megs—' I argue.

'You can buy dinner.'

'It's only gonna be pizza.' Braden turns his blue eyes to me and smiles.

'Pizza is fine by me. I love pizza.' She turns and flounces down the hall to the elevator.

'Uh, Meggy?' Braden raises an eyebrow and takes my hand. 'Is it just the three of us?'

'Don't be silly. Lila, Ryan and Aston are already downstairs.'

'Let me guess – Kay's still out?' I roll my eyes.

'Of course she is,' Megan says it like I shouldn't even have to ask.

I shouldn't have to ask, to be honest.

The elevator doors ping open, and I spy the others sitting by the main doors. Aston looks like he'd rather be anywhere other than here, Ryan looks like he needs more sleep than he's got, and Lila looks like Lila. She's the only morning person out of us – and it's already nine a.m.

'It's a good thing it's your birthday,' Ryan says as we approach. ''Cause otherwise I'd have to kick your ass for having me up at this time to go out for breakfast. Go out.' He shakes his head.

'Right, man,' Aston agrees. 'What's wrong with fuckin' room service?'

'What's wrong with room service is they don't have soap to wash your mouth out with like I do.' Megan smiles sweetly at him, and Lila flicks Ryan's ear.

'You miserable shit,' she scolds, then looks at Braden. 'Happy birthday.'

'Thanks,' Braden half-smiles.

We all make to leave the hotel, and the dry desert heat hits us as soon as we step outside. There's no sea breeze, no reprieve from the heat that's already burning down on us.

'Sheesh.' Lila fans herself. 'I think I just stepped into the desert.'

I look down at the sidewalk to hide my smile, and Braden laughs silently. I elbow him.

'Um, Lila, honey?' Megan says softly. 'You are in the desert.'

'Oh shit.' Lila laughs at herself, and when I look back up, Ryan's head is shaking. There's always one – and it's nearly always Lila.

We walk for what feels like hours, and after a while I start wondering how anyone knows where we're going. I mention as much.

Megan replies by holding her phone over her shoulder. On the screen is Google Maps.

'You planned our route on Google Maps?'

'I did.' She winks.

'And you didn't think it would be easier to oh, I don't know, call a cab?' I raise my eyebrows, and Lila stops.

'Why didn't we think of that?' She looks back at me.

'I didn't know it was so far away.'

'It's round the corner,' Braden says. 'Is it really that far?'

'Yes,' I grumble, walking again.

He drops my hand and wraps his arm round my waist, pulling me to stop. He bends and hooks his other arm around my knees, sweeping me up into his arms. I shriek and grab his neck.

'What are you *doing*?'

He laughs, burying his face in my hair as we walk. 'I'm making sure you're not too tired for later,' he whispers.

'And what would that be?'

'Whatever you want it to be,' he breathes, kissing my ear. I shiver and tug a lock of his blond hair at the bottom of his head.

'It's too early for dirty thoughts.'

'Hell no it isn't.' He glances down at my chest and legs before looking back ahead. I sigh and shake my head. Sometimes I know I won't win with him so I'll just leave him to it.

Besides, I can't exactly see another round of sex with Braden Carter being too much of a hardship.

Chapter Thirty-Four

Braden

I'm falling in love with Maddie Stevens. I know it. It's her laugh, her smile, her everything. For something that started off as a game, it's damn real now. It's more real than anything I've ever felt in my life.

It's not even sex – although that's fucking amazing. A part of me knows I could live without sex if it meant I could be with her. And I wouldn't give up sex for anything.

Especially not when a red dress that hugs every inch of every curve I've touched is being worn by the girl in question.

But no. Maddie is more than that. She's just more. She's a little broken, a little cracked, but she's also a whole lot of something I can't even describe. She's filling a part of me I didn't even know was empty.

I slink up behind her, sliding my hands onto her hips and kissing the exposed skin of her neck. She finishes brushing her hair and turns her face into me. A small smile graces her glossy pink lips.

'What?' she asks.

'I like this dress,' I reply.

'So do I.'

'I think I'd like it better on the floor, or slung over that chair over there, though.'

'I'm sure you would,' she says dryly. 'But since everyone is waiting for us, it's gonna have to stay exactly where it is for now.'

'Damn,' I mutter, leaving a trail of kisses across her neck. 'Are you sure they can't wait a little longer, Angel?'

'Braden,' she scolds, wriggling from my hold. She turns and

looks up at me. 'If this dress comes off now, you won't leave this room.'

Truth.

'So it's staying on.'

I groan and she laughs quietly, touching a hand to my cheek. She presses her lips against mine, hot and sweet, and I groan again.

'Do that again, and it won't be fucking staying on, Maddie.'

She grins and turns, bending over to take her shoes from under the bed. I watch her as she slips each foot into the black heels, the material of her dress barely covering her ass when she's bent over like that. A scrap of silky black material peeks out from under it, and my dick jumps to attention.

Okay. No one said the dress *had* to come off.

'Braden,' she says in a no-nonsense voice.

'Maddie,' I reply innocently, taking in the view as she straightens.

'You know what I'm going to say—'

'I'm ready.' I stand and move towards her. 'But you,' I mutter, running my hands down her sides. 'Need to avoid bending over tonight.' I tug her dress down.

'And why is that?' Her voice is breathy.

'Because only one person will be seeing that tiny scrap of material you call underwear tonight, and he won't be seeing it in public.' I tilt my hips towards her, and she inhales sharply. 'Deal?'

'Deal,' she agrees, stepping away from me. Her green eyes flicker down to my pants. 'And put that thing away.'

I smirk. '"That thing" agrees, but only because he knows he'll be out later.'

The twitch of her lips gives away her amusement. 'Stop it.' She grabs a small black purse from the side and walks over to the door. 'Are you coming?'

'If I'm not already,' I mutter. 'I will be later.'

In the VIP viewing area for the Sirens of TI show, I realize this must be Aston's idea. He's the only one who would plan this –

and since only Ryan and I aren't single, I know all the guys would have agreed. Kay would have agreed, leaving Megan to chaperone her. Of course, I'd be here since it's my birthday weekend, so by default so would Maddie, Ryan and Lila.

And I know exactly what the sneaky little fucker is doing.

Send Braden to a sexy show and remind him he's sexing Maddie, not falling for her. Too fucking late, dude. *Too fucking late.*

Maddie looks down and smiles as if she can sense my annoyance. Ryan nudges me.

'Aston's a fuckin' joker, right?'

'You're tellin' me,' I mumble.

He shifts. 'I dunno how I'm gonna get through this without dragging Lila back to the room.'

I don't intend to get through this. Dragging Maddie back to our room sounds promising already. Very promising.

'Right,' I agree, rubbing my face as the show starts.

Several incredibly hot girls run across the stage in the bare minimum of clothing. Is it wrong I'm imagining Maddie as one of those Sirens? Shit. I have this bad.

I shift in the seat as the girls begin to prance around the stage, grinding their bodies. Y'know what? I'm not even sure what they're doing. It's kinda blurry because they all look like Maddie to me.

Fuck this shit.

Maddie's mouth opens and closes, and she casts her eyes downwards. A quick glance to the other side of me shows Lila in the same position and Ryan shaking his head. I nudge Ryan and tilt my head towards the door. He nods once and leans into Lila.

'Angel, we're going,' I say in Maddie's ear.

'Thank god,' she mutters, taking my hand and standing with me.

We follow Lila and Ryan out into the foyer and both of the girls sigh with relief.

'That was a live porn show,' Lila says, unimpressed. 'I'm not a prude, but Jesus Christ. How can they stand that?'

'He probably booked it before I started dating Maddie.' I kiss the side of her head. 'I probably would have enjoyed it before this.'

Ryan's eyes meet mine, and he nods, ever so slightly. He gets it. He knows it's over. He winks.

'Well, baby,' he says, turning to Lila. 'Shall we get an early night? It was late last night, and we do have to drive back tomorrow.'

'Sure.' She kisses his cheek and turns to us. 'You two sleep well.' She winks at Maddie, and they walk into the elevator behind them, disappearing behind the doors.

'What about us?' I run my nose down Maddie's cheek. 'Shall we get an "early night"?'

She pulls back, a smirk on those lips I love. 'I'm sure your early night isn't the same as mine.'

'Hell no it isn't.' I reach behind me to the wall and press the elevator button, turning her with me. The doors ping open and we get in to the empty elevator.

I run my hand around her side, my fingers smoothing the material of the tight dress she's wearing. She shivers, turning her body into mine and resting her hand on my chest, her fingers splayed.

'I'm pretty sure our early night is running on the same schedule, now, Angel.' I trail my lips down her earlobe and walk with her as the doors open on our floor.

She slides her hand round my back into the back pocket of my jeans and pulls out the room card, turning so she faces me fully. She slides the card through the lock behind her back and nudges the door open.

She walks backwards into the room, slipping the card onto the dresser in the corner. Maddie flicks her shoes off as she walks and turns, reaching behind for the zipper on her dress. I swallow and shut the door.

She pulls the zipper down and reveals her smooth skin beneath the bright material. I slide my shoes off and cross the room, undoing the buttons of my shirt.

My lips find her hot, bare skin, and I wrestle the zipper from her grip. I put a hand on her hip, and pull the zipper down, my lips trailing after it across her skin. Her hand clasps mine on her hip and I slide them round her stomach, straightening up.

I pull one side of the dress down, kissing along her bare shoulder. She turns her face into me and takes her arm from the dress. I take my hand from her hip and do the same to the other side, leaving her to roll it down her body.

I spin her, my eyes roaming down her black lacy underwear. Her eyes clash with mine. I explode.

I grab her against me and push her back against the bed, my lips melding with hers. The decorative pillows fall off the bed with the force of our fall. Maddie nips at my bottom lip and slides my shirt down my arms, leaving it to fall to the floor. Her legs hook around my waist and as I stroke her sides and probe at her skin with my fingertips she whimpers and pushes her hips into me. I undo my jeans and boxers, letting my hand glide up her leg to the satin underwear covering her.

I stroke the sensitive area through the material and she clenches her legs, pulling me in closer to her. I meet her eyes as my hands travel up her body to her bra, my fingers dipping inside the cups to tease her. Goose-pimples erupt on her skin and I kiss her bottom lip softly.

'Braden,' she whispers, her breathing heavy.

'Maddie,' I whisper back, my lips caressing her jaw.

'Please.' Her hands stroke my back. 'Please.'

I kiss her again, harder, and reach for the condom packet I put under the pillow earlier. I slip it on without looking and after sliding her underwear down her legs, I push into her. She grips my back tightly and moves with me, sweat glistening against her skin.

One of my hands holds the small of her back as we move together, and I know, right now, is the exact moment I fall the rest of the way in love with Maddie Stevens.

Chapter Thirty-Five

Maddie

The urge to rip down the multicolored poster on the wall is almost stifling. It feels . . . wrong . . . to have it up there. Especially since it should be coming down anyway. After all . . .

Challenge complete.

I'm pretty sure he's in love with me, and we definitely had sex. Very good sex. Done. I should be laughing with the girls, drinking a celebratory bottle of whatever we want and remembering all the times. Instead, I'm remembering every touch of his skin on mine, every whispered word and how he held me so closely, how he looked at me as if I'm the only girl in the world.

To him, I could be.

The problem . . . He's pretty much the only guy in the world. And I never planned on that, so I'm pretty screwed.

I never planned on him being so different to Pearce. I never planned on everything I thought I knew about him, all my pre-conceived notions about how he should act being stripped away and leaving him completely bare like a blank canvas. He took that blank canvas and painted it into something so beautiful, all without realizing it.

He also destroyed every idea I had about love. Three weeks. That's all it took for me to fall in love with Braden Carter. How did it change so quickly? He's gone from nothing to everything.

Like Pearce did for Abbi.

At what point do I start losing myself the way she did? At what point am I in too deep?

Am I already in too deep?

Braden is not Pearce.

Goddamn my asshole of a brother! I clench my fist and punch the pillow instead of ripping down the poster like I want to. I want to rip it into a thousand pieces and yell at the girls. I want to yell at them that it's over, the game is over and I lost. I lost because the loser falls in love, and I did that.

How can I do what they expect and not hurt myself in the process? *I can't.*

I have a week to figure out how to explain that I fell in love with the person I was definitely not supposed to.

Shit.

The dorm door bangs open, announcing the girls back from their Starbucks run.

'Update,' Megan demands, handing me my coffee and muffin. So what if I had one earlier. I totally get the comfort food thing now.

I settle onto my bed. 'Same as it was last weekend,' I lie.

'Really?' Lila's eyebrows shoot up. 'You guys didn't have sex?'

I shake my head. 'No sex. Almost, but not quite.'

'Interesting,' Megan mumbles, kneeling next to me and tracing her finger down the poster. 'He's in love with you.'

I drink my coffee to hide the crazy stop-start thing my heart just did. Yeah, I suspected it, but hearing his lifelong best friend say it is a little different.

'You think?' I look around the room.

'Oh yeah,' Kay agrees. 'That guy has gone three weeks without sex, Maddie. He's fuckin' head over heels for you, baby girl.'

I smile. 'Mission half accomplished, then.' Mission accomplished.

'Now just the other half.' Megan sits back down.

'Seven days,' Lila says softly. 'Can you do it?'

I look at her. Her dark eyes are focused on me and full of questions. 'I can do it.'

'And you're not in love with him?'

'Not even close.' Lies.

★

I sweep my hair up, securing it with a band, and yawn as I lean against the wall near the main campus doors. Meet me here at eight a.m., he said. Damn eight a.m. I yawn again and look up, smoothing my hair.

He's casually leaning against a tree across the sidewalk, his bright blue eyes trained on me. His hands are in his pockets, and his lips are curled up slightly. Damn. He is gorgeous – there's no doubt about it. *And he's mine*, a little voice in my head reminds me.

I fold my arms across my chest and stare him down, letting my hair hang over my shoulder. His eyebrow quirks, and I fight my smile. Him and his silly games. From one game to another . . .

Braden straightens and walks towards me. When he reaches me he looks down, sweeping some stray hair from my eyes.

'Good morning, Angel,' he says softly.

'Is it? I don't see a coffee in your hand,' I tease.

He smirks and leans in, touching his lips against mine. I stand on tiptoes, and my body presses against his as I kiss him back. I taste chocolate chips.

'You've already been to Starbucks,' I accuse, narrowing my eyes.

He chuckles. 'You've turned me into an addict.'

'Where's my coffee?'

'In Starbucks,' he replies. 'Let's sit in instead of standing out here.'

I nod. 'I can't believe you got me up at this time and didn't have coffee in your hand immediately.'

'Hey, you.' He sweeps an arm around my waist and pulls me against him. 'You're grumpy before you get your coffee, aren't you?' He's grinning.

'You should know this.' I trail my finger up his chest. 'Didn't you discover that the last two days?'

'Mmm.' He sucks my bottom lip between his teeth. 'And what a weekend it was.'

I half-heartedly slap his arm. 'I want my coffee.' I pout.

He kisses me again and tucks me into his side. 'Come on then, grumpy.'

I settle my arm around his waist and poke his side. 'I'm not grumpy.'

'You're always grumpy.' He kisses my head.

'Psssh.' I shake my head, and he laughs.

Braden reaches for the door and shoves it open. The smell of coffee hits me full force, and I breathe it in, sighing in happiness.

'Nice to know coffee makes you feel good on a morning,' Braden mutters.

'If you'd been there when I woke up this morning, you could have been the feel good,' I mutter back, silently laughing to myself.

His step falters, and I bite my lip, amused.

'Did you just say that?'

I look up at him wide-eyed and blink twice. 'Well it wasn't the barista that said it.'

'One weekend of hot sex and you've turned into an animal,' he whispers in my ear.

'Not quite.' I giggle. 'I was merely making a statement.'

'Maybe tomorrow morning?' he asks hopefully.

'Maybe.' I laugh.

As he orders our coffees, I ignore the barista's evil looks in my direction and curl in closer to Braden. His arm tightens around my waist, and he carries the tray she gives him in one hand. Ignoring her flirty glances, he leads me over to the plush sofas we were sitting on last week, laying the tray on the table and dropping us both onto the sofa.

'Sofa this week,' he mutters.

I laugh and swing my legs over his, resting my head against his shoulder. He passes me my cup, and I wrap my hands around it, sipping it slightly. 'That's better.' I sigh, feeling the warmth from the hot drink slipping down my throat.

'So . . .' Braden begins after a few moments, resting his hand on my thigh. 'Have you, er, heard from your brother?'

'No,' I say softly. 'Not a thing. I spoke to Dad when we got back yesterday night, and he hasn't seen him since he left Brooklyn to come here. I . . . I think I want to care, but I don't know if I can. Does that make me a terrible person?'

'No, Angel, God no.' His lips brush my forehead. 'He put you through a lot, and sometimes, family or not, you have to say goodbye to people.'

'I hate it because we used to be so close. I remember helping Mom in the garden. Granted, Pearce was more of a hindrance than a help, but it was something that happened every year. We'd all go swimming once a week at the local pool, dinner . . . Then after what happened, it all kind of . . . disappeared.'

'It's okay to miss him.'

'I don't know if I do. I don't know if I miss him or if I miss the memories. Maybe it's just the person he *used* to be that I miss.' I look at a spot on the wall. 'I don't know who he is anymore. Maybe that's why a part of me finds it hard to care. I guess I lost my brother the same day I lost my Mom and most of my Dad.'

I sigh and rest my coffee on my legs. Letting it out feels good. I know I have to let go. I know, after three years, if I ever want to move on with my life I have to put it all behind me as best as I can. Mom will always be in my heart, but as long as I hold my brother there too, I'll never move on. I'll never live.

'The thing with memories is, they never die. You can keep them and relive them, and that's okay because they're the happy ones,' Braden muses. 'Like the ones we make. Just replace the bad memories with ours.'

I smile and lean my head back up to look at him. 'I'll try to do that.'

'And while you're trying, we'll make even more.' He smiles back.

It's strange to have someone understand you.

Chapter Thirty-Six

Braden

In approximately two days, this relationship should be over.

But it won't be. I can't see myself letting her go now.

Ever since we returned from Vegas, we've been together almost constantly. It's as if me realizing I'm in love with her has changed everything.

She's changed, too, though. She laughs more now. She smiles more. Maddie has a little light in her eyes that wasn't there before.

She presses a soft kiss to my lips, and I circle her waist with my arms, pulling her in closer to me. She squeals a little and puts her hands on my shoulders to steady herself. Her fingers dig in, and it makes me pull her closer. Her knees bend, and I open my legs so she can rest them on the chair. She does, and I slide my hands down to her hips.

'Can I help you?' I pull back slightly and smile at her. Her eyes flutter open, and she nods, pulling the corner of her top lip into her mouth. 'What is it, Angel?'

'Let's dance.' She straightens, taking my hands from her hips and linking our fingers.

'I don't dance,' I protest lamely, trailing behind her.

She flashes me a coy look over her shoulder. 'You do now.'

'Really, I don't.'

She pulls me into the throng of grinding bodies and drops my hand. Her fingers hook into the waistband of my jeans. My dick twitches. She yanks me towards her, right up against her. Her boobs press against my chest, and she looks up into my eyes slowly. It's a seductive move that would be wrong on anyone but her.

Her lips curl upwards slightly. 'Really, Bray. You do dance.'

She trails her hand round my body, her fingertips brushing the skin beneath my shirt. Her hand comes to rest on my back, the other up on my shoulder. She looks at me expectantly.

Slowly, I trail a finger along her arm to her shoulder. I let my hand fall down her back to cup her hip. The other follows the same pattern but instead of her hip, I cup her ass. I pull her even closer to me and breathe into her hair. My head ducks until my lips brush her ear.

'Okay, Maddie. I dance,' I say. 'Only for you, though.'

Her hips begin to sway with the beat of the music. They move side-to-side and her breath is heavy on my neck. Her whole body rubs against me, and when her hips grind against mine, I hold her in place against me. My rock solid dick presses into her hip and stomach. Her breath catches. Her hand moves to my hair, and she fans her fingers in it, holding me to her.

She moves again, and her leg rubs my thigh. I move my hand from her ass and grip her thigh, guiding it to hook around my hip. She lets me. I reposition myself so I press against the center of her pelvis and she gasps. I encourage her to move again, to the beat of the music.

She does. Shy Maddie has gone, and in her place is a Maddie I didn't know existed. As her hips writhe against me, I clench my teeth. I want to push everyone out the way, hold her against the wall and fuck her. *Hard.*

Her breathing quickens against my neck, and her leg clenches.

'Braden,' she whimpers. 'No . . .'

'Yes.' I kiss her neck, cupping her ass with both hands. I move my hips against her, and she whimpers again, burying her face in my neck.

'Come on, Angel,' I whisper against her skin. 'Let go.'

She does.

I lean back and capture her lips with mine as her body tenses all over. She quivers in my arms and I swallow her cry, sweeping my tongue through her mouth.

'Upstairs,' I mutter. 'Fucking now.'

I pull her through the crowd on shaky legs. Need for this

girl is overtaking me and I'm pretty damn sure I can't hear a thing apart from the pounding of my own heart.

I press her against my bedroom door and kiss her deeply. She winds her hands into my hair as I feel blindly for the handle. She slips her hand into the front pocket of my jeans, brushing my dick, and extracts the key. I take it from her and pull away for a second to put it in. I turn the key, pull it out, and turn the handle.

My lips meet Maddie's again greedily as she walks backwards through the door. I push the door shut, and her hands have moved down. She rips my top over my head. I grab the hem of her dress – thanking her silently for wearing one – and pull it off her. She pops open the button of my jeans and falls backwards to the bed. I barely stop to pull my clothes off.

Absently, I open the drawer, grab a condom, roll it on, and peel Maddie's underwear away from her. I lean over her, and she opens her legs, instantly wrapping them around my waist. She reaches out and positions me, her hips off the bed.

I move into her in one swift movement, hissing at how slick and wet she is from her orgasm downstairs. She wraps her legs tighter around me, and her hips meet me thrust for thrust. She scratches at my back as hers arches into me.

She tightens and relaxes around me as we move hard and fast. Sweat slicks our bodies. She digs her fingernails into my skin to keep hold of me as she begins to cry out. I clench my teeth, and she screams out my name. I move again, faster. I grunt out her name and collapse on top of her, absolutely exhausted.

Her heart pounds against her chest, against my chest. I lift my head and kiss her slowly.

'Okay?'

'Mmhmm,' she replies in a sleepy voice. She smiles slightly and shuts her eyes again.

I chuckle and pull out of her, taking off the condom and throwing it in the trash. 'C'mere.'

I pull the covers back, and she scuttles under them. I climb over her and pull the covers over us, pulling her into my arms, both of us oblivious to the music pumping downstairs.

'Bray?'

'What, Angel?' I run my fingers through her hair.

'I . . . Never mind.' She shakes her head and curls into me. I sigh and kiss her temple, holding her tighter.

Yeah, I think. *I love you, too.*

I wake to the smell of coffee and hair tickling my face. I open my eyes and look straight into Maddie's grinning face. She's straddling me, fully clothed and looking fresher than possible.

'Good morning!' she chirps, leaning forward and pressing her lips to mine.

'Mm,' I mumble, my hands sliding up her thighs. 'Can we wake up this way every day? Maybe a little less material, though?'

She laughs and rolls to the side, flopping onto the mattress. She grabs a take-out cup from the nightstand, and rolls back, resting it on my stomach. 'For you.'

'You're very happy this morning,' I say, studying her. 'Not that I mind.'

She grins again. 'Dad called early – I think he forgets the time difference sometimes – and told me about his doctor's appointment on Friday. Doc changed his medication again. Dad's not happy but they should help him more, give him more of a drive to do things, so I'm happy. I think that when he's used to it he'll be happier.'

'That's awesome news.' I grin and lean over, kissing her gently. Her dad isn't someone we've spoken about a lot, but I know how important he is to her. I know, like with everything else, she'll tell me more when she's ready.

She nods happily, her curls bouncing around her face. 'Yes!' Her face drops a little. 'They've tried so many times but nothing works. But it's not really a case of mental health with Dad, it's more a case of a broken heart. You can't cure a broken heart with anything but the love that broke it in the first place. He'll always be a little broken, I think.'

'Hey.' I lean round her and put the coffee down, propping myself up on my elbow. 'It's okay to be a little broken, Maddie.

Your Dad is a little broken for your mom but is a lot whole for you.'

She brightens suddenly, leaning forward and touching my cheek. 'Thank you,' she murmurs, brushing her lips against mine. 'How do you always make me feel better?'

I drop down and grab her waist, pulling her on top of me. She sweeps her hair to one side, letting it fall down over us like a fiery curtain.

'It's because I like seeing you happy.' I sit up, tightening my hold on her. Her arms wind around my neck, and she smiles shyly.

'Maybe I like being happy.'

'Good.' I dip my head and kiss her, tracing the seam of her lips with my tongue.

'Hey,' she mutters, pulling back. 'I have work to do.'

'A work-out?' I grin wolfishly.

Her lips twitch upwards. 'No. Schoolwork, Braden. Remember that?'

'No.'

'Maybe you should try to.'

'When I could work you instead? No thanks.'

She laughs and shoves me backwards, dropping down and kissing me one last time. 'Get your lazy ass out of bed.' She jumps off the bed and grabs her purse from my desk.

I roll out of bed and run across the room.

'Braden! You're still naked!'

I grin and grab her, linking our hands and kissing her. I graze my teeth along her bottom lip, and she shivers, stepping back.

'Have fun, Angel.' I wink at her and launch myself back on the bed, pulling the covers over me.

She smirks at me over her shoulder and opens the door. 'Try to do something productive today.'

'I will.'

She closes the door, and I reach for the coffee. Lying in bed thinking about her counts as productive . . .

Right?

Chapter Thirty-Seven

Maddie

I relax back on the bed a little. For the first time in months, I feel like I can actually let go.

Pearce has left California – I don't need to be a mind-reader, but he has no reason to stay here. I made it clear that he wasn't getting any help from me anymore. I have my own life to think about now, my own growing up to do. I can't be the grown-up for both of us anymore.

And judging by the still-untitled essay on the page in front of me, I have a long way to go on the growing up scale. But life is like an essay: you just have to find the right words to put it together.

Someone knocks at the door quietly. I frown and look at Megan. She shrugs a shoulder and focuses back on her school work. I move my books over and slide off the bed, wondering who it could be. Lila would walk right in and Kay . . . Well, it's no surprise we have no idea where she is.

Braden's bright blue eyes crash into mine when I open the door. *Shit shit shit shit!*

'What are you doing here?' I hiss, pulling the door closed behind me.

'I came to see my girl.' He kisses me.

'Braden, this is the girl's dorm! You'll get your ass kicked by Kay if she finds out you've been here.'

'You could at least act happy to see me.'

'I'm a little surprised.' And panicking. Panicking, yes. Yes. Ah. Shit.

'Can I come in?' He knocks on the door, and springs creak inside. 'Who's that if Kay's not here?'

'Megan,' I squeak out. 'We're doing school work.'

He frowns. 'Angel, are you okay? You sound a little . . . Off.'

'I'm just worried you'll be caught.' Or that I will be.

'Let me in then. She won't find out.'

'We could always go out,' I offer.

Braden frowns and moves around me. Before I can say anything, he pushes the door open.

Megan is scrunching a large piece of paper into a ball. That and a corner of paper on the wall are the only telltale signs anything was there.

'What are you doing?' Braden says with a hint of amusement, looking at Megan.

'Nothing.' She smiles nervously. 'Just, er, collecting some trash. Maddie has loads of it in her room.'

I follow Braden's eyes as he looks around the room. The spotless room.

'This room is cleaner than a hospital, Meggy,' he says. He turns to me. 'Is everything okay?'

I nod. 'It's fine. Meg, why don't you put that *trash* in the trashcan?'

She beams. 'Good idea, Maddie. Good idea.' She throws it across the room and it lands in the basket Kay and I use.

'You two are acting weird. Are you sure that was trash?' Braden looks between us.

'Positive.' I nod again.

It doesn't stop his suspicious look. Megan fidgets uncomfortably.

'Why do I get the feeling you're hiding something from me? Especially you, Meggy,' Braden asks.

'I don't know,' she squeaks.

'Let's go out.' I pat his arm and slip my feet into some pumps.

'You *are* acting weird. What was that? Really?'

'Nothing!' I tug at his arm.

Braden shakes me off and crosses the room towards the trashcan. I look at Megan, panic welling inside me. She returns my fearful look with wide eyes and a gaping mouth. I stare at her, unable to move my eyes towards Braden as I hear the crinkling of paper being unwrapped.

My stomach is churning. Great big elephants are somersaulting in it. I want to be sick.

"'Operation Play the Player?'" He looks at Megan first then me. 'Enlighten me, girls. What exactly was the point? I think I have a pretty good idea.'

Breathe, Maddie, breathe.

'Come on!' he says loudly. 'What are you so desperate to hide?'

'To make you fall in love,' Megan says softly, dragging her eyes away from me and towards him.

'With Maddie?'

'With Maddie,' she clarifies, looking down.

'The whole time? That's what it was? A game?'

'Yes,' she whispers.

Tense silence spreads through the room, and I still haven't let my breath out. I can't. I meet his eyes, finally. I . . .

'Congratulations, you won.' He looks at me, his eyes raw with pain yet his face completely blank. 'Consider it a success, Maddie. You got what you wanted.'

He sweeps past me, and the breath finally whooshes from my lungs. That movement jolts me into action, and I realize.

He knows. He's leaving.

It's not true. It's not a game. It's real. It's as real as anything I've ever known.

'Braden!' I yell, turning from Megan and flying down the dorm stairs after him. 'Braden!'

I shove the heavy main door open, and he's walking down the pavement towards the frat house, his head hanging.

'Braden!' I yell one last time, desperation tinging my voice.

He stops, looks over his shoulder at me, and shakes his head. He keeps on walking. He disappears around the corner.

I collapse back against the wall and cover my mouth with my hand. Tears brim in my eyes, and I shake my head the same way he did. A heavy feeling is settling in my chest with the weight of the elephants that were somersaulting in my stomach earlier. My stomach clenches and I know . . . I know whatever we had is gone. It's lost.

Because I didn't remove that stupid poster six days ago, when I should have.

Chapter Thirty-Eight

Braden

Something in me shatters as I walk away from her. I don't know what it is, and I can't think straight enough to even care what it is. I just know it was a big part of me – a big part of me that was all about her.

'Fuck!' I punch the wall outside the frat house and rest my head against it. 'Fuck,' I mutter more quietly, pushing off of it and storming through the door.

The door slams into the wall behind it, the noise rebounding off the walls of the hallway. I kick it shut behind me, seeing red everywhere. Anger is all I can let myself feel.

But anger at what? Her? Me? Anger because I fell? Anger because she played me like I should have her?

'What the hell?' Aston's face appears at the top of the stairs. 'Braden?'

I look up at him, my chest heaving as I try to control the bubbling emotions in my chest. I grip the banister with a shaking hand and run up the stairs two at a time, my shoulder knocking into Aston as I pass him.

'Dude? What?' He throws his arms out and follows me up the second staircase. I reach my room, shove the door open, and slam it in his face. Of all the people I want to see right now . . . He's not one of them.

'Braden!'

'Fuck off, Aston,' I hiss the words out between my grinding teeth. My fists clench at my sides, and I drop my head back, looking up at the ceiling.

'What's happened?'

What's happened? She happened.

'This . . . challenge fucking happened.' I turn to look at him, and he flinches slightly at the venom in my tone. '*She* happened. All this "make her fall in love" bullshit is just that. Fucking bullshit! 'Cause guess what? I got played when I was tryin' to play her. She fucked me, in more ways than one, 'cause it was all a damn lie. Now it's over. It's fuckin' over!'

I grab the lamp from the desk and chuck it against the wall. The china base smashes, pieces flying across my room.

'Dude, you have to calm down.' Aston steps forward warily, holding his hands up.

'You know what, Aston? You go out, fall in love with someone and when she breaks your heart, you tell me you can be fuckin' calm!' I yell. 'Get the fuck out of my room. Now!'

He nods once and steps back. My door shuts with a click. Alone.

Me, the four walls, and a shattered lamp.

A game. Was it as much a game for her as it was for me? No. Because it wasn't a game for me, not in the end. It was real, maybe it was always real. But not for her. No. It was a game to fucking *all* of them. And Meggy . . .

My best friend. My. Best. Fucking. Friend. She knew what she was doing. Double the betrayal.

I lie back on my bed, my hands linked behind my head. My feet are crossed at the ankles, and I'm staring at the ceiling numbly. Last night's anger has subsided, courtesy of two hours sleep, and I'm fighting the sting left by the loss of Maddie. It's Saturday, and I should be meeting her for coffee right now.

Of course, that won't be happening today.

My door opens, the squeak of the hinges giving it away. My eyes flick over, a part of me stupidly hoping it's Maddie. What for? An explanation?

I look back to the ceiling, disinterested, when I see Megan. I don't exactly want to see her any more than I want to see anyone else right now.

'I'm sorry,' she whispers.

'What are you sorry for, Megan? You did what you wanted.'

'I'm sorry because until last night, I assumed she was still just sex to you,' she admits. 'But I was wrong, wasn't I? She's more than that.'

I roll my head to the side, meeting her baby blue eyes. 'Look at me, Megan. Do I look like I want to discuss Maddie, you, or any of that bullshit right now?' She shakes her head sadly. 'Then you know where my door is.'

'Bray—'

'Here's a hint. You just walked through it. Goodbye, Megan.'

She sighs sadly and turns. She stops, her hand poised on the doorknob. 'She's hurting, too, Bray. At first, it was all a game, but it doesn't take a genius to see that it's not for Maddie. Not anymore. She was crushed last night, and I haven't even seen her yet today.' Her voice is soft. 'I've read a thousand books and watched all the romantic movies in the world, but nothing has ever been as real as what you two had. Nothing has even come close to it.'

She opens the door and passes through, letting it shut behind her with a soft click. I stare at the door, tracing the pattern of the wood with my eyes.

Eventually, I return my attention to the blank canvas of the ceiling, fighting down the same old sting yet again.

Chapter Thirty-Nine

Maddie

I haven't seen him for five days. I haven't been to English because I'm not ready to see him. The pain without him is bad enough. That all-encompassing loneliness. I didn't realize how much he took away the pain until . . . Until he stopped being there to take it from me.

I think seeing him now would make it impossible. It's bad enough in my other classes – snide, triumphant looks from other girls, appreciative glances from the guys – all because I'm not his anymore. All because it went the way everyone always thought it would.

I never imagined it'd hurt so much.

But Braden was right. I got what I wanted – what I originally wanted. Right now, I'd like nothing more than to have him wrap his arms around me and kiss the corners of my eyes, like he always used to whenever I was upset. But it's not like that anymore.

I hold my books tighter to my chest and duck my head, hiding behind my hair. I've dealt with pain before. I've suffered loss and heartbreak, I can do it again. It's a different pain, granted, but I'll survive. I have to. Losing my mom and best friend didn't break me, so losing him won't.

Because through all the death and pain in my life, I've survived. That's how I know I'll always survive.

Nothing can break you unless you let it.

A hand grabs my arm and steers me away from the crowds and through the side doors. I glance up – Kyle. As soon as we get outside, he wraps an arm around my shoulders and pulls me close to him.

'Don't be so sad,' he says softly. 'A girl like you doesn't need a guy to be happy.'

'I know that, Kyle.' I tuck my hair behind my ear and rest my head against his shoulder. 'But just because I don't need him doesn't mean I don't still want him.'

He tenses slightly but nods anyway. 'He said it was all a game. It wasn't, was it?'

I sigh and step out of his grasp, my legs carrying me over to the picnic table under a large tree. I slide onto the bench and drop my books on the table. Kyle sits opposite me.

'At first it was a game,' I say honestly. 'Kay, Megan and Lila challenged me to play him – to "hump him and dump him."' Kyle smiles dryly. I shrug a shoulder. 'I agreed. What else could I do? He was too much like . . . my brother . . . for me to imagine ever getting feelings for him. But I did.'

'Because he isn't the asshat we all think he is?' Kyle raises an eyebrow, and I snort.

'He's an asshat, all right. He's egotistical, cocky, and smug.' I trace the wood on the table. 'But he's also patient, gentle, and caring. He listened when I needed to talk. He was there. He wiped the tears and held me when I needed it. He made me laugh and made me forget. Before I knew it, I'd gone from hating him to liking him.' A tear makes a slow trail down my cheek. 'To loving him. I don't know how it happened. Somewhere between all the laughs and tears, I fell in love with him. And I don't know how to get back up again.'

We're both silent for a minute as he processes what I just said.

'But I will.' I wipe at my cheek and smile weakly. 'I've been knocked down before, and I get back up each time. I won't stay down for long.'

Kyle smiles reassuringly and nods in the direction of the building. 'I see Kay moving her ass over here, so I'll leave you.'

'Thanks for listening, Kyle.' I reach over and squeeze his hand as he stands.

He squeezes back and leaves, turning and hesitating. 'It's always gonna be him, isn't it, Maddie? No matter how high you climb back up . . . It'll always be him.'

His words shock me until the truth of them sink in.

Braden was – is – the first guy I fell in love with. He's the first guy I ever gave myself to – not sexually, but emotionally. He knew everything about me, and if he's to be believed, he loved me anyway. For that, a part of me will always hold him close. Maybe I'll never stop loving him completely.

I nod slowly. Kyle smiles, nods once and waves to Kay, throwing me a wink over his shoulder.

'Did you just tell that hot piece of ass "no" again? 'Cause I'm tellin' you, baby girl, if you don't have him, I will.' Kay takes Kyle's seat and puts a coffee and muffin in front of me. Something in me twists and I force myself to accept them.

'I told him no. For the last time, I think.' I glance over her shoulder at his still-retreating figure. 'He's just not the one for me.'

'But Carter is,' she says nonchalantly.

I blink. 'I don't think so.'

'Oh, I do.' Her eyes pierce mine. 'You been mopin' since he hot-tailed it outta our dorm room – and believe me, I'm pissed he saw my frilly pink boobie holder. But what can you do? Anyway,' she redirects herself. 'I ain't gotta be damn Einstein to see you're in love with him. I gotta be honest, I don't understand what it is, but you love him, baby girl. Now, question is, what are you gonna do about it?'

I smile at her words. 'Nothing,' I say and pick at my muffin. 'Because nothing can right what I did.'

'But love don't get that. I'm no cupid, I tell ya, but you two are like peanut butter and jelly. You're pretty shit on your own, but get you together and actually, you're kinda good.'

I laugh a little. 'Thanks, I think.'

She winks and waves her hand. 'You're welcome. So, I'm gonna ask you again. What are you gonna do about it?'

I sigh and twirl the coffee cup round. 'Nothing,' I say again. 'Don't you see, Kay? This all started as a game. It was never meant to last forever because someone always has to win the game. Love or not, we were always destined for disaster. He was always gonna be the murderer in Clue, I'd always win the most money in Monopoly. Braden would always hold the most cards at the end of the round of Old Maid, and I'd always top him at Jenga. Not everyone has a "one", Kay, and whether he's mine or not, it doesn't mean we have to be a two. I did this because you guys asked me. I didn't want to – and I didn't want to fall in love. I was always going to have to deal with the fall out of this game and this just happens to be it.'

'Then you won't mind if we go to the frat house party tomorrow night.'

I stop breathing, my whole body freezing for a second. 'No,' I lie eventually. 'No, I won't mind.'

I'm torturing myself being here – especially before the party actually starts. Every place seems to have a memory of us, and even though I know it's my fault, it doesn't stop the sting that still accompanies each thought of him.

'Ryan, what do you mean?' I hear Lila ask as I pass the front room.

'I . . . Shit. You weren't meant to find out, babe.'

'Obviously.'

'It's no different than what you guys did!'

'Oh, really? 'Cause it is. We planned to get Braden to stop sleeping around. Your plan was to get her to fall in love just so he could sleep with her. Vile, Ryan!'

I gasp. I slap my hand over my mouth to stifle it, but Lila turns her head towards me.

'Maddie? Oh, crap,' she whispers, her soft eyes filling with regret. 'I'm sorry.'

I'm shaking. Anger is flooding my body, red hot and ready to burst out of me. It's coupled with the dull pain of betrayal, the pain he felt.

The pain he lied about.

'Fuck!' Ryan looks at me.

I spin and storm off into the kitchen. He's at the bar, drinking a beer and talking with the guys. I can't see straight. I can't think straight. All I can see, all I can think, it's all him.

I grab his arm and pull him from the stool.

'Maddie? What the fuck?'

I look up into the blue eyes I fell in love with, and the anger increases. I shove his chest. 'You!'

'What?' He looks at me, behind me, and I take a step closer. He steps backwards, and I keep stepping forward until he's backed against the wall.

'Congratulations, you won,' I mimic. 'Remember that line, Braden? Remember the bullshit you laced in it? Remember every goddamn, fucking *lie* you've fed to me over four weeks?'

His face pales slightly, his eyes sparking with recognition. 'Shit.'

'Shit is about right.' I'm shaking. Bad. I can't stop, because if I stop shaking the anger stops, and if the anger stops the tears will come. 'Shit is about right because you played me all along, didn't you?! A quick fuck. That's all I ever was, isn't it? Well, did you enjoy it?'

'Maddie,' he says quietly. Sadness is in his eyes. 'That's not how it was—'

'Lies. Don't fucking lie to me, Braden. I've heard enough of them recently, don't you think?'

'Angel—'

'I'm not your damn angel. I'm not your anything, other than the last person to warm your bed.' I shake my head and step back. My eyes meet his again. 'Everything was a damn lie! I guess you played me as well as I played you, huh? 'Cause guess what? You got what you wanted. You won.' I walk backwards slowly, tears springing to my eyes. 'I guess we both won.'

I turn from him and run through the house, shoving my way through the crowds forming at the front of it. I need to get away from this place. From this house, this campus, and this state.

My feet pound angrily against the floor as I run back to my dorm. I slam my door behind me and grab my cell, doing a quick Google search. Satisfied, I follow through the process on screen and pull my suitcase from under the bed. I shove random belongings into it, needing to leave.

Ring.

Reluctantly, I grab my phone and look at the screen. Kyle.

'What?' I wipe under my eyes, brushing away the hot tears there.

'Are you okay?'

'What do you think?'

'I'm sorry, Mads. If I'd have known . . .'

'You'd be too damn clever for Berkeley,' I reply. 'Do you need anything, Kyle? I have a place to be.'

'Where are you going?'

'It doesn't matter.'

'Do you need a way to get there, wherever there is?'

'I can call a cab.'

'No. I'll come and get you. I'll be outside your dorm in five minutes.'

'Thank you,' I whisper and hang up. The background image of me and Braden smiling into the camera laughs in my face. I'd only put it on there for appearances, but then I couldn't change it.

I still can't change it. I stare at it, numbly, remembering that this particular picture was taken after Pearce's visit. My smile wasn't fake.

I don't think my smiles ever were.

A horn beeps, and I grab my suitcase handle, giving a cursory look around the dorm room. I leave, the door clicking shut behind me, and I bump my case down the stairs to where Kyle is waiting. He grabs it from me, hoisting it into his trunk. I get in the car silently.

'Where to?' He catches my eye.

'Promise you won't tell? Not even after you've taken me there. If anyone asks, say you don't know.'

'Maddie—'

'Kyle, please. I need to get away from here.'

'Fine,' he grumbles.

'Promise!'

'I promise. Where to?'

'The airport.' I gaze out of my window and hear his sharp intake of breath.

'The airport?'
'I'm leaving for a week. I'll call in sick at school.'
'Where are you going?'
'To see my Dad. I'm going home. To Brooklyn.'

Chapter Forty

Braden

Fuck. Fuck fuck fuck and another fuck.

I stare at the space she just left through. A great, big, gaping hole. That's what she does.

She comes into your life in a wild burst of color, filling an empty space you didn't know was there. And when she leaves, she takes it all with her, painting it in shades of black and white.

I push off the wall. I'm determined to find her and explain. Two hands grab my arms.

'Braden, leave her, bro.' Aston tugs me back. 'Let her calm down.'

Calm down? 'No. Fuck no.'

'Bray.' Megan appears in front of me and I try to focus on her. 'He's right. She needs to calm down.'

'No,' I argue. 'She needs to know the truth, Meggy! She needs to know the damn truth!'

'And she will.' She cups my face and makes me look at her. Makes me focus. 'She will, when she's calm. She's hurtin', Bray. Let her deal with it.'

Hurt. Hurt that I put there.

Prick.

I shake off Ryan and Aston and head for the backyard, slamming the door open hard. I storm to the side of the house and lean my head against the wall, feeling like the biggest asshole ever. A car starts from the front of the house. I look up – to see Kyle's car go past.

'Fuck!' I yell and punch the wall. Blood trickles from my already grazed knuckles, but I don't care. I don't give a flying fucking shit about anything other than the girl that just walked away from me.

Because through it all, all the kisses and the laughs, the playing and the joking, I never bothered to tell her how real she is to me.

All the times I've held her close at night through her nightmares, all the times I wiped away her tears and put a smile back on her face – they're the times that made it real. Seeing that light spark in her eyes when I did something that made her laugh, the pain in the same eyes when she remembered the past – they're what made her real.

But none of that matters now. She's taken it all with her. Every last bit followed her out of the frat house ten, fifteen minutes ago. I don't even know. I don't even know how long I've been out here. But I am alone.

I can go.

I—

'Don't even think about it.' Ryan's face is in mine as I turn from the wall.

'Fuck.' I spit and shake my fist, my brain registering the first tinges of pain from my bloodied knuckles.

'Inside. Ice on that and a beer,' Ryan orders, grabbing my arm and pulling me back towards the house.

'I can fuckin' walk, Ryan.' I yank my arm from his grip. 'I've got bloody knuckles, not broken feet.'

'Really?' he drawls. ''Cause you look pretty fuckin' broken to me.' He shoves the door open and crosses the kitchen towards the freezer. He grabs an ice pack and hands it to me. I rest it on my knuckles, flinching at the cold. Ryan grabs two bottles of beer from the cooler and nods towards the door, meaning we should go upstairs. It's better than being down here.

I push my way through the crowd when I hear my name.

'At least someone finally did to him what he's done to half the girls in freshman year,' a voice I've never heard before states.

I see red. I've had about as much as I can take today, and I spin. Ryan stops me and through the angry film covering my eyes, I see Aston's fist fly into the speaker's face. It cracks into his nose, and he staggers backwards.

'Shut your fuckin' mouth,' Aston warns. 'Anyone else wanna say somethin'?'

No one says anything.

'That's what I thought.' He shakes his fist out and looks at the guy he just hit in disgust. 'Goddamn. You got a nose of fuckin' granite?'

Ryan snorts and pushes me back towards the door.

'Move it. Down here is the last place a live wire like you needs to be.'

Chapter Forty-One

Maddie

The house is the same as I left it, and a half shiver runs down my spine as I step from the cab. I wave to the driver in thanks as he leaves and look at the house properly.

Built just outside of city limits, our two-story house has been home my whole life. I played on the now yellowing grass in the front yard, planted the wilting flowers and, with Pearce, helped Dad paint the little fence that surrounds it.

A white picket fence. Cliché, but it was what Mom wanted – and Mom got it. It was the perfect family home. Until she died.

Now, the house is a shell of what it once was. There's no laughing in the kitchen at breakfast, no water fights when the flowers needed watering, and no Candy, Mom's cocker spaniel, there to greet you at the front door. Candy went not long after Mom.

I unhook the gate and walk to the front door, tugging my suitcase along after me in the darkness. I knock once on the door and step inside, noting the gentle light coming from the front room.

'Dad?'

'Maddie?'

I shut the door, stand my suitcase against the wall and take off my coat. Walking into the peach-colored front room, Mom's haven, I find Dad sitting in her chair in the corner. His hair is a little grayer, his cheeks more sunken, and his eyes a little duller than when I left – but he's still alive. Just.

He's holding on, barely, living every day without the person he thought he'd spend his whole life with.

I touch my lips to his cheek and take his hand. 'How are you?'

'Better for seeing you, Maddie.' He smiles. There's a little light in his eye that lets me know it's true. 'But what are you doing here?'

'I missed you, of course.'

'You don't have time off yet.'

I shrug a shoulder and look down. 'I just wanted to see my Daddy.'

Gently, he pats the top of my hand. 'Well, okay, sweetie. How about you go ahead and pop that kettle on?'

'Sure.' I stand and enter the white and red kitchen. There's a few dishes by the sink, only a day old, and I let out a breath I didn't realize I was holding. He's eating. 'Do you need your tablets soon?'

I bustle around the cupboards and pull out my Piglet mug, giving Dad's a quick rinse under the tap.

'Please,' he replies.

I make two teas – no matter what he protests, he's not having coffee at two a.m. – and take them into the front room, handing him his pills. He takes them without complaint.

'I wasn't expecting you to be up,' I say as I look out of the window.

'Just as I wasn't expecting my daughter to arrive in the dead of night.'

I look at him, and he raises an eyebrow. I nod slightly. 'All right, old man. You win.'

'I'm not asleep because the new tablets Doc gave me have a couple side effects, insomnia being one, but you?' He shakes his head. 'I can't believe my daughter missed me enough that she'd turn up in the place of her nightmares at two a.m.'

I smile sadly, still focusing out the window.

'So what brings you here, Maddie? Your old man isn't stupid.'

'Y'know what, Dad? I'm really tired.' I drink the last of my hot tea, stand, and stretch. 'I think I'll head on up to bed. You try and get some sleep, okay? Goodnight.'

I kiss his forehead and leave the room. I bump my suitcase

up the stairs and push open the door to my room. The white and pink room is untouched. I shut the door and after changing into some pajamas I left behind, I climb into bed, sinking into the rose-smelling fabric.

He still uses her favorite softener.

My phone vibrates from its position on my nightstand, and I grab it. Megan's name is on the screen.

Where are u? Everyone's trying 2 find u. Bray's going crazy.

I bite my lip.

I'm in Brooklyn. I caught the next flight out. I needed to get away. I'm sorry. Don't worry xo

She responds immediately.

Shit the bed, Mads! Brooklyn? When will u be back? Xo

I'm not sure. Night, Megs xo

I turn the cell off and put it face-down, pulling my covers up to my chin.

Why would Braden be going crazy? It's painfully obvious he doesn't care about anything other than sex.

I choose to block all the memories away in a box and close my eyes, a single tear slipping out and falling onto the pillow.

I wake to a silent house. Well, an almost silent house. I open my bedroom door, and I can hear light snoring coming from Dad's room – no surprise there.

I pull my old robe tighter around me and silently pad down the old wooden stairs. Somehow, they never creak. I'd asked Mom about it once, and she said the fairies had come in as a favor and magicked them to silence. She'd apparently left a chocolate cake at the bottom of the garden in thanks.

I was seven, so I believed it. I also searched relentlessly for said fairies for the next six months. Unsurprisingly, I never found them.

In the light of day, in the old kitchen, the temperature difference suddenly hits me, and I shiver, making a beeline for the kettle in the corner. As it boils, I look out at the garden and the weaker winter sun shining on it.

Memories crash into me with the force of a tidal wave. They

flit through my mind one at a time in quick succession. So quick I forget to breathe. I see Mom and Abbi . . . Pearce and Dad . . . Smiles . . . The princess party I had when I was six . . . The flowers Mom and I planted when I was ten . . . The rose bushes Dad put in, saying '*two rose bushes for my two beautiful girls*' . . . Everything . . .

I hold onto the counter and press my temple with my other hand. Tears stream from my eyes, and I try to breathe deeply, to control it, the overwhelming feeling of loss sweeping through my body. It rises higher and higher until I feel choked. More recent memories flash in my mind . . . And there's one constant. Always one thing, just the one thing I see.

Electric blue eyes. *Braden.*

I give in to the pain. I let myself let it go, and I slide down the cupboard to the old, stone floor as the kettle reaches its bubbling crescendo.

Brooklyn . . . California . . . The pain is always there.

Chapter Forty-Two

Braden

'Brooklyn? She's in fucking Brooklyn?' I yell at Megan and kick the bar in the kitchen. 'Why is she there?'

'Because she doesn't want to be here,' she replies simply, sipping a lemonade.

'Have a fucking point for your smart-ass board, Megan,' I reply. 'How are you so calm? She's in fucking *Brooklyn*!'

'I know where she is. She's at her Dad's, and she's safe. She needs to—'

'Don't you fuckin' dare tell me she needs to calm down! You told me that last night, and now she's not even here! If you'd just let me go after her—'

'You would have done something stupid, like pin her against a wall and force her to listen to you.' Megan looks at me pointedly.

'Well,' I say uncomfortably. 'It wouldn't be unrealistic to say I'd do that.'

'Thank you.'

'But that's not the point,' I protest. 'The point is, she's in Brooklyn. I'm in fucking California. How am I supposed to tell her the truth?'

'Which is what?'

'You know, Megan. Don't treat me like a fool.'

'Y'know what, Bray?' Her blue eyes are clear, and there's a hint of ice in them. 'I don't know, because you've never actually been truthful when you've told me how you feel about her. You've fed me bullshit, and now? I still don't know. I know what I see, not what actually is.'

I sigh and sink onto the stool next to her, resting my elbows on the bar top and putting my head in my hands.

'I love her. I'm in love with her.'

Megan slurps as she sucks the last of her lemonade through her straw. She stands, putting a hand on my shoulder and leaning close to me.

'Then when she comes back, you better be ready with a whole damn production to let her know.'

She kisses the top of my head and leaves. The front door closes, and since it's still early, I'm the only one up.

I'm also the only one who didn't sleep last night.

I rub my eyes and look at the clock. Nine a.m. There's no point going to bed now, so I get up and flick the coffee machine on.

'Enough in there for two?'

My body tenses. 'Depends. Any room in your car for two?'

'You know then.'

'Don't have to be a fuckin' genius to work it out, Kyle. Maddie's in Brooklyn, and you drove away five minutes after she left here last night. You took her to the airport.'

'She asked.'

'I don't give a fuck.' I turn and look at him. He steps back. 'I don't give a fuck that she got there, or how she got there. All I care about is that she's there, and not *here* where she damn well should be. She hates that city, so right now she must really hate me if she'd rather be there than here.' I turn back to the coffee pot, slamming two mugs on the counter. I fill them and slide Kyle's along the counter, stepping to the side.

'Well, shit,' he says, taking the mug.

'What?'

'I never thought I'd see the day Braden Carter cared about a girl for more than what's in her pants.'

I put the mug down. 'You sound surprised.'

'I'm surprised you care. Am I surprised it's Maddie you care about?' I look at him and he shakes his head. 'Nah, man. Not at all. Much as I hate it, you're good together.'

I snort. 'Just got to convince her of that, now, right? 'Cause that's a walk in the fuckin' park.'

'You weren't the only one that played a game, Braden.' Kyle grabs his mug and stands up straight. 'You both set out to play each other, and you did. You wouldn't listen to her when you found out, and now she won't listen to you. I'd say that's a level playing field, wouldn't you?' He quirks his eyebrows and walks past me, slapping my shoulder once.

A level playing field.

'Hey, Kyle?' I turn. 'Thanks, man.' He salutes me and turns.

A level playing field. Another round of the game. Except this time, the stakes are a lot higher.

Because it's two hearts invested into it.

My foot taps against the back porch as I lean against the wall, staring out at nothing in particular. It's been a week since I walked out of Maddie's dorm, and I didn't think it was truly possible until now, but I miss her.

I miss her so fucking much, it hurts.

But it's not as if I can cross the road and talk my way into the dorm block to speak to her. Well, look how that turned out last time. No, because she's in fucking Brooklyn. *Brooklyn.*

I don't want to think of the pain it must have caused her to go back there, to a place she hates so deeply. She left because of me. Because I ran off and had a bitch fit for her doing exactly what I was doing.

What I was doing. Whether we both played a game or not, at some point, we would have had the same result. At some point, we would have fallen in love. Because, like Megan said to me, your forever person could be right there in front of you the whole time.

I'm nineteen. I don't do forever.

At least, I didn't. And then Maddie let me in. Whether she meant to or not, game playing or not, she let me in. And I saw it in her eyes last night. It was no game to her, and goddamn it all to hell, she's the realest fucking thing I've ever known.

Chapter Forty-Three

Maddie

After scrubbing the kitchen to work out the breakdown of this morning, I grab my coffee mug in both hands and sink into one of the kitchen chairs. It's not quite Starbucks, but for the first time in a year, I don't have the energy to make the run two blocks across to the nearest coffee shop.

The floorboards creak from upstairs, and a few seconds later Dad shuffles into the kitchen. He's already dressed – I guess I blocked everything out when I was cleaning.

'Morning, Maddie.' He kisses the top of my head and stops, looking around. 'Kitchen looks clean.'

I shrug a shoulder. 'I needed something to do.'

He glances at me as he pours a coffee. He takes four tablets from the bottles lined behind the kettle and throws them back, washing them down with the coffee. Dad makes his way to the table and sits opposite me, his gray-blue eyes studying me.

'So,' I say to break the silence. 'Do you usually sleep this late?'

He grunts. 'Like I said, damn tablets give me insomnia. So lately, yes.'

I nod. 'Has Doc said how long it'll be for the side effects to wear off?'

'Few weeks. Like normal.'

I know it's a touchy subject for Dad. As much as he hates the fact he's living without Mom, he hates appearing weak. To him, depression is a sign of weakness.

It's not. Depression is a sign of strength – because it means no matter how weak your mind might be to you, your heart is still strong enough to feel.

'That's not too bad then. Hopefully you'll be back to normal in a few weeks.' I reach over and pat his lightly wrinkled hand. He looks at me, and I notice the little lines around his eyes, the faint indents around his mouth that should be proper laughter lines.

'As normal as I can be, Maddie,' he replies sadly, turning his hand under mine and squeezing my fingers.

I nod softly, knowing his words are true. Without her, he'll never be the same person he was when she was alive.

'So. You never did say why you were back,' Dad hedges.

I grimace slightly. 'Like I said, I missed you. You must get lonely being here by yourself.'

'I might be alone, Maddie, but being alone doesn't mean you're lonely.' Dad sips his coffee. 'In fact, I'm never alone. Your mother lives on in my heart. She's always with me.'

I blink back the tears that rise in my eyes.

'Nice save, by the way, kiddo.' He winks at me. 'I get it. You don't wanna talk right now, but Maddie? By the time you go back to Berkeley, whenever that is, we will be talking.'

I sigh and run my finger around the top of my mug. 'Okay, Daddy. Have you . . . Er, have you heard from Pearce?'

Dad nods sharply. 'Couple days ago. He got picked up for possession on his way back here. He was in downtown Brooklyn just about to hail a cab. Cop smelled whatever crap it was he'd been smoking. You know it ain't his first offense, Mads, so he's waiting for bail. If he gets it. He called here asking me to bail him out and I refused. Time that boy stopped being babied and helped by us.' He gives me a pointed look.

'I'm sorry, Dad,' I say sadly. 'I just . . . I didn't want Abbi to get hurt anymore, you know? That's why he was in California, though, he wanted money to pay off his debts. I sent one lot up thinking it was for you and it wasn't . . .'

'Your mom always used to say you can't help someone unless they wanna be helped, baby girl. Your brother is one of them people, as much as I hate to say it. He's gotta find his way outta this by himself. Nothin' and no one will be able to pull that boy out of this rut he's stuck in.'

I look towards the window and into the yard. 'And no one will be able to right his wrongs.'

'You got that right.'

I've put this off for three days. I don't know why I'm here – maybe it's closure, maybe it's a reason so cliché I'm not even sure how to word it. But as I kill the engine on Dad's old car, I find myself staring at the large, white building that is home to my best friend.

I didn't even set out to come to St. Morris', I just arrived here. I rub my forehead and climb from the car, pushing the door shut. The gravel path to the main door is the same as I remember, and the oak door still has the same rusty, golden knocker on.

I take a deep breath, smoothing my hair back with shaky hands, and I press the buzzer on the intercom.

'Welcome to St. Morris' Institution. Please state your name and who you're here to visit,' the voice says.

'Maddie Stevens, and I'm here to see Abigail Jenkins.'

A few seconds pass, and the door buzzes. 'Come on in, Maddie.'

The warm peach of the front office surrounds me in a fake comfort. I approach the desk and see a nurse I know – Nurse Jayne.

'Maddie!' She stands and smiles at me. 'We haven't seen you in a while.'

A raincloud of guilt has just pissed on me. 'I've been to school – in California. This is the first time I've been back.'

Jayne nods as if she understands. 'I'm sure Abbi knows that.'

She waves me on to follow her, like I don't already know the way to her room, and I tuck my hands in my pockets as I do.

'Is she any better?' I ask hesitantly.

Jayne is silent for a second, and I know that means no, no matter what she says next. 'Some days are better than others. I think her therapy sessions with Dr Hausen are helping her, but she's still very down.' She turns to me and puts a gentle hand on my arm. 'She's not eating much, so she's lost a lot of weight. Try not to show your shock. It alarms her, and she can be hard to calm then.'

I nod. I know the rules. Don't upset her. Don't talk about Pearce. Don't mention guys or sex. Don't do anything I should be able to do with her.

Jayne knocks on room 18 and pushes the door open a crack. 'Abbi? Abbi, love, you've a visitor today!'

Her voice is so cheery, and I try to swallow the panic creeping in my throat. Jayne sighs quietly and turns to me.

'She's having a small response day today, so don't be offended if she doesn't really acknowledge you. She knows you're there,' she whispers, stepping into the room as she pushes the door open. I nod again, my own responses muted, and walk into Abbi's room.

Her room has always been as close to her own bedroom as me and her Mom could do it. I remember bringing all her pictures over, her closet, the stuffed animals we'd won at funfairs. Even her desk is here, tucked in the corner.

Abbi is sitting in a plush armchair by the window. Her blonde hair hangs limply past her shoulders, and her hands are folded demurely in her lap. Her dull, gray eyes are focused on the activity going on outside. She'll never join them. You can see it in her eyes that she wants to – but the death grip that is her depression won't let her.

I nudge another armchair closer to her and sit down slowly. 'Hey, Abs. How you doing?'

Nothing. I tuck my hands under my legs.

'You look well.' I'm lying. It's all a lie. The cheeriness in my voice, the calm outer shell. Inside I'm shaking, I'm crumbling, and I don't know how much longer I can hide it. I want my best friend back. It's childish but I do, dammit!

'Jayne says you're doing well. I've been in school, in California. I remember telling you I was going. It's not too bad there. I mean, I have some friends.' Her head turns towards me slightly. 'But it's not home, you know? Sometimes I miss Brooklyn, and I miss you too. I'm glad you're doing okay.'

I'm babbling. I'm babbling so much, but it's all I can do.

Her fingers twitch, and her attention is back on the activity outside.

'I think they're silly, the ones outside. It's freezing cold out there. You're much better off inside here, in the warm.' I chew the inside of my cheek. 'Has your mom been by lately? I gave her a call yesterday. She said you're doing well, too. Everyone's said so.'

Abbi's lips move, ever so slightly. I lean in a little. 'What was that, Abs?'

'Outside,' she whispers, not taking her eyes off the yard.

'You want to go outside?'

'Please.' Her voice is so faint I'm straining to hear it.

'Of course,' I say, standing. 'Let me go and ask Jayne—'

'You,' she says, turning her face to me. Her eyes focus on mine. 'Me and you, Maddie.'

I take a deep breath and nod, letting her hook her arms around mine. She stands up on weak legs, and I guide her to the door where she has a puffy coat hanging. I help her into it.

'Let's take a walk to the nurse's station and let Jayne know, okay?' We walk slowly down the corridor, her slippers shuffling along the linoleum. Jayne double-takes as we approach her.

'Abbi's asked to go outside,' I say carefully. 'She wants me to take her. That's okay, isn't it?'

Jayne nods enthusiastically and smiles widely. 'Of course it is! I'll pop the time on the board, and you let us know when you come back so we can jot it down. You girls have fun.'

I didn't know fun was possible in this place.

'Come on, Abs. Let's get you some sunshine, okay?' We move towards and through the glass doors, letting a small winter breeze blow into the building.

Abbi stops as soon as we step outside. She closes her eyes, and I watch her take a deep breath. I wonder when the last time she came outside was.

'Where do you want to go?'

She opens her eyes and looks over at a bench surrounded by rose bushes. I nod and help her down some steps. The

activity is still going on and we ignore it as we cross the grass.
I pull my coat a little tighter around me with my free hand and
help Abbi sit.

'It's nice outside, huh?' I lower myself to sit next to her.

Abbi nods slowly, her hair swaying. 'The noise is nice,' she
says quietly.

'I bet.' I reach over and touch her hand. She grips it with
her bony fingers.

'What is college like?'

I inhale sharply and look at her. Her eyes are watching the
group activity, the only indication she's giving I'm here apart
from talking is the way she's holding my hand.

'It's . . . different to high school. I mean, there are less classes
and more free time. And a Starbucks just around the corner.'
Abbi's lips twitch. 'I've made some friends, like I said, but I
wish you were there.' She nods.

'Me, too. We would have killed Cali, right?' She looks at me
again.

'We still will,' I promise. 'One day, Abs, me and you will
show Cali the time of its life. Okay?'

Her lips twitch again. 'Deal, deal, pig squeal.'

'Deal, deal, squeaky eel.' I smile at our childhood rhyme.

'Who is he?' She tilts her head to the side, her eyes finding
a spot behind me.

'Who is who?' I say tentatively.

'The reason you're sad.'

'I'm not sad.'

She nods, her eyes unfocused. 'You are. I can see it. What
did he do?'

'He didn't really do anything. It was both of us.'

'What's his name?'

'Braden.'

Her head bobs. 'Tell me.'

'Are you—'

'Tell me. I want to know, Maddie.'

I take a deep breath, and I pour out the story. I start at the
challenge and finish at my arrival to St. Morris'.

Emma Hart

We're silent for a while after I finish, the only noise the fall birds chirping in the yard and the wind whipping around us.

'Can we go back?' Abbi asks.

'Sure, Abs. Come on.'

We make our way to her room, stopping off at the nurse's station to check in with Jayne. I help Abbi from her coat and back into the chair.

'You love him,' Abbi says matter of factly, settling into the cushions. She's looking out the window again.

'Yes, I do,' I admit, standing beside her.

'So tell him,' she replies simply. 'We have to tell people sometimes . . . Because they don't always know. It's a little word that means a lot. Sometimes, love is all you need, even when you think you don't. Sometimes, you just have to say it.'

I beat back the rising tears desperately, refusing to cry in front of her.

I bend over and kiss the top of her head. 'I love you, Abbi.'

'I love you, Maddie.'

'I'll see you soon.' I choke the words out and head towards the door. As I open it, I know Abbi is lost back in her own world again, where the only constant is pain. I'm glad I could give her the freedom from it she so desperately needed.

I acknowledge Jayne at the desk and all but run back to the car. I yank the door open and slide in, pulling the door shut with a bang behind me.

Finally, I let the emotion overtake me. Tears spill over my eyes, and I rest my forehead against the steering wheel, holding it tightly. The tears drip down onto my legs and I know she was right. Even in her 'damaged' state, my best friend can still talk more sense than I can mentally healthy.

So tell him. It's not that easy, but what if I did? Would that make me like Abbi?

Maybe getting out now was for the best. A month – any longer, and I might have become dependent. But . . . Braden isn't Pearce and I know that.

Besides, if it was all bad, then I wouldn't be hurting so much.

Chapter Forty-Four

Braden

It's Thursday night, and some prick – I don't know who – had decided to have a party at the frat house. I'd put my money on Aston. He's been trying to get me out of my 'fuckin' ridiculous mood' since Maddie left.

But it doesn't work like that.

She's been in Brooklyn for five days now. Every day she's there, she's not here. I know, Captain Fucking Obvious with that statement, but I want her here.

I want her here in front of me so I can cup her cheeks and wipe away the tears. I want to hold her and promise her the world, apologize for everything. I want to know she feels the same. I want to know it wasn't just a game for her, either.

The worst part is I'd play it all over again if it meant another few weeks where we were happy.

'Look, I'm not interested.' I gently push yet another girl away from me. She pouts and sticks her chest out, batting her eyelashes. I sigh and shake my head, turning my attention to where Megan is throwing back shots with Kay. The girl behind me disappears.

Megan catches my eye and smiles sadly. I stand and push my way over to her.

'Have you spoken to her?' I ask hopefully. She hesitates. 'Megan!'

She nods. 'Today.'

'And?'

'She'll be back tomorrow,' she answers softly. 'She's done everything she needed to.'

'What does that mean?'

'I don't really know what rights you have to ask that question, Carter.' Kay raises an eyebrow at me.

I look at her. 'And I don't get what rights you have to bitch to me, considering you're part of the reason we're both fuckin' miserable – and why Maddie is in Brooklyn.'

She looks away, ashamed, and Megan flinches.

'Meggy, I know you never—'

'But we did,' she interrupts me. 'We did hurt you, and we hurt both of you. If anyone is to blame, it's us, and Ryan and Aston. They have to accept their part in it.' She scowls over my shoulder. 'Especially Aston.'

I don't even wanna look.

'We're all a little to blame, I guess.' I shrug. 'I just have to hope I can make it up to her when she gets back. If she wants to talk to me.'

'If she wants to see you,' Kay reminds me. 'Hey, I'm just sayin', ya know? She didn't before.'

'Thanks, Kay,' I snap and turn, pushing my way through the kitchen to the yard.

Ignoring a couple making out against the wall, I jump from the porch and head towards the trees at the end of the grass. I lean back against a tree and pull my cell from my pocket, scrolling through the numbers until I reach hers. My finger hovers over the call button, but I eventually settle on sending a text. I write several and delete them all, settling on three words – three secondary words, 'cause I'm too damn chicken to send the real ones.

I miss you.

Chapter Forty-Five

Maddie

Pushing my thoughts of Braden to the back of my mind, I pull my suitcase down the stairs. It's been a strange few days at home, rife with emotion and thinking. And the worst is yet to come, because I still haven't admitted to Dad why I came home so quickly. I know he's about to find out.

'Well, you have a safe trip back home, Maddie,' Dad says and hugs me tightly.

'I'm home right now, Dad. I'm just going back to school,' I reply and extricate myself from his arms.

'Oh, no, honey. Wherever your heart is, that's where your home is. I think you left your heart in California. University of California, Berkeley, to be exact.'

I narrow my eyes and look at him. 'What?'

'It doesn't take a genius to work out you fell in love and ran, Maddie. Your Mom did the same thing when we were younger. But you know what, Mads? You have to fight for love, because it doesn't come easily, not the real thing, anyway. I don't know who this guy is, or what's happened, but running won't make it better, baby.' He touches his fingers to my chin and lifts my face slightly. 'Truth of life is that no matter what it is – loss, heartbreak, happiness, love – those emotions are so damn strong they'll follow you no matter where you go. You could go to the ends of the Earth and love would still follow you there. It's not a place or a memory, oh no. Love is something inside you, something that only you can feel, because your love is yours. You'll never leave it behind. You could go cross-country, cross oceans or travel to the moon and that love? It'll still be there, tucked away in a dark corner of your heart just waiting for you to acknowledge it.'

A horn beeps outside.

'Don't you run from it, Maddie, because runnin' never did anyone any good. I may not know much anymore, but I'll always know love. Your mom taught me that, and she taught you it too.' His eyes glisten with tears and I know he's looking at me and seeing her. 'She left you her spirit, baby, in all those memories and in that love, she left you it. She'd tell you to go and run into love with your arms wide open. Whoever this guy is, he's a damn lucky guy to have you in love with him, so you make sure he knows it.' He kisses my forehead. 'Go on with you, now. Your ride is outside. Let me know when you get there.'

I nod, my throat filled with a lump of emotion. Mom, Braden, and love all in one sentence is too much to swallow. Literally.

I hug Dad one last time and kiss his cheek before wheeling my suitcase away from the house I've loved my whole life. I pop the trunk of the cab and lift it in, eventually moving to the back seat. I look out the window and wave to Dad as we pull away.

Away from one home, ready for another.

There's a serious damn temperature difference between Brooklyn and California, and I've never been happier to change into some shorts and a tank when I finally get back to my dorm room. I tie my hair on top of my head in a messy bun and decide to head down to the laundry room tomorrow. The time difference will mess with me today.

Honestly, I just want to nap right now.

The door opens, and Lila flies across the room, pushing me back onto the bed. She squeezes me tightly, babbling about how good it is to have me back and she's so glad I'm okay and she's so sorry she started this all in the first place.

No nap for me then.

I pat her back. 'Lila? Lila, you're squashing me.'

'Oh my god! I'm sorry! I didn't think!' She scrambles off me and bounces on the bed, sitting next to me. I pull myself up. 'When did you get back?'

'Er, to Cali or back in this room?'

'Here here.'

'About five minutes ago.'

'And I totally just ambushed you! Oh, gosh.' She shakes her head at herself. 'I just wanted to see you before anyone else. I want to apologize for, you know . . .'

'It's okay, Lila.'

'No, no it's not, okay? It's absolutely not okay. You should know I absolutely kicked Ryan's ass for that shitty stunt they pulled. It's not cool, at all.'

'We did the same thing, Lila. That's why I went away. We didn't really do anything different at all.' I smile sadly.

'Well.' She pauses. 'I guess, but I'm still sorry you found out that way.' She purses her lips.

'It's okay. I'm over it.'

'Are you?' She raises her eyebrows.

'Eh. No.' I shake my head. 'But I can always pretend, right?'

'Then pretend and come party tomorrow night.'

'Honestly, Lila, let her get through the door!' Megan exclaims and kicks the door shut. I didn't know it was open.

I look up at my blonde friend. 'Hey, Megs.'

'I'm so glad you're back.' She hugs me tightly, and I return the gesture. 'But don't you dare run away like that again, do you hear me, Maddie Stevens? Don't you freakin' run from me that way! We crapped our pants, actually crapped our pants! I thought you'd been picked by a serial killer or something!'

'The only serial killer I came across was my Dad. He's been known to bash a box or two of cornflakes in the past.' I grin and she looks at me, hiding her own grin.

'Gah! I'm just glad you're back. Did Lila tell you there's a party tomorrow night?' She sits on Kay's bed.

'Ah . . . Yeah. I don't think I'm going.' I chew my lip. 'I don't think I'm ready to.'

'It's been two weeks. You have to see him at some point,' Lila says softly. 'I know you don't want to—'

'You're right, Lila. I don't want to see him. I'm not going. Not yet. I still need some time. I need time to process every-thing that happened in Brooklyn. At least let me have that.'

'Fine,' she huffs. 'But you have to start going back to your English classes. You can't keep skipping because of him.'

I finger a loose thread on my shirt. 'I'll go back to English.'

Chapter Forty-Six

Baden

My eyes traveled around the frat house a million times on Saturday night, yet I didn't see her at all. She's here, but she wasn't there. But she's here – in California.

My Maddie is back in California.

And it's taking every ounce of self-restraint I have not to run over to her dorm block like my ass is on fuckin' fire. Because, like Megan said, I'd probably end up pinning her to a wall – and that's never good.

My leg shakes as I sit in English class, and my eyes are traveling the room again. I can't help it. She didn't show before she left. I want her to now. I need to see her.

The door opens, and Aston walks through. He crosses the room and sits next to me. 'She's coming.'

I nod once and fix my eyes on the door. If she's coming, then she'll be here –

Now.

She's here. Megan's arm is linked through hers, but Maddie is smiling. It's a weak smile, and I hate myself for that. My hands tighten their grip on the edge of the desk, and I clench my teeth together. Aston kicks me.

Maddie's hair falls down and blocks her face from my view as she sits, not making eye contact with me. In fact, she didn't look anywhere close to me. I can't pretend that shit doesn't hurt, 'cause it damn well does.

I watch her all lesson instead of paying attention. How am I supposed to concentrate on anything but her? All there is, is Maddie. All there is, is everything that could have, would have, and should have been.

When class ends, I push my way through towards her table, catching them as they leave. Aston shakes his head, but I don't care. I have to talk to her.

'Meggy.' I nod at her and look at the person I'm really there for. 'Maddie.'

She looks straight ahead, clutching a book to her chest. 'Braden,' she says softly.

'How was Brooklyn?'

'It was . . . Fine, thank you. How are you?'

'I'm . . .' I catch the warning look Megan shoots me. 'I'm good. I guess.'

She nods slightly. 'I've gotta . . .'

'Sure.' I open the classroom door for them, wanting to rip it off its hinges. 'See you later.'

'Yeah, see you,' she whispers and leaves quickly. Megan shoots me an evil glare and points her finger.

'Not what she needed,' she hisses.

'I needed to see her, Meggy.' I meet her eyes, and they soften. 'I needed to speak to her. She is . . . She's okay, right?'

She sighs, her whole body sagging. 'I don't know what you want me to say, Bray. But . . . Sure, if it makes you feel better, she's fine.'

'And if it doesn't?' I clench my teeth.

'Then she's still fine.' She turns around and runs after Maddie.

I make a sound of disbelief and anger. Aston grabs the door to stop me slamming it and gives me a look.

So I get a little crazy where Maddie is concerned.

I avoid the cafeteria like a plague knowing she'll be in there. It was more painful seeing her than I thought it would be. Instead of going there like I normally would, I head back to the frat house. I dump my backpack on the floor by my desk and drop back onto my bed, my hands clasped behind my head.

I had so many grand plans of how I'd get her to talk to me. I was determined to make her listen, make her believe I love her, but then . . . I see her, and all that disappears because I don't wanna talk to her.

I just wanna grab her. I wanna hold her tight and stroke her hair. I want to kiss the corners of her eyes and never let go of her. Because she's mine.

Goddammit, Maddie Stevens is mine. And that's the bottom line. It always will be.

She'll always be mine – and I'll always be hers.

Chapter Forty-Seven

Maddie

Two days after speaking to Braden after English, and I still haven't recovered. Where the crap has my 'bounce-back' mechanism gone? The freakin' springs are probably broken, actually. It's been used so many times, it's probably fed up of bouncing my ass when I fall on it.

This time it's on me. This time, it's on me to pull myself together and get up from the low I seem to have sunk to emotionally.

I also need to magically grow a pair of balls and actually go to the frat house for the books I left there because staring at it sadly from my bedroom window isn't bringing them to me. Seeing Braden – in a classroom I can deal with, but in the frat house? His house? His room?

Could I ever deal with that?

If I went, would I come back even more broken than I am now?

No, no, I'm not broken. I'm strong, just like he said. And I can go over there. I can do it.

I slip my pumps onto my feet and run my fingers through my hair anxiously, shutting the door behind me. My feet seem to echo in the empty hallway as I slowly make my way down the stairs. I shiver despite the warm evening air, and wrap my arms around my body.

I pause on the sidewalk next to the frat house for a second, and the door opens. Kyle.

'Maddie?' He frowns, doing a double-take.

'I, er . . . Is Braden there?' I ask softly.

'Yeah, he's in. I thought you—'

'We're not. I just . . . I left some books here.' I look down.
'I need them back.'

'Oh, sure. Give me a minute, I'll get them.'

I nod and hear the door shut. I bounce uncomfortably, bending my knees and study the cracks in the sidewalk.

It was once perfect, flawless, but now it's cracked and broken. Just like me.

'Maddie?' Braden's voice is hesitant. It's a tone I've never heard before.

'Hi.' I look up and fake a smile. I hide the frantic beat of my heart and shaking of my hands.

'I've got your books.' He steps out and holds them out. I grind my back teeth together and reach out, cursing my shaking hands. 'Are you cold?'

'Uh, a little. I think the change in air is making me sick,' I lie. 'I should get back.' I tuck the books against my chest and make to move.

'You're okay? Your dad . . . He's okay?'

I wish he didn't care. 'Yeah. I'm good. Dad's good,' I smile slightly and make the mistake of meeting his eyes. 'What?'

He sighs. 'You're lying.'

'Why would I be lying? I'm fine, Braden, just like you are.' The words sound hollow even to my ears. 'I needed to get away and now I'm back. I'm fine. I'm sure your life is how it was before both of us started those games—'

'You're wrong.' He slams the door behind him and storms down the steps. I step back.

'Braden—'

'It's not like it was before you, Maddie, not at all. I might be just as lonely and just as pathetic, but it's not the same because there will never be another you. It's not fucking possible.' He stops in front of me and looks down. His hands are clenched tightly in fists at his sides. 'You . . . It's just you. No one else. Without you, it's all fucking pointless. Without you . . .' He growls in his throat and touches the side of my head, his fingers sinking into my hair. I swallow the lump in my throat and hold back the tears forming.

'Without me, your life is better,' I choke out and step back, turning and running across the road.

'Without you it's all bullshit, Angel!' he yells after me. 'You give it all meaning. You make every day worth it so you're wrong! Before . . . Before was before I had you. Now I've had you and I've lost you, and nothing can ever compare to having you, Maddie!'

I shake my head and run faster, leaving him standing there. Tears stream freely down my cheeks, and I hiccup a sob, covering my mouth with my hands. I punch the code into the keypad through blurry eyes and climb the stairs two at a time.

My dorm door opens as I reach it, and Kay holds out her arms. I let the books drop to the floor and collapse into her comforting embrace.

'I'm done!' Lila yells, throwing her pen at the wall behind my head. 'I'm done!'

'Shut up!' Megan holds a finger up. She mutters to herself and scribbles something down on the book in front of her. 'Okay, carry on.'

'So kind,' Lila snaps. She turns her eyes on me. 'You! I'm done.'

'Me? What have I done?' I look at Megan. She shrugs.

'You, being a miserable bitch!' Lila exclaims. 'I am so done. I'm not taking it anymore. I'm gonna put a goddamn smile on that face even if it's a forced one!'

'I'm fine, Lila.' I turn my attention back to the laptop in front of me. 'Really. You don't need to put your fingers in the corners of my mouth and pull it up.'

'You are a liar. And do not tempt me, Maddie Stevens, because so help me, I will do it!' she threatens.

'I have no doubt of that,' I reply dryly. Megan giggles.

'There is a party tomorrow night, at the frat house. You. Are. Going.'

'No. I'm. Not.'

'Oh yes you are.'

'I'm not going, Lila. It's not about Braden, or even about

seeing him. I just don't want to go, okay? I have loads of schoolwork to catch up on from last week. I have to catch up.'

'Bullshit!' Megan cries, her pen flying across the room. 'I call bullshit! You've already caught it up. The biggest load you'd have is from English and you already handed that in. Excuses!'

'It's not excuses,' I argue lamely.

'Just because you don't want to see him—' Lila starts.

'I've seen him four times this week and spoken to him twice.' I raise my eyebrows. 'I have no issues with seeing Braden Carter.' My jaw is tight.

Lila shakes her head. 'You still don't wanna see him.'

I sigh. 'I do want to see him.' I look away from them. 'But after the "thing" outside the frat house, I'm scared that when I do see him, I'll jump on him and kiss him instead of kicking him in the balls like I actually want to.' I shrug a shoulder, and Megan giggles.

'Then you have to come because either one could be amusing.'

'You're going to make me go, aren't you?' I look between them.

'Maddie, honey,' Lila begins in a softer tone. 'I love you, but it's been three weeks. I'm not letting you mope anymore. You're going.'

That settled that, I guess.

Chapter Forty-Eight

Braden

I grab a beer from the cooler in the kitchen and head into the front room, taking a seat in the corner with Aston and Ryan. Neither say anything. What can they say? We're all expecting Maddie to turn up tonight with the girls. Megan and Lila will drag her along because Lila's fed up with the – and I quote – 'goddamn miserable look on her face all the damn time.'

I guess we're both gonna be forced here tonight because I'd rather be anywhere but here.

I take a mouthful of beer and swallow it heavily, just waiting. I don't know what I'm waiting for.

Maybe I'm waiting for her pretty green eyes to meet mine. Maybe I'm waiting to hear her laugh and see her smile again. Maybe I'm waiting for a moment I can approach her – in a totally non-caveman way – and just . . . see her. Without the shouting about how shit my life is without her. I can do without that, and she probably can too.

The house fills up as the guys and I sit in silence. I don't touch the beer again. I have no desire to get drunk tonight. The only desire I have is –

Laughing in the kitchen.

Fuck.

That sound – it cuts me to the core.

Ryan is looking at me sympathetically, and Aston isn't even looking at me. I drop my eyes to the floor and twist my untouched beer bottle between my fingers. How can I enjoy this stupid fucking party when the only person who makes it enjoyable is laughing on the other side of the room? It was one thing being here without her and letting it pass me by, but knowing she's here . . . Knowing that makes me hypersensitive to her.

She laughs again, and I grit my teeth, turning sharply to look at her. She's standing next to Kyle. His arm is around her shoulders. What the fuck?

Maddie glances up quickly. Her green eyes meet mine for a split second – long enough for me to see the complete sadness there. I might be the reason she's so damn sad, but I'll be fucked if I'm letting that punk comfort *my* girl. I slam the bottle on the table and cross the room in a few quick strides.

'Excuse me,' I say, even though I don't care.

I take Maddie's arm and pull her away from Kyle, ignoring his cry of protest, and yank her through the room.

'Braden, let go of me!' she cries, trying to loosen my grip on her. 'Braden! You're being an asshole!'

'Fuck this!' I stop and grab her waist, hoisting her over my shoulder. She squeaks out a scream and begins to smack me in the back, wriggling and kicking me for all she's worth as I carry her upstairs.

'Let go of me! You're being a caveman again!' she yells.

I shove my bedroom door open, walk through and deposit her inside. Turning, I slam the door shut, pocketing the key.

I turn to her, trying to stay calm. 'That's because you're mine, and I'm not watching you laughing with him down there! You don't belong to him, Maddie! You never have and you never fucking will!'

'I. Am. Not. Yours!' she hisses, pointing at me. 'I may have belonged to you once, but I don't anymore! Remember that?'

'If that's what you wanna believe, Angel, then you believe it.'

'It's not what I believe! I know it!'

'See those eyes, Maddie?' I cross the room, stop in front of her and look down at her. 'They tell me a different story, so why don't we give up the game?'

'The game has been played,' she says acidly. 'We both won, Braden, and now it's over.' She sighs. 'I don't know what I'm supposed to say to you. Regardless of how either of us feel . . . It's over. *We* are over. I'm not yours anymore. Do you get that? I'm. Not. Yours!'

'But I'm yours!' I grab her face and tilt her head back, making her eyes crash into mine. 'I'm yours, Maddie. I always have been, and I always will be. Yours. Do you get that? Do. You. Get. That? I'll always be yours!'

Her lips part slightly, but she says nothing.

'Huh?' I prompt her. 'Fight it all you want, Maddie. When it comes to me and you, we'll always belong to each other. Whether you like it or not, I. Am. Yours.'

Chapter Forty-Nine

Maddie

Inside, my body is in overdrive. My heart is pounding, my blood is rushing through my body, and adrenaline is filling every spot possible. I'm so angry – yet I'm so broken and I want him.

Outside, I'm frozen to the spot.

'No,' I say, looking away from him.

'Yes.' His voice is begging me to believe him, to believe he still wants me.

That he loves me.

'We both played the game,' he says softly. 'Both of us, Maddie. We both had the same goal, and we both achieved it. Don't you get it yet? I fell in love with you, Angel. I'm still in fucking love with you. What did you think would happen? Did you think I'd just let you walk right on out of my life like you were nothing?'

I nod.

'Shit, Maddie!' He lets go of me and turns, rubbing his face. A tear drips from my eye. 'Did you really fucking think that? That I'd let you go from everything to nothing? 'Cause that's what you are. That's what you have been. Everything. You're fucking everything.'

He steps towards me and cups my face again. He pulls my face up until my tear-filled eyes meet his unusually dusky blue ones.

'Maybe this is what I should have said the other day. You know I'm no good with dating. I had to look on Google for where to take you for our second date, for fuck sake.' I smile a little. 'I'm no good at this, Maddie. I've messed up big time and it probably won't be the last. Maybe shouting at you about how crap my life is without you wasn't my smartest move, but damn it . . . I'm so lost without you around. I can't let this go, Maddie, and I'm not going to. You can run all you like, but I'll catch up with you every time, and when I do I'm gonna try and prove to you how right we are together.'

A tear drops from my eye, and he dips his head, kissing it away. He rests the side of his forehead against mine.

'I love you, Angel. I can't stand there and watch you with Kyle acting like everything is all right, 'cause it ain't. The only way it can be all right is if you're by my side. In some fucked up way, me and you, we're perfect for each other.'

I half-laugh, half-sob. 'I don't care about Kyle. Not like that. He knows that.'

Tears spill from my eyes and Braden pulls me close. My arms wrap around his waist and my face presses into his hard chest.

'I love you,' I whisper through my tears. 'But I'm scared, Bray, I'm scared everything I think I know about us is wrong. I'm scared that maybe it's always gonna go wrong.'

'I'm not Pearce,' he says into my ear. 'I'm not him. I'm never gonna hurt you, control you or lie to you. Anymore,' he adds about the lying.

'We both did that. We both lied. We were both wrong,' I admit sadly.

'It brought you to me, Maddie. Something that does that can never be wrong.'

I look up at him, and he brushes his lips against mine. I stand on my tiptoes and kiss him a little harder.

'Mine, Maddie.' His blue eyes are clearing, the electric blue I know so well returning. 'You will always be mine.' He wipes the tears from my cheeks softly.

'Yours,' I agree with no other choice. I can't ever see another choice. My hands move and I grip his collar pulling his face to mine. I graze his bottom lip between my teeth. 'But that means you're mine.'

'Are you going cavewoman on me?' He smirks slowly.

I smile, the first genuine smile since I saw my dad. 'Me, Maddie. Braden, mine.' I kiss him again.

His arms circle my back, and we move sideways towards the bed. I spin us and push him back onto the mattress. I fall on top of him and straddle him, my dress rising up my thighs. Braden's hands stroke my thighs, his thumbs probing the insides of them.

I sink my fingers into his hair and hold on tightly, kissing him for all it's worth.

My past doesn't matter. It may always haunt me, and I know it'll always be in my mind and my heart, but I can't let it control me anymore. If I let it control me, it'll control my relationship.

We might not be forever. Our first love might not be our last. I can't predict where we'll be five, ten, even fifteen years from now, but I can't let my past rule my future. My past has shaped me into the person I am today, and knowing that means I can let go of all of my doubts and hold onto what I have. I can let go of my thoughts of my brother and hold onto Braden as tight as he'll let me.

Because, sometimes, letting go is the key to holding on.

Epilogue

Braden

In the two days since I dragged Maddie back to my room in a move that would put Fred Flintstone to shame, she's barely left my side. Brooklyn was too far – too fuckin' far – and I'll be damned if I'm giving her the chance to escape again.

Paranoid? Probably, but when you have it, you have it. And I have it.

The door clicks open, and Maddie comes flying in. She launches herself on the bed and sits in front of me, grinning at me like a madwoman. Her eyes are shining, her cheeks are flushed, and her hair is mussed. It makes me think about us just having sex, and I grab her waist and lie back, settling her on top of me.

'Guess what?' she says, excitement and happiness threaded in her tone.

'What?'

'I just spoke to Jayne – oh, that's Abbi's nurse – and she said that Abbi asked to join in with a group activity yesterday!'

I slide my arms around her waist, and she kisses me firmly.

'That's good, right?' I double check. Hell, I have no idea.

Maddie nods, her hair bouncing with the movement. The ends tickle my face and I sniff a little. 'It's amazing,' she squeals. 'It means she's broken through whatever wall was holding her back, whatever was keeping her lost inside her mind and her memories. Their hope now is she'll start talking more to her doctor, and they can really help her.'

Her excitement and happiness is infectious, but I can see the shadow of sadness in her eyes. 'Hey,' I say softly, trailing my fingers up her spine. 'You know you couldn't stop what happened to her. You already saved her life, Angel, and you going to Brooklyn probably saved it again without you even realising you were doing it.'

She breathes in deeply, and her lips curl up slightly. 'It's scary how well you know me.'

'Not scary.' I grin. 'Totally natural if you're in love.'

'Oh, in love are we?' she mocks, raising an eyebrow. I growl playfully at her and flip us over so she's lying under me.

'Yes. *In* love.' I look down into her green eyes as they search my face, and I dip my head so my lips press against hers. She tastes sweet, and chocolate chips linger on her tongue as she flicks it against my mouth.

'Fuckin' Starbucks,' I mutter. 'You spend more time there than you do anywhere else.'

Her eyebrows shoot upwards. 'Oh, because I've spent absolutely no time in this bed in the last forty-eight hours. I haven't skipped three classes and missed an assignment deadline or anything, have I?'

My cheeks twitch as I fight the grin wanting to break out. I brush my nose up her cheek. 'It's not my fault. I was having so much fun I forgot to tell you we had to go to class.'

'You forgot, did you?'

'Absolutely.' I kiss her again, and she sinks her fingers into my hair.

'Thank you,' she whispers.

'What for?'

'Always making me feel better. You're a total pig—'

'Hey!'

'But you're the best kind of pig.' The smile on her face wins me over, and goddamn, I know I'll never be able to stay mad at her.

'I guess that's a compliment.'

'Oh, it is.' She nods. She bucks her hips so I fall off her, and gets up.

I reach forward, grabbing her waist, and pull her back down. 'Where are you going?'

Maddie slaps my hands. 'I'm going somewhere where I'll

see something other than these four walls and the underside of your sheets, Braden Carter.'

'Nothing wrong with the underside of my sheets,' I grumble as she gets up.

'I never said there was.' She opens the door. 'But you should know that Aston was making sexy eyes at Megan when I came up.'

'What the hell is Megan doing here at this time of the morning?' I sit up. Making sexy eyes?

'Okay, one, it's ten a.m., and two . . .' She laughs a little. 'Megan is always here at this time of the morning. Don't ask why, but she is. You just don't usually drag your ass out of bed till gone lunch.'

I grin wolfishly. 'Why would I get out of bed when you're usually in it?'

She shoots me a look, hiding her smile. 'Just move your ass before Aston sweet talks his way into Megan's pants.'

'Over my dead fuckin' body!' I jump from the bed, and she laughs as she shuts the door. 'Tell her she better be on the opposite side of the room from that son of a bitch when I get down there, or I'll go caveman on *his* ass!'

I hear her laughter down the hall, and I yank some jeans on. I shove a shirt over my head, and follow her out. She's standing at the bottom of the stairs, looking over her shoulder. She winks, and disappears around the corner into the kitchen.

I run down the stairs, my feet barely touching the steps, and slide across the floor into the kitchen. I stop at the doorframe and lean against it casually. Maddie smirks at me across the room, hugging a cup of coffee. I grin at her a little, and notice Megan sat next to her. Aston is at the other end of the bar in the kitchen.

But he's looking at Meggy.

I knock him on the back of the head as I pass him, and snatch Megan's toast from her hand. She stares at me open-mouthed.

'Excuse me,' she sputters.

'You're excused.' I grin, and rip a bite of toast off. I lean against Maddie, and she rolls her eyes. Megan looks at her.

'What?' Maddie shrugs. 'He's already stolen it. What do you expect me to do? He's like a big kid.'

I poke her side. Megan looks at me, smiling.

'She's got your number, Bray,' she says happily.

I glance over at Aston and back to her. The smile slowly drops from her face and she coughs a little. I lean in closer, and crook my finger for her to move in.

'And I've got yours, Meggy,' I warn her quietly. 'Aston might be one of my best friends, but if he so much as blows a goddamn kiss in your direction, I'll kick his sorry ass.'

'It may have escaped your notice, but I'm more than capable of taking care of myself, Bray,' she says through clenched teeth. 'I appreciate it, really, I do, but if I want to get involved with someone, I will.'

'But that someone won't be a guy with a dick bigger than his brains.'

Maddie sighs, and pushes me back. 'For God sake, Braden. Who's said Megan is going to sleep with Aston? He hasn't. She hasn't.'

'But you said he was making sexy eyes at her!'

Megan's lips curl upwards. 'Aston makes sexy eyes at himself when he looks in the mirror. He's a pretty boy.'

'You sayin' I'm not a man, Megan?' Aston calls over.

Megan looks up, her eyes wide with innocence. 'Would I ever?'

'You know, if you were anyone other than Braden's adopted sister, you'd be slung over my shoulder right now.' The guys around him holler.

'Really?' Megan twirls some hair around her finger, and all eyes are on her. 'I might have liked that. Shame.'

I look at her in shock, and Maddie sniggers into her hand.

'You would have liked what would happen upstairs even more, babe.' Aston winks. I turn, glaring at him.

'Keep it in your fuckin' pants or lose it, dude,' I threaten.

He looks at Megan and back to me. 'I'm pretty attached to my dick, so I think I'll keep it in my pants. Only where she's concerned though.'

Megan's lips purse. 'You're a pig, Aston.'

'They all are,' Maddie mutters, smiling innocently at me. I half-grin at her.

'You know,' I say quietly, putting my arm around her as the conversation starts back up and Megan disappears into the yard. 'I'm a little wary about going to my parents' house next weekend. There's no telling what would happen without me being here and keeping an eye on her.'

'Are you her best friend, or her Dad?' Maddie looks at me knowingly. 'You care about her, and I love that, I do, but you gotta let her have her fun. Let her make mistakes. Besides,' she glances at Aston. 'He's not a bad mistake to make . . .'

'Maddie,' I growl.

'I'm just sayin'.' She grins. 'He won't do anything. He respects your friendship.'

'It's not him I'm worried about. It's Megan I don't trust.'

Maddie reaches up and touches a hand to my cheek. 'Don't. Let her be Megan. Then, if anyone fucks her around, you can go alpha-caveman-protective-big-bro on their ass. Okay?'

I pause.

'*Okay?*' she says forcefully.

I grit my teeth, and damn this love shit, because this girl has me wrapped around her little finger and then some. 'Fine,' I grind out. 'I will let Megan make her own mistakes.'

'Do you mean that?'

'Yes. I will try not to be so alpha-caveman whatever it was on her.'

Maddie moves her hand from my cheek and replaces it with her lips. 'You're making the right decision, Bray. You can't protect her forever.'

My eyes find Aston again, and I watch him steadily. His back is turned, and he's joking around with the guys. He's got more charm than a group of snake charmers, and I've seen the shit he's caused in the last couple of months with girls. The idea of that happening to Megan . . .

I look back at Maddie, meeting her beautiful green eyes. 'That's exactly what I'm afraid of.'

PLAYING FOR KEEPS

Megan

'You do realize your mom will ask her one hundred questions about you, right?' I glance up at Braden from my stretched out position on his floor.

'No shit,' he mutters. 'That's why you need to tell her what to say.'

I pause my aimless flicking through my magazine. 'Let's think about that for a second.'

'Meggy.'

'No.'

He shuts his closet door and drops to the floor in front of me. His dirty blond hair flops into his eyes and he levels them on me, pleading with me silently. I shake my head.

'Braden Carter, you chose to take Maddie home for the weekend. You have to deal with – and field – your mom's endless questions.'

'Meg,' he draws my name out, sounding like a petulant toddler begging for candy.

'It would happen sooner or later.' I shrug and sit up, tucking my legs under me. 'You might as well get it over with now. Besides,' I grin, 'I'm sure she'll give the questions a break by telling her childhood stories.

'Fucking hell,' Braden grumbles and sighs. 'At least I have comfort in the fact you were with me for most of my stupid moments. Hell, you probably caused most of them.'

'I so did not!' I pause, and he raises his eyebrows at me. *Actually,* there was that time I ran off with the ladder and left Braden stuck up a tree. We only had the ladder because we had to go to some work thing with our parents, and they didn't want us to be covered in scrapes and grazes. Braden got cocky and thought he could jump – and he could, but not without breaking his arm. We never did get to the work thing . . . 'Okay. At least a third were caused by me. Don't go twisting it, because I will correct her when you come back.'

'Yeah, yeah. Whatever you say.' He stands and grins. A knock sounds at his door seconds before it's pushed open.

Aston walks in shirtless, his jeans hanging low on his hips. Every inch of his body is exposed, from the curve of his biceps to the dip of his v muscle beneath his pants. My gaze flits over him, taking in his wet hair sticking up, and the small towel slung around his shoulders is almost an afterthought. His gray eyes interrupt my perusal of his body, and he smirks when he realizes.

'I'm starting to wonder if I'll see you anywhere other than a guy's bedroom,' he drawls.

'Just because you haven't seen me in yours,' I reply, leaning back on my hands. 'And I'd imagine that's something you're not used to.'

Braden looks to the ceiling and shakes his head, rubbing his hand over his face as if he'd rather be anywhere other than here.

'I don't think you'd fit in in mine.' Aston leans against the doorframe. 'It's not up to the standards a pretty little rich girl is used to.'

'I can't say fitting in with your bedroom is on my to-do list.' Even if the person is . . . 'And pretty little rich girl I may be, but I'm not a snob.'

Aston snorts. 'So if a guy from, say, a shit-riddled and utterly fucked-up background chatted you up, you wouldn't run ten miles in the other direction?'

I stand, staring at him. 'Just because someone's past and upbringing is fucked up doesn't mean the person is, Aston. The way someone was brought up doesn't define them as a person. Whatever perception you have of me, however stuck up you think I am – my upbringing doesn't define the person I am now. I'm not as shallow as you'd like to think I am.'

He tilts his head to the side for a moment before his lips twitch up at one side. It's a cocky, smug grin that tells me I walked right into his trap.

'Oh, it's easy,' he says through his smile. 'So, so easy. You're a little ticking time bomb aren't you, Megan?'

'Any reason you're here?' Braden interjects before I can respond.

'Yeah. I need that English book.' Aston looks around.

'Which one? I've got more fucking English books than I have classes.'

'Shit, man, I dunno.' Aston shrugs. 'The one from last class.'

I roll my eyes and perch on the edge of Braden's bed. 'The Shakespeare one.'

Both of them look at me blankly, Braden more so. Aston at least looks like he knows who Shakespeare is.

'You know, Bray. The guy who lived "years ago and can't fuckin' talk properly".' I give Braden a pointed look, and his face breaks into a big grin.

'Oh, that guy. Yeah. I pretty much reworded Maddie's work.' Braden turns to his desk and grabs the textbook. He shoves it in Aston's direction.

'Cheers, dude.' Aston looks at me and winks, and I try not to roll my eyes again.

He's so damn infuriating. He really does wind me up just 'cause he knows it's easy, and he's starting to learn that referring to me as 'a little rich girl' is the easiest way to rile me. It's not my fault I was born into an upper middle class family – Braden was too, and he doesn't get the rich boy treatment.

Oh, that's right. He doesn't get it because eighty percent of the guys in this house are from the same background.

I reach down, grab my magazine from the floor and roll it up. I swing it in Braden's direction, smacking his back with it.

'Ouch! What the fuck was that for?' He frowns at me.

'Thanks for backing me up, dickhead.'

'Hey – I shut him up.'

I scoff. 'Only because you were getting annoyed that I and his bedroom were put in the same sentence.'

'At least I shut him up. Now you can tell Maddie what to say to my mom.'

Oh, I'll tell her what to say alright.

I sigh, looking into his wide, pleading eyes, and shrug. 'Fine, I'll tell her what to say.'

'I think you were playing your own game all along.' Lila twirls a bit of hair around her finger.

My lips quirk behind the safety of my book, and I glance at her over the top of it. 'I have no idea what you're talking about.'

'You're a terrible liar, Megs. You know exactly what I'm talking about.'

'If I knew I wouldn't have asked.'

She reaches over and tugs my book down, catching my smile before I can hide it again.

'See!' she exclaims. 'You do know.'

'Okay, okay. So what if I was? It all worked out in the end, didn't it?'

'But it nearly didn't. Maddie ran back to Brooklyn, or did you forget that?'

'No,' I reply slowly. 'I didn't forget that. She came back and they kicked each other's asses.'

She purses her lips. 'You weren't worried at all were you?'

I shake my head. 'Not really. I know that makes me sound horrible, like I don't care, but I knew they'd sort it out. You can't tell me you believed her when she said she wasn't in love with him?'

'Well no . . .'

'Precisely. She fell for him as hard as he fell for her, Lila.'

'Then why Brooklyn? I just don't get it. We all know they were doing the same thing.'

'You weren't here when Braden found out.' I chew on my bottom lip. That was the worst moment – none of us ever thought he'd turn up at her dorm room, least of all me. It was a bad call on my part, and despite my best efforts to get rid of the poster there was no way to do it quietly. 'He was mad. So, so damn mad. I sat there and watched his heart break, Li, and I felt so shit. Hell, I watched both their hearts break. What did it for Maddie was Braden went crazy over what she was doing, then she found out he was doing the exact same thing. She was embarrassed over the whole thing and angry over how he'd acted. But most of all she was heartbroken over it – that moment shattered every belief she had that he'd fallen in love with her. The only thing she could do was run.'

'Huh. And she told you that?'

'No, but you don't have to be cupid to figure it out.'

'How did you figure it out?'

I shrug a shoulder. 'It happens when your favorite aunt is qualified in three areas of psychology.'

Her mouth drops open. 'Three?'

'I know, I know. I come from a family of overachievers. I think I'm somewhat of a disappointment with my little English major and book writing ambition.'

'At least you're doing what you love. And, for the record, you'd be a terrible cupid.' She giggles.

'Well, thanks.' I throw my pillow at her, smiling. 'But like I said, it's all okay now, isn't it?'

'I have to admit, I never thought I'd see the day Braden Carter took a girl home.' Lila hugs my pillow to her chest.

'You and I both.' I smirk.

I never truly thought I'd see the day he'd be as in love as he is. Braden and Maddie have the magical kind of love every little girl dreams of – at least I did. I spent hours upon hours dreaming of the guy that would give me butterflies and sweep me so high off my feet I'd never go back down. My dreams were only fueled by Mom's extensive library in her home office. I can't count the times I used to sneak books out to read about the kind of love my best friends are experiencing now.

'Whatcha readin'?' Nanna peered over my shoulder.

I jumped, snapping the book shut. 'Nothing.'

'Why you readin' it then?'

'Dunno.'

She leaned over the back of the sofa and snatched the book out of my hands. My eyes widened as she took in the book. 'Huckleberry Finn? You're hiding for this?'

'Um, yeah.' I swallowed.

Nanna opened the book. Her eyes flicked across a page before she closed it again and pulled off the dust jacket. 'Megan Harper. You sneaky devil.'

I smiled warily.

'Does your mother know you've stolen her copy of *Pride and Prejudice* when you should be reading *Huck Finn*?'

'No. Please don't tell her, Nanna! *Huck Finn* isn't terrible, but I don't want to read it. I'd much rather read about Lizzy and Darcy.'

She didn't respond.

'Please, Nanna.'

'I won't say a word, girl. Between you and me, Huck Finn isn't nearly as exciting as Mr. Darcy. Just don't tell your mother I approve of your stealing her romance novels.'

'I won't.'

Nanna gestured to the book. 'Has he kissed her yet?'

I nodded happily. 'It's my favorite part.'

'Mine too.' She winked.

Our dorm door opens, snapping me out of my inner musings, and Maddie comes bursting in in an explosion of fiery hair.

'You have to make me ill or something. Or pretend I am. Or – oh! Cover me in face paint,' she babbles, slamming the door and pressing her back against it.

'Eh? Face paint?' I frown.

'Yep. I'm allergic.' She gestures to her face. 'Makes my face go all puffy and spotty and stuff.'

'Aside from the fact face paint isn't something I keep under my bed,' Lila comments. 'Why on Earth do you want to be ill?'

Maddie slumps down the door, hugging her knees to her chest. 'I've never . . . You know. Done the meeting the parents thing before.'

'Ohhh,' Lila and I say in unison.

'His parents aren't bad at all.' I look at her. 'Honestly, they're some of the nicest people I've ever met.'

'He's your best friend. You have to say that,' she groans.

'Well, he is, but I don't. Really, Mads. You don't have to be worried about anything.'

'What if they ask me a hundred questions?'

'His dad won't. His mom will, though – but not about you. About Braden.'

'And what do I say?'

'The truth.' I grin. 'Aha! I win!'

Maddie and Lila both look toward me, their eyebrows raised.

'I told Braden I'd tell Maddie what to say to his mom, and I'm saying to tell the truth.'

'Smart move,' Lila acknowledges.

'I guess he didn't tell you to convince me to lie?' Maddie sits up and smiles.

'Of course he didn't. He naturally assumes I will do that, and more fool him.' I grin. 'When are you going?'

'After English. We have it last tomorrow, don't we?'

I nod, and Lila frowns. 'I thought you were going Saturday morning. Something about Braden not wanting to leave Megs for two nights to party in a house full of horny frat boys.'

I drop my head back. 'For fuck sake,' I mutter to the ceiling.

'Oh, that was the first plan,' Maddie explains. 'I told him he was being damn ridiculous, and Megan was more than capable of looking after herself in a house full of animals.'

My head moves forward, and I smile gratefully at her. 'See.' I glance Lila's way. 'This is another reason I knew they'd be perfect for each other. She kicks his ass, and I get a break from his adorable protective act.'

'Adorably annoying,' Maddie corrects me. 'It drives me mad, so I have no idea how you put up with it.'

'It's normal for me. He's always done it, so it doesn't really bother me anymore. It's a bit like white noise now. Besides, I already begged his mom to give him a baby sister when I was thirteen, and she refused.'

'Wow, was he really that bad?' Lila snickers.

'You really want to know?' I glance between them, and they nod. 'Okay, we were six and it was fall. We'd spent all weekend collecting conkers for school on Monday, and I had the perfect one. Braden always won against me, but I'd won our practice battle on the way to school with it. There was this boy who had a kiddie crush on me – Adam Land. I challenged him to a conker fight and won. He hated being beaten by a girl, so threw another one at my head. Braden jumped on him and bit him.'

'He bit him?!' Maddie shrieks, and Lila laughs.

I put my hand to my mouth and giggle silently as I nod. 'He bit him so hard he drew blood. His mom went crazy when the principal called her.'

'That's brilliant. I wish my brother would have done that. He would have laughed,' Lila muses.

'Okay, now I'm really glad I talked him into going tomorrow no matter how worried I am about it.' Maddie tries to muffle her giggles.

'Does this mean I get to see a different side of Megan?' Lila asks, a glint in her eyes.

'Hey, it doesn't mean I'm gonna grab some guy by his collar and drag him to bed just because Braden isn't here.' I drop my eyes to the floor. 'Maybe.'

Besides, I flit through a perpetual state of love-hate where the guy I want to take to bed is concerned. I live the Elizabeth and Mr. Darcy kind of love in *Pride and Prejudice*. Luckily enough everyone else only sees the hate.

The fact crazy little butterflies fire up in my stomach whenever Aston Banks walks into a room is my secret. And I don't intend to share it anytime soon.

Aston

Her blue eyes are focused on the words on the page in front of her like they always are. I've never known anyone to spend as much time with their nose between the pages of a book as Megan does. Everywhere she goes she has one – in her bag, in her lap, next to her.

No one else notices. And no one else notices the fact I do.

Her brow furrows, and she sucks her bottom lip into her mouth as she sweeps her long blonde hair from her face. She gathers it at the back of her head and snaps a band from her wrist, tying it up and exposing the sleek curve of her neck and the skin there. I spin my pen between my fingers and glance at my own book.

Off limits. That's what Megan Harper is.

I knew the first time I saw her I could never have her. The way she holds herself and the sarcastic yet polite comments – she has endless amounts of 'screams rich girl', a class I never have and never will be in. It's engrained in her to treat everyone with respect no matter what you think of them. I'm certain she could face a serial killer and have at least one nice comment for him.

She does for everyone.

Everyone is treated the same way, and every sarcastic, almost bitchy comment is followed by a softer one. Every frown or fleeting dirty look is followed by an apologetic smile and every slap is a playful one. Everyone is equal until they prove her otherwise.

Except me.

I'm the exception to her rule. And I fucking love it. I bring it on myself, but I can't help getting under her skin and shaking her up. It's addictive, sparking a fire in me I can't put out once I've started. She bites so easily and her voice snaps a reply to me sometimes before I can even finish what I'm saying.

It makes it easier to keep away from her. Makes it easier to take a random girl I don't give a shit about to my room every weekend and fuck her instead. If Megan showed even one ounce of interest in me for something other than a battle of words, I'd be next to her like a damn gunshot.

I'd have her in my bed and underneath me quicker than a fucking bullet.

'What's the matter? Bored of looking at your usual tarts?'

I blink. Her face is turned toward me, her large, bright eyes questioning, and I smirk.

'Depends if you include yourself in that statement.'

'I don't exactly have a high opinion of myself, Aston, but I don't think quite that badly of myself either.' She bites the end of her pen. 'The last thing I'd want is to be one of your tarts.'

Ouch.

'That's a shame.' I lean in closer. 'I think you'd fit in perfectly.'

'Really?' She smiles insincerely. ''Cause I'm afraid I don't quite make the cut. For one, my panties tend to still be on by the end of the night.'

'It could be arranged for it to be otherwise.'

'The only way they'll be coming off is if I take them off myself.'

I grin. She's getting the tell-tale flush to her cheeks, and her eyes are shining a little more like they always do when she's annoyed. Shit, I've been on the receiving end of this look enough times.

'Hey.' I lean back, resting my foot on top of my other knee. 'Whatever floats your boat, babe. I'm not against a little strip-tease.'

Megan runs her tongue across the top of her teeth and stares me down. 'Then go and look in your goddamn mirror, 'cause you aren't getting one from me.'

I can't help the upturn of my lips just like I can't help the images in my head. Her jeans are tight enough, I don't need to imagine the curve of her ass, but I do imagine it minus the jeans and her bent over, pulling her underwear down.

Blood rushes down my body and I shift. Jesus – a hard-on in English isn't what I need.

'Another shame.' I drop my hands to my lap. Fucking thing has a mind of its own. 'You have just enough ass to get it right.'

'So do you, but I don't see you standing in front of my table and ripping your clothes off to a cheesy tune.' She barely bats an eyelid, taking her eyes from mine and going back to her word. 'And thank God I don't.'

'Braden goes tonight,' I say, changing the subject completely.

'I know.'

'Are you coming over?'

Her eyes scoot from the page to meet mine. 'Why?'

'Because I was wondering if I could get that striptease,' I reply sarcastically. 'Fucking hell, Megan. I was just asking.'

She rolls her eyes – something I'm sure she has reserved for when she talks to me. 'Alright! Yes, I am. I'm coming over with Lila and Kay.'

'Your little sidekicks.' I smirk.

'Says you,' she mutters.

I'll ignore that. 'So you'll be at a party without Braden. How will you cope?'

'Fuck you, Aston.'

'Sore spot, huh?'

She spins in her chair and fully levels her gaze on me. Sparks fire in the blue, and I know I've really pissed her off this time. Just as well I like it when she's mad at me.

'I'm not a china doll, much to everyone's disappointment,' she snaps. 'I don't need Braden to hold my hand when I'm at a party, thank you very much. I'm more than capable of keeping away horny assholes. I'm not sure where you've gotten your perceptions of me from, but they're so wrong it's unreal.'

She slams her books shut as everyone gets up. She storms past me, then pauses a second and looks back at me over her shoulder. Her lips part, but she shakes her head, turning around and walking away instead.

My perceptions of you are just fine, I want to say as I watch her leave. I just don't say what I really think, because that would be counter-productive to keeping away from the one girl I really want.

Same shit, different night.

The house is full of people, some from Berkeley and some not. I'm getting to the point where I don't even fucking know. The only reason I'm in this damn frat house is because Gramps was and it was what he wanted. Hell, the man has done enough for me. The least I could do was apply and get in here for him.

Girls flutter their eyelashes, flick their hair, and skim their eyes through the people to find a guy to take home. The guys do their version of it; standing against the bar, walls, in door-ways, drinking beer and picking out a girl to take wherever the fuck they want to. And I'm doing it too.

Same as always. Friday and Saturday nights equal meaning-less sex. Focusing on that, the meaningless fuck, means I can't focus on the shit that means something. And it's so easy.

Pick a girl. Hand her a drink. Tell her she's pretty. Take her upstairs. Fuck her. Make sure she's gone by morning.

I'm not the only one that keeps to that. Braden used to, and half the guys in this house do as well. The girls know exactly what they're getting themselves into, at least with me – they know I want nothing more than a couple hours.

I don't even want to know their damn name.

I bring my beer bottle to my lips and glance at a tall, dark-haired girl walking past. Her eyes skirt down to me and her lips curl. She's not perfect, but she'd do . . . If I wasn't so aware of a pair of eyes on me.

I fight the impulse to meet the gaze across the room but lose. I let my eyes jump from the girl to Megan's. She's sitting at the bar, her body facing it, the angle almost begging me to take note of the way her dress hugs her body. I trace my eyes over it, and I love the fact she's got more curves than most of the girls here. She's not the skinniest girl but she's confident in her body and it shows.

Confidence is pretty hot on any girl, but on Megan it's just downright sexy.

I smirk at her, my lips moving slowly, and raise an eyebrow. Her foot taps as she holds my gaze, neither of us willing to look away, and something shifts between us. She swallows and runs her fingers through her hair, her eyelids drooping. The movement is so slight I only notice because I'm looking for it. Because I'm looking for any little thing that will show me the shift is attraction.

And it is.

She purses her lips around the straw in her glass and questions me with her eyes. This is different – it isn't us trying to piss each other off. It isn't us throwing sarcastic comments at each other. It's something new.

Something raw.

Something dangerous.

Something that could fuck me up.

The smirk drops from my face, and she looks away. She swirls the ice cubes round the bottom of her empty glass and her shoulders relax slightly. I spin the beer bottle between my fingers.

I know the risks. I know if I go over there the sex tonight won't be meaningless. It won't be a casual fuck where it doesn't matter in the morning. It'll be giving in to the one weakness I have.

But fuck. I want to.

Megan

I want to be the girl going upstairs with him instead of the one watching him go.

He drives me crazy in the worst kind of way. Every comment, every smirk, every cocky raise of his eyebrows. Each thing affects me, especially the way he clearly doesn't know me even though he thinks he does. He's so wrong about me in every way, and it pisses me off so badly, yet I don't think I could say no if he walked up to me right now and invited me to his room.

The one not fit for a little rich girl like me.

The one I'd probably feel totally at home with.

But I don't know if one night would be enough. When you want someone so badly you have to work to hide it, just one night of letting go of that restraint wouldn't be enough. If he came up to me now and I let go, I don't think I'd be able to hold on again. I don't think I'd be able to leave it at one night of casual sex.

Hell. I don't know if sex with him would be casual.

I know one night can't hurt, but I also know it can't do any good.

'Sex doesn't make love, Megan. If you want to give physically, that's up to you, but don't give it all up emotionally just because a guy has a few smooth lines or is good looking. Real sex is the whole package.'

And Mom's words remind me I want the whole package now.

'I don't think I've ever seen you alone,' Aston's voice crawls over me smoothly, making the hairs on the back of my neck stand up, and he sits on the stool next to me.

'It doesn't happen often.' I turn my face slowly, finding his gray eyes for the umpteenth time today. 'I could say the same to you.'

'It doesn't happen often,' he parrots, a half-smile teasing his lips.

'So why are you here with me and not in a dark corner with your usual company?'

'Ouch, Megan. Is that bitterness in your voice?' His knees brush mine. 'Don't tell me you're jealous.'

'Disgust,' I mutter, looking away from him so he doesn't catch the lie. 'Don't confuse it with bitterness or jealousy.'

'You know something?' He leans in closer, his breath fluttering my hair as he places his mouth close to my ear. 'I think you're fooling yourself. Ten minutes, Megan.'

He gets up and disappears, leaving me shaking my head after him. I need to shake my head – I need to do something to hide the temptation running through my body.

Kyle wordlessly removes my glass and pours me another drink. 'You're quiet tonight.' He leans against the bar opposite me.

'It has been known to happen.' I smile.

'Odd without Mads and Braden, huh?'

I shrug a shoulder. 'A bit, I guess. At least all their shit is sorted out now. We can all get on with our lives.'

Kyle snorts. 'Right. Braden took every guy in this house down with him when she went to Brooklyn. It was like living with a woman with fucking PMS, and shit, I moved away from home to escape that. My sister is a demon then.'

'You should try being around guys that don't get laid enough,' I comment dryly, sipping my drink. 'They beat girls with PMS hands down.'

'I don't doubt it.' He smirks. 'Just so happens there's none of those around here.'

'Huh. You're probably right.'

'You look like you need to get laid though.'

'And here I was thinking you were a nice guy. You had to go and blow it by saying that, didn't you?' I sigh playfully. 'You all are the same.'

'Hey, I'm just saying.' He leans forward and grins. 'I bet you wouldn't be short of offers since the caveman isn't here.'

I bite the inside of my cheek, fighting my smile. 'The caveman thing is really sticking, huh?'

'You have no idea.' Kyle's eyes twinkle.

Why can't I want Kyle instead? He's a damn nice guy, and he's not exactly bad looking without his unruly dark hair and hazel eyes. He's leanly built, his muscles not showy but clear to see. He'd be such a great distraction – if I wasn't already so distracted by Aston.

I finish the rest of my drink and push the glass toward him. 'Do me a favor? Tell Lila I'll see her tomorrow sometime. I'm heading back to the dorm.'

'Got it.' He nods and turns away.

I glance around the room and scoot out of it. This is a risk. A big risk, but I don't care.

Aston's words were full of promises when he sat next to me on the stool, and his eyes were full of mysteries I want to unravel between his sheets. Paranoia attaches itself to me as I push my way through the living room and up the stairs. I run my fingers through my hair as if I'm just heading to the bathroom and glance around on the landing. My fingers grasp the bottom of my dress and tug it down as I climb the final staircase to his room.

Someone grabs my arm and spins me into the wall. Their mouth covers mine, swallowing my shriek, and their swift movements thwart my attempt at kneeing them in the balls.

'You're not being attacked,' Aston mutters lowly against my mouth. 'Unless you want it.'

I open my eyes to his in the dim light of the hallway. 'You're a pig, you know that?'

'Yet you're here.'

'Apparently.' I drop my eyes.

He cups the side of my head, threading his fingers through

my hair, and tugs my face upward. His lips touch mine again, soft but forceful, and I slide my hands up his arms to grip his collar. I hold his face against mine, parting my lips for his probing mouth, and push my body into his. He flicks his tongue against mine, before biting on my bottom lip and sweeping it across it. Tremors fall down my spine, and he reaches around to slot his key into the door, breaking the kiss.

He shoves it open, his hands trailing down my back, and I let him pull me into his room. He slams the door at the same time he yanks my body against his, his breath fanning across my lips. My eyes drop to his mouth and close as he dips his head to kiss me again. This time it's firmer, more needing, and my fingers creep below his polo shirt and onto his hot skin. I spread my fingers out, my thumbs brushing the solid muscle on his stomach, and he releases me to pull his shirt over his head.

I run my bottom lip between my teeth and run my eyes down his torso. He's perfect, beautifully so. His skins stretches over each pack of muscle, the shadows in the indents between them like a light engraving on his skin.

I step forward and touch my mouth to his chest, and he cups the back of my head. He kisses my earlobe, running his lips down my neck, and my trembling hands reach up between us.

What am I doing?

'Megan?'

I open my mouth to speak but no words come out. Instead I swallow, stepping back. His hands fall away from me and hang limply at his sides.

'I . . .' I swallow again, trying to control the crazy buzzing in the back of my mind. 'This . . . This can't happen.'

Can't happen? What am I doing now?

'Can't happen?' He looks like he's at a complete loose end, unable to work out what I'm saying. Hell, I just followed him up here and now I'm refusing. I don't get it myself.

'Yep.' I back toward the door, pushing my hair from my face, and tug my dress down a little. 'This can't happen. At all.'

My hand finds the handle and opens the door. And I walk away, leaving him staring after me.

No one knows.

I remind myself of this as I stare at Lila's sleeping body. I keep expecting her to wake up and yell at me for being so dumb. But no one knows – not that it's stopping the intense feelings of near-peace and guilt warring inside me.

The old age cliché. Your head vs. your heart. My head is telling what I already know – I'm a terrible person. I betrayed my best friend by kissing his best friend when I know it's the last thing he wanted me to do . . . But my heart tells me differently, what I should know. It's telling me I'm not a terrible person. For once I went after what I wanted without thinking of the consequences.

It doesn't make me reckless and unfeeling. So unfeeling is probably an exaggeration, but reckless? Yes. It was reckless, and probably a little selfish.

Then again, you don't get anywhere in life without pissing off a few people.

Was last night a mistake? I did the one thing I said I wouldn't do, the one thing I promised myself I wouldn't fucking do. Don't get involved with your best friend's best friend – it's simple. Something so simple that became incredibly compli-cated the second I looked into Aston's misty gray eyes the first day of college. I always knew there'd be something between us, I just didn't know if it would amount to anything.

And here we are.

After all my attempts, all my fighting to keep away from him, I've still somehow ended up falling for his cocky smile and man-whore ways. Not that I love the man-whore ways – I want to set fire to the fake hair, fake nails, and fake eyelashes of every girl that sleeps with him. That's what they are, and he knows it. Fake.

Jesus Christ, Megan, it was a freaking kiss. One little kiss. Not a goddamn proposal.

But . . . Maddie said Braden would never fall in love but she was wrong. He did, but Braden and Aston are in different leagues. Braden's heart was never truly in the sleeping around, he just did it because he could. Something to pass the time – I know that as clearly as I know Aston likes the sleeping around and never-ending attention he gets from girls.

How has one little kiss ended in me dissecting his behavior? A kiss!

I don't have any expectations for an 'us'. I have wants but no expectations. I may be a hopeless romantic happy to get lost between the pages of a hot and steamy novel or a sigh-with-sweetness one, but I'm not naïve enough to believe that those kinds of things happen all the time. Some people will get that kind of love that makes guys wonder and girls swoon, but not everyone.

Love is a fickle thing. Just because you have a person out there that compliments you, that calms your storm and feeds your fire, it doesn't mean you'll always have them. You might never meet them. You might meet them – but it just might not be the right time for you.

I'm nineteen. I know love and lust. I know the difference – and I know that for some strange reason, Aston is my storm calmer, my fire feeder. I also know it isn't the right time for us. It might never be.

Though after the way he held me to him and kissed me last night, I'm not so sure I'm okay with that anymore.

Aston

I'm fucked. And it's all my own fault.

I had to do it, didn't I? I had to go over to her and say what I did. I didn't expect her to do it – I never thought she'd actually come upstairs, but she did. And shit; it felt so wrong but so right at the same time.

She's so dangerous. She's the one in this whole damn college, hell, in the whole damn state, that could strip away my devil-may-care attitude and put me on my sorry ass. She's the only girl that could make me feel again. She could take everything I've tried for so long to stick back together and shatter it into more pieces than it was in in the first place.

I should have stayed the fuck away from her, but I didn't. And now I know the sweet taste of her mouth as she kissed me. I know the softness of her lips as they moved across mine, and I know the feel of her hands gripping my hair.

I also know what it's like to be so close but so far away. 'Cause damn it all to hell, she had to stop and walk away, didn't she? She had to fucking go and leave me there, as hard as a rock, staring after her like a lost little sheep.

Shit. Even though it was just a kiss, it's gonna take nothing short of a goddamn miracle to get me to stay away from her now.

I grab my cell from the side and scroll to her name.

I'm pretty sure I showed Old Maid up last night. Bet the old girl can't kiss the way I can. I press send, remembering the conversation in Vegas, and my lips curve.

Learn some tricks from the big boys in Vegas, did you? She retorts. I'd bet anything she's smiling that smile that lights up her whole face. The smile that makes her looks so damn beautiful she'd put every girl in the country to shame.

You tell me, babe. I grin wider.

I roll over in bed and hit the empty side – the empty side she lay on last night before she left while I was sleeping. My eyes find the calendar on the bedside table, and I shove it off the top to avoid looking at the date. But I know it.

I always know it. It's impossible to ignore – it creeps up on me silently then hits me with a big fucking bang. It's always the hardest this time of year. This week, the one that shaped my life, is the one I love and hate. It changed me for the better but forever destroyed my Gramps.

One person's blessing is another person's curse.

I jump out of bed, get dressed, and grab my car keys. It's earlier than usual and Gramps will probably whack me with his stick for turning up before lunch, but I have no desire to sit here in my room and wallow in my own bullshit self-pity.

I slip out of the front door before anyone stops me and climb into my car, quickly pulling away from the large house. It can become stifling all too quickly, and it's easy to get buried under the weight of your own feelings. It's not too far to Gramps' house, his insistence on moving us away from San Francisco but not out of Northern California the reason I'm at college in Berkeley and not there. San Francisco holds too many memories. Too much shit to ever go back to.

I pull up outside his house, the sun crawling over the front yard an indication I'll spend my day working in his back yard doing what he can't. The rich smell of smoke wafting from his cigar hits me as soon as I open the door, and my face wrinkles up like it does every Sunday.

I hate it, but it's safe – and there's comfort in safety.

'I wish you'd stop smokin' those damn things, Gramps.'

His low, raspy chuckle reaches me through the house. 'You say that e'ry week, boy, and I'll keep on saying the same thing back – I wish you'd stop goin' on about me smoking these "damn things".'

I grin and make my way into the front room, letting the

front door swing shut behind me. The old, wrinkled man I call my Gramps is sitting in his usual spot in front of the window. The floral chair is as old and weathered as he is, but there's definitely more life left in Gramps than in his ratty chair.

'I know. It's worth the shot, though, right?' I shrug, dropping onto the sofa across from him.

He smiles as he turns his face toward me, his dark gray eyes crinkling a little in the corners. 'If you say so, boy. What are you doin' here early, bugging me?'

I look out of the window. 'Got nothin' better to do on a Sunday.'

He chuckles. 'Never know, do I? Probably did what you had to do last night.'

'Gramps. Someone your age shouldn't be making comments like that.'

'Why? Because I'm wrinkled? Find me a nice bit of stuff on a Friday at the Bingo, and I'll put you to shame. Ha!' He puffs one last time on his cigar and stubs it out in the ashtray on the table next to him.

'So many things wrong with that damn sentence.' I shake my head.

'So, who'd you annoy this time?'

'Who says I annoyed someone?'

'You're here at half ten in the mornin', boy! Something is up. You never get your sorry ass out of bed earlier than twelve on a Sunday.'

'I didn't annoy anyone. Besides, I knew you'd want my "sorry ass" in your yard today.'

Gramps' knowing gray eyes settle on me. He taps his fingers on the arm on his chair, each knock of his fingers grating on me. Time stretches as he searches my face, coming to his conclusion. I swallow and shake my head.

'I know what you're gonna say, and you're wrong,' I say firmly.

He starts softly. 'You've never spoken about her.'

'I don't want to speak about her. I have *nothing* to say about her.'

'I think you do. I think you just pretend you don't.'

I shake my head and look away. 'And I think you're shittin' me, Gramps. I get it, alright? You miss her and you wanna talk about her, but I don't. I can't relate to the Mom you knew. She was never, and I mean *never*, that person to me.'

'You can't live in hate forever, boy.'

'It's not hate, Gramps. It's pity, pure and simple. I pity her and I pity the life she forced me to lead until she died – until you took me in.'

'For all your schoolin', for everything I taught you, you never learned to forgive and forget?' he says in a softer voice, his tone coaxing my eyes back to his.

'Forgiving and forgetting are two very different things, Gramps. You can forgive, you can forget, but rarely are they done together. I can't forget my childhood and I can't erase the scars. I can't change the things it's taught me or burn those images or memories from my mind. They mean I'll never forget, and because I can't forget, I can't forgive. It's that simple.'

His gray eyes darken slightly with disappointment and sadness. The usual pang of guilt hits me – guilt for hating the person he loves. Guilt for relief in his despair.

'Gramps—

'No.' He drags his gaze back to the window, his focus on the yard outside. 'I understand. I just wish I understood you, boy.'

'Nothin' to understand,' I reply. 'I'm just getting on with it, Gramps. I can't let myself live in the crap of my past. Not now, not ever.'

'There's some weedin' that needs doing in the far corner, by my vegetable garden. When that's done, I need some holes diggin' for some bushes I'm getting this week.'

I take the subject change – and the escape. Both of us, we're always running away from what we want to say. What we need to say.

'Bushes?'

'For your Nan. Hydrangea. Always Hydrangea,' he mutters

to himself. 'For devotion and understanding. We all need a little of that.'

I nod although he's not looking at me. His way of remembering her. I wonder if he's glad that Nan never saw what happened to her only daughter. I wonder if he's glad that for all the pain she suffered, she never had to watch her baby destroy herself and die.

I wonder what she would think of me now, if she'd look at me and be happy I'm her grandson, or find comfort in my plans for the future. I wonder what she'd say about the way I cope and how I act.

I grab the trowel from the shed, crouching by the vegetable garden, and the truth smacks me full in the face.

Nan would probably be disgusted by me.

God knows there isn't much to be fucking proud of.

Megan

My eyes scan the room, and I sigh in relief when I see I've beaten both Aston and Braden to class. Every part of me wishes it was a day where we didn't share a class, but it just doesn't work that way. This is real life, and as my Nanna always says, real life likes to kick you when you're down.

I sit down at my desk and remember who sits with me. Shit. I drop my head, resting it on the table.

'Crap,' I mutter.

The chair next to me squeaks. 'If you're trying to hide, babe, then you're doing a shit job. I can see you.' Aston's words curve around me, wrapping me in a smooth caress, and my throat goes dry.

'Why would I be hiding?' I sit up and forward, determined not to meet his eyes.

He shrugs a shoulder carelessly, grabbing his pen and twirling it between his fingers. God – I hate it when he does that. I catch his every movement from the corner of my eye. His eyes are burning in the side of my head, begging me to turn, begging to look at him.

'Because you want me so badly you can't even look at me,' he says in a dramatic tone, arrogance weaving through each word.

My back straightens. 'Clearly someone's been feeding your damn ego again. I remember being the one who walked away – and I don't remember ever telling you I want you.'

He leans forward and his bicep brushes mine, the heat from the fleeting touch sinking through the sleeve of my sweater. 'Is that so?' he asks, his voice low and barely perceptible.

I fight the urge to drop my eyes to the desk. 'Damn right it is.'

He trails his fingertip down the back of my arm, the tickling feeling leaving me tingling and fighting a shiver. 'I think you're wrong,' he whispers. 'You might have walked away, Megan Harper, but you were also the one that walked toward me.' His eyes flick to my lips. 'And it was a damn nice walk, don't you think?'

My head snaps round, leaving our faces inches apart. His lips are curled in a slightly smug smile, and I curse myself for that being the first place my eyes fell. I drag them away from his mouth and across the sharp planes of his face until they meet his smoky eyes.

And I remember why I didn't want to look at him. His eyes have the power to entrance me, to hold me captive in his gaze, and they are. The silvery hint at the edge of his irises is pulling me in and trapping my eyes in a silent battle with his. Like this, when I'm unable to focus on anything but the swirling mass of gray in front of me, I remember why nothing could have stopped me following him and kissing him on Saturday night.

'Is he being an asshole again?'

My eyes shift from gray to blue as Braden's voice cuts through the fog Aston put me in. 'That's a stupid question, Bray. He's always an asshole.'

Braden grins and jabs Aston in the arm. 'Get your slimy mitts away from her, dude. I told you in Vegas, she's got more fucking class than your usual lot.'

'I know that,' Aston replies, moving his gaze across my face.

I tear my eyes away, trying not to laugh at the irony of Braden's statement. I might have more class than his usual weekenders, but that doesn't mean I'm not one of them. I just won't go and beg for more.

'Coffee?' Maddie mouths across the room, catching my eye. I nod – I want to know how the weekend went for them. Braden's mom can be a little . . . eccentric sometimes.

'I take it he doesn't know?' Aston nudges my foot with his.

I jolt, glancing back to him as Braden sits next to Maddie. 'Um, no. Aside from the fact that's the first time I've seen him, I can't just drop it into a conversation, can I? That would be fun.'

'I guess not.' He rubs his thumb over his mouth. 'Besides—'

'Let me guess,' I deadpan. 'Your face is too good to be messed up by the fist that would inevitably meet it?'

He pauses for a second and smirks. 'I wasn't gonna say that, but I'm glad you think so.'

'You know, Aston, Braden isn't the only one capable of messing up your pretty face.'

'I like a girl feisty.'

'And you also like to discard them after a quick and meaningless fuck, never mind a mere kiss against a wall, so it doesn't really matter, does it?' I raise an eyebrow, feeling the pang of my own harsh words.

He stops, and I turn away. My own words have stung me more than I thought they could. No matter how many times I tell myself I don't care, I do. I care more than I want to. No one wants to be tossed aside like a ragdoll by the person they want to care.

'I never said you were a mere kiss, Megs, neither would be a quick and meaningless fuck. Don't put words in my fucking mouth,' he whispers as the lesson starts. He leans forward, still twirling his pen between his fingers. 'I'm many things and not all of them are good, but I'm not a liar. I'd be lying if I said that kiss was nothing.'

A lump rises in my throat, full of hope and wanting . . . And reality. It's full of emotions that have no place in this conversation. I swallow the words forming in my mouth, the ones full of truth that have no place in a time of doubt, and I swallow the question I don't want to hear the answer to.

All I want to do right now is ignore him and focus on class, but it's nearly impossible. I can feel every inch of him beside me, I can see each movement of his body and I can sense every flicker of his eyes to me.

Aston stretches his leg out under the table and knocks his

foot into mine. I tuck my feet under my chair and sweep my hair to one side so it falls into a curtain between us. I need something to block us – I'm too aware of him and the way he makes me feel.

A tug on my hair pulls me from my forced state of concentration, and my neck almost snaps with the force of my head turning.

'What?' I hiss.

'Are you avoiding me?'

'I'm sitting right next to you. How the hell can I be avoiding you?'

'Well would you be sitting here if you didn't have to?'

'No. But the same applies to every time I have to sit next to you, so today isn't anything special.'

He sits back, his face deathly serious. 'You think I'm a total jackass.'

'Do you want a gold star? I thought it was obvious.' The lessons ends, and I shove all my things in my bag. I stand and hoist it over my shoulder when he grabs my arm.

'Just remember, Megan,' he whispers from behind me, 'who came to who on Saturday night. And I bet you'd do it again in a heartbeat.'

Fuck. Smartass little dick.

I watch him go and I hate that he's right. He might have put his cards on the table, but I'm the one that collected them and shuffled them. That stupid, stupid kiss was my own doing, and we both know it.

We both know I can pretend to hate him. We also both know it's a big bag of bullshit.

'Ready to go?' Maddie holds the door open, and I glare at Aston's retreating back.

'As long as we don't run into anymore assholes while we're there, then let's go,' I mumble.

'What did he do?' she asks with a hint of laughter.

'He's just being Aston.' I shrug. 'You know – his usual Gods-gift-to-women self.'

'Mmph. Was he like that all weekend?'

'I have no idea. I barely saw him,' I lie and inwardly flinch. Damn. I hate lying, yet here I am.

'Probably just as well,' she muses, smoothing her hair back from her face. 'Braden nearly combusted this weekend with the thought he'd left you here in Berkeley around his, and I quote, "will fuck anything with a pulse" friend.'

I force a laugh. 'You'd think Braden has no faith in my ability to stay away from someone like that.'

And rightly so.

Maddie shrugs. 'You know what he's like. Of course his mom heard his frequent use of vulgar words and handed him his ass on a silver platter.'

I laugh loudly and this time it's real. 'Oh, man. I wish I could have seen that!'

'It was hilarious.' She giggles. 'She kept asking me if he's that vile at college.'

'What did you say?' I peruse the board in Starbucks. 'Caramel macchiato, please.'

'I said no and discreetly nodded a yes.' She grins and orders her usual.

'Damn. You know him almost as well as me.'

'I'd take a chance and say I have you beat on that.'

'And you can stay that way in that department,' I mutter, grabbing my coffee.

'Honestly though, I thought he was gonna kill his mom the amount of times she embarrassed him.' She giggles and we sink into armchairs. 'I've never seen a guy before.'

I smile, the caramel scent drifting up from my cup. 'Braden is a serious blusher. You'd never believe it, but if you get it right you'll have him blushing like a high school freshman who just found out her skirt has been tucked into her panties all day.'

Maddie snorts. 'So I found out. It's cute. And, Megs . . . Did he really shave her cat?'

I choke on my mouthful of coffee and nod, hitting my chest. 'I wanted a poodle, but my parents refused. Braden thought he'd be my savior and he shaved the cat. It looked nothing like a poodle, and we both ended up getting grounded for two weeks.'

'His mom told me that. She also said you both spent half that time in your rooms, leaning out of your windows and yelling at passersby in the hope that she and your mom would get so annoyed they'd unground you.'

The smile on my face widens as I remember. Our houses are set so they face each other, both with huge yards wrapping around. We both had the side rooms, the ones that faced the main street, and we'd lean out of them talking to each other all day until someone walked past. Then we'd shout and scream about how we'd been locked away unfairly by an evil witch.

Needless to say, I wasn't allowed to watch *Sleeping Beauty* or read *Rapunzel* for a long time. In fact, my parents confiscated all my fairy tales for about a month. That didn't go down well. At all.

'So, did anything happen here?'

'The usual. Nothing exciting.' I shift in my seat.

'In other words, Kay drank too many shots and offended someone, Lila sneaked off with Ryan, and Aston took some girl back to his room and pissed her off two hours later.'

'Pretty much,' I agree, choosing not to correct her about Aston. It's only a half lie, anyway . . .

'And you, as always, turned down advances from the numerous hot guys and disappeared back to your room. Right?' She raises a skeptical eyebrow.

'Right.'

'Braden wasn't here breathing down your neck and you didn't take advantage of that?'

'Nope.' Kind of no, anyway.

'Wow.' She cocks her head to the side and smiles. 'You really do need to get laid.'

'Wow.' I mirror her movement, trying not to laugh at her. 'You really do spend too much time with Braden.'

She opens her mouth, pauses, and closes it again, her eyes widening. 'Oh my God. You're right. He's turning me into a female Frat brother!'

'Join a sorority?'

'I don't think I'm quite sorority material. Plus a good half of them have likely slept with my boyfriend and hate me because I'm the one that got him.'

'Ah, that would be awkward.'

'Mhmm.'

'Where is Braden anyway? Not like him to let you leave his side,' I tease her.

'Ha ha.' She rolls her eyes but smiles. 'He's gone to sort all his crap out. In other words, interrogate Aston and make sure he didn't pull his usual tricks and get into your pants.'

Wow.

'And he thinks Aston would tell him even if he did?' My eyebrows get stuck somewhere between a frown and raising in disbelief.

'Apparently,' she mutters. 'Just like you'd tell me if you did, right?'

'Uh, no.' I laugh, biting back the uncertainty that tried to creep into my words. Dammit.

'So you might have slept together?' Maddie's green eyes sparkle over her cup.

'No.'

'Right. So you might have because you're gonna tell me no anyway.'

'Maddie, stop putting words in my mouth.'

'It didn't work, did it?' She pouts.

'No, because nothing happened.' I bang the table. 'Nothing.'

Nothing anyone needs to know about. And no one needs to know, so nothing happened.

That logic works a lot better in my head than I'd imagine it would outside of it.

Aston

I glare at Braden. 'For the tenth fucking time, I did not sleep with Megan this weekend.' But not for a lack of damn well trying.

Braden folds his arms across his chest. 'She seemed more pissed at you than usual in class.'

I shrug a careless shoulder. 'Probably because I pissed her off more than normal on Saturday night.'

Ryan grins. 'She did look like she wanted to wring your balls after you spoke to her at the bar.'

'Yeah well, even if she did wring them, I wouldn't have been hard pressed to find someone to kiss them better afterwards, would I?'

'Shit, man.' Braden shakes his head and sits down. 'Was I really this much of a fucking asshole before Maddie?'

Ry throws his cell in the air and catches it. 'Yep.'

'Difference with me and you, dude,' I say, 'is that *I* can admit I'm an asshole. You thought you were fuckin' Jesus or somethin'.'

'That's because I am – behind closed doors.' He grins like the smug bastard he is. 'At least you didn't try it with Megan.'

'I don't know why you're so worried. Megan has more brains than to give the goods to this dickhead.' Ry cocks his thumb in my direction, and I flip him the bird.

'You say this, but I'm the only one here with my freedom left. Your girls have your dicks in the palms of their hands,' I remind them.

'And what magical damn hands they are.' Ryan snickers.

'What? You never felt a magic hand before Lila?' I throw at him. 'I guess I'm the blessed one.'

'Blessed with the ability to snake your way into bed with anyone you want to,' Braden continues.

'Because you didn't have the same ability. I must have imagined all the half-dressed girls doing the sweet walk of shame from your bedroom.'

'One day, Aston, you're gonna end up just like us.'

'If I ever end up as pussy-whipped as you, please, fuckin' punch me.' I snort. 'But that's not gonna happen, trust me.'

Being pussy-whipped means feeling – and I don't do that. I don't let myself do that. Feeling means remembering, and remembering is a load of shit. Besides, the one girl that could make me is the one girl that's off-limits.

And that's a damn good thing. If I can't have her, I can't feel for her, and if I can't feel, I can't hurt her. Because I would. Eventually. Eventually the walls would build back up, push her out, and I would fall back on the only feelings that matter.

The physical ones. The ones that involve a pair of legs around my waist.

You're just like her. It'll be all you're fuckin' good for.

'Dude?' Ryan claps his hands once. 'You there?'

'Yeah.' I pull myself from my head. 'Thought I saw somethin'.'

'You say you won't find anyone, but you will,' Braden continues. 'Trust me. And it'll be the girl with balls big enough to stand up to you and put your spindly little dick in its place.'

'If there's a girl that can tame me I'll welcome the challenge.' I lean back. 'I'd like to see someone try. Gotta feel to be tamed, boys, and I don't feel a thing except for whoever it is in my bed on a weekend.'

'I didn't feel anything. Then I had to play Maddie.' Braden pauses, running his hand through his hair and focusing on me. 'Some things are just too real to be ignored.'

'See? Pussy-whipped.' I snort. 'Don't you two fuckers have something better to do than sit here and tell me I need love in my life?'

'Probably.' Ry grins again. 'But this is way more fun.'

'What's fun?' Lila asks, strolling into the room and looking at Ryan.

'Annoying Aston.' He reaches for her, gripping her hands and pulling her down onto his lap.

She groans. 'You do realize an annoyed Aston usually equals sex, which means there'll be a pissed-off girl hounding us?'

'Really?' I sit up straight. 'Girls do that?' *Well damn. I knew I was good, but . . .*

Lila's eyes are as flat as her voice when she turns to me. 'Yes. It's like they think that because I'm Ryan's girlfriend, I have a VIP pass inside your head. I don't, thank God, but they don't get that. They all want to know why you don't call.'

'Hey, I never promise to call them. I don't offer and they don't ask. Half of them don't even leave their numbers!'

Lila raises her eyebrows, and both the guys laugh.

'They don't!' I insist. 'It's not my fault. How the fuck can I call if they don't leave their number?'

'Maybe they want you to ask for it.'

'If I ask for it, then they'd expect me to call.'

'The problem is—?'

'I won't call. If I ask for it then they have a real reason to be pissed off when I don't.'

She sighs and drops her head, looking back at Ryan. He fights his smile. 'Is there no way to attach a warning to him?'

'Like what, babe?' Ryan sputters.

'"Sex addict asshole who won't call, so don't even bother?"'

'That would seriously damage my reputation!' I protest.

Lila rolls her eyes and shoves herself off of Ryan's lap. She heads toward the door, stopping and looking over her shoulder at me before she passes through. 'You hardly have a stellar reputation, Aston. What you need to do is have one night with a *nice* girl. You never know – you might like it. It might change your asshole perspective on things.'

'Eh, she's got a point.' Braden shrugs.

'Assholes.' I stand and follow her through the door, taking the stairs two at a time up to my room.

I'm so fucking done with that conversation.

I nearly had one night with a nice girl. That *almost* ruined me because I can't imagine being with anyone else other than her now. I can't stop thinking about what would have – and fucking well should have – happened after that kiss. Whenever I look at her now, I picture her lying on my bed beneath me and wrapped around my body.

The guys see the Aston I want them to see. They don't see the fucked up mess inside – they don't see the real Aston. I don't intend to show the real me to anyone. Ever.

You aren't worth shit.

I let my bedroom door swing shut behind me, pushing back the echo in my mind.

I know I'm not worth shit. I don't need a ghost from my past to remind me of that.

I had shivered in the corner, waiting, wondering. The thin blanket I wrapped around my body did nothing to block out the chill coming from my open window – the open window my six-year-old body was too small to reach.

She said she'd come back. She'd promised she would, but she took too long and he went to find her. I didn't know his name, but he said she was gonna get it this time. He was angry.

I rubbed the top of my leg, flinching and trying not to cry at the stinging pain there. It was always my fault. This time it was because Mommy took too long and I cried. I don't know who he is but I don't like him. He hurt more than the last one. He had bigger arms to hit me with.

'Mommy?' I whispered into the silent darkness. I was scared. Alone and scared. Where was my mommy? Why wasn't she home yet? I rubbed at my eyes to stop myself crying.

I wanted Mommy to come home before he did. If he came home first he would hurt me again.

'Mommy?'

Megan

'He really is an asshole,' Kay says, spying Aston across the yard.

He's standing in front of a girl with more highlights than my e-reader, and she's doing her best to push up her chest into his face. He smiles slowly at her, resting his arm against the tree next to him. She twirls some hair around her finger, attempting what she thinks is a demure smile, and looks into his eyes.

'I see he took the conversation we had two days ago to heart,' Lila remarks.

'What conversation was that?' Maddie asks.

'I told him he needed to find a nice girl.'

'You obviously have different definitions of the word "nice",' I say, harsher than I mean to. 'Because the only thing nice about her will be when she turns around and leaves.'

Kay snorts. 'I freaking love it when you guys get jealous.'

My head snaps round. 'Who said I was jealous?'

'You're so green you're practically blending in with the grass.'

'Right. Because being jealous of anyone with Aston is so likely.'

Yet I am jealous. I'm pissed. I'm disgusted. And I'm even more annoyed at myself for the clenching in my chest. I knew he'd be back to his usual tricks straight away, but seeing him this close to another girl when that was me just days ago pisses me the hell off.

Seeing him with another girl when he was mine, even if just for a few minutes, is like a clawed hand reaching into my chest and ripping out my heart. Even if I walked away from that kiss.

And that's all it was. A kiss. When will I get this into my thick damn head?

Aston nods to the girls, smirks, and walks across the yard. He drops onto the ground next to me and looks at me.

'What?' My eyes flick over his face.

'Nothing.'

'Did Barbie have to go get her implants adjusted or something?' I snap, shifting away from him. Ugh.

Hello, irrational Megan.

It would be easier if I could get a little box to stuff this jealousy in. We'll bundle it in with the rolling stomach and clenching heart. What a tidy little package that'd be.

'She's not my type.'

'Are you gonna call her?' Lila asks.

'Yep, we're going.' Maddie grabs Kay's arm and pulls her up and after her.

Aston snorts and glances at me. 'No.'

'Does she think you are?'

He shrugs. 'How am I meant to know?'

I disguise my snort by covering my mouth with my hand. My half-annoyed, half-amused snort.

'What?' he asks.

'Nothing.' I shake my head. 'You get with stupid girls, y'know.'

'I do, huh?' He turns his face toward me slowly, his gray eyes challenging me.

'Yeah, you do.' I run a thick blade of grass between my fingers, focused on him. 'If I were them, I'd be shocked if you *did* call – hey, I'd be shocked if you even text. I mean, the girl who speaks to you the day after sleeping with you would have to be something, right? Hell, the girl who speaks to you after kissing you would have to be someone pretty damn special.'

'Depends when I spoke to her,' he replies evenly.

'The morning after?' I vocally challenge what's in his eyes and silently send him one of my own.

You told me it meant something. I call bullshit.

'If I spoke to her the next morning, then it'd mean she's

more than a fuck – or a *mere kiss*. It'd mean she meant some-thing. That she was someone pretty damn special.'

Throw my words back at me, you bastard.

I guess I lose this round.

My heart pounds painfully in my chest, twisting and scrunching as what I can never have is dangled openly in front of my face. *We* are being dangled openly, for everyone to see, but they'll never know. An open secret, a complete contradic-tion of itself.

'Then it's a good thing no girl has ever got that morning chat, huh?' I ask quieter, forcing the hard edge into my voice.

Gray eyes flick to my lips, making me part them and draw in a breath at the intensity in his stare. Every time. Every damn time those eyes get me.

Aston rubs his chin, studying me carefully. 'Yeah, it is, isn't it?' he replies just as quietly as I did.

Lila coughs and I look away from Aston. Her eyes flick between us and I grab my bag strap.

'I have to get to class. See ya later.' I get up and leave without looking back.

Lila is the teenage girl version of Sherlock Holmes. If she has any suspicion someone is up to something she'll follow your ass around until she's got to the bottom of it. If we're not careful, she'll have us figured in a heartbeat.

But, as I walk back onto the main campus, I can't stop thinking about what he said.

He said I meant something. A kiss meant more than the endless stream of one-night stands he's had over the last few months. How is that possible?

Huh . . . It doesn't matter anyway. It can't happen. That mind-blogging, knee-quaking, heart-pounding kiss shouldn't have happened, so anything else definitely shouldn't happen.

But what if 'anything else' is sex? I walked away from that once. Stupid or smart, I don't know. Yet . . . what if we both want that more? And what if sex turned into more? Like a relationship . . . Or love. What would happen then?

Psh. Love and Aston in the same sentence? If there was such

a thing as too many books, I might agree with Lila when she says I read too many. People don't just change and neither do their actions. I don't believe for one minute he could flip a switch and go from man-whore to a one woman man.

Knowing this makes it all the easier to fight my want for him.

But in the slim chance something did change – and we're talking very freaking slim here . . . There just isn't a chance on this Earth I'd be able to fight anything if he wanted me the way I do him.

Maddie and Lila loop their arms through mine, and I'm not surprised when we begin to head in the direction of Starbucks.

'Why do I get the feeling I'm not going to like whatever conversation we're about to have?' I groan.

Maddie shrugs. 'I have no idea.'

'It could be, oh, I don't know . . . Maybe the fact you've both grabbed me and directed me toward the "chat room" of Starbucks?' I deadpan, looking to Lila. 'And the fact Lila has that grin on her face means she's up to no good.'

'Okay.' Lila sighs as she pushes the door open. 'Go sit down. I'll get coffee.'

'This is not good,' I mutter to myself. 'What did she do? What did she break? Oh, hell. Don't tell me she deleted my essay from my laptop again.'

'Nothing.' Maddie pushes me down into an armchair and sits opposite me. 'She didn't *do* anything. And you know that was an accident.'

'Mmph. Well she's about to do something, and if she's buying me coffee I don't think I'm gonna like it much.'

'Well, it's a "maybe baby" situation.' She taps her chin. 'You're either gonna love it or hate it, but I don't think it matters—'

'Because I'm gonna do it anyway,' Lila sings, setting a tray on the table in front of us.

'I'm not going to lie to you, I'm starting to get a little scared.' I look between the two of them, from Maddie chewing her lip to Lila's sparkling eyes.

'Just tell her, Lila!' Maddie cries. 'Before she takes that coffee and throws it on you!'

I grab my coffee and point it in Lila's direction. Nothing like making a point.

'Okay! So, I've been thinking,' she begins.

'Which is never a good thing,' I interrupt.

'Whatever. I've noticed you're the only single one bar Kay – and I'd never dream of doing this to her.'

'Damn, you noticed I'm single?'

'She's always off with some, er, someone, I'm with Ryan, and Maddie with Braden, leaving you all alone.'

'Oh no.' I know exactly where she's going with this.

'So I was thinking you need a guy—'

'No.'

'So then you won't be all alone. Obviously Aston is out of the question . . .'

Obviously. 'No.'

'And Braden will kick your ass if you try and set her up with anyone in the frat house,' Maddie points out.

'But the frat house is only a small portion of the incredibly yummy guys in this campus. I mean, come on.' Lila looks around a little and leans forward, lowering her voice. 'Have you seen James Lloyd lately? Holy shit! He's in my math class and he really is hot as hell.'

'Boyfriend,' Maddie reminds her with a sigh. 'Point is, Megs, we don't want you to feel left out.'

'Have I ever said I feel left out?' I look at them both again. 'Well, no . . .'

'But I feel like you are,' Lila presses. 'And I don't want you to be. Y'know, in the name of friendship and female loyalty everywhere, it really is in your best interests to let me set you up with some hot guy.'

'In my best interests or in yours?' I raise an eyebrow.

'Yours, definitely yours.'

'And what if I say no?'

'Oh, that doesn't matter.'

Oh no. I sit upright and my hands grip the arms of the chair as I stare at her. 'You haven't, Lila. You haven't.'

'She has.' Maddie nods her head.

Lila grins. 'You have a date tomorrow night to Mark's party.'

I can't think of anything worse than Lila setting me up with someone. Her taste in guys is questionable. Very questionable. I've been here twenty minutes and I'm starting to feel like Harriet in Jane Austen's *Emma*. God knows Lila's matchmaking skills are on par with Emma's. They're both crap. The only thing Lila has going for her is Ryan – she figured her love life out way before Emma did.

I know every single date Lila sends me on is destined to crash and burn because of the way I feel about Aston. Of course there's no way to explain that without digging myself a giant hole. There's no way to explain every guy will pale in comparison to his cocky, self-assured smirk and forceful, needing kiss. Goddamn that kiss . . .

Six days, and I'm still here grasping onto a memory of what could have been. Six days, and the knowledge I did the 'right' thing is slowly turning into regret for not doing the wrong thing. Knowing I did the right thing is twisting my stomach.

But who is it the right thing for? Braden?

Something might be the right thing for someone else but that doesn't mean its right for you.

Right thing or not, I'd still be here having this date. I'd still be sitting mere meters from Aston sweeping into the kitchen, pretending to give a crap about something that isn't his eyes burning holes into me.

I slam the shot glass down on the bar after emptying it. Christ, I've become that girl. Alcohol to tolerate a date.

'So,' the guy opposite me says. 'You look a little bored.'

I laugh lightly. 'No, I'm sorry. I just had a rough day, y'know?'

He nods. Shit. What's his name? Ugh, stupid frat boys are

rubbing off on me. I sweep my hair to one side, smoothing it away from my face, and lean in close. 'Why don't you tell me more about yourself?'

And your name. Please.

'Well, I'm majoring in Biology . . .'

And I've switched off. I don't mean to, I really don't, but science is pretty much Chinese Mandarin to me. It's too realistic; I deal with fiction. I do swoon-worthy scenes, heart stopping declarations of love, and incredible guys that give girls like me unrealistic expectations.

Disney, I'm looking at you.

I pull my glass toward me and take a drink through my straw, nodding my head and pretending to be interested in Mr. Biology. Pretending because my attention is on the dark-haired girl standing in front of Aston. Closely. Very closely.

He picks up a bottle of beer and looks up. As if he can feel me looking at him, his eyes slam into mine. They're flat, almost emotionless, almost dead, and I go cold. Nothing. That's what I get from this. Nothing.

I smile but I don't feel it. I only feel an irrational annoyance bubbling in my stomach and that coldness from his gaze spreading through my body.

'Hey.' I lean forward and place a gentle hand on Mr. Biology's arm. 'I'm so sorry, but I'm not feeling great. I'm gonna head to my dorm.'

'Oh. Um, sure. I can walk you back.' He makes to move.

'No!' I take a deep breath. 'No, I'm okay, thank you. It's not too late.'

'Oh, sure.'

'Thank you for a nice evening.' I smile weakly and get up, spinning around.

Nice, Megan? Is that all you have? God.

My lack of convincing adjectives aside, I need to get the hell out of this frat house.

He – Aston Banks – is taking me over. He's grabbing hold of me and shaking me like a martini.

I push open the front door and step into the mild California evening air. I take a deep breath, heading back to the dorm room with a hasty step.

I need to make like Cinderella at midnight.

Aston

Time goes too fast. Too fucking fast.

Since I kissed Megan, I've slowly retreated into my own mind. Every day brings a fresh set of memories, slicing open a fresh set of scars. Every day cuts open a new wound that bleeds for hours. Every set of memories starts a fresh onslaught of cuts inside my mind that will never heal. Each one has its own shape, its own meaning, its own pain.

Each one is a reminder of why I can't give Megan what she deserves. Each one is a reminder why I should have stayed away from her in the first place and why I should now.

Broken. Shattered. Mismatched.

They're the first three words I think of when I have to describe myself. They spring to mind instantly.

Useless. Worthless. Nothing.

They're the next three. The words that were drummed into my mind so many times, by so many voices, for so long. They're the words that creep under your skin, worm their way into you and never leave.

A good word can linger with you for a few fleeting moments while a bad one will never leave.

It's too close to the words that both shattered and made my life. The words that broke and saved me.

She's gone.

I rub the heels of my hands in my eyes, bending forwards, and take a deep breath. This . . . Thinking of her this weekend, the woman who was supposed to protect me no matter the cost, is inevitable, I know. That doesn't mean I want to. It doesn't

mean I have any fucking intention of remembering the woman
I have to call my mother.

I stand abruptly, storming across the room and yanking open
my door. I leave it to slam behind me as I fly down the stairs
to where music is pounding for a sophomore, Mark's, birthday
party, and grab a bottle of beer from the fridge. I uncap it,
raising the rim to my lips and letting the cold liquid run down
my throat. I need to forget. I don't care who I forget with, I
just need to forget all the shit of before.

It'd be a lot fucking easier if Megan Harper hadn't ruined
me for all other girls. It would certainly be a lot fucking easier
if I wasn't comparing all girls' lips to the soft, rosy pinkness of
hers, or their eyes to the never-ending blue of hers.

Yeah. It'd be a lot easier if last weekend had never happened.

I catch the gaze of a girl across the kitchen. Her dark eyes
give me a once over, and she flicks her black hair over her
shoulder curving her lips into a smile. I lean against the end
of the bar, taking in her slim figure. She saunters over to me
confidently and gives me a dazzling smile.

'Can I help you?' I smirk, twirling the beer bottle between
my fingers.

She steps closer, and my eyes drop to her chest. Her boobs
are almost spilling from her top, black lace creeping up above
the neck of her shirt.

'I'm not sure,' she says in a sultry tone. 'But I'm pretty sure
I can help you.'

She trails a fingertip down my arm, leaning in even closer.
Woah – I'm all for forward girls, but this chick has never heard
of personal space.

I step back slightly. 'And how can you do that?'

'Wouldn't you just like to know?' She runs her tongue across
her top lip in a move I'm sure she thinks is sexy, but it just
isn't doing it for me tonight.

I catch the bob of a blonde head over her shoulder and flick
my eyes there. Megan downs a shot and slams the glass on the
table, glancing over her shoulder and glaring at the girl in front

of me. The guy next to her says something, and I hear her laugh softly, the sound riling me. She leans in closer to him, smoothing her hair round to one side. Her legs are crossed on the stool, her tight black skirt riding up the smooth skin of her thigh.

The thighs I want wrapped around my neck and my waist.

I drink a little, ignoring the girl in front of me, and watch as Megan purses her lips around a straw.

The lips I want against mine.

Her hand runs through her hair, fluffing it up and letting it fall down in a messy style.

The hand I want to thread my fingers through while I hold her under me, messing up her hair in a totally different way.

God. Fucking. Damn.

She glances back over her shoulder, her blue eyes icy as they meet mine. She smiles but there's nothing genuine about it. Her head turns, and she says something to the guy before she disappears through the crowd.

I give my attention to the girl in front of me, not really seeing her. 'Look, babe, you're not really my type. Try that guy at the other end of the bar. He looks like he could use some of your help.' I nod to the guy Megan was just talking to and take off, leaving the girl disgruntled behind me.

I leave the frat house, the air outside getting colder as Berkeley slowly moves into winter, and cross the street to the main campus – and the girls' dorms. Thanks to her sharing with Lila, I know her building and her room number and I know that's where she'll be.

I'm not thinking about what I'm doing. I'm not thinking about who this could hurt, what could happen after this, or even how I'm gonna feel. All I can think about is Megan and her helping me forget.

If I can't forget about her, I need to forget my past *with* her tonight.

Tomorrow, I'll deal with the shit fallout that's bound to come. I'll deal with the crap in my head from yet another bad decision.

I wink at the pair of girls that let me into her dorm block

and take the stairs two at a time to her floor. I knock on her door twice and lean against the doorframe.

'There's no one here,' she shouts.

I bang again. 'Open this fucking door, Megan, or so help me, I'll break it down.'

The lock clicks and it creaks open. She pokes her face through the gap. 'What the hell are you doing here?'

I nudge her into the room and shut the door, turning to twist the key in the lock. Her room is tidy, a stark contrast to the mess of mine, and it's so Megan. Books are piled high on her desk, both schoolwork and otherwise, and although she's hiding it, I can see the stuffed toys under the bed. Clothes are strung over the chair in the corner, and judging by the tidy bed next to it, I'm guessing they're Lila's.

'Hello, Aston? What the hell are you doing here?' she repeats.

I look down at her and run my hand through my hair. 'Honestly? I have no fucking idea.'

'Was that girl not "your type?" Her boobs too far inside her top for you?' Megan raises her eyebrows.

'Jealousy isn't a good look on you, Megs.' I spin so I'm right in front of her and her back is against the door.

She tilts her head up, looking at me defiantly, and her shirt slips off her shoulder slightly. 'I'm not the one who looked like they wanted to rip someone's head off at that party.'

I flatten my hands on the door either side of her head, boxing her in, and move my face toward hers. My eyes search the blue in front of me. 'And I'm not the one who looked like they wanted to rip out someone's extensions,' I say quietly. 'Who's the jealous one, Megan?'

'You,' she whispers. 'I have nothing to be jealous of.'

'You're right.' I drop one of my hands to her waist, flexing my fingers. She clenches a fist, looking at me steadily. 'You don't have anything to be jealous of, because I'm here and not there.'

'And why exactly are you here?'

I stare at her, barely breathing, not moving, and the words burn their way up my throat with a feral need to get out.

'Because I need you. I need to feel you again. One kiss . . . One poxy little kiss . . . It wasn't enough. It was nowhere near fucking enough, Megan. It won't ever be enough, not with you. I don't know if anything will be enough.'

Her lips part slightly and her body relaxes a little. Her chest heaves as she takes a breath in. 'You . . .' She swallows, putting a hand against my chest. 'You shouldn't be here.'

'I shouldn't be, but I am.'

'This is wrong.'

'Yep.' I bend my head toward hers. 'But I'm here, Megan. Think whatever the fuck you wanna think, but I'm not going anywhere until I get to kiss you senseless again.'

'I'm not blind, Aston. There's more than just kissing on your mind.'

'I'm not denying that.'

She pauses and closes her eyes for a second. 'You . . . Argh!' She opens her eyes. 'You need to go. I can't . . .'

'Can't what?'

'I can't stand here with you looking at me like that and not do something I'm going to regret.'

I cup the side of her head and stroke my thumb down her cheek. 'You already have though, haven't you? You regret walking away last weekend. I can see it.'

'No.'

'If you didn't regret it you would have kicked me out by now. You wouldn't have even let me in here.' I tilt her face up. 'You know why I'm here and you did before you opened that door.'

Her blue eyes are fixed on mine, and whatever it is she's doing to me wrecks me a little more. Whatever fucked up hold I've allowed this girl to have on my fucked up self has just strengthened a little more.

'Why are you here?' she demands.

'You know.'

'Tell me. God dammit, Aston. Don't hint with me. Don't stand there, pull your usual tricks and think I'll fall into your lap with my knickers down. If you're here for a reason then you tell me now. Are we clear now?'

'Fine,' I whisper, dipping my head so my face is so close to hers you couldn't get a breath between us. I can still see her eyes, though, and they're raging. 'Because it obviously isn't fucking obvious enough – I'm here because I want to finish what we started last weekend. I want to push you into this wall, kiss the crap out of you, then I wanna throw you on your bed and kiss the crap out of the rest of your body. And then, Megan, then I'm gonna sink so deep inside you you'll forget where you end and I begin.'

She swallows, her eyes widening. Her tongue darts out and licks a trail across her lips, sending all the blood in my body down to my cock.

I lean my body into her. 'Are we fucking clear *now*?'

Megan crashes her lips into me, hot and hard. Her fingers dig into my shoulders and her body presses against me, molding to the shape of me. I kiss her harder, making her lean into the wall even more, and I'm straining through my jeans with the force of my need for her.

I move my hands across her body like I'm starved, which I am. I touch and hold, smooth and grip, probe and tickle. I sweep my tongue into her mouth, deeply, desperately, needing and wanting to taste every inch of her mouth. Her back slams into the door, and she whimpers.

Her bottom lip is soft and swollen between my teeth as I tug on it slightly, and groan breathlessly as I release it. She opens her eyes, the heaviness of her lids adding to the fire raging in them. My gaze is steady, my grip on her anything but. I hook my fingers under her shirt, shaking slightly, resisting the urge to rip it away from her beautiful skin. Her heavy breathing races between her lips, and we're so close I can almost taste it.

'Megan,' I whisper, my heart pounding. I know how bad this is. I know nothing good can come from this. Three days ago she was cursing me, hating me, and now she's pinned against her door by me. I embody everything she hates.

But I don't give a shit right now. I need her. I need her so fucking badly it scares me.

Her hands slide across my shoulders and up my neck to the back of my head where she sinks her fingers into my hair, winding it round them. 'Don't,' she breathes out. 'This is wrong. So wrong. But I can't stop myself. I can't stop this time.'

Air rushes from my lungs at her words, and I take her mouth with mine harshly. Her tongue slides across my lips, wriggling slightly at the seam of them. I slide mine out, caressing hers, and I stroke my hands up her back, pulling her from the door slightly. Her kiss is demanding, asking and telling me what she wants at the same time.

I'm powerless to deny her it.

I'm powerless to deny her anything.

Megan picks herself up on shaky arms and legs, and I don't want to let my arms drop away from her the way they do. She grins at me, grabs her clothes, and heads for the small bathroom to the side of her room.

I push myself up onto my elbows, letting my head drop forward for a second, accepting the reality of the situation. The reality being that I am well and truly fucked – and not just in a physical sense. I'm fucked in every way possible.

I shove myself upwards, roll off the condom, and dump it in the trashcan. I wipe myself off with some tissue and get dressed. I'm just about to pull my shirt over my head when I hear the door open and Megan speak in a small voice.

'We have to go and pretend, don't we?' She looks at me, her face earnest. 'We have to go pretend this never happened. Just like last time. But worse.' She drops her eyes to the floor.

I pull my shirt over my head as I cross the room. I stop just in front of her, taking a deep breath.

'Yeah. That's the general idea.'

She sighs heavily, dropping her hand from the doorknob. 'I figured as much.'

'But it doesn't mean we don't have to pretend we don't exist.' I touch her waist before she can move, and she turns her face up to me, her brow furrowed.

'What?'

'I don't feel like getting my ass kicked by Braden, but for some crazy reason me walking out of here without me knowing you'll still be here drives me fucking insane,' I admit, holding her gaze. 'I won't leave here without you promising me you'll still be here, Megan.'

'Here for what? Sex? 'Cause I can get that anywhere, Aston. It's not exclusive to you,' she snaps, pushing me away. 'I'm not gonna do that.'

I grab her back to me, holding her against me. I lower my mouth to her ear and feel the slight tremble in the way she's holding herself.

'I said I needed you tonight. I never said it was just sex. Assuming, Megan. We all know what happens then.'

'Yeah, but you're already an ass, so I didn't think it would make much of a difference.'

My jaw tightens. 'Face it, baby, you need me as much as I need you. Maybe I need you more. I haven't figured that out yet, but believe me, Megan Harper, if I have to walk out of this room without you promising me you're mine, I will come back and chase you down. I will chase you down and if I have to, I will pin you and your naked, trembling body to that damn bed until you say it.'

She heaves in a breath and shivers. Her body relaxes against mine slightly as she wraps her arms around my waist.

'I'll be here,' she says into my chest. 'I don't know . . . I don't know if there was any chance I wouldn't be.'

I tilt her face up and press our lips together. I could regret this. I *will* regret this. Because she makes me feel. She makes me feel human again, like a person instead of like an empty, soulless shell. She makes me feel real, even if it's only for a short time while I'm with her.

I nip her top lip. 'Good,' I say against her mouth. 'Because I was seriously debating the bed pinning.'

She smiles. 'Maybe next time.'

Megan

My bed smells like him, and I'm being a total teenage girl by snuggling under the covers instead of getting up. It's a spicy scent that's so out of place in California, but so right for him.

I feel a little like Juliet right now, secretly in love and holding onto it desperately. Of course that's probably much more suitable for a thirteen year old to do than me, but I'll take it because it's all I have.

The idea of telling Braden crosses my mind. Why not? That's the decent thing to do – the right thing to do. I should just tell him and get it over with. He'll probably ignore me for a few days and okay, punch Aston, but surely that would be easier than pretending?

No, it wouldn't. Telling him would mean admitting that both of us lied about last weekend – kind of. A lie of omission. Telling him would just cause unnecessary pain for all of us. It would tear Braden up and it would tear Aston and me apart before we'd even been together.

But are we even together? I have no idea. No point in telling Braden until I'm completely, absolutely sure, right? There's no point in getting him annoyed over something that might not even be.

Yes. That makes me feel better. A little.

Relationships are shit. They're so much easier to comprehend when they're not real. They make much more sense when I'm lying in bed with my covers over my head, a torch in hand and sneaking another chapter.

★

I snapped off the torch and lay down as Mom opened the door. 'Well? Has Jo realized it yet?'

I took a few deep breaths.

'Megan Harper, you're the worst pretend sleeper this side of the Pacific, so give it up.' She turned on my light, and I sat up.

'Why doesn't she get it, Mom?' I held the book up.

'Jo was a tomboy. She wanted to be fighting with her father, not sitting pretty and looking for a nice man to marry.'

'I know that!' I sighed. 'Laurie is so in love with her and she's blind to it. And anyway, it's not like she went looking for him. She found him by accident.'

Mom laughed quietly and a smile crept onto her face. Her blue eyes regarded me with tenderness and an understanding of my frustration.

'Oh, Meg,' she said softly. 'The best kind of love is the kind that happens by accident.'

I smile at the memory and breathe in deeply, taking one last smell of Aston, and climb out of bed with my selfish decision made. I beat back the guilt bubbling up and step into the shower. The hot water runs over my body, alleviating the tightness from my shoulders. But not the tension. That's still there – but that tension is inside, somewhere the relaxing pounding of the water can't reach.

I climb from the shower and dress quickly, shoving my wet hair up on top of my head with a few clips. The dorm is still quiet, and I expect the only person up in the Frat house will be Lila – if only because she spends more time there than in our dorm room.

My arms hug my jacket tighter around my body as I cross from the main campus to the house. The temperatures are quickly dropping and it's obvious. It's a far cry from Southern California, that's for sure.

I grasp the door handle tightly and pull open the door at the same time it's pushed from the inside. I squeak a little, jumping. Two hands land on my arms, hands I know. I look up straight into gray eyes.

'Careful,' Aston mutters with a smile, rubbing his thumbs across my arms.

'What are you doing up?' I ask. I've never seen him out of bed before eleven unless he has class.

'Going for a run. I can do that, can't I?' He raises an eyebrow, still smiling, and drops his arms. His palms brush my arms and his fingers trail along in their wake. Goose-pimples rise as if it was skin on skin, and my breath catches slightly. His fingertips brush mine as his hands fall away from me completely.

'Of course,' I manage and decide to ask my next question silently. 'Is anyone else up?' I mouth. He nods. 'I'm just surprised you're up this early. I mean, aren't you usually recovering from whatever you dragged upstairs with you last night?'

A muscle under his eye twitches, and it actually hurts me to say it.

'Oh, last night was different to every other night,' he says in his cocky voice. The eyes fixated on mine are softer than the edge in his tone. 'In fact, I don't think I'll be forgetting it any time soon.'

'I'll leave you to your remembering then.' I step to the side, fighting the urge to reach for him the way I did last night.

He moves in closer, his lips brushing my ear. 'Good choice.'

I watch him over my shoulder as he runs off. His shirt is clinging to his body, his legs strong as they beat against the pavement.

Running – that explains that lickable washboard of abs he has going on.

'If he pulled that shit around Braden, his ass would meet the sidewalk.'

I turn around abruptly, coming face to face with Maddie. She's leaning against the banister casually, her eyes on me.

'In fact,' she continues. 'I'm surprised you didn't put him on his ass.'

'What's the point?' I shrug and enter the house. 'It wouldn't bruise his overly large ego any, neither would it slice some of it off.'

'Never stopped you before.'

'I'm learning to pick my battles.'

'And putting an egotistical, arrogant asshole on his ass isn't one of your battles?'

'Nope. Not anymore.' I slide onto a stool in the kitchen and look around. 'Wow. This place was trashed last night.'

'You have no idea.' Maddie starts up the coffee machine. 'So let me guess – Braden was the last egotistical battle you fought?'

'No. I didn't fight that – I merely passed him on to you.' I grin.

'Talking about me again, girls?' The topic of our conversation strolls into the room wearing just a pair of sweatpants. He tosses his shirt at me as he passes. 'I would have thought you'd be doing something productive. Isn't that usually what you two do?'

'Ew. Put that on!' I chuck his shirt back at him. 'I don't want to see you half-naked this early in the morning. In fact, I'm pretty sure I don't ever want to see you half-naked.'

Braden grins and pulls his shirt over his head. 'You're just jealous because you don't have a kickass body like mine.' He wraps his arms around Maddie and pokes his tongue out at me.

I poke back. 'I don't want a body like yours. I'm happy with the girls, thanks very much. You can keep your show-off muscles. And by keep, I mean keep them under your shirt, Bray.'

Maddie rolls her eyes and wriggles out of his hold. 'I don't know how I cope with you two. I'd say you're like brother and sister, but that's true. You bitch like it.'

'It's because despite DNA differences, we are brother and sister,' Braden protests.

'And thank God for those DNA differences!' I take the cup of coffee Maddie offers.

'I agree. Fuck knows what I would have done had I ended up anything like you.'

I purse my lips. 'Watch it, Carter. I know all your dirty little secrets, remember?'

'And I know yours.' He waggles his eyebrows.

No you don't.

'I don't *have* any dirty little secrets. You made sure of that.'

'Damn right I did. But you think I don't know about Sam Carlton in senior year. I do.'

I tilt my head to the side. 'So that's where his black eye came from.'

'Damn right.'

'Are you for real?' Maddie looks at Braden. 'You gave him a black eye because Megan had sex with him?'

'No. I gave him a black eye because *he* had sex with *Megan*,' Braden explains. 'There is a difference.'

I sip my coffee, and Maddie blinks at him. 'You really have been reincarnated from the Stone Age, haven't you? Did you get your big club and swing it at him? Maybe you rode up on the back of a sabre tooth tiger, growling at him?'

I snort, covering my mouth with my hand so I don't spray coffee everywhere.

'There's only one club that gets swung around here—'

'Uh-uh.' She holds her hand up. 'Don't get sexual on me, Braden Carter. No wonder Megan is so uptight. She's not getting any because you're still scaring everyone away!'

'I am not uptight!' I squeak. And I am getting some. So there.

'I don't scare them off!' Braden argues. 'I merely warn them that they could end up meeting my fist should they get her to scratch their itch . . .' he finishes in a mumble against his cup.

'You've been saying that since the beginning of college?' I jump up and touch my forehead. 'Oh my god, Bray!'

'Just a warning,' he mumbles.

'Just a warning?' Maddie shrieks. 'No wonder why out of the four of us girls she's the only one not in a relationship!'

'Hey! Kay isn't in a relationship,' I point out.

'She's in a relationship with sex.' Maddie shrugs. 'Same difference.'

'I haven't warned anyone since . . .' Braden pauses.

'Since we went to your parents' and you told every guy in

this house if they touched her, you'd personally castrate them,' Maddie offers.

'Well, yeah. Then.' He lowers his mug and nibbles at his thumbnail. 'It's the thought that counts, right?'

I narrow my eyes at him and lower myself back to the seat. I can't believe he's actually done that. I knew he was protective of me, but holy shit! This is a whole new level.

This is cementing that what happened with Aston and me has to stay a secret for as long as possible. However uncertain 'we' might be. I can feel the heaviness of the thought solidifying in my mind, getting stronger and stronger until it's a certainty.

'You do realize I can take care of myself, right?' I question him. 'You do realize I'm not nine years old on the monkey bars anymore?'

'I know,' he replies in a slightly softer tone, turning to look at me. 'I just don't want anyone to hurt you, Meggy. You're my best friend. I want you to find the perfect person to fall in love with.'

'What if I have to have a few imperfections on the way?'

He shrugs a shoulder. 'That's what I'm stopping. None of the guys here are good enough for you.'

'You always said you weren't good enough for me,' Maddie mutters.

'I wasn't, Angel, and I'm probably still not. Difference is, I knew I was slowly falling in love with you every day. I can't guarantee that for the asshats in this place. I want someone to love Megan as much as I love you. Hell, I want someone to love Megan as much as *I* do, and if that means I have to fight off every guy that comes calling for her until he comes along, then I will. If there's two people I'll always protect, it's you two.'

Yep. I hate it and it's tearing my insides apart, but Braden can't find out.

'No, Mom, I'm not falling behind.'

'Well, it sounds like a lot of partying goes on at that college.'

'Mom. My grades are fine.'

She exhales, the phone crackling. 'I believe you, Megan, I

just don't like the idea of my baby girl getting herself pregnant by a horny teenage boy.'

'You've been watching too much TV.'

'Well, that *16 and Pregnant* is on just about everywhere these days. It worries me.'

My lips curve. 'No getting pregnant, Mom.'

'Well, at least you're using protection.'

'I never said I was having sex.'

'That will please your father,' she says in a chirpier voice. 'Talking of your father, we're off to dinner tonight so I need to go.'

'Okay. Have fun, and give Dad a kiss from me.'

'I will, Megs. You behave yourself.'

'I always do,' I reply dryly. 'Bye, Mom.' I hang up and drop my phone on the bed, shaking my head. Honestly. It's times like this I remember why I came to Berkeley in the first place.

Close enough to visit, far away enough for freedom. Far away enough not be the perfect little girl I was always expected to be. Granted, I failed that majorly as a kid.

I change into a tank top and bed shorts, ready to settle on my bed with some schoolwork. Mom may believe there are parties every weekend and she may be right there, but it doesn't mean I'm at every party every weekend. Just one a weekend.

I blow out a long breath, ready to tackle the English essay awaiting me, and sit Indian-style. A knock sounds at my window before I can start, and I frown. My window?

I crawl over my bed and push open my curtain and—

Stare right into Aston's face.

He grins.

'What the?' I push the window open. 'Just . . . What?'

'Open the window before I fall out of this fucking tree!' he mutters, still grinning. I open it fully and sit back. He looks around quickly before hooking his leg over the windowsill and launching himself into my room. He falls face first onto the bed, and I lean over his legs to pull the window and curtains shut.

'Um,' I say as he gets up.

'What?' He kicks his shoes off and sits in front of me.

I look at the window and back to him, pointing between them both in confusion. 'Did you actually just climb up a tree and through my window?'

'Yep.'

'Why?'

Aston puts his hands flat either side of me and leans forward, the tip of his nose barely touching mine. 'Because I wanted to come see you.'

I raise an eyebrow, not moving. 'Mhmm.'

'So since this whole thing is secret I thought I'd pull some ninja moves. I always wanted to be a *Teenage Mutant Ninja Turtle*, y'know.' He leans forward, pressing his lips to mine, and I smile at his touch.

'Who were you?'

'Who was I?'

'Which turtle were you? Don't you know you were defined by your choice of turtle?'

He sits back a little, his head tilted to the side. 'Really?'

I nod. 'Oh, yeah. You had to be the right turtle, or you weren't cool at all. Who were you?'

His brows draw together slightly as he frowns. 'Donnatello.'

'You were cool.' I press my hand to his cheek and smooth out the wrinkle in his forehead. 'Why did you frown?'

'I don't remem . . . I was thinking.' He shakes his head a little and takes my hand from his face, linking his fingers through mine. He looks at our clasped hands for a second, turning them slightly. His palm is rough and his hand is a lot bigger, almost encompassing mine completely.

Silence stretches between us for a second, and I flick my eyes up to his. He's frowning again, his light gray eyes darker. His lips are pursed and his grip on my hand tightens, making me flex my fingers.

'Aston?' I ask softly, my free hand hovering between us, unsure of whether or not to touch him. I want to. A part of him looks vacant, so incredibly lost it's not even there, and I want to grab him and keep him in together.

He loosens his grip on my hand and focuses his eyes on

mine. 'Sorry . . . I just . . . thought of something. It doesn't matter.'

'Are you okay?' I shuffle a little closer to him, my hand deciding to rest against his neck.

He nods. 'I'm . . . fine.'

I pull his face down to mine and touch my mouth to his softly. His hand snakes to my back, pulling me against him, and I find my body flush against his. He leans me back, slowly lowering my body against my bed, and lies over me. I run my foot along his leg as he runs his tongue through my mouth, kissing me the same way he did last night.

Deeply. Desperately.

And he pulls away, resting his forehead against my shoulder briefly, and he takes his hands from mine. He shoves himself up and walks across the room without a word.

What? What just happened?

I sit up, my confused eyes on him as he presses his hands against his forehead and takes a few deep breaths. 'Aston?'

'I won't do it,' he mutters, digging his hands into his forehead. 'I won't do it.'

So many things are going around my mind I don't even know if I can put them into words. I'm staring at him and his hunched shoulders, his tensed muscles, and I have no idea what he means.

'Do what?' I ask quietly.

'I won't . . . use you. Not like that. Not. That. Way. Not anymore.' He drops his hands and exhales raggedly. 'Not you.' His hands are shaking by his sides, and as if he knows I can see it he clenches his fists.

I stand and quietly move across the room, stopping just behind him. I wrap my hand around one of his clenched fists and lean my cheek against his shoulder, my other hand wrapping around his front. I splay my fingers against his stomach, feeling his whole body heave as he takes deep breaths. He drops his head back against my shoulder, turning his face into my hair, and shudders.

This is a side I've never seen. Granted, I've never seen the side of Aston that climbs through a window, either, but this . . . This feels like a stranger. This feels like an Aston that should only exist in a parallel universe. This feels like nothing I ever imagined he could be.

Only I don't know what he is. I thought he was a 'get what you see and see what you get' kinda guy. Now I think I was wrong. Now I think – no, I know – there's a side to him he's never shown anyone, that he keeps buried deep inside. Judging by the tightness of his body, the pounding of his heart, and his slightly erratic breathing, it's a side he doesn't want shown.

But it's a side I want to see. A side I want to know. A side a part of me wants to fix, because something tells me it's a side that's a little bit broken.

Aston

You're worth nothing. You're no better than your whore of a mother.

Her body against mine. Hand on hand. Skin on skin.

You think anyone will ever want you, you brat? They won't.

The softness of her hand against mine.

You are nothing.

The gentle aroma of vanilla that's settling on her hair.

No one will want you. Megan. You're no better than her. I'm not there. Little rat. I'm here. With Megan.

Megan.

The warmth of her body against my back grounds me, holding me in the now when all my mind wants to do is give in and go back. Give in and go back to the time of my life I don't want anyone exposed to. The time I don't want Megan exposed to.

I know I need to leave. Now. I need to push her window open and climb down that fucking tree.

Instead I turn and hold her to me.

My hands splay across her back, my fingertips digging into her skin, and she wraps her arms around my waist. Her face presses into my neck and she brushes her lips across my collarbone, a feather-light touch. My grip tightens on her and I push my face into my hair again, the ends tickling my nose. I shake my head slightly, holding her ever tighter.

Sex. Sex doesn't hurt – it can't hurt anyone. *It's all you'll be good for.* My fall back and way of coping. *Just like her.* The thing that keeps the demons at bay and stops them clawing at the corners of my mind.

This weekend, thirteen years since Mom died, the demons are stronger than ever. The memories of that weekend flood my mind and there isn't anything I can do to stop them.

Except hold Megan.

I have no idea what it is about her, but I know that I need her. And I know that for all my forgetting over the years, she makes me remember. For that, I should push her away. I should run away screaming.

But the pain from remembering is nothing compared to the softness of her touch when she takes that pain away.

And that's why I won't use her, not in the way I've become so accustomed to.

I breathe in deeply and turn my face toward Megan's, nuzzling the side of her head with my nose. 'Lila will be at the house tonight?'

She nods against me. 'Always on a weekend.' Her hands rub along my back in a soothing motion, slipping under my shirt, her hands like silk against my skin. Her fingers probe gently, coaxing my clenched muscles into relaxation.

'I want to stay,' I whisper. 'Let me stay.'

She pulls back, taking one hand from my back and running it around my body. It climbs up my stomach and chest, finally resting against the side of my face. I open my eyes to meet her wide blue ones, the soft safety of them drawing me in.

'Of course,' she replies quietly. 'Whatever you need.'

I let out a shaky breath. 'I just need to be with you.'

Megan reaches up on tiptoes and kisses me softly. 'All night?'

I can't miss the wariness of her tone, two simple words riddled with uncertainty. My hands frame her face and I rest my forehead against hers.

'All night.'

Just Megan.

We move back to her bed and climb under the covers. Her body tucks into mine perfectly, my arms circle her like they were made to, and my heart pounds to a beat only she can hear.

My fucked-up coping mechanisms are trying to take over

and it's hard not to give in. Hell, I want to watch her give herself over to me. I want to watch her body arch and feel her muscles tighten as she lets go. I want to see the sparkle in her eye, hear the cry leave her body, feel her nails in my back.

But I have to remember it's Megan. She's more than any other girl. She's something I don't deserve yet, something I can't give up.

I pull her tighter to me and bury my face in her hair. The soft strands tickle my face and I breathe in deeply. She stretches an arm over my stomach and threads her legs through mine, tangling us together, and leans her head back to kiss my neck softly.

In this moment she is mine. She might not be tomorrow, next week, next month, but right now . . . She's fucking mine.

So I let myself hold her, wondering if there's a chance she'll ever know the peace she brings me.

Megan eyes me speculatively. 'I have a question.'

'It's never good when you have a question.' I grin.

'It's not that bad!'

'Oh, yeah? Like that time in English when you promised it wasn't a big question and kept the prof talking for half the class?'

She shrugs a shoulder, smiling a little. 'Hey, it made for an easy class!'

I lean forward, putting my face to hers. 'And a fuck-off essay after.'

'Um, yeah.' She smiles cutely, wrinkling her nose. 'Anyway . . .'

'Go on, then.' I hope to shit she doesn't ask—

'Yesterday, when I asked which turtle you were.' Shit. 'You . . . You seemed to go somewhere else. Like . . . you had no idea what I was talking about.'

I sit back, words and excuses swirling in my mind. 'I was home-schooled,' I answer tentatively. 'So I never really knew all that stuff. My Gramps taught me.'

'Your Gramps? Why not your mom? Or dad?'

Of all the days she asks me today. She asks me on the one day I can't talk about it.

'I can't . . .' I get up. 'I can't have this conversation today, Megs. Any day but today.'

'He's in here somewhere.'

I had moved further into the corner of my bedroom, hugging my blanket tighter. Mommy still wasn't home. I was still waiting, and now some funny lady was in my house talking about 'he'. Was she here for me?

No. I didn't want to leave Mommy. They always said it would happen, the big men. They always said that one day they would take me from my mommy.

I covered my face with my hands so they couldn't hear me breathing and slipped under my bed. I moved back to the darkest corner, shaking and trying not to cry.

I don't want to leave my mommy. I don't want them to take me away.

My bedroom door opened, and I shook harder. No. Don't let them find me. Please. The light flicked on, and I could hear their footsteps across my bare wooden floor. I could see the shadows as they walked further.

'Have you checked under the bed?' one woman asked.

'No. I'll do that.'

Nonononono. Don't find me. Please don't find me.

A kind face appeared and morphed into a gentle, coaxing smile. The woman held out her hand. 'Come on now, honey. Let's get you out of here.'

I shook my head, shrinking back further. 'I want Mommy,' I whispered.

'I don't have her, sweetheart, but I can help you. You're shaking, are you cold?'

I nodded.

'I have a nice thick blanket here for you. And some cookies – you like cookies?'

'Cookies?' I frowned.

'Yes. They're really yummy and these ones have chocolate chips. Would you like to try one?'

I had no idea what she was talking about, but I was hungry. I scooted forwards a little bit. 'A cookie?'

'Yes. Come out from under your bed, we'll get you warm and you can have a cookie. Okay, Aston?'

'You know my name?' I bit my lip, my eyes wide, and moved back a little.

'Yes, I'm here to help you. I won't hurt you, I promise. We can be friends, yeah, buddy?' she asked softly.

She wasn't a man. She didn't look horrible. I couldn't see any pictures on her skin and she didn't smell like the men.

I shuffled across the floor and out from under the bed. Another woman was standing there and I flinched away as she moved closer.

'It's okay, sweetheart. I'm giving you this blanket to keep you warm.' She smiled encouragingly, and I took the blanket, not wanting her to touch me.

The other woman bent down and looked me in the eye. I clutched Bunny tighter to me.

'How about that cookie?'

I nodded, climbing onto my bed. She reached into her purse and pulled out a red shiny packet. She opened it and pulled out a round, light brown circle with dark spots on. I took it from her tentatively, still scared of her. My eyes were flicking between the two women in front of me, being nicer to me than anyone ever had before.

'Try it,' the first woman coaxed. 'Just a little bite?'

I brought it to my mouth and nibbled at a dark spot. The sweet flavor exploded in my mouth and I gasped, biting into the cookie. My stomach rumbled as the crumbs flooded my mouth. I'd never tasted anything like it. It was the best thing ever.

'My god,' the second woman breathed. 'The neighbors were right. The system has failed this kid. He's never even eaten a cookie at six years old.'

The first woman looked at me. 'Is this the first time you've had a cookie, Aston?'

'Yes,' I whispered. 'I like it. It's yummy.'

'How about another one?'

I nodded, staring into the face of the woman who was my childhood savior.

'Just, not today.' I repeat, breathing deeply as I let the memory go. Thirteen years, and the main marker I have of this day is the first cookie I ever ate. 'I need to go. I have to go see my Gramps.'

Megan looks at me worriedly, sadness in her eyes, and I cross the room to her. I cup her face in my hands, rest my forehead against hers, and exhale.

'It's not you, Megs. There's a lot about me you don't know – a lot I don't want you to know. It's not nice stuff, it's not good, okay? Today isn't a day to talk about it. Maybe there won't ever be a day. I don't know.'

'I want to know,' she whispers, resting her hands on my arms.

'I don't want you to know.' I kiss her and quickly move away. I push open her window, make sure it's clear, and jump out onto the tree branch.

'Then whenever you're ready,' she whispers. 'I'll be here. Waiting.'

I glance over my shoulder, and she's watching me go. I make eye contact with her for a second. Set on seeing Gramps, I jump down the tree.

'Didn't think I'd see you today.' Gramps' voice grumbles through the house.

'It's Sunday,' I reply simply, crossing the front room and sinking into my usual seat opposite him.

'Ain't just any Sunday.' He twists his lit cigar between his weathered fingers, staring at the smoke rising from it.

'Doesn't mean I'm not gonna see you.' I watch the twirling smoke.

'Thought you didn't wanna know today.'

'I don't, but I'm still gonna come see you. You need me.'

'I need to look at your face and know you look exactly like her?' He puffs on his cigar, the end of it glowing bright orange. 'You do, you know. You look exactly like her.'

'I . . .' I drag my eyes to his and see the pain there. 'I know.'

'You're smart, too. Just like she was. I could tell that when I started teachin' ya. Picked up your numbers like Einstein. Of course, she was good with numbers in a different way.'

The numbers of the street.

'I hate that so much of me reminds you of her.'

'Why? 'Cause you hate the memories? Your memories and mine, they're different, boy. If you'd let me share mine you'd see a different side to your mom than the one you know. You'd see that she ain't all bad. She just jumped on the wrong train and couldn't get back off.'

'And that's what she turned our life into. A damn train wreck. Everything . . .'

'And today is a day to remember it, however you want to.'

'You think I don't, Gramps? You think I'm not haunted by the memories of the past every day? You think I don't remember? I don't want to remember it. Not at all. But I do.'

'It's good to remember,' he pushes on, twisting his cigar in the ashtray. 'You gotta remember where you've been to see how far you've come.'

Megan

'Come on!' Kay begs. 'It's Sunday. Who the fuck does school work on a Sunday?'

'I do,' I tell her. 'It has to be in tomorrow, so I have to do it.'

'Didn't you stay in last night to do this?' She raises her eyebrow.

'Yes.'

'So why didn't you do it?'

Because I was busy with my sort-of-almost-boyfriend. 'Because I fell asleep early.'

'You never go to sleep early.'

'Oh my god! What is this? Interrogate Megan time?' I slam my pen down and look up at her. 'Do you want me to tell you my turn-on spot while you're here? Shit, Kay!'

She snorts. 'No offense, babe, but I'm not really into you like that, so we'll pass on the turn-on spot. But why were you asleep early?'

'Gee, I don't know, Kay. Why do people usually go to sleep? Could it be because they're tired?' I sigh.

'Shit the bed, someone is expecting Mother Nature!'

'Not for two to three weeks.'

'Then you must be pregnant . . . Oh wait—'

'Kay? Go fuck yourself.'

'I'm going,' she mutters, pulling the door open. 'Try not to get your panties too twisted, my little hormonal bag of joy!'

I throw my pen across the room, hitting the shut door. I stare at it blankly for a second, then shake my head. I'm actually trying to write the essay – trying being the main word in that sentence.

I'm trying and failing because my mind is stuck on Aston and the way he acted last night. And this morning.

The Aston I've always known – and the one I fell for – is cocky. Egotistical. Pig-headed. He's devil-may-care, flighty, and doesn't think about anyone else. But that wasn't the Aston I saw this morning. I could see it in his eyes – a deeper, darker part of him that makes me think his act is just that. An act. A charade put on to fool people.

A game he's playing with himself, constantly fighting for the winning spot. A game he's unwilling to lose, whatever the rules may be.

I get up to retrieve my pen and settle back on the bed, twisting it between my fingers. I have no idea why he said he needed me or why he said he wouldn't use me. I have no idea why he's acting the way he is.

Hello, he climbed through my freaking window.

Is it too much to think that – maybe – I could make him better? Whatever it might be that haunts him, whatever it is that makes his eyes darken the way they do . . . Maybe I make it bearable.

But what is it about today that's haunting him so much? I wish he could have said. I wish he would have just told me.

I wish I knew if he was okay. And I wish I had the balls to pick up my phone and find out.

But I don't.

'So you ran out on Charlie on Friday night, went to bed early on Saturday, kicked Kay out of the room last night, and still didn't finish the essay?' Lila raises her eyebrows.

'Yup,' I sigh. 'That pretty much sums it up.'

She frowns, chewing on a Twizzler. 'Why?'

'Because I just didn't.' I shrug. 'I don't have a reason. I guess I wasn't in an English essay mood this weekend.'

'What kind of mood were you in?'

'Apparently, a sleeping one.'

'And your excuse for running out on your date?'

'He's not my type.'

'He's hot, muscular, *and* his dad is kinda rich. How can he not be your type?'

We get up from the lawn and make our way to the main building. Lila throws her empty packet in the trashcan before we pass through the double doors and hoists her bag onto her shoulder.

'That stuff doesn't mean anything to me, Li, you know that. Money is money. It talks but it lies, too. And looks are crap – the hottest guy could be the biggest asshole in the world. It just . . . It doesn't matter.'

'Let me guess – there was no magical spark and unrelenting passion as for Mr. Darcy and Elizabeth?'

'Absolutely,' I agree, my lips twitching into a smile. 'He pales in comparison to the wonderful Darcy.'

'You and your books.' She shakes her head.

'There's nothing wrong with my books. They give me what I don't have in real life.'

'Like the perfect guy?'

'Exactly! And until I have my Mr. Darcy, I won't stop reading. Charlie was definitely not Mr. Darcy.'

'You know something? You're a really bad liar,' she says out of the blue.

'Hang on – what? How did you come to that conclusion when I'm not lying?'

'And again.' Lila laughs. 'I don't know what you're lying about, but you're not telling me the complete truth. At least not about this weekend.' She stops outside her class and tilts her head, studying me. 'Got anything you want to share?'

I look at her, taking in her upturned lips and curious eyes. 'Nope.' I hug my books to my chest. 'Nothing I want to share.'

I'm not lying. I don't want to share what happened in the slightest.

'I guess I'll just have to find out by myself.' She grins and disappears into her class.

I take a deep breath in. See? If Sherlock Holmes and Cupid could have babies, the baby would be Lila.

An arm rests on my shoulders. 'Smile, Meggy,' Braden chimes, steering me toward our class.

'Where's Maddie?'

'She's in bed. She's sick.'

'She better just be sick.' I look at him pointedly.

'Fuckin' hell, you sound like Mom.'

'It's because I learned it from her.' I smile sweetly at him and push my way up the staircase, shrugging his arm off.

'You seem different.'

What is it with people today? 'Do I?'

'Yep.'

'How?' I look at him like he's crazy and enter the room.

'You seem . . . Distracted? Yeah, distracted.' Braden chews his thumbnail.

'I'm always a little scattered, Bray, you know this. Maybe it's just pronounced today.' I shrug and slide into my seat next to Aston. Braden perches on the edge of my desk.

'Why are you still sitting next to this ass?' Braden looks at me, grinning.

I roll my eyes. 'Because even sitting next to this ass is preferable to you telling me how "different" I seem today. I've had it from Lila all morning.'

'Different?' Aston questions. 'Different how? Hey, Megan, did you finally get some?'

Smart boy.

'Hey, Aston, I see you finally managed to get your dick back in your pants long enough to make it to class.' I smile at him, exaggerating it for Braden's benefit.

'Well, you know . . .' He leans back in his seat, linking his fingers behind his head. 'Sometimes it's a fucking hard call, but I thought I should probably make an appearance. Wouldn't want you missing me now, would I?'

'I'd miss you like I would a lego under my foot. Oh, wait, I wouldn't miss that!'

'Do you two even know what you sound like?' Bray looks between us.

'I have ears, Braden,' I retort. 'I can hear, funnily enough.'

'You sound like an old married couple.'

'I said I can hear.'

'I know. I chose to ignore you.'

'Well isn't that a surprise?'

'You two sound like a couple of kindergarten kids,' Aston offers.

'You two sound like you want my knee in your balls,' I say, following suit. 'This is why I sometimes wonder if Kay is the smartest person I know. Guys are annoying.'

Braden snorts, jumping up. 'Of course we're fuckin' annoying. We have to be to put up with *your* annoying whiny asses.'

I scrunch up a ball of paper and launch it at his head as he walks to his desk. It bounces off the back of his head and he bends down, scoops it up, and throws it back at me. I catch it and grin.

'He's got a point,' Aston mutters.

I turn, looking at him blankly. 'I meant what I said about a knee in the balls.'

'You're really fucking hot when you're mad.'

I swallow the bubble of laughter inside my chest and fight the smile my lips are twitching into. 'I'm not mad. I can always get mad though, and when I do I'll be so hot I'll burn your damn ass.'

He grins slowly – that sexy grin he does – and lowers his eyelids slightly. My heart pounds a little harder when I recognize that look as his bed look.

'Is that an offer?' he says in a low voice.

I can feel Braden's eyes on us. 'Even if it was, it wouldn't be much of an offer because you wouldn't be able to pay the price.'

'Try me,' he offers, his smile turning cocky as we both put on the charade. As we both play for the silence of the secret we have. As we play for keeps.

For keeps of each other. For keeps of the secret that binds us together. For keeps of the lie we're now committed to telling.

The lie that breaks my heart a little every time I play this game.

I flick my blonde hair over my shoulder and smile, resting my chin on my hand, and cross my legs. 'How about the price would be so high that you'd be ruined for all other girls – and you'd never have an opportunity to put it back in your pants?' My stomach twists with my own words.

He runs his teeth across his bottom lip, his gray eyes darkening a shade as they flick down my body and back up. When he looks at me the way he is right now, I feel naked. Like he can strip away the layers of clothing I'm wearing to my body beneath with a mere glance.

'I don't think that would be such a bad price,' he mutters, stretching his arms out in front of him and tapping his fingers against the edge of the table. 'In fact,' he says even quieter as the class finally starts. 'I think I've paid that damn price.'

I almost choke as I breathe in sharply. *Only I could choke on air.* Aston raises an eyebrow, and I do the only thing I can do. I spin abruptly in my seat, focusing on the front of the room. It's not what I want to do . . . but that's an 'if only'. If only. If only.

I keep getting caught up in games. First, Maddie and Braden's – and now my own, however voluntarily. Both a game for love, but each with their own set of complex yet easily broken rules. Both with the ability to make or break the players. And both with the same prize.

The one thing coveted above all else, for however long it lasts. The one thing we all want regardless of who gets broken along the way. The one thing that no matter the cost, no amount of money could ever buy it.

The grand prize we play for.

Love.

'I went to the supermarket and I bought an apple.'

My lips curl to one side and I look behind me at Braden. 'What?'

'I went to the supermarket and I bought an apple,' he repeats, sitting opposite me on the picnic bench.

I know this. We used to play it all the time when we were kids – usually when we were hiding from our parents because we'd done something wrong. By the time we'd finished it, they'd forgotten we were in trouble because they were so worried.

We were the biggest little shits ever.

I close my book and resign myself to the fact he won't let it go until I play. 'Okay. I went to the supermarket and I bought an apple and a beer.'

He raises an eyebrow. 'I went to the supermarket and bought an apple, a beer, and a crotchless thong.'

'What?' I cover my face with my hands and shake my head. 'I cannot believe you just said that.'

I guess this game has evolved a little over the last ten years.

'You know the rules.' He kicks me under the table.

'Fine. I went to the supermarket and I bought an apple, a beer, a crotchless thong, and a dildo.'

He pauses before bursting into laughter. I grin at him, propping my head on my hands.

'I really wasn't expecting that,' he admits.

I shrug. 'Bit of a change from bananas, carrots and donuts, right?'

'Just a fucking bit.' He laughs again. 'For once I'm going to quit. I'm a little worried about what we could come up with.'

'You and I both, Carter.'

'So, Harper.' He leans forward, studying me. 'What's up?'

You're kidding me. I appreciate the concern, but sheesh.

'Mom set you on my case, didn't she?' I raise my eyebrows again. 'She was going on about me getting pregnant this weekend.'

'What the fuck?'

If the twitching of my lips didn't give me away, I so would have followed through with that.

'I'm not pregnant. She's worried about me getting pregnant.'

'No. Well, yes. She did call me.' He rubs his hand down his

face. 'For what it's worth, I reminded her you have to have sex
to get pregnant, so you're definitely safe there.'

This is becoming a common theme for my conversations.

'Gee, thanks,' I reply sarcastically. 'Was that all?'

'No. Y'know, sometimes I think about when we were kids
and think we were right little fuckers.'

'We were. It's a wonder our parents hadn't killed us by age
ten.'

'Shaving the cat . . . Climbing trees . . . Flushing your
cousin's diaper down the toilet . . .'

'That was you!' I poke his arm across the table. 'I had nothing
to do with that.'

'It absolutely fucking stunk, Meggy!'

I'll give him that. Ever smelt a diaper done by a ten month
old? They're not pretty.

'Thinking back I don't think Mom was as bothered about
the toilet being blocked as she was about the mess on the sofa.'
I look at him pointedly.

'Damn,' he mutters. 'I was eight. How was I supposed to
know the kid would pee everywhere? I could control that shit.
I thought I always could – I didn't realize it was like a special-
ized skill.'

The worst thing here is he's telling the truth. He genuinely
didn't know my cousin would pee everywhere without a diaper
on.

'I'm surprised she let you in the house again after.'

'I didn't pee on the sofa.' He grins. 'I'm house trained.'

'Oh, gee, I'll be sure to let Maddie know.'

'You're cocky, Meggy.'

'I learnt from the best.' I smile sweetly at him as we get up.

Braden laughs, wrapping an arm around my shoulders again
and squeezing me. 'I miss being kids. It was so damn easy.'

Me too. No work, no future to worry about, no feelings to
hurt.

No lies to tell.

Aston

'Remember where you've been to see how far you've come,' I mumble to myself, pushing the psych paper aside. 'Yeah alright, Gramps. Fuckin' helps if you've actually got somewhere, though, doesn't it?'

I push the heels of my hands into my eyes, rubbing harshly. Hear something enough and it'll be burned into your body, scarring your skin and tattooing itself in your mind. It doesn't matter how long ago the words were said. It just matters that they were.

Thirteen years and I don't feel like I've got anywhere. So what if I'm not the scared little boy in the corner anymore? He's still inside. He's still afraid, still shivering. He's still bruised, he's still broken, and he's still beaten.

Just because I appear not to give a fuck doesn't mean I actually don't. Not everyone is what they seem, and I'm one of those people. I don't even know who I am, because I spend so much time fighting against who I don't want to be. I have no time to be who I want to be. I have no time to be who I could be.

I spend too much time fighting against the memories that are buried deep down. But it doesn't always work – occasionally they creep up on me faster than I realize and consume me, taking me back to the place I hate more than anything. It's always voices – always whispers lingering on the edge of my consciousness. Sometimes a whisper is worse than a scream.

Just like her . . . No good for anything . . . Worthless . . .

I shove away from the desk, my chair getting caught on the carpet. It tips backwards as I stand. I ignore it, slip my feet into my sneakers and grab my wallet.

I need to prove them wrong. I need to prove myself wrong.

I ignore everyone on my way out of the house. If I speak to anyone, if I stop, if I think for even a second, I'll be back in my room still swirling in the same pool of fucking self-doubt.

My engine whirs to life, and I pull away from the frat house. There's a bar just outside the city, set away from the roads leading to the interstate, and it only takes one glance at the bar to know it's a run down, no ID, shabby place.

The kind of place my mom would have worked at. The kind of place she would have been picked up at. The kind of place her dead body was found at.

I push on through the city traffic full of perfect people driving back to their perfect families in their perfect little goddamn houses.

You're not worth anything.

I flick the radio to 'on' and *Trapt* blares out, the beat of *Headstrong* fueling the feelings running rife through my body. A mixture of anger, determination, frustration, and a sliver of helplessness.

Because they still control my life. No matter what I do or where I go, the bastards that controlled my early childhood control me even now.

I take the turn off to the small road that will lead me to the bar. The road is deserted, no cars, nothing, until the bar comes into view. The parking lot outside is half full with rusted, run-down cars that need more than a fresh coat of paint. My car looks out of place here.

I look out of place here.

I *am* out of place here. Mom wouldn't have been; this would have been her idea of heaven. Here is where she could have arranged a meeting with a rich guy – the guy that would probably pay over the odds and then some, all because of the privacy.

I pull a cap onto my head and get out of the car, staring at the exterior of the bar. The sign is slightly broken, one of the lights flickering pathetically against the darkening of the sky behind it. Eighties music hums from inside, and a woman's voice screeches. A scratchily written sign proclaims a karaoke night.

I push open the door and get hit by the smell of stale smoke and beer. A woman in a barely there outfit passes in front of me, a tray raised above her head as she weaves her way through the patrons gathered about the bar. It's far from busy, but everyone is focused on the thirty-something woman trying to sing in the corner of the bar.

I adjust my cap and order a beer. I was right. This place doesn't care about ID. A beer is put in front of me and I hand over the cash. No one gives me a second look apart from the waitress cleaning glasses at the opposite end of the bar.

Her eyes flick up and down me and she runs her tongue across her lips. Her clothes barely cover any skin, leaving her body on show.

It's all you'll be good for.

Her bleach blonde hair is flicked over her shoulder as she bends over to put glasses away, causing every man at the bar to look at her ass.

You're just like she is.

She straightens, sending me a suggestive smile. She's not much older than me, maybe one or two years. I drink some of the flat beer as she meanders across to me.

'What's a guy like you doing in this bar?' She leans forward, resting her elbows against the sticky wood. Her tits squeeze together, almost popping from her top.

You're nothing, just like her. It's all you're good for. You're worthless. Useless. A pile of shit. You're just the son of a whore, born to be a whore.

There's no stirring in my dick, no attraction toward this waitress flaunting herself right in front me. There's no desire at all, except the one to get the hell out of here.

'You know what?' I push the glass toward her and stand. 'I have no fuckin' idea.'

I don't wait for her reaction, instead I turn and leave the bar within minutes of my arrival. No one notices me getting out except her. I was invisible.

My car is comforting. I rest my head against the steering wheel, fighting against the constant voices swirling in my head.

'I'm not,' I say quietly. 'I'm not like her. I'm *not* like her!'
And I'm not.

If I was, I'd be waiting for that girl to finish her shift so I could fuck the shit out of her. That's what my mom would have done, except she would have sold her body for money or drugs. She wouldn't have thought about what she was doing or how it was affecting those around her.

But I am thinking. And I'm not waiting for the waitress.

I'm driving away from the seedy, run-down bar full of everything that's bad.

I'm heading back to Megan. To something good.

Seeing her face, even if it is across a crowded hallway, makes the day brighter. Seeing the guy next to her, making her laugh, makes the day turn darker than the dead of night.

It drives me fucking crazy. I should be the one walking beside her, making her laugh and wrapping my arm around her shoulders. Not that fucking asshole.

I lean against the wall, waiting and watching as they come closer. She shrugs his arm off, adjusts her books and rests them against her hip. The hip that's between them. She tucks some hair behind her ear, making her face more visible to me.

Her blue eyes collide with mine for a second, but her facial expression doesn't change, and neither does mine. Any twitch of lip, any blink of an eye, any movement of our bodies is all it would take to out us. We both know that.

The stakes of this game are high.

They're too high, and it makes me wonder if it's worth it. If it's worth the lying and sneaking around. Then I look at her. I get a glimpse into her eyes and a twitch of a smile from her, and I know there's no chance I can stop playing this fucked-up game.

She drops her gaze as she walks past, and I drop mine to her ass. Her jeans hug it tightly, and I remember what it's like to hold it as she moves against me.

The more time I spend around her or thinking of her, the

more I need her – the more I need the peace she can bring me. The more I need the complete and utter silence she brings me when she's tucked tight in my arms. The more I need to prove that I'm not my mom, that I'm more than a whore's son, born to be a whore myself. The more I need to prove to myself that I'm more than that – just like I did last night.

I'm not good enough for Megan. I know that. I'll never be enough for her, and it's best for her if she packs her bags and runs in the opposite direction screaming for her life. I don't know if I'll ever be able to let her in the way she wants. I don't know if I'll ever be able to tell her all of me, let her know all of my past. I don't know if the shaking little boy inside, stuck in a hall of horrifying memories will ever be able to break free from that and let me be with her completely.

But I still won't use her the way I've used girls for so long.

I would rather lose her entirely than use her for my own selfish needs.

The halls are almost empty when the dick walking with her disappears into his class and leaves her standing alone. I grab my cell from my pocket.

You have class?

I watch her as she takes her own from her bag. *No*, she sends back instantly, leaning against the wall. I shove the phone back into my jeans and walk in her direction.

'Football field,' I mutter. 'Five minutes.'

I can't look back to see if she responds no matter how much I want to. I just have to hope she'll get that pretty little ass down there.

I push open the double doors and almost walk into Ryan.

'Took your fuckin' time,' he mutters.

'Don't start your girly shit with me today, man,' I warn him. 'I never said what time I'd be done.'

'What? Didn't bag a girl in class to scratch your itch?'

'Why would I? You know I only pull that shit at weekends. You aren't the only one with grades to keep.'

'You mean you actually have grades?'

'You're a dick, Ryan.' I shake my head. 'And yeah, if you

must know, I graduated high school with a GPA of 3.8, so fuck you.'

'Shit! That's higher than mine!' he exclaims. 'I barely scraped a 3.4 to get in here from out of state! How the hell did you manage that?'

'My gramps was probably a better teacher than the poor shits that got stuck with your ass,' I reply. 'That's how I managed it.'

'Did you not go to school at all?'

'I went the last two years, and that's it. It was easy as hell. I'd already learned most of it, so I spent it fucking about and surprising the hell out of my teachers with near perfect scores on most tests.'

'I never knew that.' He pushes the door open and we step into the house.

'Why would you? You all assume my brain is in my dick. Hey,' I pause and shove my book in his direction. 'Take these.'

'The fuck?'

'I left something in class rushing to meet you. I'll be back in a minute.' I spin and leave the house. All I can focus on is getting to the football field – and if I'd stayed two seconds longer Ryan would have kept me there.

When I'm out the view of the house I break into a jog, detouring around the campus buildings instead of going through them. Fucking hell, why does the damn field have to be on the other side of this place?

There's some guys running around on the field, but I can't see Megan anywhere until I scan the bleachers. She's standing under them, looking between the seats on to the field.

I smirk and silently jog to her, placing my hands on her sides. I touch my lips to the side of her neck, and she turns her face into me.

'You know,' she whispers, 'I feel like I'm back in high school.' She spins in my hold and looks up at me.

'Who were you meeting under the bleachers in high school?' I raise my eyebrows.

'Only every guy I've ever dated. And apparently you're no exception.'

'So we're dating?'

She slips her hands up my chest and clasps them around my neck, her face coming close to mine. 'Unless you're in the habit of creeping through girl's windows, I'd say so.'

My lips twitch on both sides. 'No habit here.'

Apart from her. Megan Harper is my habit and she's one I stand no chance of breaking. I have yet to decide if it's good or bad.

'Why are we here?' she asks and pauses. She smiles. 'Oh. I get it. You've got a case of the caveman.'

'Bullshit,' I fire back, pulling her body closer to mine and kissing her. 'I wanted to see you without us bitching at each other. You complaining?'

'No.' She kisses me again. 'But admit it, Aston. You saw Tom with his arm over my shoulders and got pissed off. That's why you text me.'

Her eyebrows are arched over her amused blue eyes, her lips half-pursed and half-smiling. I stare at her for a moment and give in.

'A little,' I admit. 'I fucking hated seeing that prick with his hands on you.'

Megan brings her hand to my head and touches my cheek. 'A lot,' she corrects me. 'You looked like you were ready to drag me out of there by my ear just to get me away from him. I hate to say it but you'll have to get used to it.'

'Fuck that,' I mutter. 'If that happens much more I'm gonna stand in front of Braden and gladly take his shit for being with you. I can't fucking deal with seeing that all the time.'

'You have two choices. You can see me with them and know I'm with you, or you can see me with them and wonder which one I want.'

Fuck that for a laugh. I take a deep breath and lean my forehead against hers. 'Fine. I'll deal with it. But I don't damn well like it, Megs.'

'I know.' She smiles. 'I don't like it much either, but if it makes you feel better, Tom's a jackass.'

'So am I,' I mumble.

Her hand snakes into my hair and she holds me tightly. 'Yep. But you're a special kind of jackass.'

'Yeah?' I dip my head and brush my lips across her. 'What kind is that?'

'My kind of jackass.'

'It just occurred to me I don't know your major,' Ryan throws at me as I walk into the frat house.

I grin, still buzzing from being around Megan, and sit down. 'Psychology.'

'Are you for fucking real?' He sits up.

Braden walks in, eating an apple. 'Is who for real?'

'This dick is majoring in psych. Did you know that?' Ryan cocks a thumb toward me and looks at Braden.

'He can't be.' Braden looks at me and I smirk. 'Are you really?'

'Pretty damn sure that's why I do the classes the course requires.'

'Well, fuck me.' He leans against the doorframe. 'What you studying that for? To understand why you need so much sex?' Him and Ryan chuckle.

So I can understand why my mom was the way she was and stop other people going that route. So I can help stop other kids dealing with the shit I had to.

'I know why I need sex, asshole,' I retort. 'I'm doing it to work out why people like me hang around with fucktards like you two.'

'Oh, that's easy,' Ryan shrugs. 'We make clever dicks like you look good.'

'True that,' Braden agrees.

Ryan looks at him. 'You know something? I don't even know what your major is.'

Braden shrugs a shoulder carelessly, chewing. 'You know something?' He grins. 'I don't fucking know either.'

I laugh at the smile on his face. 'Ryan, man, you might just have a point about you two making me look good.'

'I'm majoring in engineering, if either of you dicks care.' He shrugs.

'Hey, that's supposed to be pretty tough. All that math and stuff,' Braden says vaguely.

'Math was all I could do well in school. It made sense.'

'Yeah, well.' Braden straightens, dropping the apple core in the trashcan. 'The only math I know is that me plus Maddie, minus clothes, equals a product not even algebra can create. Shame we can't major in sex. I'd walk away top of the class.'

I smirk as he leaves with a satisfied smile on his face, and Ryan snorts.

'That's some pretty sweet math . . . One I think this whole house can appreciate.' He grins.

I nod in agreement, thinking of Megan.

Fucking right I can appreciate that.

Megan

I must be the only person in my class that will read a classic novel for anything other than requirement. I can't think of anyone I know that would pick up *Jane Eyre*, *Little Women*, or *Tess of the D'Urbervilles* for pleasure.

In fact, they're not even my first choice. *Little Women* comes in a close second, but *Pride and Prejudice* will always win out. There's something beautiful about a couple from two different backgrounds traveling along the bumpy road of love until it's undeniable, and there's something even more beautiful about watching that journey happen. Flicking through the pages anxiously waiting for that sweet first kiss, the passion filled argument, the final declaration. There's something that pulls me in and takes me away from the real world.

There really is no place like the one you find between the pages of a book.

The only place that comes close is in the arms of the person you love.

Perhaps that's why with Braden in class all day, I'm sitting on the corner of Aston's bed reading – and swooning over – the beauty that is Mr. Darcy. I'm pages away from one of the best scenes in the book – the rain scene where everything is so passionate and wet and *oh my god, get together already!* And I'm not ashamed to admit it, but I'll happily yell at the characters until I get what I want.

That love. That all-consuming, overwhelming, never-ending love is what I want. I want to feel what Darcy and Elizabeth feel. I want to look into someone's eyes and know I'm looking at my happily ever after.

The door opens, and I keep reading, my eyes skittering across the page and drinking in every word.

The door is open. Okay. So this is gonna be kinda awkward if this isn't Aston. Damn, why didn't I think of this before?

I slowly raise my eyes over the top of the book. Aston clicks the door shut behind him, smirking at me with a cocked eyebrow.

'Not that I'm complaining, but is there any reason you're on my bed?' he asks smoothly.

'I'm reading,' I reply, dropping my gaze to the page again. 'And I need to be comfy when I read, which will explain why I'm on your bed opposed to that horrible chair at the desk.'

'I can see you're reading, Megs, but why are you reading in my room and not yours?'

'I can go if you'd like me to.' I dog-ear the page and tuck the book under my arm.

'Hey, no! No, I didn't say that.' He drops his bag and walks toward the bed, putting his hands either side of me. 'I didn't even fucking think it.'

'Oh. Well.' I smile sweetly. 'I'll just get back to my book, then.'

'Hell fucking no,' he mutters, grabbing the battered book and dropping it on the floor. My mouth drops open.

'You did not just throw my book on the floor.'

'I dropped it.'

'No. You threw it. I should bitch slap you for hurting Mr. Darcy that way.'

'Right. Because Mr. Darcy and his pompous ass will appreciate it.'

I narrow my eyes a little, half-surprised he even knows who Mr. Darcy is. But then again, I'm quickly finding out that Aston isn't what he seems, and I like it. There's a whole other side to him I'm quickly coming to adore.

'You don't throw my books. Ever,' I tell him firmly. His lips twitch. 'I mean it. Next time you throw one of my babies, especially a favorite, I *will* hurt you.'

He schools his face into a serious expression and climbs onto the bed, kneeling in front of me. 'I'm sorry, baby,' he murmurs, cupping the side of my face. 'I won't throw one of your books ever again.'

I smile at him, turning my cheek into his palm. 'You damn well better not.'

Aston touches his lips to mine and slides his hand round to the back of my head. He lowers me back on the bed slowly, his mouth moving against mine tenderly.

'I just realized that Braden is in classes all day. Which means I have you all to myself for a while.' His lips travel along my jaw. 'So there's no damn way you're reading a fucking book when you could be doing this.' He runs a hand down my side and slips it under my shirt, his hand rough against my skin.

I arch my back into him slightly, my hands easing their way up his arms to his shoulders and neck as his lips find their way to mine. The hairs at the nape of his neck tickle. I curl my fingers around them, holding him against me. My leg bends and my foot travels up the back of his calf, his jeans rough against my bare toes.

His tongue explores my mouth, diving in and out, swirling in the same way desire is in my lower stomach. His probing hand below my top does nothing but ignite the fire inside me. It does nothing but continue to feed and fuel the storm of feelings I have whenever he's near me.

Aston trails his lips along my jaw to my ear, letting them fall away from my skin and resting his head next to mine. His breathing is heavy and full of pain.

'I still don't understand why you're here,' he whispers.

'I'm here because I want to be.' I trail a hand down his back, rubbing in slow, circular motions, and I know the demons inside him are rising up. The demons that keep him from me completely.

'But I don't understand why.'

'Not everything needs an explanation. This is one of those things.'

'What if a part of me needs one?' He pulls back, releasing me and kneeling up again.

I sit and cross my legs. My eyes find his, and I'm lost in the swirling torment that's in the shadows of them. His emotions are all battling each other with the force of a tornado – the color of his eyes darkened to the shade of a storm's heart. I'm aching to reach out and touch him but something tells me not to. Despite the lingering temptation tingling my fingers, I know I have to do this on his terms. I'm so angry at him and I don't even know why. I'm so confused about everything. I want to understand. I want to know what he keeps so buried down inside him, and I want to make it better.

'Then that's something I'll never be able to give you,' I say quietly, sadly.

'Why?'

'Because my reasons for being here – the way I feel inside, what I feel about you, about us, about all of this – I can't put them into words. I could sit here for hours and try to explain, but I can't. They just . . . are.'

He stands and turns away from me. He pulls his shirt over his head and tosses it into the corner of his room carelessly, the muscles in his back and arms flexing as he runs his hands through his hair.

'Aston. Talk to me,' I say softly.

'Why? What difference would it make?'

'Because I need to understand! I need to understand you – all the difference faces of you. I know three. I know the guy, I know the lover, and I know whatever side of you this is, but I don't fucking understand them!' I stand. 'One minute you're climbing through my bedroom window, then you're kissing me, then you're walking away from me. I don't get it!'

'Some things can't be explained,' he says tightly, throwing my own words back at me.

'Bullshit! *Bull. Shit.* Aston!' I walk toward his turned back. 'Absolute crap! The way you act the way you do, the way you hide a part of yourself from everyone, all that has an explanation, it could be explained! You just choose not to. For some reason, you don't.'

'Maybe I can't!' He turns to me, his eyes raw and his body

taut. 'Maybe I can't explain it all. Maybe I can't. Maybe it hurts too much. Did you ever think of that?'

His eyes drop, and I want to kick myself. I never thought of that. I never thought whatever it is he's keeping inside that haunts him so much is too painful for him to talk about. This whole time I've been thinking about how I feel about what he's going through. I've been so occupied with what his secrecy is doing to me, I haven't stopped to consider what it's doing to him. I haven't thought for one second about how he feels. God.

My hands reach out for him, and he grips my wrists in a lightning fast movement. 'Don't,' he whispers, his face hard. 'Don't.'

A minute passes between us, stretching out for an infinite amount of time. Neither of us move, the only sound between us the heaviness of his breathing, until he looks at me slowly. His eyes are filled with sadness, and I've never seen him look so vulnerable. I want to shake his hands off my wrists and touch him, soothe that pain, but I can't. I've tried.

Whatever he's going through he has to share for both of us. I can't think about me or him as separate people. When it comes to the pain shining in his eyes, something has to give, because I need to know why, because the game isn't between us. The game is the show we put on for everyone around us. There's no charade when we're standing face to face like we are now. There's no charade when everything we feel is so, so real.

'You're so desperate to keep hold of me, yet you're so determined to keep me at arm's length,' I whisper. 'Why? Why can't you talk to me? What are you scared of?'

'I'm scared of keeping you and I'm scared of losing you. My whole life I've looked after myself, depended on myself, and I've kept everything at bay. All the feelings, everything. And then . . . Then I met you and everything changed. Everything I thought was real turned out to be a load of bullshit. The only thing that's real is you.'

'Why me? Why do I make such a difference?'

He exhales slowly, resting his forehead against mine, his eyes burning into me. 'Because I've *never* needed anyone as much as I need you. If I let you in, if I tell you everything, then you might not need me, too – and that is the fucking scariest thing of all. As much as I wish you'd walk away, as much as you should walk away, I don't think I'll ever be able to let you.'

'Why would I go?' I frown.

He sighs, finally releasing my wrists and linking our fingers. 'Because my past is different to yours, Megan. We come from two different places. We have two completely different stories—'

I shake my head. 'You really believe that shit? Do you?'

He doesn't move.

'You think your past will change the way I think about you? The way I feel? Because it won't. It won't change a goddamn thing!'

'Megan—'

I shake my head again, snatch my hands from his, and shove him away. I lean against the window and look out between the gaps in the curtains. 'I'm not gonna walk away, Aston. I couldn't even if I wanted to. I'm in too far already. Whatever it is that's inside you and that's eating away at you . . . I want to *know*. I need to know for *us*.'

I hear his steps as he crosses the room and feel the warmth of his body as he presses against my back. He rests his hands on my hips. They slowly creep round to my stomach, flattening out, and he buries his face in the side of my hair. I lean back into him, struggling with the rollercoaster of emotions running through my body.

'We're different, Megs,' he whispers. 'Too different. Even now we have to hide this.'

'We only have to hide it because Braden will kick our asses, but we can't hide it forever.'

'I don't want to hide this. I don't wanna hide you. Every guy that looks at you . . . I hate it. I hate the way they look at you like they just wanna fuck your brains out. It drives me fucking insane.'

'The way you used to look at me, you mean?' I tease, smiling a little.

He laughs hollowly, turning me around. I wrap my arms

around his waist and lay my head against his bare chest. I listen
to the beating of his heart, harsh and frantic.

'Yeah, the way I used to look at you until I did sleep with you.
Fuck, Megs, when I kissed you I realized that wasn't all I wanted
from you. It wasn't all I needed from you.' His voice rumbles
in his chest and he presses his lips to the top of my head.

'Then let me be what you need,' I beg. 'Don't think about
Braden, or keeping this a secret, or where we come from. All
that matters is we're here now and I'm here now. Let me be
what you need me to be. Stop pushing me away, Aston, 'cause
even though I should let it go I can't. I'll always come back.'

His chest heaves with the force of his breath. 'I will. I'll tell
you everything. But not today, Megs. Soon. But not today.'

I shut my eyes briefly. 'You promise?'

Aston slides a hand up my back, over my shoulder, and cups
my chin. He raises my face slightly, bending his down, and I
meet his gray eyes. 'I promise.'

This is a mess.

I smile politely at the guy across the table from me. Date
two on Lila's 'Operation Get Megan a Boyfriend' and it's no
better than the first. If I'm honest, it's even worse.

And it's not even the guy. No, Callum is lovely. He's sweet,
he's hot, and he's funny. He's pretty much the perfect guy – but
he's just not *my* perfect guy.

'Lila said you were an English major?' he asks, dipping his
spoon into his ice cream.

'Yeah. I've always loved literature so it makes sense to major
in it.'

'What do you plan to do when you graduate? I know it's a
while away.' His lips quirk up to the side. 'But it's good to have
a plan, you know?'

'Oh – I think I'll probably end up teaching it.' I shrug. 'Maybe
I'll go into publishing, I'm undecided exactly what. I'd like to
write a book one day though. What about you?'

'I hope to get into Harvard Med. It's not easy to do but I'm
on the right track.'

Well done, Lila. Not only do you set me up with a junior, you pick the one that's planning on going to the opposite side of the country in eighteen months.

'Wow. Quite the goal.' I smile.

'Hey – yours isn't bad. At least you get to do what you love. My career choice is largely influenced by my family.'

'Oh.' Awkward. 'It can't be that bad, right? Or you wouldn't do it?'

'No, it's my second choice career, so it's not hard.'

'What was your first?' Oh, god. Am I acting too interested? I don't want to be rude but I don't want him to think I'm interested. Dammit. This whole thing is one giant clusterfuck.

Aston walks past the window and double-takes. My eyes flick toward him, and I'm aware of Callum talking but I can't really hear him. I'm too focused on the clenching of Aston's fists and tightening of his jaw. He's pissed off.

Really pissed off.

'Megan?' Callum waves a hand in front of my face and I look back at him.

'I'm sorry – I just saw a friend I've been trying to call. It's kind of important.' I inwardly flinch at my own lie. 'Do you mind if I run after him?'

'Um, sure. Not at all.'

'I'm so sorry.' I get up from the table and put a bill down. 'Here – toward lunch. I'm sorry.'

I run out of the diner and after Aston, turning the same corner he did to leave the downtown area. I get to the end of the street and sigh. I can't see him or his car – and I have no idea when I'll get a chance to explain why he saw me having lunch with some other guy.

Damn Lila and Maddie and their stupid ideas!

I turn. Since I bailed on Callum heading back to campus is my best decision. And texting Aston would probably be a good idea. Damn secrecy.

I'm pulled down an alley and my back presses against cold bricks. Can't move – someone's heavy weight holds me back. Gray eyes capture mine before panic sets in.

'Do you make it a habit of sneaking up on girls?' I mutter.

'Only you,' he responds. 'But I'll be honest – I wasn't expecting to come downtown and find you having fucking lunch with another goddamn guy.'

'Aston—'

'I'd be lying if I said I wasn't pissed, but then we're not exactly exclusive so I guess—'

'Lila set it up,' I blurt out, silencing him. 'She's going all Austen's *Emma* on me. She has this crazy idea that I need a boyfriend and is setting me up with guys she thinks Braden will be okay with. I can't refuse or she'll know something is up. I just turn up, talk, and that's it. I don't even give them my number. It's all fake.'

'Fake?'

'Uh-huh. I just go so she doesn't get on my case about it. Besides, if it was a real date I wouldn't have left him there to come running here after you, would I?'

His body relaxes, tightness leaving his muscles, and he pulls me from the wall into his body. He presses my face into his neck. The way his arm is wound tightly around my body lets me know he wasn't lying when he said he didn't want to lose me.

And this wasn't anger. This was fear – of that exact thing happening.

I wrap my arms around his waist, holding him tightly.

'I don't know why I thought . . .' he trails off. 'I'm such a fucking dick. I'm sorry, Megs.'

'It's okay.' I kiss his neck softly. 'I probably would have thought the same if it was the other way around.'

'No, baby, it's not fucking okay. I can't accuse you of that shit just because of my own issues—'

'You didn't accuse me of anything.' I pull back, looking into his eyes. 'If it was the other way around, I probably would have gone in there and ripped out her extensions.'

He smirks. 'I don't know how I didn't go in there and knock him out.'

I run my fingertips across his back. 'I don't know how you

did it either. I hate even seeing other girls look at you,' I say quietly.

'If Braden was anyone other than my best friend . . .' He shakes his head. 'I'd tell him, but it ain't that damn easy.' He sighs heavily. 'I guess we're just gonna have to deal with Lila's bullshit plan and get on with it.'

'But what if it's obvious? That there's a bigger reason I'm turning them down?'

'Then we cross that bridge together when we get there.'

'There's only so many guys that can't be my type.'

'Listen here.' He turns my face so it's against his, our noses brushing. 'There's only one fucking guy you need to worry about being your type, so every other dick can take a running jump off a cliff. In case you need reminding of that, baby, here's your reminder.'

His lips crash into mine, his tongue forcing its way into my mouth possessively. He runs it along the length of mine forcefully, his hands pulling me ever closer to him. My own slide up his back, gripping onto his shoulders, and I let him claim me. I know this is what he needs, and the deepness of his kiss that tugs on my lower stomach muscles proves me right.

'I think I'm good on the reminder,' I whisper as he pulls away, pressing our cheeks together. 'But any time you feel the need to remind me fully . . .'

His fingers dig into my back. 'Any time I feel the need to remind you fully . . .' He turns his face, his lips barely touching my ear. 'It'll be a reminder you'll never fucking forget.'

Aston

Seeing her with another guy – no matter how innocent or friendly it was – put a part of my brain into overdrive that's only ever roared to life for me. The need to grab her arm, drag her out of that diner, and pin her against the wall while I kissed her senseless almost took over. The need to protect her from every other ass in this town, hell, in the state, was almost our undoing.

It's something no one would understand. For the first time in my life I've started to let someone in, let them *be* there, all while taking what they have to offer. And that's the problem. I'm taking from Megs but I'm not giving back to her – I'm not giving her what she deserves, yet, somehow, she knows exactly what I seem to need. All the time.

For the first time in my life I've let myself feel something other than the things that fuck up my mind. I've let her in. The one girl I knew could undo me with a simple smile or one glance into those little blue eyes – and she does. Every single time, she undoes me like she's tugging on a loose string of a hand-knitted blanket, and all I can do is unravel in front of her.

The craziest thing is that I want to unravel. I want to tell her everything she wants to know. I want to tell her why I'm a fucked up mix of hot and cold toward her, why I pull her into me and then push her away. But telling her . . . Telling her might just push it over the edge.

Telling her could push her away and make me permanently cold.

Telling her would mean accepting. Reliving. Remembering. *Feeling.*

Apart from Gramps, she is the only person I've ever felt something for. She's the only person I've wanted to feel for, and what I feel is spiraling out of my control. It's growing along with my need for her, which is way stronger than it should be, way more addicting than it should be.

Because that's what she is. She's addicting. The vanilla smell of her hair, the light in her eyes, the brightness of her smile, the soft skin of her hand; every part of her is addicting to me.

And even more than that . . . She sees me. She doesn't see the jackass who fucks everything with a pulse, or the cocky, arrogant bastard who cares about no one other than himself. Or maybe she does see that – she just sees what's under it, too. She sees the real me, the one that no one else ever bothered to see.

She sees the broken. She sees the mismatched. She sees the fucked up.

And pretty soon, she's gonna grab hold of that fucked up and pull it out of me in a gut wrenching conversation.

'It's not working,' Megan's voice echoes down the hall. 'Make her stop with her stupid dates.'

'There's nothing I can do,' Maddie replies. 'You know what she's like. She thinks she's damn cupid or something.'

'One success – a third of success – with you and Braden doesn't make her cupid! It doesn't make me cupid, either. Shit. Has she ever thought maybe I'm happy as I am?'

'You'll have to ask her. I just yes or no to the guys, Megs. Seriously, you should see some of the dicks she had lined up. It would have been like walking into a strip club – just without the sexy.'

'Ughghghghgh.' Megan bangs her head on the table as I walk into the kitchen, grinning.

'What's up? Being forced on dates such a hard life?' I smirk as she lifts her head.

'How would you know?' she throws back at me. 'I wasn't even aware you got your "date's" name before you ripped her panties off her.'

'Touché,' Maddie mutters.

'Oh, I do, sometimes. But that's usually all I get.' I shrug and lean against the counter. 'Better to be nameless and get fucked than forced onto dates with a bunch of pretty boys.'

'Oh, because you're not counted in the pretty boy category? How long did it take you to do your hair this morning?' She raises an eyebrow. 'Probably longer than it took half my dorm combined, Mr. Maybelline.'

'I could probably make you come quicker than I could do my hair,' I respond, watching her cheeks flush slightly. 'But that doesn't mean I'm a fucking pretty boy.'

'Let me guess – it makes you a sexy boy?'

I grin. 'I'm glad you think so.'

'I never said I thought so, asshole. It was a question, not a statement. Still learning the difference?'

I move to the table, leaning across it toward her. 'No, but with your sass, it looks like you could do with a lesson learning the difference between a slapped ass and a spanked ass. Want a teacher, Megs?'

Her mouth drops open, and I fight the urge to lean even closer to her and make her close it. I see Maddie smirk, amused, out the corner of my eye, and let my own lips curve into a smirk.

'If I ever feel the need to be taught a slightly kinky side of sex,' Megan says in a lower voice and leans forward slightly, pushing her boobs together. She's pushing this right to the fucking limit. 'Then I'd find a teacher who could play my body like a guitar, strumming all the right strings at the right times, not a horny college boy just looking to get off.'

'How do you know I'm not the guitar player?'

'How do you know you are?' she challenges, sitting back and letting her mouth curve upwards.

'It takes me ten minutes to do my hair. I could make you come in half that,' I threaten and promise her, my eyes still fixed on hers. 'If you can find a damn guitar player that can do that, then I'll salute you, Miss Harper. Until then, you can imagine *my* fingers plucking your body like the strings of a guitar.'

I scoop an apple up from the bowl in between us and take a bite, winking at her as I leave the kitchen.

'Pig!' she yells after me. I hear Maddie's quiet laughter, and grin to myself. Sometimes, being known as an asshole who likes to get into girls' pants is a good thing – and in a situation like that when she's turning me the fuck on, it's definitely a good thing.

I rest against the wall outside the frat house, finish the apple, and throw the core in the bin. I spy Braden stretching round the side of the house and jog over to him.

'Ready to run?'

He looks up, grabbing two water bottles. 'I thought your lazy ass was still in bed.'

'Yeah it was, but pissing Megan off was so much more fun.' I shrug, grin, and take off with him behind me.

'I dunno why you do it, man. One of these days she will hand your balls to you.' He shakes his head.

'She's too irrational for that. She gets pissed off way too easily to even consider ripping my balls off.'

'Yeah – but you've heard Kay's revenge methods, right? I heard her last week seething to Maddie that she wanted to "take a butter knife to the underside of that fucking asshat's balls and put them on the school menu as a special with a side of fish to represent the whore he thought he could fuck right before her."' He takes a deep breath, and I flinch a little.

'Ouch. Who pissed her off?'

'Dude, I don't know, and I don't think I fucking want to.'

'Wait,' I muse. 'I thought she was a lesbian?'

'Bisexual,' he corrects me. 'She likes both.'

'Oh, man. So none of us are safe from her loud-mouth ass?' I shake my head. 'Damn.'

'Right?' he agrees. 'So, me and the guys were thinking of heading into San Francisco tomorrow night for the weekend. Maddie and Lila are coming – not sure about Megan, though.'

My muscles instantly tighten, my stomach clenching at the mention of my home city. It's so close to Berkeley, yet so far away. The six year old Aston that left San Francisco is a completely

different person to the nineteen year old Aston living in Berkeley, but that doesn't mean it's a place I can even consider going.

'Don't think so,' I reply, trying to keep my shaking voice even. 'I gotta see my Gramps on Sunday. Old coot nearly whacked me with his fucking stick for not showing up that weekend we went to Vegas.'

Braden laughs, taking me at my – very true – word. 'Alright, alright. You stay back here like a good little dickhead and fuck some other poor girl.'

'That's the plan.'

Or it's not. But he doesn't need to know the real one.

We stop for a second to drink and catch our breath, and I take my cell from my pocket.

Are you going to SF? I send to Megan.

She replies instantly. *I don't know. Are you?*

No. Don't go.

Okay. I won't.

I slip it back into my pocket, looking up into Braden's curious face. 'What?'

'I don't think I've ever seen you text anyone. Girl finally get your number out of you?'

I snort. 'Don't be so fucking stupid. If I did that I'd never get any damn peace between them and you and Ryan.'

'True that.' Braden nods, and we start running back in the direction of the frat house to get ready for class.

We change quickly, meeting back outside to head into the main building for English. Maddie and Megan are waiting for us when we get downstairs, and Megan's tapping her foot impatiently.

'Are you girls ready? Some of us actually want to pass this year,' she says sarcastically.

'Oh, Meggy,' Braden mutters, taking Maddie's hand. 'You could pass this class in a fucking coma. You've probably read everything on the semester plan already.'

She slaps the back of his head, and he curses.

'The fuck was that for?'

Maddie slaps his chest with her books. 'Language!'

'You sound like my mom,' he mutters.

Megan grins at Maddie, her eyes flicking to Braden. 'Just because you're right about the reading thing doesn't mean I have to like it. Maybe if you paid a bit more attention to the class you'd pass without looking over my shoulder when we have work due in.'

'Why did I never think of that?' I look at Braden.

'Because you're apparently a fucking genius in your own right,' he grumbles. 'Am I the only stupid one here?'

'Oh, you're not stupid,' Maddie soothes him. 'You're just a little bit slower than us.'

'You know what, Angel? It's a really good job I love you.'

'I think so, too.' She smiles. 'It means I can say exactly what everyone else is thinking.'

He gives her a look that says she'll get it later, and she smiles wider.

'Hold up,' Megan pauses, staring at Braden. 'Did you just call *Aston* a genius?'

'I did.'

'They're not words I'd ever expect to hear in the same sentence.'

'Fuck off.' I tug on her hair, and she swats at me. 'I'm not jokin', Meggy. This kid graduated with a fucking 3.8 GPA.'

Megan looks at me now, her eyebrows raised and surprise in her eyes. 'You did?'

I shrug. 'One of us assholes has to be smart.'

'No, really? You did?'

She's not acting here. She's genuinely surprised, and I don't know whether or not to be pissed she doesn't believe me. 'Yeah.'

'I can't believe you have the same GPA as me. You don't look that smart.' She smirks wickedly, and I know the smile is for Braden and Maddie's benefit.

I hold the class door open for her, looking down as she pauses in front of me, and my hand brushes her hip. 'Not everyone is what they seem, Megan. You should know that by now.'

She looks up at me, her startling blue eyes full of questions I know I have to answer.

'I know that. I just wish those people could trust in the people that care a little.' She sweeps past me to our desk. I bite the inside of my lip and follow after her.

'Maybe it's not that they don't trust,' I say. 'Maybe it's that they've forgotten how to.'

She straightens her books on the desk, slowly turning her face to me as I sit next to her. 'Then maybe they should open their eyes and see that the person they need to trust is right in front of them. Maybe they should open up and share so they don't have to bear the burden alone.'

'Not everything is made to be shared. Not every scar is on the body. Some scars are on the mind. Some scars can't be seen. They're inside, burned in so deeply that they'll never be healed.'

Her eyes are earnest and soft. 'Just because a scar can't be healed doesn't mean it can't be soothed,' she whispers.

Fuck. She's so right, and this weekend is the perfect time with everyone gone. But am I ready? I don't know. I don't know if I'll ever be ready to talk about my childhood, but I don't have a choice if I want to keep her. If I want to keep this girl in my arms, secret relationship be fucking damned, I have to be honest with her.

I take a deep breath and make a decision I know I'll regret. A decision that will change everything.

A decision that will change me.

'Sometimes the dark truth is too much for some people,' I warn her.

A decision that will change her.

'Sometimes a light dusting of the truth isn't enough,' she responds.

A decision that will change us.

'Is the dark really better than the light?'

She nods. 'Sometimes. Sometimes you need to get lost in the dark to truly appreciate the light.'

'This weekend,' I drop my voice so it's barely audible. 'I

can't promise everything. I can only promise what is there to give.'

She blinks once, her hand twitching. She clenches her fist and puts it in her lap. 'I've only ever had half of you. I'm sure I can wait a little longer for all of you.'

A night of fitful sleep, recurring nightmares and horror flashbacks aren't how I wanted to start my day. Now, with the guys off to SF, Megan can get in and out of the house fairly unbothered. If anyone asks, she has a spare key to Braden's room and left some books there. If anyone asks why she's in my room, I borrowed one of the books. It's hardly foolproof, but then again, no one here will care that much.

They all secretly want in her pants.

'You really wanna know?' I look at her across the room.

Her light blue eyes are wide and earnest as she meets my weary gaze. She pulls her knees to her chest and bites her thumbnail, nodding slowly. I sink onto the bed opposite her, the springs creaking under the heaviness of my body, and gaze out of the window.

'It's not an easy thing to listen to,' I warn her.

'I want to be there for you,' she replies softly, shifting a little closer to me. 'But I can't be there if I don't understand, not really. And I want to, Aston – I want to understand. I want to know all of you.'

I take a deep breath. It doesn't matter if I'm ready or not anymore – it's too late to back out. I have to tell her everything, tell her things I've never said out loud before. And somehow, when I look into her eyes, I find the strength within me to say the words.

'I have no idea who my father is. My mom got herself knocked up at seventeen to a guy whose name she didn't even know.' My voice is hard, bitterness coating every word thickly. 'She palmed me off on my Gramps whenever she could; she wasn't cut out to be a mom – at least at seventeen. Gramps insists she suffered from post-partum depression, but she didn't care. Not really. If she did, she would have seen a doctor instead of medicating herself with alcohol and the cheapest drug she could get ahold of.

'CPS kept in contact with us until I was sixteen and considered "stable" by them. I stole my file once and read it. It says that "Mom" moved us into a stingy little apartment when I was two, and although there were complaints from neighbors about hearing a child screaming and being left alone, whenever they visited everything was perfect. I was clean, the apartment was clean, and she was clean. They couldn't do anything without proof.' The view from my room is a far cry from the dirty alleys of the Tenderloin district in San Francisco. 'Despite the area we lived in she always managed to make it seem like we lived somewhere else whenever they showed up.

'I didn't need to read the report much further. I have memories from when I was about four, spanning the next two years. "Stepdads" that came and went repeatedly. All the same. All big, tattooed, and more stuck on drugs and alcohol than even she was. They all hated me with a passion.'

Dirty little son of a bitch. Fuckin' runt. You piece of shit.

'They showed it whenever she went out to earn money – when she went to sell her body to some rich prick to fund the drug habit for herself and whichever poor bastard she was fucking at the time. That's when it would start.'

'Mommy,' I had whimpered, cowering in the corner of the kitchen and hugging the smelly rabbit to my body. He leaned over me – I didn't know his name. I never knew their names. They were never there long enough for me to know them.

'Your mommy can't hear you,' he mocked. 'She's busy being a whore to get me the good shit. She's good at that.'

'I want my mommy.' I pushed back further into the corner, the cable jack cutting into the bare skin on my back. Tears formed in my eyes and I curled up tighter, scared of the big man in front of me. The smell of alcohol on his breath fell over me and I covered my nose and hid my face.

It was pointless. I knew, even then, that he wouldn't touch my face. They never did.

'Face hits were too obvious. A bruise on the back? On the legs? Even the stomach. They were safer for them. They weren't questioned, and when they were, it was the same answer.'

'Oh, that?' Mom had gently stroked my back, her eyes steady on the social worker's. 'We went to the park a few days ago and the silly boy thought he could swing off the big monkey bars. I turned away for a second – a friend called me over – then he was on his back on the floor. He's got no sense of danger. I've tried to explain, but he is only four. We came home and cleaned it up good, though. Didn't we, little dude?'

Her blue-gray eyes found mine, a spark of fear in them. I nodded.

'Mommy made it all better.'

'I fell off the table. I tripped on a crack on the sidewalk. I slipped on the stairs outside the apartment. There was always an excuse. Never a hospital visit. Always my fault. Never theirs.'

The glass had hit the wall hard enough that it shattered. I screamed, slipping on a wet patch on the floor as I tried to escape to my room for an extra second of relief. I fell to my knees, fear pulsing through my body. I sobbed, cried, whimpered. I gulped desperately at air, my throat tight. I pulled myself along the floor, scrambling to escape the angry shadow approaching me.

The glass cut right through my palm, and I screamed again. Blood mixed with the clear alcohol on the floor, swirling in patterns, and someone banged on the door.

'Fucking nosey bastards,' the man grumbled, picking me up. I fought against his hold, and he lowered his mouth to my ear. 'Don't fuckin' fight me, rat, or you'll have my belt across your back.' I stilled. 'Good boy.'

The door opened and the old woman across the hall was there with a worried look. 'I heard a smash and a scream – is everything okay?'

'Fine. The boy knocked my glass off the side while I wasn't in the room and tried cleaning it up – cut his hand a couple times. If you don't mind, I need to clean him up.' He shut the door on his lies.

'Every time. She knew. She never cared enough. All she cared about was sticking another ounce of shit into her bloodstream or snorting another gram. All she gave a fuck about was the bottom of her glass.'

One day, maybe you'll be useful and we can send you out to earn the money instead of your whore of a mother.

A fist. Another bruise.

That's all she's good for. Fucking. It's all you'll be good for one day.

A kick to the back.

No one is ever gonna want you. Not when they find out how much of a fucking slut your mother is.

A bang of the head on a chair leg.

You're only good for what she is. No one will ever care about you.

'Stop,' a soft, pained voice whispers. Hands press tenderly against my cheeks, lips brush my forehead. 'You can stop now.'

I open my eyes that must have closed while I was lost in my head. Megan's blue eyes are brimming with tears.

'You can stop,' she repeats. 'You're safe here. You're safe with me.' She strokes my cheek as a tear rolls down hers. 'You're safe.'

The fog begins to clear, the memories pushing back, and I see her clearly. The pain etched on her face is something I never want to see again. It's something I put there. This is why I never wanted to tell her. This is why I never wanted to get this close to her.

'Don't cry for me, baby.' I brush my thumb under her eye. 'I'm not worth your tears.'

She nods. 'You are. You're worth every last tear in my body.'

'I'm not,' I argue, moving away from her. I shove off the bed and begin to pace the floor, the old words reopening the scars and reinforcing everything I've tried to push back. Reminding me of what I am. Reminding me of the worth of my life, of my body. 'I'm not worth you. Don't you get it? They were fucking right, Megs. I'm not worth anything. I'm too fucked up. Everything they ever said – every time they told me I wasn't worth shit, every time they told me no one would ever want me—'

'They were wrong,' she says in a small but strong voice. 'They were *wrong*. All of it. It was all lies.'

I press my hands against the wall and clench my jaw. 'Nah. They were right. Every fucking one of them. I'm fucked up. I'm broken, a bunch of mismatched pieces stuck together in a shit attempt at being fixed.'

The bed springs squeak and the floorboards creak. A soft hand touches my back, another wraps around my tightened bicep.

'They weren't right. They were far from being right.'

'You don't know that.'

'Yes I do.' She wraps her hands around my arm and rests her head against me. 'They were wrong, because I want you. I want all of you – even the broken parts and the mismatched parts.'

I find her eyes. 'Why? Why? I can't give you what you really want. I can't give you sunshine and fucking rainbows. I can't give you puppies and fluffy bunnies. I can't give you the perfect you deserve.'

'I don't want perfect, and if I want sunshine and rainbows, I'll go to the local elementary school and visit the kindergarten class.'

I push off from the wall, her hands falling away. 'It'll always end up as sex. There's nothing inside, baby. I'm fucking empty.'

'You're lying and you know it.'

'Am I?' I turn, pinning her with my gaze. I am lying – but

it's better this way. 'Am I lying? You think I feel anything when I take some girl back on a Saturday night? You think I feel anything other than sex?'

Silence stretches, and I fucking hate myself for this. I hate myself for pushing away the one person I want to pull into me.

'I know you don't feel anything other than sex when you take a girl back to your room on a Saturday night.'

That's more painful than the physical kicks to the stomach I used to get. 'So why are you still here?'

'Because I'm not just any girl,' she says with certainty, her eyes boring into mine. 'Do you think I'm dumb, Aston? You just bared your soul to me – the deepest, darkest parts of it – and now you're trying to push me away. Who are you really trying to protect, huh? Is it me or is it you? Do you feel nothing for me when you call me "baby"? Do you feel nothing when you hold me against you? Do you honestly feel nothing when we're together? Go on. Tell me! Tell me that right now, with me looking into your eyes that you feel nothing, and I'll walk out that damn door. Tell me you don't care.'

I can't.

'Tell me!'

And she knows it.

'Go on!'

'I can't!' I yell. 'I can't fucking tell you that! And that's the problem. You have to go. You have to walk away, because I can't. You have to protect yourself from me, because I can't walk away from you.'

'I don't want you to!' She storms across the room. 'I don't want you to walk away from me!' She stops in front of me, her chest heaving, and continues in a quieter voice, 'I don't want you to walk away.'

No one will ever want you. No one will care. You're not worth shit. Son of a bitch. Useless prick.

I grab her and pull her against me, burying my face in her hair. I'm shaking as I hold her. I need her – I don't know what it is, but I need her more than I've ever needed anything. She's all I can feel. She makes me want to rip apart the mismatched pieces of myself and put them back in the right places. She awakens something in me, a will to live, a will to *love*. With her arms wrapped around my waist, her hands spread against my back, and her head tucked into my neck, it feels like home.

Megan feels like home to me.

Megan

'Did she really never tell you about your dad?' I ask, drawing circles on Aston's arm with my fingertip.

'No. Gramps told me a few years ago she went away for a friend's birthday and a few weeks later found out she was pregnant. She swore there was only him but she couldn't remember his name,' he replies. 'It doesn't matter, anyway. I have my Gramps, and that's what matters. He was there when no one else was.'

'He sounds like an amazing man,' I say, tilting my head back and staring into his gray eyes. 'It makes it easy to understand where you get it from.'

He makes a noise of disbelief. 'I'm not amazing, baby, far from it.'

'The beauty of being an outsider is that I can see what you can't,' I argue. 'You might not see it yet, you might never see it, but you are.' I raise my hand to his face, stroke my thumb down his cheek and across the faint stubble on his jaw. And I'm not lying – I can see everything he can't. I can see the beauty of him hiding behind the ugly memories of his past. He just needs to let it shine through.

'If you say so.' He catches my hand in his and kisses each of my fingers softly.

'I'm sorry I made you remember those things,' I say in a small voice.

'I'm not,' he replies firmly. 'I'm not sorry you did. You were right yesterday. You have to get lost in the dark to appreciate the light. My head is full of darkness, full of shadows and horrors, and then I look into your eyes. It's like finding the light at the end of the tunnel – the light I never thought I'd find.'

I flatten my hand against his cheek, his resting atop mine, and move my face forward so our lips brush. 'I like that. I love that I make you feel that way.'

'It's true. Who else could I threaten about spanking across the kitchen table?' His lips twitch, a bit of the normal light returning to his eyes as the darkness recedes.

'I'm sure you could find someone.' I shrug a shoulder.

'I probably could, but I don't want to find someone.' His face turns serious again, and his hand trails along my arm and rests on my back. 'I have to tell you something else – but you have to promise me you won't get mad and leave.'

'I'm. Not. Leaving.' I put extra emphasis on each word. 'Okay? I'm not going anywhere.'

For a second I see a glimpse of the little boy he keeps inside flash in his eyes, and my heart breaks a little. A tiny crack forms for the pain he must feel.

'A few nights ago I went to this bar. It's out the way, and I went there because I had to prove to myself I'm not like my mom was.' He closes his eyes, gathers himself, and opens them again. 'I knew if I went in there and left with someone, I'd be no better than she was.'

I swallow, trying not to let my facial expression change as a little bile rises up my throat. Even as my whole body tightens, a part of me believes he didn't. He's stronger than that. A part of me has to believe that.

'And?'

Outside my voice is calm, deceptively so, but inside my body is raging. It's raging that he'd try it, raging at the people who made him this way, raging at the words he must have heard so many times to make him believe he's no better than his mom.

'I couldn't. I was in there for maybe five minutes, tops, and I had to leave. I had to run. It wasn't me.' He looks steadily into my eyes. 'And you're the reason I left. Hell, you're the reason I went. I told myself that if I went and left alone, I was good enough for you. If I left alone, I cared, I had feelings. If I left alone, I wasn't hollow inside.'

'You're not hollow inside.' I prop myself up on my elbow and look down at him, running my fingers through his hair. 'You do feel – you must have felt to go in the first place. And as for being good enough for me . . .' I shake my head. 'Who dictates that? Society? A TV show? A romance novel? No. Not even Braden can dictate that, Aston. The only person who decides if someone is good enough for me, is me, and I say you are most definitely good enough for me.'

He tucks my hair behind my ear. 'How do you know?'

I smile a little. 'Well, you're no Mr. Darcy, but you know . . .'

His fingers move against my side, tickling me, and I fall backwards onto the bed, laughing. He leans over me, his leg slipping between mine and his hips pinning me down. His hand leaves my side and travels up my body to my hand where he links our fingers.

'"You have bewitched me, body and soul,"' he murmurs, looking down into my eyes. 'I forgot the accent, but I'm sure that'll do. That's all I can remember of the book when I look at you.'

'One of my favorite lines.' I smile. 'Do I make you forget things often?'

'All the time.' He lowers his lips, moving them softly across mine for a long, lingering moment.

'I can't believe you actually know some Jane Austen,' I muse, moving his hair from his face.

How many guys know Jane Austen? Every day he surprises me a little more.

'It was the first classic novel my Gramps made me read. I was eight.' He props his head on his hand. 'He said that although Darcy was a pompous ass in the beginning, if I grew up and loved a woman the way he loved Elizabeth in the end, then he'd done his job at raising me.' He trails a finger down the side of my face.

'He gave you the book to teach you to respect women,' I say

in awe. 'He wanted you to take Darcy's journey of respecting and loving Elizabeth and apply it to real life. Your Gramps is a genius.'

'I'll tell him you said that.' He grins.

'I'll tell him myself if I ever get to meet him.'

'You can. If you want to.'

'Really?'

Aston nods. 'I've already told you the worst. Gramps . . . Well, he'll probably be happy to have someone to talk to who actually enjoys discussing literature's greatest love stories. Hell, I don't have much patience for that shit.'

'I would love to meet him,' I say honestly. 'And discuss literature's greatest love stories.'

'Tomorrow?' Aston questions, the little boy showing in his eyes again, and I realize he's letting me in.

By taking me to meet his Gramps, he's giving me more of himself. He's letting me meet the one person who really knows him . . . The one person that knows the little boy inside.

I run the pad of my thumb along his bottom lip. 'Tomorrow. I'll be sure to bring Mr. Darcy.'

'No need.' He drops his face to mine again, taking my bottom lip between his and sucking lightly. 'I'll be a real life Mr. Darcy.'

'You don't have the top hat and tails,' I protest, clasping my hands behind his head.

'Who needs them? They'd end up on the floor anyway.'

I giggle as he kisses me again, his body pressing into mine. 'You're probably right.'

I feel like I'm fifteen and sneaking back into my room after breaking curfew.

I never intended to stay at the frat house last night – it just happened. After Aston told me everything, I couldn't leave. I couldn't walk away, leaving him with the memories I made him drag out.

So that's why I'm creeping out in yesterday's clothes to change quickly before he takes me to meet his Gramps.

Hoping everyone else is still in bed or doing what they normally do on a Sunday morning, I silently pad my way down the stairs. Kyle's deep voice makes me pause.

'A blonde girl?' he asks.

'Yeah. I didn't see who it was, though. As far as I know she was still in his room last night.'

'You mean Aston didn't come down and pull some chick?'

Fuck.

I press my hand over my mouth to stifle the stream of curse words. I glance at the front door. If I turn the corner right now, whoever is outside will see me and know *I* was the girl in his room.

'Megan?' a voice asks, and I bite my tongue.

'Nah. Braden would kill him.'

That's it.

I take my pumps off and skip up the stairs on tip toes. My hands shake as I fumble for Braden's key in the pocket of my jeans and slip it in the lock. I sneak into his room, and take one of my books from his desk.

Thank you, Braden, for your constant need to copy my English notes.

The door clicks shut behind me, and I put my pumps back on. I know I look on the rough side of human – hey, it is a Saturday – but I walk casually down the stairs anyway. Kyle and the other guy, Mark, both look at me as I appear in their line of view.

'Morning.' I smile and wave slightly.

'Uh,' Kyle says awkwardly. 'You're here early.'

I lift the book. 'Braden had my notes again. It's exactly why I have a key for his room.'

'Seriously?' Mark narrows his eyes, looking at me suspiciously.

'The book is in my hand, isn't it? Want me to take you up and show you how many of my damn books he has sitting on his desk?' I offer, pointing to the stairs more calmly than I feel. 'It's no big deal.'

'Nah, you're alright,' he replies, relaxing.

'Great.' I fake a smile. 'I'd love to stay and chat, but I have a paper to write. See ya.'

'Bye, Megs.' Kyle waves as I turn and leave the frat house.

All the air rushes from my lungs when the door shuts behind me, and I force myself to walk instead of run. *Shit.* That was close – too fucking close – and I've exhausted my number one excuse for being at the frat house when Braden or the girls aren't.

'Where the fuck were you last night?'

Kay's voice sends a bolt of panic through me. Hell. Can I get a break today?

'Why do you need to know?' I ask, letting myself into the dorm block.

'Because I came round here to bring your ass to a party – not with those dicks at Braden's house – and you weren't here. Where were you?'

I put my hand on my doorframe, grinning, and decide to play it coy. 'Wouldn't you like to know?'

She smirks. 'Fucking right I'd like to know. Did you finally get some?'

I shove the door open. 'A lady never reveals her secrets!' And slam it shut before she can question me further.

'You bitch!' she yells, banging on the door. 'I'm not letting this go!'

'I know!' But at least now I have time to come up with an excuse.

I exhale, a long, tortured sigh, and rest my forehead on the door. Who thought a secret relationship was a good idea?

Oh, yeah, me.

That was before the secret relationship became something complex, more than just a boy and a girl. Now it's entwined deeply in a past filled with horrors I can't even imagine, voices I'll never hear, and memories I'll never see fully. It's not just a passing college fling, something to pass the time.

It's real.

It's as real as a relationship could ever be.

I straighten and chuck the book on my bed, not caring when

it slips to the floor, and strip as I head to the shower. A quick
hot shower should sort me out and relax me from this morning's close calls. Too many in such a short space of time. There's
only so many excuses I can come up with before the truth will
have to come out, and I know that moment will be so explosive
that even the Chinese New Year won't be able to touch it with
their fireworks.

I step from the shower and run through the motions of getting
ready, standing in front of my closet for longer than necessary.
I mean, this is the equivalent of the 'Meet the Parents' moment,
right? So a good impression – literature aside – is necessary.
But what the hell do you wear to meet someone's grandfather?

The gray sky outside makes me rethink my skirt idea. I pull
out a pair of jeans instead and couple them with a colorful
shirt and wrap-around sweater. I blast my hair with the hairdryer, clipping it away from my face with a flower pin, and
smudge on some make-up.

My cell buzzes and a message from Aston pops up. *Ready
when you are.*

Give me five.

Convinced that it'll be sunny I grab a light jacket and
sunglasses, and leave the dorm room. The sky has darkened
only a little. It won't rain. Yet.

The walk downtown doesn't take long, and I find Aston
parked exactly where he said he'd be. I knock on the window,
smiling, and he leans over to open the door. I get in and he
leans over the gearstick to kiss me soundly.

'Risky,' I mutter.

'And being seen in a car with you isn't?' he shoots back,
amused.

I produce my glasses from under my jacket and slip them
on. 'See? I'm in disguise.'

'You still look like you.' He grins as he pulls out. 'We're not
passing campus, anyway. It's still early, so I doubt many people
will be about.'

'You say that. If I was Pinocchio, my nose would be about
ten foot long I've told so many lies this morning.'

'Who to?' He glances at me.

'Kyle and Mark, then Kay,' I grumble. 'Kyle and Mark think I'd slipped in to grab a book from Braden's room, and Kay thinks I was with a guy all night.'

'Which is right. But she doesn't know?'

'No. She doesn't know. I slammed my door in her face.'

'She won't let that go.'

'I know. But I have time to make a decent excuse as to why I can't tell her who I was with.'

He sighs. 'You know she's gonna tell Lila and Maddie, and they'll be on your case, right?'

I tuck my hair behind my ear and chew on my thumbnail. 'I know,' I mumble. 'But I didn't have time to think. I was still reeling from Kyle and Mark. She caught me off-guard. I'm a real crappy secret girlfriend.'

'I like that.'

'That I'm a crappy secret girlfriend?' I frown at him as he pulls up outside a tidy, two-story house with perfectly pruned bushes and flowers.

'No, well, yeah.' He turns, his gray eyes light and piercing straight into mine. He smiles, grabbing my hand and tugging me toward him. 'The girlfriend part.'

I blush a little as I realize it's the first time either of us have said that word. 'Oh, um . . .'

His lips touch mine, and he mutters against me, 'Don't. I like the thought of you being my girlfriend, even if you are secret.'

'Like Romeo and Juliet?'

'Save the literature for Gramps.' He leans back and smiles. 'But, yeah, kinda. Just without the dyin' and stuff.'

I put my hand on the door handle and smile at him over my shoulder. 'I can totally go for that.'

My feet touch the ground and I realize how nervous I am. When it's me and Aston and we're messing around, talking, I don't feel nervous. But now I'm standing in front his Gramps' house, my heart is pounding and my palms are getting sweaty. I run my tongue over my lips, wetting them since they're suddenly dry, and swallow.

Aston takes my hand, linking our fingers, and pulls me toward the house. 'Don't be scared.'

'Does he know I'm here?'

He grins, his hand on the door handle. 'Nope.'

My mouth drops, and he pushes the door open, letting out the smell of cigar smoke.

'I wish you wouldn't smoke those damn things, Gramps!' he calls.

'So you keep sayin', boy, and I keep sayin' I ain't gonna stop.'

Aston grins again, and I get the feeling this is a routine for them. 'Well if you're smokin' now, put the thing out. I brought company.'

'Better not be one of those jackass frat boys you live with,' his Gramps grumbles.

'No, it's not one of those jackasses.' Aston chuckles slightly. 'Better than that. Much better.'

'What, you bring me a stripper?'

'Uh, no. Maybe next time.'

I smile, loving the easy banter between the two.

'Well? Who is it?'

We step into the front room, and an old man is sitting quietly in an armchair at the far end of the room. He turns his head from where he was looking out the window, and I can see interest spark in his gray eyes. Gray eyes the exact same shade as Aston's.

'This is Megan,' Aston introduces us. 'Megan, this is my Gramps. Just call him Gramps.'

'Hell, she's a pretty thing, ain't she, boy?' Gramps says, looking at me and smiling. 'Come sit down, darlin', and don't you mind him. His manners are a bit iffy since he started hanging around with those jackass frat boys.'

I laugh slightly and let Aston lead me over to the sofa opposite his Gramps. I sit on the cozy cushions, and Aston stops mid-sit.

'Let me guess. You want me to remember my manners and go get Megs a drink?' he asks with a raised eyebrow.

'Off you go.'

I smile at Aston's exaggerated sigh, and I can almost see the closeness in their relationship. It's not just the fact Aston is so like his Gramps, just sixty or so years younger, it's in their easy banter and the affectionate smiles they have. His Gramps' comments remind me so much of my Nan – she's a crazy old thing with a penchant for 'hot young things', as she puts it, but I love her.

Gramps looks at me and winks. 'Gotta keep the boy on his toes. So, Megan, are you the girlfriend?' He looks so much like Aston in that second I can't help but smile wider.

'That's me.'

'He never mentioned you before.'

'It's, um . . . complicated.'

'Protective older brother ready to kick some pretty-boy ass?'

I think I love this man.

'Something like that.' I grin. 'Best friend.'

'Jackass frat boy?' he questions.

I nod.

'See, boy? I told you they're all jackasses. Were in my day, still are now.'

'And you raised the biggest one,' Aston pats the old man's shoulder, putting a tray of drinks on the table and passing me one.

'Thank you.' I look up at him, feeling a little shy now we're in front of his gramps.

'Damn right. And he's a pretty boy! No one can tell me I did half a job raisin' you, kid.' Gramps grins, raises his glass of lemonade, and takes a drink before setting it back on the table. 'So, Megan, do you like literature?'

Aston smirks, resting his arm on the sofa behind me, and I smile. 'It's my major.'

Gramps' eyes light up and he sits up a little straighter. 'Favorite novelist?'

'Jane Austen. *Pride and Prejudice*, before you ask.'

'By god, boy!' he exclaims in glee and claps his hands. 'We have a keeper with this one!' He turns to me again. 'Second favorite?'

I chew my lip for a second. 'Dickens or Louisa May Alcott. It's tough, but Alcott might just win out. Her ability to create a whole cast of compelling, lovable characters – not just one or two – is something I've yet to find in another writer.'

Gramps shakes his head. 'You're telling me *Little Women* is better than *Great Expectations*?'

'Oh, no,' I say. 'Not better – the stories are on par with each other, but their styles are very different. My preference runs with Alcott's style, and I have a bit of a crush on Laurie.' I shrug a shoulder.

'How many boys in books are you dating?' Aston pokes my shoulder. 'First Darcy, now Laurie . . .'

'The proper term is book boyfriend,' I correct him. 'And there are many swoon-worthy characters in the literary world, new and old.'

'What about if I was in a book?' He grins. 'Would I be your book boyfriend?'

'God help the world if someone ever wrote you into a book, boy,' Gramps grumbles. 'That would be a literary disaster.'

Aston sticks his tongue out, and Gramps laughs.

'Be nice, old man, or I'll hide the walking stick.'

'Hide the walking stick and I'll kick your ass with it!' Gramps threatens. 'It wouldn't be the first time and I'm sure it won't be the last!'

I smile, looking at Aston and tuning the conversation out a little as they continue to banter back and forth. His body and expression are relaxed, his smile easy, and his eyes light. This is the real Aston, the one he doesn't show. He's happy and playful, yet there's an underlying shadow to him.

If I ever had any doubt whether or not I was falling in love with Aston Banks, it's been completely wiped out.

There is no doubt. Here in the place he spent the happier years of his childhood sitting across from the man who made him into the incredible person he is today, there is only certainty.

Aston's expression darkens slightly, and I listen again.

'Gramps . . .'

'I just want to know if you went.'

'No. I didn't go and I don't plan to.'

I look between the two, trying not to appear nosey – very hard when you feel like a third wheel.

'It might do you good.'

'I'm not ready.'

'It's been thirteen years, boy.'

'I don't care if it's been thirteen or thirty, Gramps. I'm not ready!' Aston stands and leaves the room, leaving his Gramps sighing.

The old man turns his face toward the window, his own shadows passing over his face. His eyes flick to me, hovering on my face for a moment. 'Did he tell you? About himself?'

'Some,' I reply honestly. 'He got so far and . . . It was too much.'

He nods his head, his gaze going back to the window. 'I got him when he was six – the day they found out his mom had died. She was my baby. My only child. Losing her near killed me but he gave me something to live for. I had to protect him and give him the life she couldn't.

'He spent two days in hospital while he was checked out. He was underweight, dirty, and completely starving. But that wasn't the worst. There was a big gash on his palm with tiny pieces of glass in that had been left, scratches, and healing cuts across his legs, and a huge bruise on his back.' He looks at me, and I don't try to disguise my horror.

'How could . . .' I trail off, putting my hand to my mouth as what he just said processes in my mind, and I shake my head.

I try to process it but I just can't imagine it. I can't imagine the pain Aston must have been in, both mental and physical. It makes me feel sick to my stomach, and I flatten my other hand over it like it'll stop the churning inside.

'He blames his mom for what happened. He blames her for never protecting him – but I'm the one that should be blamed. I knew she wasn't fit to keep him, yet I left it anyway. His gran died when he was four and I was stuck in a loop of grief.' He looks back at the window, and I follow suit, seeing

Aston leaning against a tree. 'I should be blamed for not protecting him.'

'You didn't know what was happening, did you?'

'No.'

The sadness coming off of him wraps around me and hurts me as much as Aston's does. I can see in the slump of his shoulders the guilt he's been carrying around for all these years, and in the downturn of his lips how much he really feels he's to blame. And it makes me mad. I hate that this innocent and loving old man feels that way because of the cruel and selfish actions of complete and utter bastards.

I sit up straighter. 'Then how can you be blamed for something you knew nothing about? You took him in and brought him up to be the person he is today, and as much as he doesn't believe it, he's a credit to you. He doesn't see it, but he is. You did your best to make your daughter's wrongs right again. You could have walked away and left him to the state, but you didn't, and I for one think that makes you an incredible person.'

His voice breaks. 'You're very wise, Megan.'

'It's the books.' I turn my head, and we both share a small smile. 'You mentioned about him going somewhere . . .'

'His mom's grave. I try every year to get him to go, but he always says he's not ready. Stubborn little ass.' He bangs his fist against the arm of his chair.

'I don't think he's accepted what happened to him. I don't think he's let himself deal with it.'

'I hope he can. I hope *you* can deal with it.' Gramps looks at me seriously, his gray eyes like granite. 'It's not easy, what he's dealt with. What you know is only a small part of the crap my boy went through.'

'I can deal with it,' I reassure him. 'And I can help him deal with it. I want to.'

'I like you,' he says suddenly. 'You come across as a total romantic, but you have a kick-ass, hard edge to you. You won't take his shit, will ya?'

'I never have taken his shit, and I don't intend to start now.' I smirk.

'Do me a favor?' Gramps leans forward. 'One day, get him to his mom's grave. Even just for a minute. And for god's sake, don't let the pretty ass walk all over you. He thinks he's Mr. Darcy.'

'Then call me Elizabeth.' I smile.

Aston

Why did he have to bring it up? Of all the things he could talk about, he brings her up. Every fucking time! I don't want to talk about her. Not to him. He doesn't understand. He doesn't know the same person I did. His ideals are different to mine.

His memories are a thousand miles apart from mine.

I kick at the sand, pulling my jacket tighter around my body, and Megan speaks for the first time since we left Gramps' house and drove north where no one would find us. 'You okay?'

I shake my head. 'No. Every time. Every fucking time he brings her up. I thought he wouldn't in front of you, but he did.'

'He has his own pain,' she says softly. 'It doesn't excuse it, but he does. He feels guilty for what happened to you – that he couldn't stop it.'

My mind reels, and I look down at her. 'He told you that?'

She nods, letting her hand drop from my back, and stands in front of me. I stop.

'You've never let him tell you.' She reaches up and cups my face. 'He hurts too, Aston. You both hurt. It's not something that will go away, but you can't let it rule your lives. If you let pain rule you you'll get lost in it.'

'What if I'm already lost?'

'You're not lost. You're hiding but you're not lost. I won't let you get lost.'

I let my hands come up to rest on her back and pull her into me. 'What if there's no map?'

'Then I'll get lost with you,' she whispers. 'I won't let you let them win, Aston. I won't let you get sucked in by those demons. I care too much to let that happen.'

And she does. I can hear it in her voice.

She wraps her arms around my neck, and I hold her to me tighter, our foreheads resting against each other.

'I'll try, Megs,' I promise. 'I can't say I won't, but as long as you're here, I think I'll be okay.'

'And you'll talk to your Gramps? Just once?'

'I'll think about it. How about we just focus on stopping me from getting lost for a bit?'

'You just need a place to aim for, that's all. You need a place to go to.'

'Go on then.' I smile. 'Give me a place.'

'Okay.' She pauses for a second, closing her eyes and chewing her lip.

'I'm waiting . . .' I tease her.

Her blue eyes open, shocking me with their vitality. 'Aim for the moon, because even if you miss, you'll land among the stars.'

'I don't need to aim for the sky. The only star I'll ever need is standing right in front of me.' I brush my lips over hers. 'Maybe the place I need to aim for is nowhere other than where I am right now.'

'Maybe I'd go with you wherever you ended up.'

'Maybe I'd never ask that of you.'

'Maybe you wouldn't need to ask. Maybe you'll never need to ask me for anything, because I'll always be here.' She silences my upcoming argument by pressing her lips firmly against mine, holding me prisoner in her kiss. Her fingers tangle in my hair, her body fitting against mine perfectly.

My arms tighten around her waist, one of my hands moving up her back to cup the back of her head. She stands on her tiptoes and her tongue meets mine, never relenting in the pressure of her movements.

This girl is sliding between the cracks of me and gripping hold of the mismatched pieces before tearing them apart. She's studying them, getting to know them, to know me, and then she's carefully lining them all back up and holding them together.

What she'll never know is she's the glue that holds it together.

She's the glue that holds me together.

'So it's Sunday evening and we're on a deserted, dark beach in Northern California in the freezing cold, eating ice cream,' Megan summarizes, running her finger around the top of her cone and licking it off.

'That sounds about right.'

'And why are we eating ice cream instead of oh, having a coffee in Starbucks?' She raises an eyebrow at me.

I shrug. 'I don't think they have a Starbucks in . . . wherever the fucking hell we are.'

'Wherever we are? Oh, god. Remind me never to let you drive anywhere again.'

'Let me?'

'Yes. Let you.'

I scoop my arm around her waist and pull her into me. 'You didn't let me do anything. I didn't see you offering to drive.'

'Why would I offer to drive when you could do it for me?'

'But you just said . . .' I shake my head, smiling at her playful grin. 'Never mind. I don't think it's even worth trying to fucking understand.'

'No, it's not.' She beams, kissing me quickly and scooting away. 'I'm just one of those people you'll never understand.'

'That's because you're complicated.'

'I am not complicated!'

'If you were simple, I'd be able to understand you.'

She finishes the ice cream and throws the cone toward the trash as we come to edge of the beach. 'You win.'

'You didn't eat the cone?' I ask.

'I don't like the cones.' She hops up onto the hood of the car, her legs hanging over the front.

'So why do you order ice cream cones?' I stand between her legs, and she hooks them round my waist, sliding into me.

'Because I like the ice cream,' she says with a furrow in her brow. 'Why else?'

I grin, and a fat raindrop falls on the car. Another follows it, and another, and another, and she squeals as one falls on her cheek.

Her hands push at my shoulders and she releases my waist as she tries to get away. I laugh as it rains harder, the cold drops soaking us in seconds. My t-shirt clings to my skin and my eyes flick to the drops of water sliding their way down Megan's chest, disappearing below the neck of her shirt. I take her hands from my waist and slide my fingers between hers, still laughing.

'Aston, no! Let me up! It's raining!'

'And?' I ask. 'You're already soaking wet.' She wriggles against me, her center rubbing against my jeans and causing the blood in my body to rush downwards. She wriggles once more and pauses, looking up at me when she realizes my dick is rock hard.

'Did I, er, do that?' She batters her eyelashes.

'Mhmm,' I hum out, leaning into her.

'But the rai—'

My lips capture her mouth in a crushing kiss. My body is taut against hers as I lean forward, pushing her against the hood of the car. Our wet shirts rub together and hers rides up slightly. Our hands hit the car above her head and she gasps, my tongue meeting hers as I hold her hands still, my hips pinning hers. She moves her legs up, hooking them over my hips and clutching them around my waist. Her back arches into me so every inch of us really is touching.

Rain continues to beat down, covering us both as our tongues battle each other, sweeping and caressing. I release her hands, grip her wrists with one hand, and slide my free one down her wet body. Her shirt is slightly drier where it's against the car, and I run my hand along the part of her back not touching the hood. My fingers tickle and tease her, my thumb running just inside the back of her jeans, feeling the strap of her thong. My hips press into hers, and in this second, all good thoughts are gone.

A wet Megan – in more ways than one – is sending my dick into overdrive, and it's the only part of me thinking right now.

She gasps as I run my nose down her neck, breathing heavily against her slick skin.

'Megs—'

'Do you need me, or do you need what I can give you?' she asks bluntly, making my head snap back.

I get it.

'You,' I reply honestly, looking into her eyes. 'I fucking need *you*.'

'And if someone catches us?'

'Do you see anyone around?' I let her up, holding her against me and cupping her ass in my hands. 'You're gonna have to open the car door, 'cause my hands are full.'

I carry her round, my dick straining against my jeans, and she opens the door. I all but drop her in, and she sprawls on the back seat. I climb in after her, shutting the door, and lean over her. Her breathing is heavy as she gazes up at me through heavy eyelids.

I drop my head and kiss the spot beneath her ear, letting my mouth go down and down until it reaches the swell of her boobs. My tongue flicks out and runs inside her low-cut shirt and bra, reaching until it flicks against her nipple. She whimpers, clutching at my back, and I reach in and undo the buttons down the front of her body.

Her shirt falls away, revealing her body, and I keep kissing her, even as my hands fall to her jeans and begin to peel the wet material away down her thighs. I sit up, tugging it off the rest of the way, and she kicks the ceiling.

'Shit,' she hisses, dropping her head back slightly. I laugh slightly, running my hands up her legs. She grabs fistfuls of my shirt and yanks me forward. 'You shut up and kiss me.'

'Fuck yes,' I answer, taking her mouth with mine. Her fingers flick down my stomach, slipping under my shirt and caressing my stomach until they finally unclip the button on my jeans. She pushes my jeans down with her feet and pushes her body against mine.

My dick jumps at the contact, and I mutter a garbled curse into her mouth, ripping my boxers down and sliding her thong to the side. My fingers slip along and inside her tightness easily, and in seconds I replace my fingers with my cock and push into her. Her legs tighten around my waist and she grabs at my lower back, taking me in one easy swoop.

Judging by the constant clench of her muscles and the wetness surrounding me, sex outside turns Megan on.

My fingers dip into her wet hair, my tongue dips into her mouth, and our hips grind together rhythmically.

In this deserted place where no one knows her, where no one knows me, we are as one.

And I realize it really is her I need.

Mommy was mad. I'd heard her shouting at him for a long time. I didn't know what many of the words meant, but they were words Mommy said were naughty and only for grown-ups. Words I mustn't say.

'They're coming tomorrow!' Mommy shouted. 'What am I supposed to tell them this fucking time?'

'I don't fuckin' know! He's five years old – he fell out of a damn tree for all I care!'

'And got a black eye? From what? A freakin' tree root?!'

'Think of something!' he yelled at her, his feet stomping against the floor. Mommy always said not to stomp. Stomping is naughty. 'They always believe you anyway!'

'Where are you going?'

'I'm leaving this fucking shithole before you get a black eye to match your little bastard of a son's!'

The door slammed. I jumped, rubbing Bunny's ear against my cheek. Soft.

I didn't like this man. I didn't like any of the men, but he was the most horrible. He was really big and had lots of funny pictures all over his arms. I asked him what they were once and he shouted at me. I just wanted to see the pictures.

'Fuck! Fucking useless jackass!' Mommy yelled the naughty words and the door slammed after her.

I didn't mind her going. She was going to get money for food, she said. She said she had to work, but usually a nasty man stayed with me, drinking horrible beer.

I got up and pushed my door open slightly, looking around. I was really alone and it was dark. I didn't like the dark. The horrible men said big scary monsters were in the dark ready to eat little boys like me.

I looked toward the kitchen, shaking, my stomach hurting. I wanted to eat something. I was hungry. Mommy didn't have any food this morning, apart from a biscuit she gave me. Just a plain biscuit. I wanted some gravy.

I hugged Bunny even closer and looked around again. Maybe if I looked I could find some food.

Someone knocked at the door and I screamed. The big scary monsters. I started to cry and ran back into my room, pushing the door shut. I took my blanket from my bed and crawled under the bed, moving right to the back corner. My blanket wrapped around me and I curled into a ball.

No one ever found me here.

I was safe from the monsters.

Darkness. Monsters.

I pat the bed beside me. *The bed. Not the floor.*

I lean over, turning my bedside lamp on, and look around. My room – in the frat house. At college. In Berkeley – not my tiny room in San Francisco. No monsters, no men, no Mom. Just me, alone.

I bury my face in my shaking hands, adrenaline still running rife from my dream.

Fell from a tree. And they fucking believed it. The asshole had put his fist in my face for the first ever time, and all because I'd walked in front of the television and he'd missed a touchdown. That was all it took, five seconds, and I had another bruise, another memory, another scar to add to the collection.

And she still never did anything about it. She still covered it up. She still never checked on me.

Monsters.

It amazes me I was so fucking afraid of monsters that didn't exist. The real monsters were the tattooed, alcohol and drug dependent dicks she brought home again and again. They were the monsters – not the things a five-year-old boy's mind could conjure up.

The monsters in my mind then were much less worse than the ones I faced daily. They were nicer than the monsters I still face now.

I roll over, leaving the light on, and bring my knees to my chest. My thick blankets cover me the way my thin ones used to, and I curl up the way I used to under the bed. My need to protect myself, to protect my body outweighs all else.

In my mind, I am five again.

Megan

And we're back to it.

Another day of lies. Another day of pretending. Another day of wishful glances, discreet smiles, and banter with an underlying meaning only we understand.

Another day I have to remind myself that we *chose* this. We chose to be secret and not tell Braden. I'm just not sure how much longer we can keep it this way. Someone will find out eventually no matter how careful we are.

Hell, Kay and Lila are already halfway there.

'Just tell me who,' Lila begs me. 'I won't tell anyone, I swear.'

'It's not a big deal. It was just one night. You guys are always telling me I need to get some, and I have, so leave it at that.'

'You're kiddin' me!' Kay exclaims. 'I want the details!'

'Maybe I don't want to give you the details.'

'Maybe I can keep buggin' the shit out of you until you give them to me.'

'Maybe I still won't give you the details.' I shake my head. 'Seriously, you guys, I'm not giving you what you want.'

Maddie grins. 'Stubborn.'

'No, just private.' I wink.

'Boring,' Lila counters. 'Boring is what it is.' She sighs. 'I and Maddie have shared our deets before, Kay has given us enough to write a damn book, and it's only you left to share – which you haven't this year. At all.'

'There's nothing to share!' I protest, ignoring the guilt at lying yet again. I know full well there's a *lot* to share. 'It just happened. It's not going to be mentioned again, so there we go. Conversation over.' I check the time on my watch and grab my books, standing up. 'I have to get to class. I'll see you later.'

'What are you hiding, Megan Harper?' Lila yells after me.

I shake my head, chewing the inside of my lip, and keep walking. *Nothing,* I want to yell over my shoulder. *Aston,* is the word that crawls up my throat. I stay silent, making my way through the few people still milling through the hallways laughing and joking.

I turn the corner to the stairwell, and Aston is standing at the bottom of the stairs. I double-take as he looks around the empty area and walks toward me. His eyes find mine. His broken, weak eyes. My stomach knots, and I'm relieved when he wraps his arms around my neck and buries his face in the hair falling around my neck.

My arms slide around his waist, and I hold him with the tightness he holds me, trying to ignore the heavy, deep breaths he's taking. Trying to ignore the heaving of his chest and the shaking of his body. He nudges my hair aside and kisses my neck softly, breathing in deeply. I pull my face back and look into his eyes. He blinks once and dips his head. His whole body tenses when his lips crush mine and he's shaking with more than just his pain. He's shaking with the need to let it all out but not being able to. He releases me suddenly and walks the way I just came.

I stare after him, my heart feeling like a lead weight in my chest as reality sinks in. He said I make it better, take the pain away. I'd bet anything he spent the night tormented by his past, by the nightmares and flashbacks he tries to run from. Telling me on Saturday, then the conversation with his Gramps on Sunday must have been the trigger.

And five seconds is all I get to hold him. Five risky, stolen seconds and one desperate kiss is all I can have to take the pain away.

I shoulder my bag and head up the stairs to class, unable to take him off my mind. All I can see in front of me are his eyes. Even as I sit at my desk and open my books, the words blur and I picture the pain etched onto his face. I picture the scars I'll never understand.

Because he was right. The worst scars are the ones you carry inside, the ones you hide from the rest of the world.

But I don't have the scars. I lived a happy, sheltered life in a nice area, a million miles away from the reality of some people's lives. The most horrible part of my childhood was my mom filtering my reading material and the best when Nanna told her to give it up and let me read what I wanted. I'm naïve and blind to the lives of people outside my own. I know this now, and I'll never understand Aston's pain. I'll never understand the things that circle his mind each day, the words that poison it.

"'Hell is empty and all the devils are here",' my professor quotes from her copy of *The Tempest*, the words slashing through my musings. 'A powerful statement – and very potent in a time where belief of the devil was very real. What did Shakespeare mean by his words?'

'He meant exactly what he said,' I say, my eyes focusing on the fifty-something woman pacing the front of the room. '"The devils are here." Whether or not he believed in God he would have believed that each of us have free will as the bible teaches us – the free will to be either good or evil. The people that chose to be evil, to steal, beat, murder, they were the devils. They still are.'

'So you agree, Megan?'

'How can you not? I'm by no means religious, nor do I pretend to be, but I'm not blind to the world. If there is a God, a greater good, then there must be a devil and a greater evil to balance it out. The greater evil is in the people sitting on both death row and a park bench. If there is a hell, it's most definitely empty. Ask anyone who has been unfortunate enough to come into contact with one of those people and has demons of their own left over. They'll tell you that the devils are here disguised as one of us.'

'So you're saying you could be sitting among devils and not know it?' Her eyebrow raises and she pauses in her pacing.

'You walk among them daily, whether or not you realize it. We all do, and we probably know someone that has demons inside their mind and not know it.'

My professor nods, moving onto someone else.

Demons. Just like Aston has.

Demons from the evil that spawned them.

Shakespeare was right. If there is a devil, he's definitely on this Earth.

Green-gray eyes. Chestnut brown hair with a hint of copper. Nice broad shoulders and the lingering of a summer tan on his skin. And as boring as a lecture on psychics in a monotone voice.

Which, in fact, could be what he's talking to me about right now.

I'm going to kill Lila for this one.

'I'm sorry.' I come back to the here and now. 'What did you say?'

He bristles a little. 'Did you listen to any of that?'

'Um.' A slight flush rises on my cheeks. 'Not really. I'm sorry. I'm not great company right now. I have a few things, er, going on.'

'Do you want to talk about it? It helps, you know.'

Dude, I can't even remember your name. I'm not about to tell you my life story.

'No, no, it's fine. Thanks.' I attempt a smile through gritted teeth, hoping I'm a better actress than I think I am. 'Maybe we should just finish up here.'

'Sure.' He waves toward the counter for our small bill, and I swallow my relieved sigh. He pays it despite my protests, and we step outside. 'So, Megan . . .'

Oh, no. Please don't.

'Mm?' I hope I don't look as worried as I feel. Crap. I'm a terrible person.

'I know you're not in the right kind of mood tonight, but maybe we could go out again sometime?'

Shit. 'Um.' I scratch behind my ear. What's his name? *Double shit.* 'Look, I'm not sure what Lila told you, but she's kind of setting me up. It's not you, I'm sure you're a lovely guy, but I'm just not looking for anything right now.'

He smiles widely and shrugs a shoulder. 'Yeah, she mentioned it. It was worth a shot though, right?'

'Uh, sure.' I smile again. 'I think I need to go and have a chat with her, actually. Thanks for the meal.'

'You're welcome.' He waves as he walks away, and I begin the walk back to campus, thinking over what I have to say to Lila.

I know how it will go. She'll demand to know why I can't possibly have any more dates, and I'll make up some floozy excuse that's about as believable as me saying I'm a Vegas stripper. But I can't do this anymore. I can't pretend to enjoy these dates. It's not fair on me, Aston, or on the guys I have to go out with.

I jog the final stretch to campus as rain lightly begins to fall. A shiver runs down my spine as yesterday comes back to me. Nothing can compare to the way I felt as Aston pinned me against the hood of his car, kissing me like I'm his one requirement to live.

Maybe that's why I can't consider anyone else, why every date Lila sends me on will be futile.

Maybe it's because when I look at other guys all I see is him.

I shake my hair out as I walk into the dorm room. Lila looks up from her books and grins. 'How did it go? I gotta say, I expected you to be back a lot later—'

'This has to stop,' I say bluntly. 'This dating thing. I won't do it anymore.'

'Why? Was he an ass?'

I shrug my jacket off. 'No, he was nice. Just like the last one. Shit, they're all nice, Li. I just don't care about any of them.'

'Let me guess – they're not your Mr. Darcy?' She raises an eyebrow, and I throw myself onto the bed.

'Precisely.'

'Let me help you find him.'

'I don't need your help to find him.'

'Megs, I just want you to find someone who makes you happy.'

'I'm happy!'

'I didn't say you weren't but I want you to find your Darcy. I want to help you do that.'

'I don't need your help!'

'Megs—'

'I've already found him!'

Fuckshitohmygod. I slap my hands over my mouth, my eyes widening to the size of dinner plates. Why did I say that? Fuck. Fuck. Now I've done it. This is it. Cover blown.

Well done, Megan Harper. You absolute fucking idiot.

Lila's eyes widen slowly and she drops her pen onto the bed. Her jaw drops open, and I feel like everything is moving in slow motion. *Why the hell did I have to say that?!*

'What?' she asks. 'You found him? Who is he?'

'Um. Did I say that?' I laugh nervously. 'Really? Ha. Um. I didn't. I don't. Shit.' I fall sideways on the bed and bury my head in my pillow, my heart pumping furiously.

'Nuh-uh!' she exclaims. 'You are not saying that and then just flaking on me, Megan Harper!' Her bed springs squeak and she gets up. Her hands wrap around my arm and she yanks me up. I pull the pillow up with me, keeping my face covered, but she tugs it away. I smack my hands over my face.

'Um, I lied?' I try lamely. 'To get you to stop?'

'No way! No. Way. I can't believe you found your Darcy and you didn't tell me.'

Yeah . . . 'I kinda . . . Can't. Tell you.' I drop my hands.

'I'm your best friend! What do you mean, you can't tell me?'

'Exactly what it says on the tin. I can't tell you.'

'What are you? Romeo and Juliet having a secret romance? Forever destined to be star-crossed?' She snorts, jumping back on her bed. I bite my lip, and she looks at me seriously. 'Megan.'

'Um.' Is that really all I have? Freaking '*um*'?

'Oh my god. You're not . . .?'

'Um.' Again with it! I study English every day and I can't think of a better word than that? This is going from bad to worse.

'No. Oh god,' Lila mutters. 'Oh god.'

'I have a right to remain silent, right?' I pull my knees up and release my lip, replacing it with my thumbnail. I chew on it for a moment as she stares at me in shock. 'Like in a police interrogation? I don't have to answer without a lawyer.'

'You are! You're babbling. You're such a bad liar.' She takes a deep breath and shakes her head. 'I don't know whether to hug you or slap you.'

'I plead the fifth.'

'Megs, are you and—'

'Please don't ask me anything, Lila,' I whisper, looking at her earnestly. 'I don't want to lie to you anymore.'

Silence stretches. I swallow. Chew my nail. Tap my foot. Lila stands and paces. I chew my nail. She paces.

'Aston,' she mutters, sitting back down. 'When? How?'

I shake my head.

Recognition dawns on her. 'When Braden took Maddie home. And since . . . He hasn't slept with anyone. He's always with you, isn't he? The weekends – when I'm at the frat house – he's here. That's why no one has seen him. Damn.' She shakes her head. 'You've really pulled this off without anyone finding out?'

She's not going to drop this. I know it, but this is all my fault. Time to face the music.

'Somehow. But, Lila, you can't tell anyone,' I beg. 'I mean it. No one can know. You are the only person that knows.'

'And it's the real thing? Not just sex?' She tilts her head to the side.

I nod and trace my finger along the pattern on my quilt. 'There's more to him than meets the eye. We're not just sex. I . . .'

'He's your Darcy,' she says simply. 'He's the rain to your drought. The every to your thing. Your soul mate decided by the universe, right?'

'And that's why you can't tell anyone,' I insist. 'No one. Not even Ryan.'

'And Braden really doesn't know?'

I snort. 'Do you think we'd be secret if Braden knew? Braden would flatten the house with his anger.'

'Why? You're both his best friends. Y'know what? I don't damn well understand him.'

'Because I'm like his sister and Aston is a playboy incapable of feeling anything than what's inside his pants. At least that's the case in his mind.'

Lila sits back on the bed, letting out a long breath. 'But you know Braden *will* find out, right? Sooner or later, Megs. He will know.'

'I know. I just hope it's later.'

'Why not? Why not get it over and done with?'

Because I'm a chicken. I'm a wimp. Because I know I've fucked up majorly and I can't bring myself to admit it. And finally . . .

'Because I'm gonna need a freakin' good excuse as to why we've kept it quiet for so long.'

Aston

Gramps' house has never looked more daunting. The house I really grew up in and the only home I've ever known is now one of the scariest places I'll ever have to face.

Inside this happy place is a box full of demons ready to be unleashed on the world, and that's something I can't think about. I can't think over whether or not it's a good idea for me to be here. I can't decide if this is the right decision for me right here, right now.

I just know this conversation has to happen. I can't stay locked in my past but I'll never be able to move on if Gramps can't. I won't be able to get past it if it's my own damn ignorance keeping him locked in place.

'What you doin' here in the middle of the week?' Gramps grumbles as I push the door open and walk into the house.

'Come to talk to you,' I reply, dropping onto the sofa next to him.

He drags on his cigar, the smoke swirling, and pierces me with his eyes. 'You've been sittin' out there in that pretty boy car for long enough. Whatchu wanna talk about?'

I take a deep breath and look away, knowing that the next word will change everything. 'Mom.'

He doesn't say anything. He exhales, blowing out smoke, and I see him shift slightly. 'Thought you didn't care about her.'

'Maybe I want to know, now. Maybe I'm ready to listen to what you have to say.' I turn my face back to him slowly. 'Maybe it's time we were both honest about the shit inside our heads, Gramps.'

'Megan's a good one, for sure. She made you come here didn't she?'

I shake my head. 'She made me realize I can't live in the past forever but she didn't make me do anything. I came here on my own.'

'She knows you're here?'

'No.'

Gramps shifts again and sits back, leaving his cigar to rest on the ashtray. His elbows rest on the arms of the chair and he links his fingers in front of him. 'What do you want to know?'

I tuck my hands under my legs the way I used to when I was a little boy and he was about to start a lesson or read me a story. In many ways the conversation we're about to have is both. The naked truth of the story and a lesson in that truth.

'Whatever you have to tell me. Whatever you think I should know.'

'The first thing you need to know is that your mom wasn't always the person you knew. Until she was sixteen she was the perfect daughter. A first grade student, polite, friendly . . . I couldn't have asked for a better baby girl. She was the kinda girl that would bake you sugar-free cookies if you told her you couldn't have sugar. Then she hit junior year and got mixed with the wrong people.

'Now that ain't no excuse for what she did, but they were a big influence on her. I know I can't blame them – she made the choices she did. They weren't forced upon her. There's no excusing the life she created for herself – or for you.

'The day she came home and said she was pregnant was a crazy day. Me and your Gran, we had a mix of emotions. We were gonna have us a lil' grandbaby, but it was at the cost of *our* baby. She was only just seventeen, and we'd never imagined a weekend at her friend's would have ended up that way. Still, we tried to help her any way we could.'

'When did you know . . .? About the drugs?'

'About five months in. Your Gran went with her to the scan, and you were this tiny little thing on screen. You were small the whole pregnancy. Your mom's doctor knew from blood tests she'd done them but she swore she stopped. Eventually, the doc managed to get out of her she was still doing them, and so started the program to wean her off while you were still inside her, to minimize the damage she could be causing you.'

'But they couldn't see that on the scans?'

Gramps shakes his head. 'No, boy. Physically you were fine. Small but fine. Mentally? They wouldn't know exactly how the drugs would affect you until you were older, speaking and moving and all that.'

'So you tried to stop her?'

'Course we did. She was still under eighteen so we limited the time she spent out without either of us. Somehow she still managed to get the darn drugs. She slipped them by us. The day you were born five weeks early, this tiny little four pound baby that was as long as my damn arm, was the second best day of my life. Don't you doubt that. I remember lookin' at your Gran and sayin' to her, "May, this boy here is *my* boy. When he's big, we'll go on them fishing trips I love, and I'll teach him about a real football team, then I'll teach him how to treat his lady right."' Gramps pauses for a second, swiping at his eyes, and I swallow. 'I promised there and then I'd never let anythin' happen to you, but I did.'

'It wasn't your fault, Gramps.'

'I should have taken you there and then!' He bangs his fist against the arm of his chair. 'I never shoulda let her have full custody of you, but I thought she was better. I thought my baby girl was coming back.' Tears stream down his cheeks, and I slip off the sofa and kneel in front of him. 'I thought you'd be fine. Even when she took you away and moved out when you were almost two, I thought you'd be fine. You always seemed fine. We saw you every other weekend until you were four. Then your Gram died of her stroke and I was alone. I forgot everything except the fact I'd lost my wife, my best friend, my soul mate. I forgot you.'

'You never forgot me, Gramps. You were always there, even when you weren't.'

'Anyway. Two years later the police turn up, tell me they've identified a dead body as my daughter, and there's a six-year-old boy that needs a home or he'll get put into care. No way was I letting my boy get abused by the system. I'd failed my baby girl. I wasn't about to fail you any more than I already had.'

'You didn't fail me.' I touch his arm and he looks up at me, his gray eyes watery. I bite back my own tears. 'You didn't, Gramps. You saved me – you taught me how to live. You took me on those fishing trips, taught me about football, and taught me how to treat my girl right. You took the shit my life was and turned it into something entirely different. You didn't fail me, not for a second.'

'I should have—'

'You never raised a fist to me. You never whipped my back with a belt. You never kicked my stomach until I vomited. You never smacked my head against the corner of a kitchen table.' My whole body shakes as the images flash in quick succession through my mind. Different men, different days, different times. Different ways of beating me, all leaving the same scars. 'You. Didn't. Do. That. You didn't even know. But she did. She knew. She lied to the hospital, CPS, everyone – it was always blamed on me. You didn't know. You couldn't stop what you didn't know about.'

'Doesn't stop the guilt, son.'

'Then remember what you *did* do.' My gray eyes meet his properly. 'Remember what you did teach me. I'm the person I am because of you.' I pause, knowing the next words about to fall off my tongue are the total truth, and I'm saying them to myself as much as I am him. 'You showed me Darcy and Elizabeth, you introduced me to his arrogance. Until recently, I was Darcy. I didn't give a shit about anyone other than myself. Then there was Megan. Without you showing me Darcy, I never would have thought she could have been anything more than one night. You showed me how Darcy loved Elizabeth and because of that you taught me how to love. You taught me how to love Megan the way Darcy loved Elizabeth. You did that. No one else. Just you.'

Gramps reaches forward and hugs me, his body shaking as he cries into my shoulder. This is what I've denied him because I was so caught up in my own fucking pain. My best friend – everything he kept inside to keep me happy. I hug him tighter, letting my own tear fall from my eye.

'Know something, boy?' he mumbles, sitting back and composing himself.

'What, Gramps?'

'Your Gran would be damn proud of the man you've become.'

And I believe him.

For the first time, I truly believe she would be.

Megan is sitting with her back against a tree trunk, her hair swept to one side and showing the smooth, tanned skin on one side of her neck. Her legs are bent making her jeans look tighter than they are normally, and as she wraps her arms around her waist, I want to be the one doing it. I want my arms around her waist, her back against my chest, and her head resting on my shoulder while I lean the side of my face against her bare neck.

Instead I'm lying on my side trying not to look at her. Trying to ignore her. Trying to pretend I need anything other than to hold her in my arms until the next ice age and we freeze there together.

'You're telling me the Chargers are on better form than the Cowboys?' Braden shakes his head. 'Fuck off are they! Romo is playing his ass off this season.'

Lila opens her mouth. 'It's a—'

Ryan slaps his hand over it. 'Don't. Say. It.'

'Game,' Megan finishes for her. 'A game, boys. It is *a game*. I know you're in love with your boys, and Bray, if you were gay you'd be after Romo's supposedly shit hot ass, but it is just a game. And he's playing shit, for what it's worth.'

'What is it?' I smirk at her. 'I don't think I quite got that.'

'Do I need to spell it for you? What, did you not get master hearing with your smart-ass GPA?' She raises her eyebrows. ''Cause that's gotta cause you some problems.'

'I'm pretty sure my hearing is going because of the amount of times I've had a girl screaming in my ear.'

Braden snorts, and Maddie slaps his thigh. 'Don't encourage him!'

'I was just . . . Never mind.' He hides his smirk.

'You know screaming is relative, right?' She runs the pad of her thumb across her bottom lip. 'It doesn't necessarily mean they were having a good time. I mean, don't girls usually scream in horror movies?'

Lila's shoulders shake as she laughs silently, and Maddie bites her lip. I watch Megan steadily, taking in the spark in her blue eyes and the gentle curve of her lips that only grows as I keep watching her. My own lips twitch, and I jump up.

'Watch your smart mouth, Megan,' I warn her. 'My last offer is still open.'

Megan

My mouth drops open, not from what he said, but because he threw it out so carelessly in front of the others – especially Braden.

Aston grins and winks at me. He turns, stretching his arms over his head as he walks in the direction of the house. I watch him go, struck into silence, and ignore Lila's gaze burning into the side of my head.

'His last offer?' Braden says tightly, his eyes resting on me.

'He offered to teach me the difference between a slapped ass and a spanked one,' I mutter. 'He's a prick.'

'Caveman. Rein it in,' Maddie orders, tapping his cheek and standing up.

'In,' he mutters in response.

'Good. Keep it that way.' She kisses his cheek, and Ryan and Lila stand.

'I'll see you after class, Megs.' Lila looks at me pointedly, and I nod. Yep. I'm so in for tonight.

We sit in silence as the others disappear, and I stare into the distance. It's the first time I've been alone with Braden since me and Aston got together, and for the first time in my life it feels like there's a gaping hole between us.

I know I put it there.

I also know I have to tell him. I could do it now. Without Aston here. Where there are other people around.

I open my mouth to speak, explain it, but he beats me to it. 'Where have you been lately?'

'Huh?' I look at him. 'I've been here, at college.'

'Oh, ha ha. Very fucking funny,' he says dryly, throwing a

blade of grass at me. 'No, I mean, like, SF. I thought you would have come with us.'

I shrug a shoulder. 'I just didn't feel like it. I had some work to catch up on too. Papers and stuff.'

He nods. 'Kyle said you dropped by Sunday morning to get one of your books.'

'Yep. You had my Shakespeare book. Again.'

'I will always have your Shakespeare book. I don't know how to complete a paper without your scribbled-on books.' He grins at me, flicking his hair away from his eyes.

'You need a hair cut,' I point out. 'And I know. Ever since eighth grade you've copied my crap. I have no idea why I let you do it.'

'It's because I'm fucking brilliant, and you love me.'

'And you still have the worst potty mouth of everyone I know.'

He grins again. 'It's why you love me, Megs. I'm the big brother you never had.'

'I think you're the *reason* I never had a big brother,' I reply dryly, smirking. 'Mom saw you dragging me into the mud to make mud pies and climbing trees, and decided an adopted son was more than enough.'

'I dragged you?' He laughs. 'You dragged me more times than I did you!'

Okay. So he might have a point there. 'Let's face it, we were always gonna be trouble.'

He clears his throat. 'I'm not trouble.'

'The cat, Braden. The cat.'

'That wasn't trouble. That was me attempting to be a gentleman.'

I smile, amused. 'I'm not sure your mom thinks of it that way, even now.'

'No, I explained it to her,' he insists. 'I told her it made me a gentleman for trying to give my favorite girl in the world what she wanted.' I kick his foot playfully.

'Does Maddie know this?' I tease.

'Meggy.' He looks at me seriously. 'I love Maddie, but you're my best friend. You always have been and the only person that means more to me than Maddie is you. I love you in different ways, and Maddie knows she'll never be you, but she gets that. Besides, you can be my favorite in a different way.'

I laugh and kick him again, shaking my head. 'Is sex really all you ever think about?'

He pauses for a second, chewing his lip. 'No. I just thought about food.'

'Food and sex?'

'Xbox.'

'Beer?'

'And that is why you're my best friend.' He winks. 'You get me.'

'Someone has to understand you, Bray.'

'Is Lila still sending you on those dates?'

I shake my head. 'I told her after the last one, no more.'

'Were they jackasses?'

'No, I just wasn't interested in any of them. I'm capable of picking my own love interests, you know.'

'Shouldn't have any damn interests,' he grumbles.

I clear my throat. 'Remember our conversation about this? Do we need to go to caveman-speak? Megan, big girl. Take care of self. Braden watch and shut up.'

Braden chuckles. 'Does that mean no black eyes for anyone who sleeps with you?'

You owe your best friend a few. 'No. No black eyes, no warnings, no demands of leaving me alone, and most definitely no caveman antics.'

'I think all of those qualify as caveman antics as far as Maddie is concerned.'

'I know. I was just spelling it out for you.' I shrug.

'Gee, thanks a fuckin' lot.' He shakes his head, standing up. I put my hand in his outstretched one, and he pulls me up. He starts to walk backwards toward the house. 'I have to get to class. Get some last minute caveman antics in before anyone finds out.'

'Braden Carter!' I call after his retreating body. 'Don't you freakin' dare!'

He stops at the door, grins, and disappears inside. I shake my head, detouring around the house and taking the route away from the campus toward the bay.

Yet again I failed to tell him about me and Aston. A few words is all it would take, but the longer we hide it the harder it is to find the words. The harder it is be honest.

Lying. I hate it – I hate lying to everyone about everything, because I don't want to hide us. I don't want to hide the way I feel about Aston. I don't want to hide him. I just don't want to hurt anyone and I know it will hurt Braden.

But the longer I keep it secret the more it will hurt him.

The breeze from the water drifts over me, chilling me, and I tug my sweater around my body tighter. My hair flies into my face and I push it away in vain.

Games. They're all good until someone gets hurt. Braden and Maddie's games were all good until they got hurt and both acted irrationally – him by walking away and her by running. Mine and Aston's games are all good until it gets out, which it will.

The truth always comes out.

I could walk away now. I could speak to Aston and tell him it's done, I can't do it anymore, but I'd still be lying then. I'd be lying because I can, because it's not done.

Lies. They're easy to keep track of until they begin spiraling and you begin spinning a web of them, too easy to get caught up in. Lies are all good until you look at who you're lying to.

The question is, is it better or worse to lie to yourself over your best friend?

'That was awkward today,' Lila comments as she enters the room.

I look up from my book. 'Welcome to my world.'

'A world you created.'

'Your tact amazes me,' I say dryly. 'Really, Li, just remind me. It doesn't play on my mind or anything. Nope, I'm totally oblivious to it.'

'I don't get why you don't just admit it.'

'No one asked?' I try, shrugging. I sigh. I don't know either.

'I wish I knew, I really do. It's not as simple as it looks from the outside. You see it as a simple secret, something hidden for a simple reason. Simple. And it's not. It's not just boy meets girl and they fall in love. It's boy meets girl and all hell breaks loose, in his head and in reality.'

'So you're telling me that Aston's head is stopping you being honest?' She raises an eyebrow in disbelief. I shut my book and put it on my bed next to me.

'You don't know him. You think you do – you all think you do, but you don't. To you he's just a girl-using, thinks-with-his-dick asshole to be avoided by anyone with any sense. I know different. I know he's not what he seems, and I know that what he seems is nothing more than an act to hide who he really is.'

'Okay.' She settles on the bed. 'I don't know either way, so let's go with what you said. When does your pretending become reality? When does your act end, Megs?'

I sigh and lean back against the wall. 'I have no idea. I tried to tell Braden earlier – no, I did. Maybe not hard enough, but I tried. The words just wouldn't come. I keep thinking about how he'll look when he finds out I've lied to him.'

'Doesn't matter when he finds out. He isn't gonna look any happier if he finds out today or next year.'

'I just don't know how much longer I can hide it. It makes everything so hard. I need to help Aston, Lila, but having everything secret means I can't always be there and that hurts,' I finish quietly. 'I can see when he needs me and it hurts so damn bad.'

She shrugs. 'I know now. I can help. Keep everyone away from here or make excuses for you, back you up.'

'I swear you were just telling me I needed to tell Braden.'

'And you do.' She sighs. 'But it's clear you won't – or *can't*,' she corrects at my annoyed look, 'so I might as well help you. God help me because I *will* be killed when this all comes out, but at least I can feel like I'm keeping this secret for a reason.'

'You don't have to do anything. I got myself into this mess. I just need to figure out how to help Aston, and then maybe everything else will just . . . fall into place.' I run my fingers through my hair, sighing deeply. 'Maybe. Hopefully.'

'Until everything falls into place, I'll help you. I'll make it so you can talk to Aston. I don't see it myself, I'm not gonna lie. But you care about him, and I care about you, so whatever.'

I look at her for a second, taking in her honest expression, and smile slightly. 'You're the best friend.'

'Or the stupidest, when Braden finds out,' she mutters and heads toward the bedroom.

'Li?' I ask. 'You're not gonna tell him, are you?'

She stops at the bathroom door and looks at me over her shoulder. 'I may not agree with you keeping it quiet, and I may not like the fact I know, but that doesn't mean I'm gonna tell him, Megs. I don't like your decision, but I respect it.'

'Thank you.'

'Besides,' she continues. 'If I tell him he'll kick *my* ass, and I'm the innocent one.'

'There I was thinking you were doing it out the goodness of your heart!'

'No way.' She grins. 'I'm protecting my ass – and you make sure Aston knows about this so I can call in a favor in the future.' She winks. I laugh, reaching for my phone.

Lila knows, I send to Aston.

What the fuck? How?

She guessed. It's not a total lie . . .

And?

And nothing. She's not gonna say anything. She'll cover for us.

I don't like this, Megs.

Neither do I, but it's either she covers or we tell Braden.

Let's stick with Lila for now.

We need to talk.

About?

You.

I sink into Aston's arms, sliding my hands under his shirt and flattening them against his back. His lips come down on mine firmly, and he sucks my bottom lip between his.

'What's Lila doing?' he murmurs.

'Lila took the others to crazy golf.' I shrug, looking up at him. 'Don't ask me. She kicked up a fuss to Ryan.'

'Lila hates crazy golf. In fact, she hates any kind of sport.'

'I know.' I shrug again. 'She said you owe her.'

'Figures.' He sighs and runs his fingers through my hair to the ends, kissing the end of my nose. 'So tell me. What do we really need to talk about? "You" isn't exactly informative.'

I tug him toward the bed, and he sits down against the wall. My knees sit either side of him as I straddle him and lock my hands behind his neck. His hands rest on my bed, his fingers drawing tiny circles against my skin.

'You. Everything. There's more, Aston. I know there is.'

His stomach tenses. 'What do you want to know?'

'Everything,' I whisper. 'Everything that's left. However long it takes, however much it hurts . . . I'm here.'

His chest heaves as he takes a deep breath, and his eyes fill with apprehension. Fear sparks in them. I've never thought of him as being scared of his past, of what he hasn't let himself think about, but he is. He's petrified.

'There isn't much left to tell, not about when I was a kid. It was the same thing over and over. Mom would sell herself for money, spend a minimal amount of it on food and bills if she could be bothered, and the rest on drugs and alcohol. She'd meet a guy, he'd watch me while she "worked", and I'd usually get a bruise to add to my collection for something or another. Social Services would visit, the guy would leave, and she'd meet someone else, every other night going out and fucking some poor rich guy so she could keep putting the same old shit into her veins. That was it for six years. I'm glad I can only remember two years of it, even if they were the worst years.'

His fingertips dig into my skin slightly, and I twist his hair around my fingers gently, looking at him intently.

'She couldn't parent. She didn't know how to. I was always an afterthought – and everything was blamed on me. She blamed it on me, the guys blamed it on me, and when you get taught everything is your fault, you start to believe it. Every cut or bruise was explained as me being a rough little boy to the social, and every cut or bruise was explained as me being a little no-good bastard to *me*. That was their reasoning. That I was good for nothing, no better than my mom.' He pauses for a second, breathing harshly.

I move my hands to cup his face and rest my forehead against his, letting him calm down even as my own stomach twists. He closes his eyes in pain, and I can't begin to imagine the things that are playing out behind his eyes. All I can do is sit here with him, holding him to me, and ride it out.

'That's what I remember most, the things they said to me,' he whispers. 'It's like they enjoyed hurting me with words as much as they did with their fists. It was all the time. All the fucking time, Megs. I remember them always telling me I'd be no better than her, that sex was all she was good for so it would be all I was good for. Sex and drugs and alcohol – they said that was my life, and it would have been true. She never sent me to school because of the bruises, so eventually I would have ended up the same way if she hadn't died.'

'How did she die?'

'Drugs. What else?' He shrugs a shoulder, moving his arms so they wrap around my body. 'The official report states it was from an overdose of a bad batch of heroin. The drug had been tampered with, making it even more dangerous, and she accidentally overdosed. They reckon she'd been going through withdrawals and in her confused and desperate state she used more than she normally would have. She was found three blocks away from our apartment at a seedy bar, and I was found at home a day later. That's what Gramps said anyway. I remember it all as just one blur of time. Day and night were the same to me then. Mom slept during the day and left at night. I was left alone most of the time – except for a single weekly outing to the park to keep up appearances. That was the one day she cared about me.'

His voice is so broken, so small, so lost. It's like he's regressed back into the mind of the six-year old he was and is seeing the world through his eyes again. I look at him, look into his sad eyes, and my heart clenches as a tear spills from his eye.

I've seen him angry. I've seen him fight the demons. But I've never seen him cry, and this breaks my heart.

Seeing him cry is worse than I ever could have imagined.

Aston

One tear falls, and another, and another.

The pain is real. It's old but real, always there, and it's finally breaking through. It's been held back for so long, but it's finally out. I'm starting to let go of the things that have killed me for years.

Megan's touch is warm and soft, comforting and safe, and as she pulls me into her, I let her. She doesn't speak. She doesn't do anything but just hold me. She reminds me I'm not alone, that I'm safe. As much as I need to hold her, I need her to hold me just as much. She grounds me and keeps me here. By focusing on her I'm reminded that I'm not six years old and afraid anymore. She stops the flashbacks consuming me. She makes that pain bearable.

'That's why I major in psych,' I breathe out after a while of her holding me. 'Because it means I can help kids like me that have all this shit in their heads. If I'd had someone to talk to when I was younger, I probably wouldn't be this fucked up now.'

'You're not fucked up.' She sits back and runs her thumbs across my cheeks, drying the tears there. 'You had a hard life, Aston, but now you're dealing with it. You're proving, yourself, that all those men, they were wrong. By graduating school and coming here, you're proving them wrong. You did that. No one else.'

'No. I'm always gonna be a little fucked up, Megs. I'm still gonna wake in the night and wonder if I'm hiding under my bed or if I'm safe. I'm still gonna doubt myself every day, and I'm still gonna be a little broken, no matter what I do.'

'But you'll also heal a little more every day,' she says softly. 'We'll find a way to help you deal with those nightmares and flashbacks, I promise. I'll help you, Aston.'

Her blue eyes gaze into mine and her hair falls around our faces, hiding us from the rest of the world. I could lose myself in her eyes a thousand times over and still go back again. I could fall into her touch and never feel the need to get up, and I realize that's why she's so different to everyone else. She gives me what no one else ever has. She slowly pulled me from not caring about anything to caring about her. And she's made me realize so many things.

No matter what Mom's boyfriends said, I've proved them wrong. It was my own actions that got me to Berkeley – to meet Megan. When I went to live with Gramps he taught me everything, but it was me that pushed on through it, graduated high school and came to college.

It was me that made it so I could meet Megan.

I will never be like my mom because she never loved anyone except herself. I can never be that person, destined for a broken life of sex, drugs, and alcohol.

Because I'm completely in love with the girl right in front of me.

Here we are, back at the usual Friday nights I craved so much. Friday nights meant forgetting and giving in to physical feelings only. Friday and Saturday nights were the best nights, but now I just want to grab Megan and run. I want to take her away from this shit ass party.

Especially when Lila's fucked-up plan to get her a date has made its way round the classes we all have and you have every Tom, Dick, and fucking Harry trying to get in there.

Every time one of those jackasses goes up to her, for a split second, I resent Braden and the fact he's the reason this relationship is fucking secret. I'd love to go over to her right now, grab her away from the dick in front of her and kiss her senseless in front of everyone to make my point. I'd do anything to take her away from them and show everyone where she belongs. Who she belongs to.

Because she is mine, and not in a possessive way. It's my arms she falls into, my lips she kisses, my heart she holds. All of that makes her mine.

Not the arrogant bastard's she's talking to.

I slam my bottle down, ignoring startled looks from around me, and push through the throngs of people. I deliberately nudge her back as I pass her and head to the stairs. My feet take them two at a time, flying up. I'm not watching that shit anymore. My room is silent, quiet, and I wait for her to come up.

I have no idea how long I have to wait. Too long and I'll end up going back down there, too little and people will guess she's come after me. People will wonder why . . . But I don't know if I care anymore. I don't know if I can care anymore.

My door opens and closes.

'There has to be a good reason you just stormed up here like a girl on her period with no access to chocolate,' Megan quips.

'I can't do this secret shit anymore, baby.' I turn around and pin her with my eyes, briefly noticing how well her jeans hug her hips. 'I can't be down there with you surrounded by assholes and not slip my arm around your waist and warn them off with my eyes. I can't fuckin' do it. Not now.'

'It's never bothered you before.'

'It's always bothered me! You think I've never cared when I've watched you laughing and joking with whoever it is trying to get inside your damn pants on that night?'

She steps forward. 'I never said you didn't care! I said it never bothered you – and if it did you never showed me!'

'So if I walked up to a girl and started talking to her for the sake of keeping up appearances, you wouldn't be bothered by it, huh?' I look at her helplessly. 'I can't watch them fucking ogle you, Megs. This secret relationship has gone on for too long. We have to come clean.'

Her eyes widen a little. 'We can't . . . Braden—'

'Will have to fucking deal with it!' I step in front of her, cupping the side of her face, and she rests her hands against my chest. 'He'll have to deal with it. He'll have to accept it, because I'm not pretending anymore and I'm not giving you up for shit.'

'He'll hate us,' she whispers.

'The damage has already been done, baby. It's him or us.'

She shakes her head, running her bottom lip between her teeth worriedly. 'Braden.' I hate the way she winces when she says his name.

'Then we have to tell him,' I say softly, lowering my mouth to hers. 'Now. We'll tell him now.'

The door bursts open 'Tell me what?'

Megan

I jump away from Aston, my hand flying to my mouth when I see Braden standing there. His eyes flick between us, the blue in them slowly getting icier, his expression getting harder.

The tension in the room rockets. I can almost feel Aston tensing next to me, see the anger and realization flooding through Braden's body. I'm standing frozen, unable to do anything but wait. Unable to do anything but look at the anger and betrayal firing up in my best friend's eyes.

There are a thousand excuses rolling around my mind, but the cat really does have my tongue.

There's nothing than can excuse this.

And it's time to be honest.

'Ryan thought he saw you follow Aston up.' Braden focuses his eyes on me. 'I thought he was crazy. I told him it was some other poor fucker, but when a couple of the other guys agreed I said I'd come up just for a laugh. Because I didn't actually fucking think I'd find you up here in his goddamn bedroom!'

'Bray . . .' I whisper.

'How long?' He looks at Aston, his jaw tight. 'How long have you been fucking her?'

'Braden!'

'It's not like that,' Aston replies equally tight.

'Really? You expect me to believe that bullshit?' Braden yells. 'How long?'

'About the time you took Maddie home.'

'That was the first time?' His blue eyes pierce me.

I nod, my hand falling away from my mouth. 'Just after.'

He laughs bitterly and turns to Aston. 'I go away for two days and you jump into bed with her a week later?'

'With each other!' I step forward. 'Each. Other, Braden!'

'Oh and that's supposed to make it fucking better is it?'

'No!' I move in front of Aston. 'No, it isn't. Nothing can make it better and I have no excuses for this, but you have to realize I can make my own decisions. I'm old enough to deal with the fall-out. I love that you have my back, I do, but you can't always be there to protect me! Aston didn't force me into anything. Do you get that? I *wanted* to!'

His eyes focus on me, my chest heaves, and Aston touches my arm.

'Megs—'

'No,' I say, my eyes on Braden. 'As much as he'd like to believe it, it's not just you. I'm not gonna stand here and watch him give you shit because of something we both did.'

'How long have you been sleeping with *each other*?' Braden says sarcastically. 'Because it makes the world of fucking difference.'

'*We* have been in a *relationship* since the weekend after you left,' I correct him.

'Ha!' Braden slams his hand into the wall. 'A relationship? Are you fucking serious?'

'Yes.'

'Fucking unreal. You've made some shit choices, Megan, but this tops the goddamn list!' He passes through the door. I wrench my arm from Aston's grip and follow him, not caring who can hear this conversation.

'The decision to be with Aston wasn't the bad choice! The bad one was keeping it from you – and you know why that happened? You know why I didn't tell you? Because of this. To stop this happening! I knew you'd go bat shit crazy over it!'

'So why did you fucking do it?' he throws over his shoulder.

'Because I wanted to!'

'And that makes it better?' He stops, turning to look at me. He motions in the direction of Aston's room. 'He's just gonna break your heart, Megan! That's what he does. He fucks girls and leaves them—'

'You don't know him like I do!'

'No, but there's a lot of girls that do!'

'No they don't!' I yell, my foot stamping. My hands come up to the sides of my head. 'They don't know him the way I do. None of you do, so don't you fucking stand there and tell me it was a bad decision when you know nothing – *nothing* – about my decision! You know nothing about us. You know *nothing* about how I feel, or how he feels!'

'Go on, then, Megs. If it's such a big thing, the *real fucking deal*, tell me. How do you feel?'

I look at him steadily, opening my mouth to speak.

'I love her,' Aston says from halfway down the hall. 'I can't answer for her, but I can answer for me. And the answer is I love her.'

My hands fall to my sides, and I swallow. My heart takes up a frantic beat in my chest, pounding and rattling against my ribs. We've never said it. He's never said it.

And now he's admitting it. Out loud. To Braden. And anyone else listening.

'Do you love her or what she gives you?' Braden asks uncertainly, his voice still laced with anger.

Aston steps up behind me, reaching down and taking my hands in his. His fingers lace through mine, and as his chest touches mine I can feel the vulnerability in him. The only person he's ever opened up to about anything is me, and now he has to do it to someone else.

'I love her for who she is, and who I am when I'm with her. Everything Maddie does for you, times that by a million, and that's what Megan does for me. She's right, Braden. None of you know me like she does. She knows everything about me – even the things I didn't want anyone to ever know. She knows them and she's still here. I love her for everything she gives me, every touch, every smile, I love it all.

'You can come flying at me now and kick the shit out of me. I'll take it because I deserve it for going behind your back, but I won't fucking apologize. I won't ever apologize for loving her, so don't expect me to. And don't expect me to walk away from her because I won't. I can't.'

He tightens his grip on my hands slightly, and my body shakes. Gentle footsteps on the stairs announce Maddie's arrival, and my eyes slide to hers. I don't see the anger or annoyance I expect.

I see understanding.

'And you, Meggy?' Braden questions.

Deep breath. 'I love him, Bray. I'm sorry I didn't tell you, I am. Both of us tried not to let it happen but it did, and I'm not sorry for that. I'm just sorry it hurts you so much.'

Maddie slides her arm around Braden's, leaning against him, and he heaves out a breath.

'Y'know what hurts the most?' He looks at me, anger gone from his eyes. A hint of defeat replaces it. 'You're my best friend and you didn't think you could tell me. You didn't even feel for a second that you could tell me. Maybe that's my fault, but that's what gets me. Am I pissed you lied about it? Fucking right I am. I'm fuming. But I can't be mad at you. No matter how much I want to slam my fist into Aston's face and yell at you, I can't.'

'Why not?' Aston asks. 'I'd deserve it.'

Braden's eyes go over my shoulder to meet the gray pair I love. 'Because when I look in Megan's eyes I see the same love for you that Maddie has in hers for me. You didn't hesitate for a second to tell me you love her, when she didn't even know yet. I could tell that from her reaction. You hadn't told her, and I made you tell me. I'd be a fucking hypocrite if I was mad at you for that, but just because I'm not mad doesn't mean I want to be around you right now.'

He shakes his arm from Maddie and walks down the stairs to his room. Maddie looks at both of us, a small smile playing on her lips.

'It took long enough for you to admit it,' she says softly.

'You knew?' Aston pulls me closer to him.

Her smile grows a little, and she tucks some hair behind her ear. 'Of course I did. I know pain, Aston, and pain knows pain. You have some pain deep inside you, I don't know what it is, but I know it's there. And Megs is the softest, most under-standing person I know. You two were drawn together because she could heal your wounds. I've known since we got back that you two had something.'

'Why didn't you ask me?' I tilt my head to the side slightly.

She makes to follow Braden, pausing on the top stair. 'Because . . .' She grins. 'If Braden had any suspicions and asked me if you'd said anything, I wouldn't have had to lie to him.'

I can't help but smile. She knows him so well. She knows him like I know Aston.

I breathe out deeply, letting myself relax against him. His arms wrap around me tightly, his face burying into my neck.

'That was . . . fun,' he says dryly.

'That went well,' I say truthfully. 'I was expecting Braden to punch first, ask later. That's his usual M.O.'

'Maybe he was just so shocked you were actually there that he forgot to punch me first.'

I let out a small laugh. 'I think that's probably right.'

He releases me and steers us back into his room, nudging the door shut. I rub my hands down my face.

'What do we do now?' I look at him.

Aston grins, moving toward me. 'We stop hiding, and I get to go all protective on your pretty little ass when some dickhead tries to hit on you.'

My lips curve up on one side. He cups my face and brushes his lips across mine.

'That sounds about right.'

'Yep. We just have to clear something up first.'

'What's that?'

His gray eyes clear, becoming raw and honest. 'I'm sorry I never told you how I feel.'

'I know now,' I respond.

He shakes his head a little. 'No, you don't. You don't know how just a touch of your hand can take away the pain from my past, and you don't know how lying next to you at night stops the nightmares. You don't know that you're the first person to really make me smile, and you definitely don't know that I'm so in love with you I can't see or think straight. "In vain have I struggled. It will not do. My feelings will not be repressed. You must allow me to tell you how ardently I admire and love you.'"

Damn. He gets the British accent perfect. I smile up at him, and resting my hands on his waist, I move our bodies closer. His fingers slip into my hair, curling around the back of my head, barely brushing the top of my neck.

'Even when I tried not to, I still did,' he says in a softer voice, resting his forehead against mine. My nose brushes his, and I close my eyes, just listening to him. 'I stepped over the edge and started falling for you, and I'm damn sure I don't ever want to get back up from it. I don't know how you do it, baby, but you make me better.'

Aston touches his lips to mine, a feather-light brush, and I slide my hands around and up his back to his shoulders.

'A speech worthy of Mr. Darcy,' I mutter, smiling. He pulls his face back, his eyes lighter, his lips curved upwards. My hands move along his arms, and I hold his gaze intensely. 'I love you, Aston. I don't know how or why, I just know that I do. Everything you think about yourself, everything you've been told, I see and think the complete opposite. You are worth everything to me – *everything*. Okay? And I promise you here and now, I won't leave.'

He takes a shuddery breath, vulnerability flickering in his eyes. Instead of saying anything he dips his face toward mine, and our lips meet again. His hands slide down my back, and as I wrap my arms around his neck our bodies align perfectly.

'You don't have a choice,' Aston whispers, his breath fanning across my lips. 'Because I don't think I'll ever let you leave. Besides, we never had a proper first kiss.'

'We did. Up against a wall after you attacked me, I believe.'

'That wasn't a kiss. That was a prelude to sex that never happened.'

'Yes, but kissing happened,' I remind him.

The corner of his mouth twitches slightly. 'But it wasn't a kiss – not a proper kiss.'

'You've kissed me hundreds of times, Aston.'

'I know. But we still never had a real first kiss.'

I sigh, slightly amused by this. 'Why is that so important to you?'

'Because you're the most romantic person I know, and I know it matters to you.'

'It doesn't matter that much.' I gaze into his smoky eyes. 'It's just a kiss.'

'Nothing with you is "just" anything,' he mutters, smiling. 'It's always more than it seems, and I want to give you the first kiss you deserve.'

'You don't have to do anything. Having us is more than enough.'

'Megan . . .'

'You're not going to give up on the idea of a second first kiss, are you?'

Aston shakes his head. 'I'll never give up on anything where you're concerned. So let me have my way.'

'Fine,' I whisper.

He dips his face toward me, the tip of his nose brushing mine. My eyes flutter closed.

'I hope you're ready for the best first kiss of your life,' he whispers. 'Because it's gonna be your last first kiss.'

His hand slides to the back of my head and pushes us together. Our mouths meet, a soft touch that becomes gently more probing. His lips caress mine slowly, and my body sinks into him. The taste of him, the feel of him, the smell of him – it all takes me over. With each brush of his lips I feel myself falling deeper into him, even deeper than I am already.

I feel myself crashing into him with everything I have, crashing into him and holding on tightly to everything he has to give. Because the romantic in me wants it all and it won't let it go. At all.

My heart is in complete contradiction of itself. Lying here in Aston's arms, half of it is lighter than it's been in the last few weeks. The lightness comes from the truth being told. But the other half is heavy, like a lead weight is holding it down and pinning it to the ground.

I shift, and Aston's grip on me tightens. I run my fingers through his hair, smoothing it back from his face, and study him. Now he looks like he's at peace. The lines on his forehead I've seen so many times are now completely smooth, his mouth is slightly open, and his breathing is even and steady.

But his peace has come at the torment of my best friend – who's somewhere in this house, probably awake. He'll be hating himself for being mad at me, happy I found the love he has, and guilty I felt like I couldn't tell him.

In fact he won't be at the house. I know exactly where he'll be.

I climb out of bed, and there's a light knock at the door. Crap. I grab one of Aston's shirts from the back of his chair, throw it over my head and open the door a crack. Lila's face stares back at me.

'I ran back to the dorm room to get you some clothes. I knew you didn't have any and you'd be up now.' She holds out a bag.

'Thank you,' I say quietly.

'Hey – you don't need to thank me. I don't wanna be you today. Braden isn't even here; he left Maddie a note on her cell that he needed an hour. She gets it but has no idea where he is.'

'That's why you got me clothes.'

She laughs into her hand. 'Partly. I know it's no good all of us going and searching for him – I mean, he could be anywhere, right? You're the one person who will find him.'

I nod. 'I know where he'll be. Tell Mads not to worry; I'll find him. Thanks for bringing this, Li.'

She smiles and walks down the hall to Ryan's room. I close the door behind me and turn to see Aston's gray eyes staring at me hotly. I ignore the feeling that sweeps my body and hold up the bag.

'Lila got me clothes.'

'If I didn't just hear that Braden's disappeared and you're the only person who knows where he is, I'd go and give those damn clothes back to her.' He props himself up on his elbow, his eyes locked to the top of my thighs where the hem of his shirt falls.

'You would?' I ask innocently, walking over to the bed.

'Fucking right I would.' He grabs my arm and pulls me toward him. I land half on him, half on the bed, and his hands creep beneath the shirt, his fingers tracing inside the line of my panties. 'I would absolutely say you should sleep in my shirt, but there's a slim chance of any sleep actually happening if you did.'

'I don't think I would complain,' I say against his mouth, brushing lips with him.

He kisses me hard, and at a shift of his hips his erection pushes into my bare thigh through the covers. I run my fingers through his hair and break the kiss, grinning down at him.

'I need to go find Bray.'

'I know,' he replies softly. 'It's not fair on Maddie either now. Shit. We've made a mess of this, haven't we?'

I sit up, running my fingertips down his arm to the palm of his hand. He catches my fingers with his, linking them together.

'Yeah. We have. There's no point lying about it, but honestly, regardless of when we told him it would have happened. He still would have been angry and needed to cool off. We know we shouldn't have kept us a secret and we should have told him a long time ago, but there's nothing we can do about that now. It was wrong, and now I need to go and speak to him and make it right.'

'He's a stubborn ass. How do you know he'll talk to you?'

I smile, shrugging one shoulder. 'Because if he wanted to talk to anyone else, he wouldn't have gone to where only I would know where to look for him.'

'I wondered how long it would take you.'

The wind coming in off the bay whips my hair around my face, leaving me to battle it constantly. 'Longer than it should have,' I respond, hopping up onto the rock next to Braden. I shove my hair from my face again.

He says nothing and shrugs his shoulders, looking out across the choppy water. His thumbs flick against each other, his feet tapping to an invisible beat. I know him well enough to know he's thinking about what to say, so I keep quiet, waiting for him to make the first move.

'I understand why you did it,' he says after a moment of silence. 'I mean, why you kept it secret. I don't understand why you'd sleep with that ass.'

I glance at him and catch the twitching of his lips. 'Umm . . . He's hot?' I offer, trying not to grin. Turning his face away, Braden bites the inside of his cheek. I look down.

'Yeah, well, I guess if you have to be with some fucker, it should be a fucker I actually like.'

'You'll never like anyone I date.' I rest my head on his shoulder, and he puts his arms round mine the way we used to whenever we chatted. Before we left for college. Before games started.

'True,' he agrees. 'But I can't completely hate Aston because I liked him before, so I'm fucked. Although I gotta admit I never imagined you with him. I imagined you with some rich bastard driving a soft top car, spending your days racing down the interstates between L.A. and New York for fancy dinners.'

Laughter explodes from me, and I cover my mouth as Braden shakes next to me, laughing himself.

'Right – because I absolutely have the manners and patience for that, don't I? Puh-lease, Bray, give me some credit.' I nudge his side, still giggling slightly. 'And have you forgotten your mom's charity do thing? We had to Google which fork to use because no one told us the proper etiquette. They all assumed two fourteen year olds knew that sort of thing.'

'And when we came here I had to Google dating,' he muses. 'Damn. We drew some short straws, didn't we?'

'I think it's because you were always in trouble, so by default I was too.' I smile and sit up slightly. 'I really am sorry, Bray. I never wanted to keep it from you. It was just supposed to be once and everything kind of snowballed, then before I knew it, it was too far to do anything. The longer I left it the harder it got to find the words to tell you. It makes me a total shit, and believe me when I say I feel like an utter bitch because I do. It's hurt you so much.'

'I get it, Megs. Sorta. It makes me feel like shit you couldn't tell me, but I'd probably have done the same if I was you. But I wouldn't have gotten caught.' He grins.

'I wanted to get caught.' I shrug. 'At least I think I did. If you caught us I wouldn't have had to come out and explain it because you would have guessed.'

'You always were the wimp.'

'Hey!'

'Aston is a jackass, Megs, I know that. But he loves you. I didn't think it was fucking possible, but he does.' He pauses for a moment. 'Then again this is you. You could turn a gay guy straight if you really wanted to.'

'Well . . . I bet I could give it a good go.'

'Good luck. Aston will kick his ass, gay or not. If he's anything like me he will.'

'When it comes to being an overprotective asswipe? Yep, pretty much exactly the same.'

Braden laughs slightly, then sighs. 'I'm sorry, too, Meggy.'

'What for? I'm the one who lied.'

He turns his face toward mine, blue eyes meeting blue eyes. 'Because I was so wrapped up in what I thought was best for you I forgot to stop and ask what *you* wanted. I was so fuckin' set on keeping you away from any of the walking, talking dicks in the frat house I didn't realize the best thing for you was right under my damn nose the whole time.'

'He never made it easy.' My voice softens slightly. 'Part of the reason I never told you was because he might not say it but he needs you and Ry. He needs the banter and friendship you provide him. It gives him security. I meant what I said when I said you don't know him like I do. It's not for me to tell you – I won't betray him that way – but the guy you know isn't the one I know. You just have to trust me when I say he's what's best. You know the heart doesn't lie, Bray, and my heart tells me he's what's best for me. My heart tells me he's all I'm ever gonna need, no matter how hard it gets.'

'And that's why I can't be mad. No matter how much I want to be. I trust you, girl. Sometimes I have to ask myself why, but it's no damn good arguing with your stubborn ass.'

'You taught me well.'

'Too fucking well.' He stretches and stands up, putting his hands on my waist and hoisting me up. He slings his arm over my shoulders. 'Come on, then. I ran out on my girlfriend this morning and I have to go threaten some pretty-boy ass.'

I shake my head as we jump from the rock, smiling. No good fighting it.

He still needs to be macho-man big bro.

Aston

The rough bark of the tree digs into my back. Apart from with Megan, outside is the only place that gives me peace. Even as I wait for the inevitable conversation with Braden – the one where I'll have to admit why I need her so much. He deserves that much after what we've done to him, and I'm ready for it. Because of Megan I'm finally ready to start opening up about my life.

'Still a spacey bastard.' He smirks.

'No fist in my eye?' I smirk back at him.

He shrugs a shoulder. 'I considered it. Several fucking times. Then figured it just ain't worth it since I'd probably get more punches from those damn girls than it's worth.'

He's probably right.

'But that doesn't mean I won't kick the shit out of you if you break her fucking heart.'

'I wasn't joking when I said I loved her yesterday,' I say bluntly, staring him down with the same seriousness he's looking at me with. 'She gets me, man. She gets all my shit and she deals with it. She's something out of this damn world, and I still think I don't deserve her.'

'Dude, none of us deserve these girls, but for some reason they won't leave us alone.' He winks. 'I ain't gonna lie to you – I'm pissed. I'm pissed you never told me and that you went behind my back to do it all. But at the same time I get it, yeah? You kept that fuckin' secret because of how much she means to me . . . That's why I'm not completely pissed.'

I raise my eyebrows at him, questioning him silently. He opens his mouth and closes it again.

'Fuck it.' He runs his hand through his hair. 'I don't even know what I am.'

Megan appears at the back door of the frat house and leans against the doorframe and watches us.

'Until I was six, my life was a mess of drugs, alcohol, sex and abuse. I spent my time hiding the bruises my mom's jacked-up boyfriends gave me and wondering what they'd get me for next time. I listened to her being used in the next room. I listened to her sobbing and crying every night. I watched her go too far until eventually the drugs killed her and my Gramps took me in. I've lived with that bullshit ever since, and I used sex to block it all out the same way she did. That was why I never gave a fuck. Sex meant I didn't have to feel – until Megan. She made it all real again. She reminded me of how I feel about everything, and slowly she pulled it all out of me. She made me relive all the memories and then she took it all away by just being there. The shit in my head, all that noise, she makes it quiet again, man. I'm fucked if I know how she does it.' I shake my head, watching as she makes her way over to us slowly. 'But she does. That's the shit no one else knows.' My eyes fall back on Braden's. 'That's the real me, and the least I can do after betraying you this way is tell you the kind of person she's in love with. I'm not gonna pretend anymore. I'm just gonna be fucking real because that's what Megan deserves.'

'You haven't ended up killing each other yet then?' Megan tucks some hair behind her ear and stops right between us. I reach forward and grab her hand, pulling her down. She squeals, and I catch her and gently make her sit between my legs. My arms tuck around her waist and I nuzzle the side of her head, kissing the spot below her ear.

'No, no killing. Another few minutes and it might have been a possibility.'

She turns her face toward me, and I feel the twitch of her cheek as she smiles. Her fingers link through mine.

'Good,' she mutters. 'I'd hate to have to deal with both of you.'

'See?' Braden shrugs. 'She could kick my ass better than I

could kick yours. At least I'm here to keep an eye on you, I guess. Make sure you treat her right.'

'Caveman,' Maddie reminds him, dropping onto the grass next to him.

'Whatever, Angel. I'm just saying.'

'We know.' She leans over and kisses his cheek. 'But I think Aston is aware of that.'

Braden grunts, and Maddie smiles, resting her head on his shoulder.

'This is the jackass you've been sleeping with?' Kay hollers across the yard. 'Are you fucking kidding me?'

'Uh, surprise?' Megan says weakly and shrugs.

'Surprise? Damn right it's a fuckin' surprise!' She stops, towering over us, and puts her hands on her hips. She looks at Braden. 'Why isn't his whole body in plaster?'

Braden shrugs. I'm pretty sure everyone shrugs around Kay. It's easier to do that than answer her and give her more ammunition to vomit words.

'Chill out, Bitchy-Pants!' Lila calls. 'They're just dating. No biggie.'

'You knew, didn't you?' Kay rounds on her, then on Megan. 'How could you tell her and not me?'

I smirk as Megan looks at her pointedly.

'Technically, she didn't tell me,' Lila mentions. 'I worked it out.'

'Why didn't you tell me?'

'Was it a matter of life and death, Kayleigh? Will you drop down dead now you're the last person to find out?'

'No.'

'Then that's why I didn't tell you.' Lila grins. 'None of your business.'

'You knew?' Braden asks Lila, glancing over her shoulder to Ryan. 'Did you know?'

'Why do I feel like we're in the middle of a high school drama?' I whisper in Megan's ear. She giggles silently.

'Because Kay, Braden, and Ryan are still of high school mentality?' she whispers back.

'I, er, shit,' Lila mutters.

'Don't look at me, man. It's news to me that Lila knew.'

'News . . . Knew . . . News . . .' Maddie blinks a few times. 'Um, can I just summarize here? My head is starting to hurt.'

'That'll be the shots you threw back last night,' Kay remarks.

'Nope. It's definitely from you guys.' Maddie shakes her head. 'Okay, Megan and Aston had a saucy one-nighter, leaving them dying and in desperate need of each other's company. This resulted in them starting and maintaining a secret relationship while Megan continued to fake-date guys Lila pre-approved and set her up with to keep up the facade. She then had enough, told Lila where to stick her blind dates, and spilled the beans. Then Lila covered for her until last night when they had enough, got sloppy, and Braden caught them. Now we all know, everyone is happy, and they can have unlimited one-nighters, therefore never needing to worry about being caught with their pants round their ankles while bumping uglies against a tree.'

Megan snorts. I grin.

'We have never had sex up against a tree,' she mumbles.

'Hey, not yet . . .' I squeeze her waist.

'Is that it, though?' Maddie looks at us. 'Well, basically.'

'Um, I guess so . . . Kinda elaborate, but yeah.' Megan answers for us. 'Maybe a little less desperation, though.'

'I'm not sure. I've been pretty desperate to get inside your pants since I saw you,' I tell her.

'Just my pants?'

'Well, we could go for inside you, but I was trying not to be fucking crude about it.'

Her eyes twinkle.

'Okay, usually I'd be totally up for sex talk, but the girl is like my sister. No next morning fuck stories.' Braden puts his hands up and looks at me. 'Try and keep that shit to a minimum around me.'

'You know,' Maddie muses. 'Aston doesn't swear nearly as much since him and Megan did the nasty. Maybe you should try it, Bray.' She taps his cheek, and he rolls his eyes.

'Of course, Angel,' he deadpans.

I smirk.

'I can't believe you were fucking each other and I never figured it out.' Kay looks at us.

'Relationship,' Megan corrects. 'There's a difference.'

'Sex was involved. It's all relative. I just can't believe I didn't know.'

I resist the urge to roll my eyes. 'You're not going to shut up about it, are you?'

'No,' Kay replies, leaning back on her hands. 'It's not damn likely.'

'What are we doing?' I ask as Megan tugs me toward my car.

'It's Sunday,' she says simply. 'We're going to see your Gramps.'

'Okay, but that doesn't explain why you have a damn picnic basket with you.'

'Fine – we're going to see your Gramps and take him out for the day. Better?' She raises an eyebrow at me, and I grin, starting the engine up.

'Much. But where are we going?'

'You'll see.'

She settles back in her seat, smiling to herself. If I'd hoped to get any clues from her outfit, I've definitely not got any luck. Her jeans, jacket, and boots are nothing out of the ordinary – but her tied-up hair is.

Not that it means anything in particular . . . Apart from making me want to nuzzle her bare neck.

We pull up outside Gramps' house and get out. When I open the door, I'm not greeted by the usual smell of cigar smoke. It's there, but fainter.

'Gramps?' I call out, worry trickling its way through my body. Worry shoots through my veins at a lightning speed when I see his empty chair by the window. He always sits by the window. Where is he?

'Gramps!' I shout loudly, spinning around and heading for the stairs. 'Gramps!'

'You could wake the damn dead you could, boy,' his voice grumbles from the back door. I rush through the kitchen and find him wiping dirt off his hands.

I stop. 'You were gardening?'

'No need to sound so surprised.' He chuckles. 'It's been known to happen.'

'But you haven't done it for years.'

'That's because I got lazy, boy!' He drops the cloth on the counter. 'I planted them bushes I got a couple weeks back – the hydrangea ones. For your Gran.'

'I thought you weren't ready to,' I say softly.

'I wasn't! Then me and you had our little chat, and I thought to myself what a miserable old bastard I was. Decided to get out of that damn chair and do something about it. You should go take a look at that vegetable garden. Not much growing there right now, but by spring it'll be bloomin'!' He beams, a light in his face I haven't seen for so long. He glances over my shoulder and his face brightens even more. 'And you brought Megan! Well, gardening and a chat about books with a beautiful young lady. This is the best Sunday I've had in a while.'

Megan laughs softly. 'I was hoping you'd be out of that chair. I'm taking you out for the day.'

I clear my throat, amused. 'Who's taking who?'

'Okay so you're driving, but it's most definitely my treat, Mr. Banks.' She looks at me pointedly, humor dancing in her pretty blue eyes.

'And the beautiful lady wants to take me out?' Gramps rubs his hands together. 'I best get my coat. Aston, I'm stealing your girl!' He kisses Megan on the side of the head as he passes her, a bounce in his step.

'Not a chance, old man!'

Megan smiles fondly at him, and I walk across the room to her, stopping in front of her.

'Yes?' She looks up at me.

I cup her chin, running my thumb along her jaw to her

bottom lip. I trace it softly. 'Nothing.' I smile, tilting her chin up and bending my face to meet her lips.

'Hope you're not seducing my girl!' Gramps calls. 'We have a date to go on!'

I laugh, taking Megan's hand and leading her out the house. Gramps grabs his stick and points it at the car.

'Least that beast is clean.'

'Of course it's clean. You really think I'd let her get dirty?' I glance at him.

He grunts. 'No. Guess not.'

I grin, helping him into the car, and shut the door. I get in the front next to Megan and she's smiling to herself.

'Gonna tell me where we're going yet?'

She shakes her head, eyes twinkling. 'No. I'll just give you directions. It's a surprise. Go right at the end of the street.'

I sneak glances at her as I drive and make the turns she orders me to. I'm not really paying attention to the direction we're going in. I'm too preoccupied by the excitement she's showing. It's infectious – I'm excited and I don't even know what for.

'Marina,' Gramps says from the back seat. 'We're heading to the marina.'

Megan grins and turns in her seat, nodding her head. 'Yep.'

'Why?' I frown slightly and glance at Gramps in the back seat. He taps a wrinkled finger against his mouth as he thinks, and Megan's grin grows.

'Why do people usually go to the marina?' she asks.

'Boats,' I answer. Her eyes slide to mine, her excitement really obvious now. Her cheeks are flushed, but behind the light in her eyes there's a hint of nervousness. Why . . .

'Fishing!' Gramps cries. 'You're taking us fishing!'

Megan nods vigorously. 'I wanted to do something for you both. My parents were supposed to come this weekend but Dad had a work thing come up so they canceled. He had a boat booked to go out with Braden, so I asked if I could use it instead. I'm paying him back.'

I stop the car in the parking lot near the marina and turn around to see Gramps. His eyes glisten with unshed tears, and a lump rises in my own throat.

'Thank you,' he whispers to Megan, his eyes focused on hers. 'Thank you.' She smiles in response, and Gramps shakes his head. 'I'm gonna go to that fishing place over the road and get us some bait. Megan, do you fish?'

She shakes her head. 'God, no. My dad taught Braden to fish, and his mom taught me to shop.' She grins. 'It worked out well.'

'Then make sure they have three poles on that boat,' Gramps announces. 'We'll teach you to fish!'

'Oh, I, er, um . . .'

'Nope! You're coming on that boat, so you're fishing. No just sitting there and looking pretty. You can look pretty and fish at the same time, you know.' He winks and opens the car door.

'Hang on, Gramps.'

'I can get out of a car, boy. I'm not that old yet,' he scolds me, grabbing his stick and climbing out. 'I'm getting bait. You go and sort out that boat.'

He hobbles across the street with his stick. I open Megan's door for her, pull her out, and close to me. Her arms go round my waist and she leans her cheek against my chest.

'Thank you,' I whisper, kissing the top of her head, letting my lips linger there. 'Thank you for this. You don't know how much it means to him.'

She pulls her head back and half-smiles. 'Probably about as much as it means to you.'

I nod, realizing it's true. 'We haven't fished since before the semester started.'

She runs her hands around to my stomach, her fingers splaying as they creep up my chest to my neck. 'I don't have to stay, you know. It's your day. You and your Gramps can go out by yourselves if you—'

I silence her with a kiss. 'No. No. Fishing was always our thing, just me and him, but if there was anyone in this world I want to share it with, it's you.' And it's true. She's the only person I'd dream of sharing this with.

'Then let's get to that boat. I bet he's lethal with that stick, let alone fishing poles.'

The waters of the bay are calm today, and the small boat bobs along smoothly. Megan's picnic is out of the way of any splashing water and she's looking dubiously at the fishing poles. Her gaze drifts to the tubs of worms Gramps bought for bait and she scrunches her face up a little. I can't help but smile.

'They're just worms,' I comment as I casually hook one onto my pole.

'Exactly,' she mutters, still staring the tub down. '*Worms*. If I'd have known we'd be using real live worms, I . . .' She shudders. 'I hate worms.'

I smirk. 'They're just worms, baby. You need them to hook the fish.'

'I know that.' She finally looks up at me. 'I just wish I didn't *have* to need them.'

Gramps hands her a pole. 'You need to hook the bait.'

She takes a deep breath as I hold the tub out, trying to contain my amusement. Her fingers move toward the tub before she snatches her hand back, shuddering again.

It takes her five tries to grab one. Even then, she drops it.

'Grab the damn worm and slide that hook through it!' Gramps claps his hands. 'Those fish ain't gonna wait around all day to become someone's dinner!'

'I . . . *Ewwww!*' she squeals as she grabs one quickly and slides it on. She holds the pole away from her body, the hooked worm floating through the air, and wipes her fingers on a rag next to her. 'Ew, ew, ew, ew!'

I secure the lid on the tub and Gramps and I burst into laughter.

'Come on. We gotta catch some fish!' Gramps grabs his pole, hooks his bait, and casts out onto the water.

'Yeah . . .' Megan says vaguely. 'I have no freakin' idea how that works.'

I put my pole down and pull her up. 'I'll teach you.'

'He learned from the best!' Gramps calls from the other side of the boat.

I wink at Megan and position her in front of me, wrapping one of my arms around her stomach. 'The wind is blowing from behind us, so we need to cast this way. If we try to go against it, it'll just blow your line this way.'

'Right. But how do I cast it?'

I grin. 'Patience. You need to hold the rod correctly.'

'Um, sure.'

I move my hand from her stomach and wrap my fingers around hers. 'The reel needs to be facing down, and it should sit between your middle finger and ring finger for balance. Like this.' I move her fingers. 'If that isn't comfy, you can change it until it is.'

'It's fine,' she says a little breathlessly.

'Now . . .' I move my mouth closer to her ear. 'You need to reel out until you have six inches of line hanging out, and turn the handle until the roller is directly under your middle finger.' I help her do it, my fingertips brushing against hers. 'Now hold the line against the rod, and open the bait with your other hand.'

I take her free hand from the side of the boat and put it against the bait, opening it with her.

'Now what?' She leans back into me slightly.

'Point the rod at your target.' I help her position it. 'Now we need to bring it up in a smooth, swift motion. You'll feel when the top of the rod bends and as soon as it does, we need to push it forward. Halfway to the target, let go of the line. Then we'll close the bait.'

'Up, bend, forward, let go, close,' she mutters, leaning back into me. 'I think I can do that.'

'You can.' I run my lips along her ear, nibbling at her lobe slightly. She wriggles and draws in a sharp breath.

'I can't if you do that.'

I smile against her skin. 'Ready to try.'

'No.'

'Three, two, one.' I help her lift the rod straight up and when I feel the flex I flick it forwards. She squeaks. 'Let go!'

Megan lifts her finger from the line and it flies out with rod, landing almost perfectly in the water. She grins. 'I did it!'

'You did. Now you have to wait for a fish to bite.'

'How long does that take?'

'How long is a piece of string?'

Megan

'Are you telling me I could be standing here all day and not catch a thing?'

Gramps cackles across the boat. 'That's exactly what he's telling you!'

I turn my face toward Aston, and he grins. 'What?'

'I can't believe I got roped into this.' This is ridiculous. I eat fish. I don't catch it. Hell.

'Hey.' His hands fall to my hips and he nudges my collar from my neck with his nose. His lips brush the skin of my neck. 'This was your idea, remember?'

'Yes . . .' My idea for them.

Aston's nose runs up and down my neck, his breath hot against me, and I swallow.

'So you didn't get roped into anything. You had to know that you'd end up fishing,' he reasons.

'Mhmm.'

'So why are you so surprised?'

I shiver when he takes a deep breath and exhales against my skin. His hands slide down my sides to the front pockets of my jeans. He puts his fingers in them, spreading them out and stroking my legs, before taking them back out.

'I'm not,' I whisper.

'Then don't complain.' He's smiling as he brushes his lips along my jaw lightly, and my eyelids flutter shut. Shit. He's driving me insane. 'Megan,' he whispers in my ear.

'Mm?'

'Keep your eyes on the line.'

Bastard. My eyes snap open and I look at him. The desire

in his eyes is probably equal to what's in mine, and fuck this stupid boat. Why do we have to be on a boat? 'You did that deliberately.'

He bends his head round and steals a kiss. He grins. 'So what if I did?'

I narrow my eyes and look back out at the water. 'So not—'

'Woohoooooooo!' Gramps hollers. 'We've got a big one, boy!'

'Hold that steady,' Aston tells me, releasing me and making his way across the boat to his Gramps, grabbing a net on the way.

'Giz a hand, here. Not as steady on the old feet as I used to be,' Gramps orders him. I glance over my shoulder and watch as Aston grabs the pole. It's bending a hella lot, and he whistles low at it.

'That's a good one, Gramps.'

'Don't sound so surprised,' he grunts. 'Prize fisher, me.'

He reels in the fish slowly, and as soon as it nears the surface, Aston swoops it up with the net and drops it onto the boat.

'Late salmon!' Gramps cries happily, taking a seat and bending over to look at it. 'And . . . You got a tape measure on you?'

'In the picnic bag,' I answer. 'Dad always used to take one for Braden so I thought I'd pack it.'

'Genius, girl!'

I grin, and Aston leaves the fish flapping on the deck to grab the tape measure.

'Well, is it big enough?'

'I think . . .' He rolls it out next to the fish. 'Hold him still, Gramps.' He rests his foot on the slippery salmon as they double-check the length.

'Well?'

'Just.' Aston grins at Gramps. 'Half an inch over the size limit.'

He claps his hands. 'Dinner tonight, kids!'

Something tugs on my line and my whole body twitches. I stare at the rod and the rapidly increasing line.

'Oh!' I squeak. 'Something is there! What do I do? Help!'

Gramps winks, grabs a stick and kills the fish quickly. Aston steps back up behind me and steadies my hands on the rod.

'There's a fish – has it bitten?' he asks me.

'How am I supposed to know? I can't see it!'

He half-sighs, half-laughs, and rests the side of his head against mine. 'This is gonna be a long day.'

So I'm not cut out to be a fisherwoman.

That's fine. I'm not particularly fond of the worms anyway . . . Or the shrimps. Worms are meant for gardens, and shrimps are made for eating. If you wanna catch 'em or fish with 'em, that's cool. I just won't do it.

Although I might just be tempted if Aston pressed himself up against me the way he did today . . .

Even in the cold sea breeze, I still felt like my body was on fire when he was behind me. I was so aware of him and the slightest movement of his body I don't think I actually learned a freaking thing about fishing. All I could think about was his fingers playing with my jeans pockets and his lips ghosting along my neck. Add in the warmth of his breath across my goose-pimple covered skin, and I'm ready to melt against him right now at the mere thought.

Now back in his room after eating the salmon, Aston's hands ease up my thighs and his thumbs brush along the inner side. I look into his gray eyes as he leans into me and runs his nose down mine.

'You didn't need to do that today,' he mutters as his fingers probe their way to my ass.

'I know, but I wanted to. You guys loved it.'

'It was made better by you being there.' His nose nudges at my jaw, causing my head to tilt back.

'You were pressed up against my body for most of it.' I run my fingers through his hair, and he presses open-mouth kisses along my shoulder. 'I'm sure it was better than normal.'

'It was. Much better.'

He dips his tongue in the hollow of my collarbone, my shirt catching as he moves his hands up my back. I turn my head and kiss his neck, resting my cheek against his shoulder. He breathes out heavily, shuddering slightly, and I recognize that movement. He's remembering. I hold him tighter and press my face into him.

'You don't have to leave, do you?' His voice is small and vulnerable, cutting into my chest.

'No,' I whisper. 'I'll stay as long as you need me to.'

And I mean it. If he needed me to stay forever, right here in his arms, I would. I'll stay for as long as he needs me whenever he needs me.

'Good.'

His fingers dig into my back and his jaw clenches, his whole body going rigid. I slowly smooth my hands across his back, slipping them under his shirt. His muscles are solid beneath my fingers, rock solid, and his grip on me tightens as he tries to control the shaking of his hands through shallow breaths.

I feel the burn of tears as I sit here, completely powerless to stop whatever is going through his mind. He could be remembering anything, any horror, and there's no way I can stop it. I've been here so many times already and it's ripped my heart apart each and every time.

But I won't leave. Love is stronger than hate.

Whatever hate is locked inside his body and whatever hate is burned into his mind, I know our love can push it out. I believe in the power it gives us.

And that's why I will break my heart over and over again.

I will break my heart to heal his.

'Don't go.' The words are a muffled, desperate plea into my hair.

'I'm not going anywhere,' I promise him. 'I'm right here. I'll be here as long as you need me.'

'I hate . . .'

'You're safe.' My voice is soft yet firm, my hand moving to the back of his head as I fight through the tears threatening to spill from my eyes. 'You're safe here with me.'

His body twitches and he relaxes suddenly, his breathing broken and harsh. 'Megan.'

Shit. He's so broken. His voice is so quiet, so scared. My hands are shaking and my chest is heaving. I'm still fighting the tears that surface every time he remembers.

'I'm here. I'm always here,' I reassure him.

'Don't go. Please don't ever go.' His voice is ever smaller now, barely there, yet it seems like he's screaming. I feel each word slicing into me, and a tear escapes my eye despite my best efforts.

'I'm staying. I promise. I'm not going anywhere.' I stroke the back of his head.

'I remember. Fishing with Gramps and Gran. I was four – it was just before she died. It's patchy. One of the last of her. She was wrapped in her favorite blanket on the boat. Gramps didn't want her to go and she told him to shut up. She wasn't going to miss it. She loved coming on the boat. She's the only person that ever came with us.'

Apart from me. His gramps accepted me so readily. Let me go on a trip that was reserved for them only – and his wife before she died. Today must have meant so much more to them than I thought. I hold that thought and squeeze my eyes shut.

'But then I went home. Took a fish. Mom was there. When Gramps left, she told me to put the fish in the freezer because she had to go to work, and I'd have to have toast because that was all she had. She went to work. I dropped the toast she'd made, the plate smashed, and he was angry. He was so fucking angry. He grabbed me by the back of my t-shirt and shoved me into the wall. My face smacked into it. The bastard broke my nose. Over a fucking plate!'

He tries to push away from me, and I hold him tighter.

'Megs—'

'No.'

He rips his head from my grip and stares at me, his eyes hard and cold. I wrap my legs around his, pinning him to me, and cup his face.

'I'm not letting you go,' I warn.

'I'm not fucking asking you, Megan!'

'I'm not asking you, either. I'm here, Aston. I'm right here in front of you.'

'I . . .'

And I realize. He's scared. He's scared of being the man he was told he would be. Scared of doing the things they did to him to me.

'You're not him! Any of them. You're more than that. You're *not* them,' I finish softly. 'You. Are. Not. Them.'

'You . . . I . . . *Don't.*'

'I love you.'

He closes his eyes tightly, breathing harshly through his nose, and shakes his head.

'Yes. I love you. Every broken, mismatched piece of you. I love every single freaking piece of you, even when you feel this way, and that isn't gonna change. You can be angry, afraid, sad, and I'll still love you the same way I love you when you're happy. Listen to me and believe me, Aston. I love every part of you the way you love every part of me.'

His arms shoot around my waist, and he lies me down on the bed, tucking me into his chest and locking our legs together. His body shakes as he holds me against him. I tilt my head back and stroke my thumb down his jaw and brush his lips. My fingers smooth over his closed eyes, and I press my lips against his softly.

'I'm here, Aston, and I'm not leaving you. Don't push me away anymore. We're past that now. I know all of you and you can't change that.'

'I'm scared that one day . . . one day I will be the person they tried to make me. Don't you get that? I'm scared . . . I'll hurt you one day. I'm so fucking scared.'

'You won't.'

His eyes shoot open, locking onto mine with a desperation for answers. 'You don't know that.'

I do know. I know with every part of me.

'You love me,' I say simply. 'You have what they didn't. You have love. *We* have love. Every time you feel that hate, think of me, and I'll give you love. Always.'

He doesn't move, his eyes never flickering away, his grip never wavering. The only movement in his body is the rising and falling of his chest as he regains control of his breathing. I run my thumb under his eye and across his cheek again, as if I can wipe away the pain he feels. Like if I do it enough it'll actually work.

A long, pain-filled breath leaves between his lips, and he presses his face to mine, his eyes clearing.

'And this is why I need you,' he whispers. 'It could be pitch black and you'd still break through with your light.'

'You need my love, not me. I'm just the person that gives it to you. I might be your light, but unless you wanted me to, no matter how hard I tried, I wouldn't be able to break through the darkness. You're the one that makes it better. I just help.'

He shakes his head, and I nod.

'I give you the light. It's up to you whether or not you let it break through.'

'It doesn't make sense.'

'What doesn't?'

'Why you love me.'

'There's no logic to love. It just is. Just like us. We just are.'

Everything is easier when a secret is out. Now I don't have to worry about looking at Aston wrong or saying something that might look suspicious. I don't have to watch my every movement, bite my tongue or clench my fists so I don't touch him.

And I love it.

I love that we can just be.

I don't care about the whispers from people outside our circle of friends, the ones who don't know the truth, and I don't care about the looks that come from other girls. I just care that I can fall into his arms when I find him standing outside my classroom, just like he is now.

'Shakespeare hasn't killed you yet, then,' he says as he smiles at me, taking my hand.

I look over at him. 'No, not yet, but there's every possibility of it in the future.'

'Not a damn chance.'

'How do you know? Have you ever read act after act of Shakespeare?'

'Because I'd revive you before you completely died.'

'And just how would you do that?'

He tugs me out the door and catches me against his body. 'A bit like this.' He grins and presses his lips to mine hotly, capturing me in a kiss that would most definitely revive me if I was dying.

Hell, I think it would revive me if I was freakin' *dead*.

'Think that would work?' he mutters, a smug grin on his face.

'Yup,' I mutter back, slightly dazed.

He laughs, keeping his arm locked around my waist, and steers me in the direction of Starbucks. I snuggle into his side, sighing happily. It's strange to think that a month ago we were constantly bickering, whether it was real or fake, genuine or pretense. Everything has changed so quickly.

We order coffee and take a seat by the window.

'I guess you'll be going home this weekend. For Thanksgiving?'

I look at him and shrug. 'I guess so.'

'You don't sound happy about it.'

I'm not.

'I guess it's the thought of having my mom looking over my shoulder every five minutes. I've had freedom for the last three months. Plus we usually do a thing with Braden's family, but he won't be there this year.' I stir my coffee. 'I'm pretty sure it's gonna suck without him.'

'He isn't going home?'

I shake my head. 'He's taking Maddie back to Brooklyn. She doesn't know yet. She thinks they're going to his parents'.'

Aston smirks. 'He's sneaky.'

'He always has been.' I smile. 'But his sneakiness means I have to suffer through dinner alone.' I sigh. Nothing is more tiring than the manners my mother insists on.

'Sounds like fun.'

'You could always come suffer with me, you know,' I offer. 'Mom would love that.' Once I've told her about us.

'I dunno.' He pauses, taking my hand. 'I don't wanna leave Gramps alone.'

'You don't have to. My nan will be there, and she's about as normal as a straight-sided circle. They'd get along like a house on fire. She'd probably talk him into going to Bingo with her on the Friday night. *And* she smokes like a train.' I roll my eyes.

'Perfect match,' he says dryly. 'And your Granddad?'

'He died in the Vietnam War. He was in the air force and got shot down. I never knew him so it's kinda hard to be sad about it. My other grandparents – Dad's parents – moved to Canada when they retired.'

'Canada?' Aston raises an eyebrow. 'Isn't that kind of an odd place to retire to?' A small smile creeps onto his face.

'Yes . . . But I never said they were normal.' I grin. 'I thought they might have gone to, oh, I dunno, the Bahamas or something. Even moved from Colorado to Cali to be closer to Dad since he moved here to be with Mom after college, but nope. They went to freaking Canada, and we're expected to pack up and go there every winter.' I shiver. 'It's so damn cold in Canada.'

'You really are a Cali princess.' He laughs.

'So I grew up in SoCal. Don't shoot me for liking the sun.'

'You definitely grew up on the right side of California.'

'That's why you and your Gramps should come with. He can go into cahoots with Nan and cause trouble, Mom can entertain the way she loves so much, and me and you can disappear the whole weekend.' I shrug. 'Sounds good to me.'

'I dunno. I'll have to talk to Gramps.'

'What would you normally do?'

'Uh . . .' Aston scratches the back of his neck, and my lips twitch in amusement. 'Eat take-out, watch crap television, and drink beer.'

Typical guys. I giggle. 'Okay, you're definitely coming with me.'

'That was traumatic.' I drop onto the sofa next to Braden, shaking my head. He grins, and I know exactly what he's about to say.

'She took it well, then?'

'You could say that,' I deadpan. '"You have a *boyfriend*? A real boyfriend? Oh, Megan, that's wonderful! Although, I do hope you're using protection. We've had this discussion before, and you need an education, house, and job before you get yourself pregnant."' I shake my head as if it'll clear the headache brought on by my mom's speech.

'She just cares.'

'Oh, I know. I love that she cares so much, but there's really no need to bring it up in every conversation we have. We only spoke ten or so days ago. I'm not that forgetful.'

'She means well.'

'Yeah?' I raise an eyebrow at him. 'Then why can't you stop laughing?'

He shrugs and tries to stop. 'I'm sorry, Meggy. I'm just secretly wishing I could see this meet-the-parents episode.'

'Oh, it's meet the grandparents, too. Not doing anything by half.'

'Start as you mean to go on.' He grins. 'Oh, man. I'm gonna have to call Mom three times a day for updates. How much are we betting your mom sits Aston down and gives him the pregnancy chat?'

My eyes widen and I look at him in panic. 'She wouldn't.'

Braden grins widely, amusement dancing in his eyes. 'Oh, I can almost guarantee she will.'

I grab a pillow, bury my face into it, and groan. 'This is going to be a disaster.'

Aston

'This is going to be a disaster,' Megan mutters, pulling onto a street with houses worth more than I could ever dream of making. Most are three-story buildings, all with driveways, garages and perfectly pruned front yards.

I fidget in my seat. A small voice in the back of my mind whispers about the differences in our lives. It reminds me how different it is here compared to where I started life in San Francisco. I glance at Megan and tell the voice to fuck off.

My past doesn't define who I am. The here and now does.

Gramps whistles low. 'What, you got a pool and all?'

'Hope you brought your swimming trunks,' she comments in a chipper voice.

'Good job I did, then.' Gramps pats his stomach. 'Love a good swim.'

She turns the car onto a driveway leading to one of the three-story houses. The drive is lined by circular bushes and winter flowers. I look up at the house. Painted white, it looks like something out of a movie.

You know . . . The ones where the rich, unattainable person always lives.

You're not worth anything. I clench my jaw and push the voice away. I won't let it ruin this weekend for Megan.

Megan hops out of the car. The front door opens, revealing a woman that could be Megan in twenty years' time. Looking at her mom's blonde hair, slender figure and bright smile, it's easy to see exactly why Megan is so damn beautiful.

Gramps whistles again. 'That's one hot momma,' he whispers to me, chuckling.

I roll my eyes and step from the car, turning to help him out. He waves me off, and I roll my eyes again. Damn stubborn man.

He brushes his hands off on his legs. 'I'm going to meet me some beautiful ladies.' He hobbles up the drive on his stick, approaching Megan and her mom, and promptly introduces himself. I smirk when he leans forward to kiss Megan's mom on the cheek, taking her totally by surprise. She laughs, and Megan turns to me, smiling.

My stomach jolts, and I repeat my mantra in my mind. My past does not define me. My past does not define me.

'Mom, this is Aston. Aston, this is my mom, Gloria,' Megan introduces us.

'It's lovely to meet you, Aston.' Gloria's eyes twinkle with genuine happiness. She holds her hand out, and I take it, kissing her fingers.

'The pleasure is all mine.'

She beams, leaning into Megan. 'And he's polite! I like him already.'

Gramps winks at me, and I stifle my grin as Gloria leads us into the house. Megan slips her hand inside mine, and I squeeze it lightly.

'Roger?' Gloria calls. 'Where are you?'

'In the yard, darling,' a deep voice calls back.

'He's getting the grill fired up,' she explains, leading us into the house.

It looks nothing like I expected it to. In my mind it was immaculate and filled with expensive trinkets, but it's not. The walls are adorned with certificates with Megan's name on – from swimming to horse riding, pictures of her and Braden and family photos. My eyes flick from one image to another, drinking them in.

'You were a really cute kid,' I murmur as we pass a photo of Megan with her hair in pigtails, grinning at the camera with a tooth missing.

'Shut up,' she mutters back. I grin.

The back yard is about the size of Gramps' house. He

whistles again, and I resist the urge to join him. We step onto the decking that houses the grill, a large table and chairs, and a few random plants. A pool house is at the far end next to a fair sized pool.

And you could still get another house in the free space.

I knew Braden and Megan came from money, but holy fucking shit.

'Megs!' The man at the grill calls, turning around.

'Dad,' Megan groans, and I see why. His apron is that of a naked guy's – sporting a six pack and burger bun over the space where his privates should be. I chuckle.

'What?' he says innocently.

'You had to wear that apron, didn't you? Remember? Guests?' she implores desperately.

He looks at me and Gramps. 'Too late now, darling daughter. They've already seen it!'

'And I've got a real one!' Gramps laughs throatily, patting his rounded stomach. He steps forward and introduces himself to Megan's dad.

Megan sighs and rests her forehead against my shoulder. I kiss the top of her head.

'And this must be the boy that stole my girl's heart.' Her dad turns to me, smiling widely.

'Yes, sir.' I wink at Megan. She's giving her dad the death stare.

'Roger,' he introduces himself, shaking my free hand. 'Sure is nice to meet you, Son. If she ever had a boyfriend in high school, we never got to meet him. Braden scared him off before we even got close.'

'*Dad!*' Megan gasps. 'What are you talking about?'

'The fact you never brought me some eye candy home from school,' a smoky voice rasps from the kitchen. 'About time you did. He has a nice behind. Is his front that nice?'

'Mother,' Gloria warns.

I raise an eyebrow at Megan, and her mouth drops open. A slight flush rises on her cheeks, and we both turn to look at the old woman sweeping out of the house onto the decking.

'What? I was talking about the fine gentleman sitting at the table over here.' She takes a seat opposite Gramps and runs her eyes across me. 'Although, good choice, Megan. He's a pretty one.'

'And he has brains.' Megan shrugs.

'Go off to college and you get picky. Mind you . . .' Her nan grins. 'I'd be picky too, if he was on offer.'

'And he got them looks and brains from somewhere,' Gramps butts in.

'And it was clearly you.' Her nan beams at him. They strike up a conversation, and I smile. Bringing him here was a good idea.

'So you really never had a boyfriend in high school?' I tease Megan.

She opens her mouth, closes it, and opens it again.

'Not one she brought home,' Gloria explains. 'Braden definitely scared them off, so imagine my shock when she told me about you! I thought you were definitely going to show up with a broken arm or a black eye.'

'A broken arm?' Roger exclaims, poking the coal. 'I expected him to show up in a wheelchair. Maybe that girl is good for Braden.'

'Maddie,' Megan corrects. 'Not "that girl", Dad. Her name is Maddie.'

'That's it. I knew it was an "M" name, I just couldn't think of it.' He waves her off.

'Perhaps.' Gloria smiles. 'Megan, why don't you go and show Aston around? It looks as though his grandfather is occupied for the moment.' She leans forward. 'I made the spare rooms up because I didn't know what you were doing,' she whispers. 'If you want to share, you go ahead. You're adults, after all, but just use—'

'Yes, thank you, Mom,' Megan rushes out. 'Understood.'

She tugs on my hand, pulling me away from the decking and her father's laughter. I smirk to myself.

'Good grief,' she says when we're inside. 'That went kinda well, I guess.'

'Hey – your parents embarrassed you, and your Nan eyed me up. I'd say it went pretty well!'

She pauses. 'I guess that's kinda standard.'

'I dunno. I've never met the parents before.'

She pauses halfway up the stairs, tilting her head and looking at me. 'Really?'

'Yeah. You sound surprised.'

'I kinda am.'

'Why? You know I've never really dated anyone before. It's always just been casual.'

She starts walking again. 'So . . . This is serious?' I catch the teasing lilt in her voice.

'I'm toying with the idea of it . . .'

She grins, and I pull her close at the top of the stairs. 'Yes?' She bats her eyelashes as she looks up at me.

I smile. 'Was there ever any doubt this was serious?'

'No,' she answers, kissing me. 'Not really.'

'Not really?' I raise an eyebrow.

'No,' she corrects, pulling me toward a door. 'Love you.'

Her words send warmth through my body, silencing the constant whisper in the back of my mind.

'Love you,' I whisper, kissing her nose.

'My room.' She opens the door behind her, and I follow her in.

Woah.

Stuffed toys sit on the dresser, the white rug on the floor is fluffy as hell, and the walls are painted a light purple. Two doors to the right lead to what I assume is an en-suite and walk-in closet, and fairy lights hang above her bed.

'I'm pretty sure this is the most girly room I've ever seen in my life.'

'And how many girls' rooms have you seen, exactly?' She quirks her eyebrows.

'One. This one.'

'Then your statement is ridiculous.' She laughs.

'I'm sleeping in here?' I eye up the stuffed toys.

'You don't have to.'

'I'm not saying I don't want to. I do.' I point to the stuffed toys. 'But they're gonna have to be turned around. I'm really not into being perved on by damn stuffed bears.'

Her blue eyes twinkle and she rests against the wall. 'There's nothing wrong with my stuffed bears.'

'There's nothing right with them, baby.'

'Are you making me choose between you and my bears?'

'Yes. Yes, I am.'

'I can see this being an issue, Mr. Banks.'

'Is that so, Miss Harper?' I step toward her, pulling her to me. My fingers thread through her hair, tilting her head back, and I brush my lips across hers. 'Can your stuffed bears do this?' I run my nose along her jaw, my lips peppering kisses down her neck, sucking lightly on her pulse point. Her breath catches. 'Or this?' I slide my hand down her back to cup her ass and pull her hips against mine. My erection throbs lightly against her, growing as she grinds slightly. 'Or this?' I bend my head and swirl my tongue across the swell of her breasts, teasing her by dipping it along the cup of her bra.

'No,' she breathes out. 'No. They can't do that.'

I nibble my way up to her ear, resting my lips against it. 'So what was the issue?' I whisper.

'Issue? Who said anything about an issue?' She puts her fingers in my hair and tugs my head back. 'No issues here.'

My lips twitch. 'So the bears get turned round?'

She nods. 'Hell, if there's more of that . . .' Her body pushes right against mine, aligning perfectly. 'They can live in the pool for all I care.'

'Oh, there's plenty more where that came from, and it's all yours.'

Megan runs her hand down my body, her fingers tracing the defining lines of the muscle. I sigh deeply, pulling her closer to me, and breathe in the vanilla scent of her hair. No matter where she's been or what she's done, she always smells like vanilla.

'What are we doing today?' I ask, my fingertips following the curve of her spine right to her ass.

She shudders. 'I thought we could go riding.'

'I get the feeling we're not talking about bedroom riding.'

She looks up at me, her hair messy, and smiles. 'No. Horse riding. I don't go at college and I miss it.'

'I've never ridden a horse.'

'I'll teach you.'

'Um.'

'You taught me to fish,' she reminds me. 'You made me fish!'

'I guess there's no way around this, huh?'

She shakes her head, rolling on top of me. Her knees go either side of my hips, trapping me, and her hair falls around my face. She slowly lowers her face to mine, sucking my bottom lip into her mouth and grazing her teeth across it. I slide my hands along her thighs, my thumbs coming dangerously close to the naked area of warmth between her legs.

'No way around it at all,' she whispers.

'Really? You can't ride me instead?'

'I . . .' she stops as I flick my thumb across her clit gently, making her thighs tighten. 'I'm sure.'

She grabs my hands and moves them away.

'Is it gonna be one of those days?' I sigh.

She goes to her dresser, and slides on a pair of white lace panties and matching bra. My eyes follow her every movement as she walks into her closet soundlessly. I sit up and reach forward to grab some clean boxers from my bag. Reach forward very fucking uncomfortably thanks to the hardness of my dick. I shove them on as Megan reappears wearing riding pants and a white shirt.

'Fuck.'

She might as well be naked the way those pants cling to her hips. They're molded to her body like a second skin.

'I have to watch you ride a horse wearing those pants?' I clarify, half hoping she'll be putting a baggier pair over them.

She ties her hair into a messy bun on top of her head and turns to me, her pink lips curved in a smile. 'Yep.'

I stand up and pull my own pants on. 'Please tell me it's easy to ride a horse with a hard on.'

She covers her mouth with her hand and lets out a loud

laugh, her eyes flicking to my dick. 'I've never, um, tried it. Not personally.'

I pull my shirt on. 'This is gonna be a fuckin' nightmare.'

'But I'd imagine it's pretty hard.'

'Yeah? Then at least I have something in common with it.'

Megan pulls up outside a row of old stables on the edge of Palm Springs. There's nothing beyond them except open space, and I can see why the stables were built here.

'This is the place I learned to ride. I called ahead this morning and asked them to saddle the horses up for us.' She smiles at me.

'Right.' I look dubiously at the stables.

'Come on!' She gets out of the car, and I follow suit. 'Oh, and, um, don't go caveman, okay?'

'Why would I go caveman?'

'The owner's son may have a teeny tiny crush on me.'

I look at her blankly.

'He's only just sixteen,' she carries on. 'He's crushed on me since he could walk.'

'Right.' I have to ride with a boner and deal with a sixteen-year-old guy making eyes at my girl. Who said this was a good idea?

'Oh, Aston.' She laughs, grabbing my hands. 'Don't be grumpy. He's cute.'

'Cute?'

'As in sweet-cute, not hot-cute.'

'Am I cute?'

'You're hot-cute.' She tugs me forward and kisses my cheek. 'There is a big, big difference.'

I grin as she leads me over to a stable with two brown horses. Her smile widens and she drops my hand, racing over to one of them. She runs her hand down the horse's nose and hugs its neck.

'Hello, boy,' she coos. 'Did you miss me?' She nuzzles her face into the horse's neck, and I find myself smiling. That is definitely sweet-cute.

I keep my distance. I'm really not a horse guy. I have no idea why I'm here.

Megan turns to me, a light in her eyes and a huge smile on her face.

Scratch that shit. I know exactly why I'm here. I'm here because this makes her happy, and if I wanna do anything in my life, it's make this girl happy. No matter what it takes or whatever I have to do to achieve it, I'll do my damnedest to put that smile on her face as many times as I can.

She unbolts the door and leads the horse out, patting his neck. 'This is Storm. He's my baby.' She glances at me. 'He was my sweet sixteenth present. Most people got a car. I got a horse, and worked for my Dad for a year to get my car.'

'Isn't a horse cheaper?'

'It depends, but my boy is a thoroughbred and worth more than I could have earned in the year leading up to my birthday. Besides, a car is a car. Storm is one of my favorite guys.'

'I thought I heard your voice,' a woman calls and appears from the back of the stable. 'It's good to see you, Megs. Your boy has missed you.' The woman pats Storm.

'I missed him.' Megan smiles at her. 'June, this is Aston, my boyfriend. Aston, this is June. She owns the stables and takes care of Storm for me while I'm at college.'

'It's nice to meet you,' I say.

'So you're the reason she called ahead? Learning to ride?'

'Yes, ma'am.'

She nods approvingly. 'Nice choice, Megan. He's cute.'

Megan snorts into her hand. 'I'm getting that a lot.'

'I don't mind.' I grin.

'Let's just hope Poppy thinks you're cute. She likes beginners, and if you chuck her one of these . . .' She throws me an apple I didn't even realize she was holding. '. . . she'll love you forever.'

'Where is she, then? I'll go charm her.' I wink at Megan, and throw and catch the apple.

'This is Poppy.' June unlocks a door and leads out a white horse with gray speckles. 'She's the calmest of the bunch and she's been with me for six years. She'll take care of you.'

I walk up to her, gently reaching out to rub her neck and offering the apple. She takes it, eating it in under a minute, and nudges my shoulder with her nose.

'You're not having any more,' June scolds her. 'You be nice to Aston, old girl. Megan likes him.'

Megan reaches over and pats her nose. 'Hey, girl. Ready to ride?'

Poppy neighs in what I assume is a yes, and both women lead the horses to the paddock. I follow behind, lagging slightly. Horse-riding. I never thought I'd see the day I'd be riding a horse – especially not to make a girl happy. I shake my head in a mild sort of amusement.

'Right.' June waves me over to her, and I watch Megan expertly mount Storm. Those pants are tight as fuck. Crap.

'Yep.' I stand next to Poppy, staring at the saddle.

'Gather the reins in one hand, put your left foot in the stirrup, and hold onto the wither,' June orders me. 'Then push up and swing your leg over her flank. Make sure you don't kick her.'

'What if I do?'

'Then she'll take off, and you'll land on your ass.'

Megan giggles, and I shoot her a look. 'No kicking horse ass. Got it.'

'Ready? Go.'

I do as she says, sitting on Poppy's saddle.

'Not bad,' June praises. 'Now let your legs hang down, and I'll sort out your stirrups.'

She fiddles with them and instructs me on how to settle my feet in properly. She puts a hat on my head, tightens the strap under my chin, and pats Poppy's behind. She begins to move and I grab the reins tighter.

'Holy—'

'Sit up straight!' June barks. 'Megan, he's all yours!'

'Thanks, June!' She waves her off, and Poppy follows Storm out into the paddock. Megan turns to me, grinning. 'Whatever you do, don't squeeze your legs.'

'Why not?' I mutter, wishing I could lean forward and grab the horse's neck. I admit it. I'm scared of this damn beast.

'Because she'll go faster.'

'Great. You couldn't have given me a run down on the way here?'

'Did you tell me about fishing before we got on the boat?' Her eyes sparkle, and I nod my head toward her.

'Touché, baby. Touché.'

She clicks her tongue, and Storm begins to move faster.

'I hope you're not expecting me to go any faster.'

'I'm not,' she calls. 'I didn't actually expect you to get on Poppy!'

'Nice to know you have confidence in me,' I shout dryly as she rounds behind me. Poppy's walking at a nice pace. I'm really not into taking her up into a trot. No way.

The ground is dusty as we leave the small paddock, and the sun beats down with a still hot temperature. 'Where are we going?' I ask her.

'You'll see.'

Megan

I slide down from Storm's back and pat his neck lovingly, hooking his reins around a tree branch in the shade. I take my helmet off, shake out my hair, and look under the roots for the basket I asked June to place there earlier. Storm turns his attention to the water I've given him, and I lie the blanket out on the ground on the other side of the small tree. Excited, I sit down and wait for Aston to catch up.

Palm Canyon trail is one of my favorite to take – it always has been. Sitting here by the stream and letting Storm rest was a weekly pastime before I left for Berkeley. We'd do the other trails on our other rides, but our Saturdays were always reserved for this.

And now I remember why.

The green of the fauna is a stark contrast to the barren desert beyond, and the rocks that dot the stream are just big enough to sit on. It's beautiful here. Peaceful in the winter when no one comes here.

'How do I get down?' Aston approaches.

I laugh at the sight of him. 'Click your tongue three times, and she'll stop, then get down the way you got up.'

'Not kicking her ass, right?'

'Exactly.'

He clicks his tongue and Poppy stops. His dismount is swift and it looks like he could have been riding his whole life.

'A picnic?' he smirks, hooking her reins over the branch the way I did and removing his hat.

'Surprised?' I smile as he drops onto the blanket next to me.

'Yep, but then you always surprise me.' He presses his lips to mine, and I cup the side of his face.

'You said you wanted to see Palm Springs. There's not much in the other direction you can't see in any other town, but this is my favorite place in the whole world.' I drop my hand and look around. 'I've missed it here. I didn't realize it until I was sitting here.'

'It's pretty damn nice,' Aston says appreciating the view. 'You really grew up here?'

'Pretty much. My mom has her horse at the stables, too. You didn't see him, but Midnight is—'

'Black?'

'Yep, actually.' I glance at him. 'She grew up here and taught me to ride. We spent every weekend out here until I was fourteen and she let me come alone. I didn't miss a weekend until I started college.'

'Did you not think about riding in Berkeley?'

I shake my head. 'I don't think I have the time. Besides – I can't expect my parents to pay for it as well as college. I could get a job, but then I definitely wouldn't have time to ride. It's a lose-lose situation.' I shrug.

Aston rummages in the basket. 'At least you can still ride when you get home . . . Even if it is only a few times a year.'

'True.' I smile as he pulls out the strawberries. He grabs one from the dish and brings it close to my mouth. I hold it in place, and take a huge bite. Juice dribbles down my chin and he grins, flicking it away with his thumb.

'I hope you don't think I'm feeding you,' he mutters, biting into his own strawberry.

'But you just did.' I pout, looking at the other strawberry in his hand. 'And that's a huge one!'

He looks at it, then at me and sighs. 'Fine. Have the huge strawberry.' He holds it out to me, and I lean forward, biting into it slowly, my lips wrapping around it. His eyes flick down, focusing on my mouth, and I sit back.

My lips curve up as he puts a hand just behind my back, his face coming close to mine.

'You have a little . . .' he whispers in a rough voice, bringing his thumb to my face. I glance down at it, watching as he presses it against the corner of my mouth softly, wiping along the curve of my bottom lip. I part my lips, drawing in a slow breath, and close my eyes as he sweeps his hand into my hair.

His breath is hot across my lips, mingling with mine, and my heart pounds as he hovers there above me, millimeters from touching me. It's a moment that seems to last forever, a moment filled with hope, anticipation, resolve, and *love*.

Hope for us. Anticipation for the future. Resolve to make it last. Love for everything we have and have yet to share together, and for everything we are.

And when he finally touches his lips to mine, it makes it all the sweeter.

The ride back to the stables is easy – mostly because Aston realizes he isn't going to fall off if he goes into a trot. I let him drive back to my house and that seems to make up for forcing him to sit on a horse and stare at my ass in tight riding pants all day.

It kinda makes up for it, anyway.

Everyone is out when we arrive back, and I bet Mom dragged them all to the store. Tonight is her annual Thanksgiving eve party, which translates as lots of people, lots of wine, and lots of Nan eyeing up all the younger guys.

'You were a bit of an overachiever as a kid,' Aston says as we go upstairs.

'I was?'

'Yep. Swimming, horse-riding, gymnastics . . . Anything else?'

'Hmm. I danced for a bit. Well, six months. I gave it up. I was too heavy on my feet from gym, and I was a terrible ballerina.' I grin. 'Gymnastics is a lot like dance, but apparently dance isn't a lot like gymnastics.' I shrug, walking into my bathroom and running the shower.

I toss my clothes into the laundry basket and step under the steaming hot water, letting it run over me and soothe my aches from the day of riding. My legs are stiff and I know they'll be even worse tomorrow, but it was so worth it.

It was even more worth it because Aston got to know some of me after showing me so much of him. His life is stuck in San Francisco, and while my life is in Berkeley, my heart is in Palm Springs.

He needs a little shove to let his heart break completely free from the confines he keeps it in. He might have let it go a little for me, but he needs to let it go for himself.

I just hope this weekend can do that for him, even just a bit.

I begin to hum to myself as I wrap a towel around my body, the soft melody of *Cry With You* by Hunter Hayes filling the small room. I scan the rows of bottles and tubs on my shelves, grabbing a vanilla moisturizer to match my shampoo.

The unsung words of the song haunt me, resonating through my body as I perch my foot on the edge of the bathtub and rub the moisturizer along my leg. The song reminds me of Aston, all his pain and all the pain I feel for him. It reminds me how I know I'll never leave him, how I can give him the kind of love he needs to get through whatever his past throws at him.

Just like Hunter Hayes, I feel all the pain.

I let the towel fall away as I rub the moisturizer all over my body, letting it dry the water remaining on my skin. Two rough, warm hands cup my hips and a hot, chiseled chest presses against my back. Aston's lips blaze a trail across my shoulders, his hands moving to my stomach and holding me flat against him.

'Were you watching me?' My voice is slightly shaky.

'Would you slap me if I say yes?' he replies in my ear, his hands moving up to cup my breasts.

'No,' I breathe out, pushing into his hands.

'Then yes, I was.' He kisses my neck, his hands massaging me in a way that tugs on all my stomach muscles and starts a desperate ache between my legs.

'Why?'

'Because,' he whispers. 'I couldn't not. I don't know if you realize how beautiful you are with no make-up on, your wet hair, wearing just a tiny towel or nothing at all. I've never seen you totally natural before, and I didn't think you could be any more beautiful than you usually are, but you are.'

He slides his hand down my stomach, easing his fingers between my thighs. He rubs his finger against my clit and pushes his hips into me, his erection digging in between my ass cheeks. My head drops back against him, and he blazes more kisses down my exposed neck, curving his fingers and soothing my ache. He keeps it up, holding me against him even as heat swamps my body and my legs give out. He holds me as the shaking subsides, still kissing me tenderly.

'My turn,' I whisper, spinning in his arms. I cup him with my hand, running my fingers along the outside of his boxers. He tugs us back into my bedroom, and I creep my fingers inside his boxers to touch him fully. He's rock hard, and my fingers barely go right around him as they start a steady, pumping rhythm up and down him.

Aston pushes us onto the bed, moving his hips in time with my hand, and plunges his tongue into my mouth. The ache starts between my legs again, and I involuntarily buck my hips when he groans my name into my mouth. I squeeze him in my hand, not stopping my body's responses to the desperate exploration his hands are undertaking.

It doesn't take long before he pulls away from me, rolls on a condom and positions himself against me. He looks into my eyes as he pushes inside me, my muscles clenching around him. There are so many words I could say to him in this moment, so many things that need to be said between us, but this feels like it's meant to be.

The first time since we came out. The first time since we used the word love.

After, we both shower and get ready for Mom's party. My dress swishes about my knees as I stand and check my reflection in the mirror, smoothing the skirt out. Aston steps up behind me, linking his fingers with mine, and smiles.

'We make a pretty hot couple.' He winks, and I laugh.

'I'm not used to having to share looks and brains with someone. I always assumed I'd be the smart one out of us,' I tease him.

'Oh, you're the smart one, all right.' He touches his lips to my temple. 'You've taught me a lot in the last month. A lot I wouldn't have learned without you.'

I reach up and touch his face, meeting his eyes in the mirror. 'You don't know that.'

'No, I do. When we were on the trail today and we stopped for lunch, you taught me how something barren and empty can be full of life and beautiful.'

My lips twist up slightly. 'The canyon was deserted,' I remind him.

'But it was full of life because of you,' he says honestly. 'You added to the beauty of it, bringing a desolate place alive. Just like you did for me. I always thought I was dead inside, that I had to feel that way. That I couldn't remember because remembering meant feeling, and feeling meant being. And then there was you. You made me remember what it was like to live.'

'Aston . . .' I take a deep breath. 'But none of that matters if it's all for me. You have to ask yourself who you live for.'

'At first it was you. All you. Now? Now it's a little of both. You taught me how to love, and I'm pretty sure I love myself just a little bit, now. I'll never see what you see, but it's more than I've ever had.'

I blink harshly, trying not to cry, because he can't possibly understand how much those words mean to me. He can't understand how much I wanted to make that pain better for him, make him understand he's more than he thought. And he definitely can't understand how his words seal around my heart, gripping onto it like a vice.

'Really?' I whisper.

"Her heart did whisper that he had done it for her."

'Really, baby. I live for me, but I love for you.' He kisses my temple again, and I feel every word.

He was always my Mr. Darcy.

And I was always his Elizabeth.

Epilogue

Aston

I tug the zipper of my jacket up higher as a cold wind blows in off San Francisco Bay, and fight the urge to turn and run back to the marina. I won't run. This is something that has to be done, for me.

Megan squeezes my hand, curling into my arm, and we begin to walk into the small cemetery where my mom lies.

I feel sick. Emotion stronger than I've felt in a long time swirls around my whole body, from hatred to pity, fear to anger, yet through it all . . . Through it all is a bit of love for the woman that tried and failed to give me life.

We weave silently through the graves and markers, heading to the back of the cemetery. I hold the white rose I bought tightly, clutching it to my chest, and try to breathe deeply.

I will never forgive her and I will never forget her, but I can finally be at peace with her.

The small, black marble headstone sits alongside my Gran's, and Megan places a small bunch of flowers against it silently. My eyes trace the letters of Mom's gravestone, following the engraved patterns, and it begins to blur as my eyes sting with tears.

I sink down to my knees in front of the stone, letting the tears fall as they need to, and set the rose down. The white of the rose is a stark contrast to the black of the marble, like my childhood innocence was a contrast to my mom's mature promiscuity.

Even now, it follows her. In life and in death.

'We're at peace now, Mom,' I say softly into the wind. 'Whatever it was that made you the way you were, I'm glad you're away from it. I'm sorry I wasn't enough for you. Maybe I was too much. I'll never know. I just hope you're at peace now. And I . . . I love you.'

There are so many more words. I could yell at her grave, scream at it if I really wanted, but it won't have any effect on it. She'll still be gone and it won't change anything. Hating her can't change the past, and I finally know that. Hating her won't make it all go away. It won't erase it.

I stand and look into Megan's clear blue eyes. She clasps my hand, holding on tightly, and I follow her from the cemetery. I said I'd never come back to San Francisco. I always knew I'd have to come back, and now I have. Now I don't ever have to come back. I don't have to look back. I can travel back across the water to college, and stay on that side of the water.

I can look into the blue eyes of the girl I love every day, and make the life I always wanted.

Read on for an excerpt of the third book
in the series . . .

THE RIGHT MOVES

Abbi

You just need one.

One thought. One second. One impulse. One touch. A lot of little things – little *ones* add together, snowballing and spiraling into something bigger. A big one. But one all the same. And one thing is all it takes to change your life.

Irreparably. Inexplicably. Irreversibly.

It's been two years since those little ones added together for the first time and I fell in love with Pearce Stevens. It's been two years since I felt that sweet fluttering of a first crush followed by the gentle thump of falling head over heels in love. Two years since the things that meant everything would fall apart, leaving me plunging headfirst into the dark abyss of depression.

If I knew then what I know now, I would have made different choices. Ignored the thoughts as the wishful musings of a teen heart, passed the time, fought the impulses, and shied from the touch. If I knew how the next months would unfold and the direction my life would take, I would have hopped on the next plane outta here and hunkered down in the Caribbean.

But I didn't know – and there was no way for me to. How could I know? I never imagined those little ones would grow into a big one, and I never imagined they'd come back just months after I felt them for the first time.

But the second time was a darker thought. It was a black second, a swallowing impulse, a deadly touch. The first time I watched the blood drip down my ankle from my accidental shaving cut, the newly bare razor blade flat between my fingers, was a moment that changed my life just as much as falling in love with Pearce did. It was a moment I can never change. I can't take it away and I can't pretend it never happened.

It's a part of me, just like Pearce is. A part of my past, and they are the two defining moments in my life. If you ask me where it all went wrong, I'll tell you – Pearce Stevens and the blade. And I won't be able to explain it for a second, no matter how hard you beg.

I won't be able to tell you why I fell in love with my best friend's brother, or why I didn't run before it was too late. I'll never be able to put into words why I didn't pull off my rose-tinted glasses and see him for what he really was and is.

I will never, ever be able to explain what possessed me to make the first cut on my skin. After all, you can't explain what you don't understand, and sometimes it's better not to understand.

I lean over the bathtub and watch the water run dark from my newly-dyed hair. The dark water swishes around the tub and swirls around the plug, disappearing from view with the same ease my blood did so long ago. I stay here until the water runs clear, shampoo and rinse, and wrap my hair in a dark towel.

Against Mom's wishes I made Dad take me to the store to get the dye. She doesn't understand my need to separate myself from the person I was last year. I don't think anyone does, and it's not something I can explain. I just know I'm not the Abbi I was before; the new Abbi is a different person. By separating the two halves of me, I'm moving forward with the new me. At least that's what Dr. Hausen said. She also said it was a step in the right direction – something positive.

Positive is what I need. That's why my previously pale pink, girly bedroom is now bright blue and purple. It's positive. It's different. It's new.

Just like me. I'm shiny and new.

I sit on my new beaded comforter on the bed and face the mirror. My eyes are brighter than they were before and my cheeks aren't as sunken. I touch a gentle fingertip to the hollow of my cheek and breathe in deeply. A clump of hair falls free from the towel, the almost black color a contrast against my pale skin.

I bend my head forward, roughly dry my hair, and flip it back up. My hand crawls along my bed to find my brush, and I run it through the strands. I don't really focus on anything but the repetitive motion, and I don't think about anything as I start up my hairdryer. It just is.

I don't think about the fact that the corkboard above my desk was once full of pictures of me and Maddie is now empty. I don't think about the fact all my teenage diaries were thrown out, that three-quarters of my wardrobe was re-bought. I don't think about how much of the past I've thrown away. How much of it I'm running from.

But is it really running if you still have to face up to it every day?

I don't think so. It's not running away if you know where you want to be. It's making the conscious decision to change.

I set the hairdryer down on the bed next to me and focus on the reflection in the mirror, sliding the brush through my new hair one last time. And I smile. I look nothing like the old Abbi, and for just a second, there's a spark of light in my eyes. It's fleeting, but there, and fleeting is better than not at all.

My door opens a crack, and Mom pokes her head through the gap. I hear her sharp intake of breath before I turn to look at her. Her hand is poised over her mouth like she thinks it'll hide the way her jaw has dropped. Like she thinks it'll cover her wide, horrified eyes.

'You . . . Why?'

I finger the dark strands nervously. 'I needed to change it. It reminded me too much of before.'

'Why, Abbi? Your hair was so beautiful.'

My eyes travel back to the mirror. 'Because the outside is all I can change,' I whisper. 'I can't change what's on the inside, not easily, but this I can change. So I did. I needed to, Mom.'

Silence stretches between us as she lets my words sink in. 'I don't understand.'

I shake my head. 'You don't have to understand. You just have to accept it.'

'I . . . I suppose there's not much I can do, anyway.'

I shake my head again. My fingers creep to my arm and under my sleeve, the pads of them rubbing over the slightly raised scars there. The scars I keep hidden from the rest of the world. 'It's better than the alternative. Anything is better than that.'

Mom lets out a shaky breath, and I press my thumb against my pulse point as I always do when I remember. The steady beat of my blood humming through my body reminds me I'm still alive. My heart is still beating and my lungs are still breathing. I'm still existing.

'Yes. It's much better,' Mom agrees and walks across the room before perching on the bed next to me. Our reflections are side by side and the only difference in them is our age. And our hair color. Her blonde hair is the exact shade mine was two hours ago. She reaches over and takes my hand as she meets my eyes in the shiny glass. 'Is there anything else you feel like you need to do?'

'Like what?'

'I don't know, Abbi. I just thought that maybe since you want to change a little we could go to the salon. You know, get a make-over. We both need one. Maybe our nails, too.'

I swallow, her tight grip on my hand telling me exactly how hard it is for her to suggest that. How hard it is for her to finally accept that *her* Abbi isn't coming back this time. That her Abbi is lost forever.

'I'd like that,' I say honestly. 'Maybe that's what I need. Maybe it'll change the last of it. Wipe it away.'

'No wiping away needed. We'll just make new memories to replace the old.' Mom stands up. 'I'll call the salon tomorrow. And Bianca called – you can start in her class tomorrow. A few of her girls just got into Juilliard, and she has a few newbies starting then. She thinks it would be the perfect time for you. I said I'd speak to you and call her back. Shall I let her know you'll be there?'

Ballet. Juilliard. The ultimate dream. The thing that keeps me going. The thing that saved me when I felt there was nothing left to save. 'Please, Mom. I'll be there.'

'Okay.' She backs out of my room and shuts the door behind her, leaving me to silence once again.

Silence. My best friend and my worst enemy.

I lightly brush my fingers over my wrist again and reach for my iPod. The screen glares back at me, and I click shuffle. Snow Patrol blare out, and I lie back on my bed, curling into my side.

Juilliard chants lowly in my mind as sleep begins to take me under.

I clutch the strap of my dance bag to my stomach, and the bag knocks against my knees as I tentatively push open the door to Bianca's dance studio. My stomach is rolling with apprehension, my whole body tense, but I know I'm safe here.

Bianca is one of the few people who truly knows and understands my desire and need to dance. On the day Dr. Hausen suggested using dance as therapy, Bianca arrived in the gym. One private session a week quickly turned to three, both there and here at her studio, and she helped me leave the institution. She reminded me of the freedom that comes with the stretching of a leotard and tying of a ribbon on ballet shoes. And she's the closest thing I have to a friend without Maddie here.

The familiar dance hall stares at me. The mirrors lining the wall, the *barre* on the far wall, the piano in the corner. Dexter, her disabled uncle and pianist, waves at me from the corner. I smile at him, feeling myself relax a little. Only a little, because I know soon the room will be filled with people I've never met.

Two slender hands rest on my shoulders from behind me. 'I can see your tension from the other side of the floor. Breathe and relax, Abbi, because those shoes aren't gonna dance for you.'

'I'm scared,' I whisper as the door opens.

'I know.' Bianca drops her hands and circles me, stopping in front of me and bending down so we're eye to eye. 'You're here to dance, remember that, strong girl, and you'll be fine.'

'To dance.' I let out a long breath, glancing at the growing crowd by the seats.

'And it's something you do beautifully. You're safe here.'

And I know that. I know nothing or no one can touch me here, especially not when my hand touches that *barre* and the music starts. Wherever it is I end up when I dance . . . it's safe.

I pad gently to the corner and remove my sweatpants and top, revealing my dance clothes beneath. I slip my shoes on and run my finger over the satin ribbons. Soft. Safe.

I keep my eyes on the floor in the vain hope no one will talk to me. In the hope no one will even notice me, because like Bianca said, I'm here to dance. Not to make friends, not to build relationships, just to dance.

My shoes reflect back to me in the mirror as I stop. My fingers stretch in anticipation, and I place my hand on the *barre*, letting them curl around the cold metal. Lightness spreads through my body, easing the ever-present suffocation of depression. It's only for a second, but that second is enough. In that second I feel the rush of the girl I could be, and the first easy breath I've taken since I walked in here ten minutes ago leaves my body.

The dull buzz of chatter ceases as Bianca claps her hands once. 'I'm not going to stand here and introduce myself or explain what we're doing here. If you don't know me or why you're here, then you're in the wrong studio, little chicks.

'What I am going to tell you is to forget everything you've ever learned about how dance works. When you slip your shoes on in this studio, you give yourself over to the art of ballet, not the technicalities.

'Ballet isn't about timing, getting that step perfect, or getting the best marks in class. It's about telling a story. It's about taking the feelings and emotions inside you, ripping them out and expressing them with flawless motions of your body. Ballet is a dance that stems and grows from everything we are, regardless of what it means to you, and if you believe any differently, you're in the wrong studio.' Her eyes comb over us all standing at the *barre*, scrutinizing us, like a simple glance can tell her whether or not we believe what she does.

'What you do need to know about how my class works is that you don't stop being a dancer just because you're not on the floor. I expect you to work your asses off. I expect you to be here three nights a week for two hours, then I expect you to work at home. Six hours a week in a studio will not get you to the standard Juilliard expects and demands. Damn, I spend more time than that on my hair each week.

'I don't care whether you dance in a studio, in the shower, in the middle of Central Park – hey, dance on the highway if you really want to – but you must dance. Every. Single. Day. And I will know if you don't. I will know, if for even one day, you forget to dance, because your body will show me.

'I don't want to see any of you in the wrong studio. I want you all to be in the right studio. Some of you I already know and I know you're in the right studio, but the rest of you have to prove it.' She turns and taps the top of the piano, and her uncle begins to play.

'What if we think we are, but we're not? Will you know?' someone further up the *barre* asks.

Bianca turns, her lips twisting on one side. 'Of course.'

'What happens then?'

'Then you leave my studio, because there is someone out there in this city who does deserve to be here. I only teach the best, know that, and I haven't yet had a student who didn't get into Juilliard after attending this class. There's a reason I only teach two classes a week. You are one, and the others are currently seven year olds, and the majority have been with me since they could walk at the age of one. If seven year olds can hack it, I expect young adults such as yourselves to do so.'

'Have you ever asked anyone to leave?'

'Every time I start a new class,' she responds sharply. 'Now warm up before you become the first.'

I fight my smile, training my features into a plain mask, and start my warm-up. I remember hearing the same speech when Bianca walked into the gym hall, and I remember asking her the exact same questions and getting the same answers. It's what endeared me to her so much – unlike most people who know my past, she didn't look at me any differently. To her I was – and am – a girl with a dream, everything else be damned.

The movements of the warm-up are so familiar, and the main door opens as I begin to drop into a *demi-plié*. The feeling of being watched crawls over my skin, prickling at the back of my neck and down my spine. I don't want to, I don't even need to, but I glance upwards and in that direction.

His straight-backed posture and precise steps announce him as a dancer – and a late one – as Bianca approaches him. His dark hair is short but messy, and a distinct British accent floats across the sound of the piano faintly. My eyes roam over his body from his broad shoulders to his defined arms. Dancer's arms; strong yet gentle. The touch from his large hands would be hard yet soft.

You wouldn't know he's a dancer unless you are. His build is closer to that of a football player, but he's far too pretty to do that. *Crap.* Did I really just call him pretty? *What am I even doing?* I shouldn't be standing here trying not to undress the Hot British Guy with my eyes.

He nods once and turns his face toward me. Or the class, but it's me his eyes fall on. Our gazes lock for a fleeting moment, and I almost falter in my warm-up. Even across the studio there's no mistaking the green in his eyes. There's no mistaking the way he looks me over, interest sparking in them as he does so.

And there's no mistaking the apprehension in my chest . . . Or the fluttering inside my tummy when his eyes find mine again. I swallow and look away, telling myself I'm imagining the interest in his eyes and the intensity that kept me looking at him for as long as I did.

I'm not here to eye up Hot British Guy. I'm here to dance, and nothing else.

The dream, Abbi. Juilliard.

Blake

'Shit, shit, shit, shit!' I mutter the curse words under my breath as I climb out of one of the bright yellow taxis that seem to be bloody everywhere in this city. I thought it was all put on for films and stuff, but apparently it isn't.

The strap of my bag catches on the door handle, and I almost trip as I yank it off. Being late to the first dance class is not how I planned on starting my new life in New York. Actually, I never planned on being in a damn class unless it was at Juilliard, but that's not something to think about right now. I can't think about her – if I do I'll get that stupid canary car back here, get in, and go back to my overpriced apartment.

I hoist my bag onto my shoulder and look up at the building in front of me. It's old school and doesn't look right in Manhattan. Instead of the sky high, glass buildings that seem to be the norm, this building is red brick with just a small sign proclaiming, 'Bianca's Dance Studio'. I ruffle my hair with my fingers, sighing deeply, wondering if I've made the right decision. For the millionth time.

But I am late, so there's no damn time left to worry about that. I tuck it into the back of my mind for later – for now I need my head on the dance floor and not in the clouds.

I push the door open and follow the small hallway to a large open room. A *barre* is against the far mirrored wall, and both guys and girls are lined up against it, running through the five positions in time with the gentle music playing. My eyes scan them, noting they all look about twenty or so, except the girl at the end.

Her dark hair is tucked into a pristine bun on top of her

head and her eyes are lowered as she bends her knees and moves into a *demi-plié*. She's utterly graceful, and it's plain to see she's completely at peace.

'Blake Smith?' a voice with a strong New York accent says quietly to my side. I turn to face the auburn haired woman staring at me and nod.

'Yes, ma'am. That's me.'

She smiles. 'I'm Bianca.'

We shake hands. 'It's nice to meet you.'

'And you. You're a little late, but I'd say London is quite different to here.'

I think of the twenty minutes it took me to get a taxi. 'Yeah, you're right there. Sorry – I'm still learning how to get around.'

Her laugh is gentle. 'Yes, I'd imagine it would be tough. Well, if you have any questions feel free to come to me and I'll do my best to answer them. If you put your bag over there in the corner and warm up, we'll get started.'

She silently pads back to her spot, and I look back to the girl at the end of the *barre*.

Our eyes meet.

She almost hesitates in her warm-up, but then carries on as if we're not staring at each other. As if I'm not trying to work out what color her eyes are. They're framed by long, thick lashes that curl toward her eyebrows, and her cheeks pink lightly. I run my eyes down her body, and I can't help but admire the way her leotard and leggings hug her body. She blinks when my eyes lock onto hers again.

Shit. They don't make girls like her in England. And if they do, my mother never introduced me to them.

She pulls her gaze from mine and looks to the front. Something . . . Something tells me I need to know this girl – and it isn't even something in my dick.

I run through the warm-up, half listening to Bianca talking to the class, half watching the girl with the dark brown hair. She's standing slightly back from everyone else, her hands tucked into her sleeves and her head hanging slightly, yet her poise is perfect. Her back is straight and her feet are in position.

Slowly, she moves into the basic positions and moves to Bianca's orders with the elegance of a swan floating along a river in the spring. Every move is perfectly precise – both in positioning and timing. She continues working through the moves at the *barre*, from *plié* and *tendu* to *battements*, oblivious to my eyes following her. Oblivious to my eyes following every curve of her body and every stretch of her limbs. Oblivious to the fact I've never been so attracted to a girl whose name I don't know.

I switch from the warm-up to the basic steps. I know full well Bianca is putting us all through our paces since just over half the class are new. Her eyes flick to each of us, lingering for a second or two as they examine our positioning and posture, but I'm barely concentrating. My thoughts are purely for the girl in front of me; my body is moving fluidly through the instructed steps.

For me, dancing is as natural as breathing. It always has been.

Bianca instructs us to pair off, male and female, and I move toward the brown-haired girl. How could I go to anyone else? As cliché as it sounds, she's the only person in this room I'm really aware of.

I tap her on the shoulder. 'Do you want to . . .'

A pair of startlingly light blue eyes crash into mine. *Blue. That's what color they are.* It's the kind of blue that makes you stop dead and instantly makes you think of a crisp summer's day, complete with beer and a barbecue. It's also the kind of blue that shows everything – the hue too pale to hide shadows lurking beneath – it's the flicker of darkness that makes me pause and stare at her.

I've seen those shadows before.

I know how they linger, barely scratching the surface before pulling you under. And I know the climb is always harder than the fall . . . If you're lucky enough to get a grip on the climb.

'Do I . . .?' she questions shyly, raising her hand to her face then dropping it again.

'Um.' I cough and scratch the back of my neck. Her hesitant

smile reminds me what I've actually approached her for. 'Do you want to dance together? Since we have to pair off. You know. Yeah.'

Shit. I sound like an awkward teen boy who has no idea how to speak to a girl.

Her smile stretches a little and her eyes flit around the dance hall. Everyone is paired off and talking to each other quietly.

'I . . . Sure,' she replies.

'Great. I'm Blake. Blake Smith.'

'Abbi Jenkins.' Abbi's hand slips into my outstretched one. My fingers curl around her smaller ones, but my focus isn't on the silky smooth skin against mine; it's on the gentleness of her tone and the way her lips moved when she said her name.

'Abbi,' I repeat. 'Have you danced long?'

'Since I was eight.' She takes her hand from mine and clasps both of hers in front of her stomach protectively. 'We all need a little something to escape in, right?'

Right. 'Definitely.'

Three sharp claps draw us both from the conversation, and we turn to Bianca. As she instructs us on what we need to do, my eyes trace the line of Abbi's profile. It's dainty and cute – from the way her button nose curves, to the obvious plumpness of her lips. I don't notice I'm smiling until her eyes meet mine again and she raises a questioning eyebrow. I shrug one of my shoulders, and her lips quirk.

'Shall we?'

'Uh, sure.' Shall we what? *Crap.*

Abbi lets the smile break across her face. 'Dance,' she responds with a twinkle in her eyes.

Right. Dance. What we're here for.

Shit. I come thousands of miles to achieve my dream, and what do I do? I get distracted by a pretty face. I need to be thinking with my feet not my damn dick.

For the second time since I walked into this studio, I offer her my hand, and for the second time, she takes it. She moves onto *pointe* seemingly without thinking and closes her eyes. Once again I'm struck by the ease of her movements as I fall into my own . . . With her. It's not until you dance with someone you can truly appreciate the beauty of it.

And it's been only a few seconds, a fleeting moment in the grand scheme of things, but seeing Abbi Jenkins give herself over to the music is to see true beauty.

One moment – one I'll never forget.

Until she opens her eyes as we begin to move, and I'm reminded that even shadows can fall over true beauty.

Abbi looks at me, but I can tell she's not really seeing me. There's a gloss over her eyes, brightening the blue hue of her iris through the pain lingering there. She's somewhere else, somewhere far away, but her steps never falter. She never falls out of time, never makes a wrong move. Even her breathing doesn't change.

Despite the chopping and changing of the music and movements, combined with Bianca's never-ending comments and instructions on arm positioning and timing, my blood is rushing through my body as we move together. I can hear it pounding in my ears and drowning out the music. And I'm mesmerized. I'm mesmerized by the fluidity of her movements, the ease of our dance together. It's like we've always danced together.

The music stops, and Abbi closes her eyes as we come to a standstill. When they open they're clear again, and she smiles shyly. My arms fall from her and she steps back, her fingers lightly brushing across mine. She tugs her sleeves down over her hands, clasping her fingers in front of her stomach again.

'Thank you,' she says, her eyes meeting mine.

My lips curve on one side. 'What for?'

'For the dance.' She smiles as softly as she speaks, turning back to the *barre*. I watch her go. Watch the gentle pad of her feet across the floor, the sway of her hips with each step . . .

'No,' I mutter, never taking my eyes from her. 'Thank you.'